Praise for Paul Letters
A Chance Kill

'An absorbing tale ... will appeal to readers who enjoy mystery thrillers set against a backdrop of the second world war'
— *Historical Novel Society*

Romance, war and spying – *A Chance Kill* gives you all three between the covers of this fast-paced novel. . . . What is truth and what is a lie? Who does one believe in time of war? Is a friend really the enemy? Or is an enemy really a friend? The ending is really a *tour de force.* If it does not leave you amazed, maybe nothing will!'
— *Am-Pol Eagle newspaper*

'A tense and tautly written book, sure to appeal to fans of John le Carré and Ken Follett' — *SK Mag*

'Based on true events and meticulously researched'
— *South China Morning Post*

'Whether Dyta is in Warsaw, Paris, London or Prague she is always an inspiring element in this book. She burns brightly in the darkness that surrounds her' — *Book Babe*

'An action-packed read, where an old-fashioned love story also ensues' — *Baccarat magazine*

'Ambitious storytelling' that 'delves into less well-known chapters of WWII, affording readers both new insight and distinct intrigue'
— *Flashlight Commentary*

'A thoroughly researched historical thriller, which criss-crosses the territories of Europe against the backdrop of the first half of the Second World War. It has the style of a classic British drama'
— *SK Buzz*

THE SLIGHTEST CHANCE

When your enemy is your best friend. . . .

Paul Letters

To Marj,

*Hope you enjoy this one
as well!*

Paul Letters

BLACKSMITH BOOKS

CENA, SAI KUNG 13 DEC 2018

THE SLIGHTEST CHANCE

ISBN 978-988-77927-9-6 (paperback)
© 2018 Paul Letters

Published by Blacksmith Books
Unit 26, 19/F, Block B, Wah Lok Industrial Centre,
31–35 Shan Mei St, Fo Tan, Hong Kong
www.blacksmithbooks.com

Typeset in Adobe Garamond by Alan Sargent
Cover design by Cara Wilson
Printed in Hong Kong

First printing 2018

Supported by:

香港藝術發展局
Hong Kong Arts Development Council

For Joanne

What's in a name? That which we call a rose by any other name would smell as sweet.
— *William Shakespeare*

Acknowledgements

Although Gwen Harmison is a fictional character, her escape out of Hong Kong is closely based upon the adventures of the very real Gwen Priestwood. Supplemented by archive material, Priestwood's 1943 memoir, *Through Japanese Barbed Wire,* proved an invaluable source on the only female to escape from Japanese captivity (in Hong Kong, at least). I am indebted to Hong Kong University Library (HKUL) staff for granting me access to this source, among other records that would not otherwise be readily available. Thanks go to Elizabeth Ride, daughter of Colonel Lindsay Ride – a medical doctor and POW camp escapee who founded Britain's spy network, the 'British Army Aid Group'. Elizabeth forbearingly dispelled aspects of my ignorance. Furthermore, through the careful archiving of BAAG documents, Elizabeth Ride is keeping history alive. Through archives held at HKUL, the Hong Kong Heritage Project, Hong Kong's Government Records Office and the UK's National Archives, among other sources, I was able to trace the path of the many historical characters in this novel, from Admiral Chan Chak to Morris 'Two-Gun' Cohen. The characters of Chester Drake and Dominic Sotherly/Max Holt are fictional, but the operations my characters were involved in tally with specific historical events. To the adventures of Admiral Chan Chak through to Z Force through to Eden's speeches, nonfiction dominates this novel. Regarding the places and events covered, it is easier to state what is not authentic: most significantly, the 'Jade General' and his lair are made-up (although warlord China was certainly real).

Bill Lake, a mine of historical knowledge, sources and contacts, selflessly gave me his time and introduced me to many of the other historians who helped me along the way. These include Rusty Tsoi and Kwong Chi Man (authors of *Eastern Fortress: A*

Acknowledgements

Military History of Hong Kong, 1840–1970), and Tony Banham – author of the definitive reference book on the Battle of Hong Kong, *Not the Slightest Chance.* Thanks also to Tim Luard – author of *Escape from Hong Kong: Admiral Chan Chak's Christmas Day Dash, 1941,* and son-in-law to Z Force agent Colin McEwan – for reading large sections of an early draft of this novel. Extracts from McEwan's diary, published by his daughter (and Tim's wife) Alison McEwan and the late Dr Dan Waters, helped shed light on Z Force, a lesser-known part of Britain's Special Operations Executive. Also helpful in this regard was Lawrence Tsui, son of BAAG officer Paul Tsui, who performed many heroic missions inside and out of occupied Hong Kong. Thanks also for the help of Richard 'Buddy Jnr' Hide, son of Petty Officer Steve 'Buddy' Hide – a member of Hong Kong's 'great escape'. See Buddy Jnr's website: *www.hongkongescape.org.* Thank you, Geoff Emerson, who has literally written the book on Stanley: *Hong Kong Internment, 1942–45,* and he kindly read a draft of my fictional effort.

The work of the late Steve Martin and the draft feedback of his successor Jason Burk greatly eased my research process surrounding opium. For more information, visit the website which Martin created and Burk now curates: *www.opiummuseum.com.*

The remarkable Barbara Anslow worked at the heart of Hong Kong's colonial government during the Battle of Hong Kong and experienced the rest of the war behind the wire of Stanley Internment Camp. She patiently answered my questions through numerous interviews and emails. In addition to Barbara's exceptional recall, we can also draw upon her meticulous diaries, now published by Blacksmith Books as *Tin Hats and Rice: A Diary of Life as a Hong Kong* Prisoner of War, 1941–1945. Happy 100th birthday (1st December, 2018), Barbara!

Katrina Chadwick, Nuri Mirwani, Jodi Moran and Vici Egan helped greatly with early editorial decisions, and Joanne Letters, Iain Lafferty and Kamal Mirwani kindly edited whole drafts. Without such selfless dedication and purposeful advice, my work would have never have progressed.

My gratitude goes to the Hong Kong Arts Development Council for helping to make this project viable. This novel has

Acknowledgements

also been made possible due to the passion, patience (with me) and professionalism of my publisher, Pete Spurrier of Blacksmith Books, together with editor Alan Sargent and ever-patient cover designer Cara Wilson.

Finally, thank you for the tolerance and support of my wife and son. Middle-aged men tend to buy a convertible; I've spent the last decade writing novels.

Paul Letters

For more on my work, including *A Chance Kill* – the first *Chances* novel in this unusually loose series – go to *paulletters.com*.

My son and I also run a fun history podcast for families, full of jokes, quizzes and interviews with knights, aboriginal elders and World War II survivors.

Visit *dadandmelovehistory.com*.

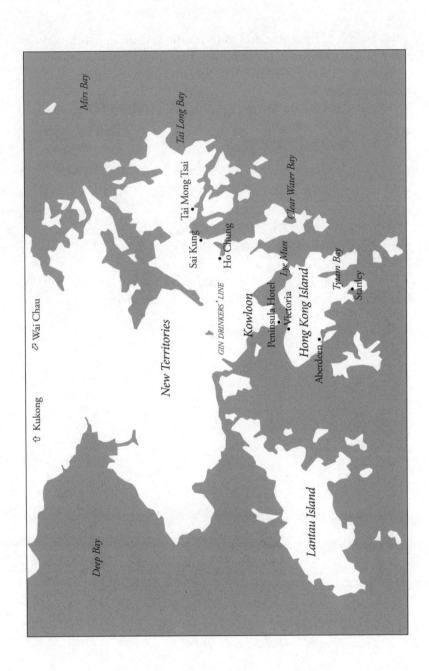

Mirs Bay

Tai Long Bay

Tai Mong Tsai

Sai Kung •

Ho Chung •

Clear Water Bay

Lye Mun

Kowloon

Peninsula Hotel •

Victoria •

Hong Kong Island

Tytam Bay

Stanley •

Aberdeen •

GIN DRINKERS' LINE

↗ Wai Chau

New Territories

⇧ Kukong

Deep Bay

Lantau Island

PART I

'Max'

Chapter 1

Saturday 15th November, 1941

Dominic Sotherly swirled his whisky and downed it in one, slamming the glass onto the marble top of the bar: he would start the evening as he meant to go on – as a work of fiction.

Dom straightened his bow tie in the mirror behind the bar. Several other drinkers had turned their heads at the gratuitous clunk of glass on marble. A wing-collared receptionist, wearing the hotel tie and blazer, entered the room and stole their stares. He approached the bar and said, 'Mr Max Holt?'

Dom was slow to nod his head, embarrassed by his assigned pseudonym.

'There's a telephone call for you, sir. From a Mr Drake.'

The receptionist led Dom along the corridor to a telephone booth. Dom paused and held a finger in the air. 'When you entered the bar,' he said, 'how did you know that *I* was Mr Holt?'

'Sir, the caller told me you would likely be sitting alone in the Long Bar, drinking a neat spirit.'

'I see. Thank you.' Dom picked up the Bakelite earpiece and braced himself for the plummy accent of the Eurasian.

'Dominic? Or should I say *"Max"*? Don't worry, old chap, she can't hear me. How the devil are you? I'm afraid we are running a tad late. Just a half hour or so. I'm sure you'll manage in a bar full of booze!'

'That's right,' said Dom, 'I like a drink. Whereas you like to shoot a bloke on your own side when you're stone-cold sober!' Money could buy anything in Hong Kong, including silence.

'Oh, good grief! Be a sport and let it lie.' Only Drake could brush off shooting a man, point blank, in broad daylight. 'In any event, technically there are no "sides" here, even now. Although I have heard—'

'Shove it up your dinger, Drake! See you later – if you feel like showing up. But if you're more than an hour late, you lose.' Dom rammed the receiver down.

That call had been contrived for one reason only – for Drake to flaunt his mysterious date. '*She* can't hear me … *We* are running a little late.' Dom would have to show up. He may have turned an order into a daft bet – daft because it wasn't for cash – but both he and Drake were under instruction from Ben.

Dom returned to the bar and let two more whiskies pass his lips before he sent the drinks bill ahead to the hotel restaurant – Drake could pay for the *whole* evening, not just dinner.

He left the bar and sauntered along to the restaurant, to secure a secluded spot. Sitting alone under softly shaded lights, he lit a cigarette. There were two groups of Chinese businessmen amid the many tables of Caucasians. The Chinese may have been banned from the clubs but at the finest hotels money spoke louder than race. Fortunately, there was no one who recognised Dominic Sotherly.

One motivation for partaking in the evening's arrangement was simply to bring Chester Drake down a peg or six. The over-priced Macallans which fuelled Dominic Sotherly's bravado could help carry off a performance as 'Max Holt'. He ordered champagne. Keeping an eye on the door, his mind was running through his cover story when Chester Drake walked in. But Dom immediately shifted his gaze. The young blonde alongside Drake dazzled in her black figure-hugging gown, flared skirt swaying as she glided past the dining tables.

Even before the girl had spoken her first words, Dom was riding high on layers of champagne and whisky, and on the thrill of being someone else. The trickiest aspect immediately became apparent: the mere presence of Drake. Beneath the charming exterior, the boy thought far too much of himself.

Drake walked ahead of the girl and yelled, 'Good evening, Max.' He sported a thin wax moustache in the mistaken belief that he was keeping up with trends in Mother England. Leaning in over his dead-fish handshake, Drake whispered, 'Word is, we'll soon be *on*. It's going to happen, perhaps within days.'

Or, thought Dom, it may never happen.

'May I present Gwen Harmison?'

Dom rolled his eyes: Drake tried too hard to be the sophisticated Englishman. Growing up, no doubt a staffroom of home tutors had sculpted and honed his accent to aristocratic heights.

'*Miss* Harmison, I presume?' said Dom. She smiled and shivered a nod. 'It's beaut to meet you.'

'Ah, tall, dark, handsome and Australian? Why, Mr Holt, how exotic!'

Dom felt himself redden. 'Please, Miss Harmison, you gotta call me Max.'

'Ah, that famous Antipodean informality. Positively charming. Then I shall be Gwen.'

They were sitting as a triangle at a circular table laid with sterling silver on white linen. Her hair worn high, her dress cut low, a string of pearls drew wandering eyes up over her collarbones to the curve of her neck. She offered around cigarettes and then lit her own: he was in danger of being out-Aussied by a Pommie girl.

'You been in Hong Kong long, Miss Harmison?' asked Dom.

'I arrived last month,' replied Gwen. 'I was living in Macao. Chester used to live there – did you know?'

'I daresay I told you, old chap,' said Drake. 'I was there until last year.' He had never mentioned it before. However, in their game, such an omission was common.

Chester Drake was half British – as was Dominic Sotherly – but Drake's Britishness fortified the confidence gained from being the son of a self-made millionaire.

'I originally went over to Macao to help my father's construction firm with its accounts.' His father's success had afforded Drake a more British education in Hong Kong than most

Britishers received in Britain. 'But, well, then one thing led to another. . . .'

Dom inclined his head a little. Was Drake talking about work or play? Surely he and Miss Harmison were no more than mates?

'Let me order you champagne,' said Dom. 'Such a wonderful aperitif.' And the Achilles' heel of many a good girl before her.

'No, thank you.' She turned to the waiter. 'I'll have a gimlet. Heavy on the ice, light on the soda, extra lime on the side.' A girl who knew exactly what she liked. Gin could well grease the wheels of Dom's ambitions better than mere champagne.

He ordered foie gras followed by Lobster Thermidor, determined to thicken Drake's bill. Then he set about quizzing Gwen about her life.

She exhaled a deep breath of cigarette smoke. 'There's not much to it, really. My work experience in England amounts to little more than a spot of nursing. I came to China several years ago, looking for adventure. Now, with the Japanese threatening Macao, I sailed over to Hong Kong in order to secure onward passage.'

'Where to?' asked Dom.

'Ideally, back to the motherland. But every man I meet tells me I mustn't take my chances against the Nazi U-boats in the Atlantic, so perhaps I'll book a steamship to Vancouver. To stay with Auntie Val.'

'So you came to Asia for adventure, a beautiful young woman all on your Pat?'

Gwen's blue eyes sparkled. 'On my Pat?'

'Sorry – Pat Malone. It means—'

'Alone.' She smiled. 'Why, yes.'

'That's all there is to it, old chap,' chipped in Drake. 'We met in Macao. I did a little bookkeeping for Gwen—'

'You helped me with more than that, Chester.' She smiled.

'Well, financial and sundry advice, shall we say, old girl?' He smiled back at her. Drake basked in knowing so much about both Dom and Gwen while they knew so little of each other.

'And what of you, Mr Holt?' asked Gwen. 'Tell me about you.'

Over more champagne and then a bottle of Chablis, Max Holt's background came to life. He tried to weave an outdoor, adventurist lifestyle – to substantiate the later claims which he knew he must make – with the relative sophistication of an upbringing in Australia's capital city.

'And I suppose Australia is just a hop away on a modern steamship,' said Gwen. 'So, for whom do you work here, Mr Holt? Every chap I run into seems to be either Jardines or Hongkong Bank.'

'Dull as a wombat's arse?'

She giggled. 'I couldn't have put it better myself!'

He narrowed his gaze on her. 'The answer to your question is not for public knowledge, if you get my meaning?'

She gaped her mouth in shock and then leaned forward, unashamedly intrigued. 'Why, of course. I shall live out the very definition of discretion.'

Drake grinned on throughout, sipping his water, nursing his wine, delighting in Dom's performance, and possibly Gwen's.

Dom took a slow drag on his cigarette. 'It's just that you get these bloody reporters – always looking for a story. . . .'

She turned her torso fully towards him. 'Why then, you must be somebody awfully famous?'

He feared he had overplayed his hand. 'It's not so much that *I'm* famous. It's who I work for.'

Her eyes widened. 'King George?'

'Oh, far more fun than him!' Dom cleared his throat. 'Ernest Hemingway.'

And that was it. The first of the three criteria Drake had prescribed – on top of the false name itself – in order to ensure that Max Holt's backstory was anything but dull: Max would work for an American celebrity. Under the assenting eyes of the boss earlier that day, Dom had agreed to the enterprise partly for the fun of it, as well as for the pleasure of getting the best of Drake.

'Gosh! My goodness. Well, you're not his butler, so possibly you're an awfully well-paid driver? Or perhaps you're his ghost-writer?' Gwen may have been *awfully* English, but that didn't prevent her from laughing at her own jokes.

'Strewth, you're not bloody far off! I'm his bodyguard.' Gwen squealed in delight, as though she had been let in on a naughty secret. That squeal was the moment Dom knew he had her. Her eyes stuck to his. 'I've been working for him for four years, off and on. While he's taking a break now – he's had a gutful of travel – so am I. Y'see, I'm only needed when Ernest travels to dangerous places – warzones, in the main, or game hunting over in Africa.'

'Upon my word, that sounds tremendously exciting!' She gripped the sides of her chair and shimmied a little closer. 'And what a writer Papa is!' she continued. 'I do so love *The Sun Also Rises,* don't you?'

Earlier that day, as Dom's mind had scrabbled around trying to form a feasible and interesting story to meet the bet's criteria, he had become grateful he had at least opened the latest novel by the American writer.

'Well, now, I'll have to confess that I've not read *all* of his books.' Or even *one.* Hemingway had stayed a month in Hong Kong earlier in the year, and *For Whom the Bell Tolls* was hard to avoid on the newspaper vendors' stalls. It was a soporific slog through the first fifty pages, and then the betting-slip-cum-bookmark had not budged for months.

'So,' said Gwen, 'if Hemingway lives in America, or Cuba, now, I believe' – Dom nodded along encouragement – 'then where do you live, Mr Holt?'

And so it was that she inadvertently steered them into the second pre-negotiated criterion – Max Holt was to be homeless.

'I live nowhere and everywhere.' He waved his open palm around the room.

'You mean you live here in the Peninsula?'

'Crikey, no. I find it kinda vulgar, don't you?'

Gwen stymied a grin.

'When I'm in town I prefer the Gloucester, on Hong Kong Island,' added Dom.

'Really?' she said. 'Why, I'm staying next to the Gloucester, in the Hong Kong Hotel.'

Only now did it dawn on him that to invite her back to what he had just declared to be 'his place' would be to invite disaster. A room in the Gloucester was unaffordable – never mind the need to explain away a total lack of personal possessions, all of which, of course, remained in a less than swanky Kowloon apartment. She would have to be more than rotten drunk not to notice.

A masterful solution came to mind. 'But, currently,' said Dom, 'I'm doing a mate a favour – house-sitting his apartment in Kowloon while he's away.'

'You're a beacon of kindness, Mr Holt.' Gwen smiled and then rose from the table. 'You must excuse me: even the Hoover Dam couldn't hold back this much drink. Where might I find. . . .'

Dom offered no directions as he hadn't seen a lavatory, but the waiter soon obliged.

'What a performance, Dom!' Drake grinned his superior grin. 'Simply marvellous.'

Dom never knew how to respond to Drake's false positives, so he lit a cigarette. 'I hope you've brought your bloody cheque-book, cobber.'

'Steady on, old chap. So long as Gwen doesn't directly question if you really are who you claim to be, I'll pay for the whole evening. My little treat.'

Treat? It was a fair bet, not a treat. Dom gushed out cigarette smoke in Drake's direction, closed the packet and returned it to his pocket.

'You never know, it could be the last Saturday night soirée for quite some time,' said Drake, and he lit a cigarette of his own. 'Things are going to get rather hot around here any day now. When they do, old chap, remember we're on the same side – for the good of the civilised world.' Drake tipped his head back and funnelled his smoke up into the air.

Dom frowned.

Drake spoke softly. 'Our little group could be Hong Kong's best chance.'

'Huh!' Drake loved melodrama as much as he loved himself. 'You think you're the bloody bees' knees! Really, you're just a cut-lunch commando!'

Drake carried on talking on his own plain. 'Dominic, do you really think you can kill a man?'

He glared through Drake's black eyes. 'That really depends on who the man is, *Chester.*'

'Steady on, old chap. I—'

'Cut the crap, Drake.' He jabbed a finger at his adversary. 'You've gotta—'

'You've got to what?' asked Gwen, reappearing at the table. 'You've got to wait for Gwen to sit down before you say anything too interesting?'

Dom smiled.

The conversation sailed calmly on, although Drake could be relied upon to stir up the odd squall.

'Max, where on earth did you first meet Hemingway?' asked Drake.

'Yes, where did you meet him, Max?' Gwen's voice rose as the sentence progressed.

'We share the same manicurist.'

'Really?' asked Gwen.

'No, not all!' Max laughed, then he fixed his eyes on Gwen's. 'Spain. During the civil war. After uni I did two years in the National Guard.' Not a complete lie – Dom had joined the part-time Queensland Militia. But he had never been to Spain. 'You know, I had all this training, and the poor people of Spain needed all the help they could get.'

'Which poor people?' asked Gwen. 'Did you fight for the Communists or the Fascists? For the wicked or for the iniquitous?'

'The Republicans. My band were fighting for freedom and democracy, not for communism or dictatorship.'

'I'm so glad to hear it, Mr Holt.' She smiled. He had surely gained points for displaying a social conscience. She raised her full glass – wine was a drink she appeared to tolerate more than devour – and proposed a toast. 'To honourable Spaniards.' Gwen chimed her glass against his and giggled. 'All three of them.'

Dom laughed and slugged back his wine. Diners milled around behind his back, taking seats at the table next to theirs. It would take only one piece of bad luck – just one mere acquaintance of Dominic Sotherly – to lose both the bet and all hope of the girl.

Drake held Dom's gaze. 'So, Max, why don't you regale us with what you do with your time, when you're not away on an adventure?'

'Crikey, well, um, I've begun to work as something of a social reformer.' A clumsy introduction to the third and final of Drake's criteria. 'I do hope you don't think me too pious – *frightfully dull,* as you English might say – but I campaign on behalf of addicts.'

'Addicts? Addicts of what?'

Dom could not bring himself to the jugular. He would ease her in. 'Gambling.'

'Gosh! Gambling in all its forms?'

'Well, its more public forms, perhaps. It's mainly the nags in Hong Kong, of course.'

'You campaign against horse racing? How odd!'

'Not against the racing, just against unrestrained gambling.' He tried to hide his frustration. 'One wonders whether many in the world would be better off without all these addictions? I mean, without opium or gambling – or alcohol?' There was no easier way to have said it, to complete the final pillar of the biography of Max Holt.

Her eyebrows jumped up towards her hairline. '*You* are a member of the *temperance movement*?' Dom could only nod. 'A *prohibitionist*? Ha! I can see how you disregard alcohol, Mr Holt! You look more like you campaign *for* it!'

Drake chuckled.

'It's a battle best fought from a position of experience,' said Dom, smiling. 'More, seriously, I'm for temperance, *not* prohibition. I can handle my grog, but millions of others can't. I simply wish that society would do more for true addicts.'

Gwen pursed her lips and, for once, said nothing. But what was she thinking?

'Of course,' said Drake, 'Hemingway is one for enjoying a drink!' He appeared to be basking in the growing safety of his bet.

The call of nature resembled as good a reason as any to excuse himself from the conversation. Dom walked out of the restaurant in a languid search for the bathroom. He glanced at his watch: another half an hour and the bet would be over. He found himself wandering the main corridor, which, further along, met the top of the Peninsula's grand staircase. He overheard voices from out-of-sight figures climbing the stairs. A Chinese-accented female said, 'Regarding Admiral Chan Chak ...' Dom paused in the corridor, just yards from the stairs, and pretended to inspect a Chinese vase. 'Major-General, you can, I hope, reassure me that you will keep your promise to my sister and the Generalissimo?'

Admiral Chan Chak: the one-legged Admiral was known to have been a close confident of Kuomintang Party founder, the late Sun Yat-sen, and was trusted by his successor, Chiang Kai-shek. Indeed, the Admiral had even saved both of their lives once – it was all over the newspapers. Sun and Chiang had been besieged by a warlord army when Chan Chak broke through by boat and whisked them away to safety.

'Of course, Madame Sun. And I do hope your sister is well?' asked the General.

Madame Sun? Madame Sun – Soong Ching-ling – one of the two sisters who had married the two progenitors of Nationalist China.

'Quite well, thank you,' she replied, her voice lowering as they reached the corridor at the top of the stairs. 'Please be aware, Major-General, that Great Britain shall have the eternal gratitude of Generalissimo Chiang Kai-shek and all Chinese, if you take good care of our Admiral. His importance is unparalleled. We – and you – cannot afford to let him fall into Japanese hands. Too much would be lost.'

Surely this Nationalist Admiral wasn't in Hong Kong? The British outlawed all Chinese Nationalists, for fear of stirrings of insurrection.

They rounded the corner, turning towards Dom. He left the vase and walked on ahead. The well-groomed man in full service regalia was indeed *the* Major-General.

'Well, Madame—'

He glanced at Dom and stopped talking. Major-General Maltby, Hong Kong's Commander-in-Chief, avoided eye contact, whereas the delicate-looking Chinese widow smiled at the passing stranger. Dom walked on. His alcohol-blurred mind replayed the scene as he strode back towards the restaurant. He was unsure what to make of it, but Ben might know.

When Dom returned, Drake was holding up Gwen's coat for her.

'We really must be going,' said Drake. Gwen, still seated, hardly looked convinced. 'I've paid the bill, old chap.'

Dom glanced at his watch and smiled.

'Must you go?' he said, addressing Gwen.

Drake answered. 'Ah, well, Do— *Max,* it's just that, er, in these times, we need to consider Gwen's safety . . . in this precarious political situation. I have a duty of care.'

Dom saw a glimmer of resentment in Gwen's eyes, yet ultimately her own sense of duty prevailed. She slipped on her fur coat and kissed Dom goodbye. 'I do hope we'll meet again, Mr Holt.' And then she was gone.

Still standing at the table, Dom stared at his watch. The rules of the bet dictated that Max would have to maintain the charade through to at least eleven o'clock: it was only 10:40pm. Chester Drake's priorities had become clear: he did not care about the bet as much as he cared about the girl.

Chapter 2

Monday 8th–Tuesday 9th December, 1941

Late in the evening, the Bison arrived with a job – a job of life and death. Hong Kong's longest day was ending, and yet for 'Max Holt' it was just beginning.

Dom and Ben set off in brilliant moonlight. They hiked up the ridge from Gin Drinkers' Bay, long a feeding ground for pirates whose work was not unlike their own. Ordinarily, the view across the harbour was a stage setting of lights back-dropped by majestic mountains. That night, however, in the foreground Kowloon's beard was more than singed, its waterfront ablaze. Smoke shrouded Hong Kong Island, across the channel. The Japanese had obliterated Hong Kong's entire air force on the ground on that first morning – if half-a-dozen Great War biplanes constituted an air force. And throughout the day, Victoria Harbour had hosted a shoot of the Royal Navy's sitting ducks.

They climbed the trail that ran up the barren hillside behind Kowloon, towards the rear of the British frontlines.

'So, this is it.' Ben 'the Bison' Randall was more gang leader than superior officer. 'The first day of our war, and your first day as a professional . . . *soldier*, Dom.'

The pause was telling. *Z Force* – you could not have made it up.

'Correction: I mean *Max*.'

Britain and America had gone from peace to war with Japan on the same dive-bomb of a morning: simultaneous attacks unleashed on two harbours whose names sounded more like a pair of doughty old aunts: – Victoria and Pearl. Dom wondered, would Uncle Sydney be next?

'I hope you realise you've been well trained.' Ben grinned. Dom took great strides to keep pace. Ben may have been the older man, but rarely would he need to catch his breath on a hike.

'Yeah,' he winked, *'they* trained me bloody well during that fortnight in Malaya.' Ben had taught him weaponry and communications but sent Dom overseas for jungle warfare and explosives.

Ben landed the ball of his fist on his comrade's shoulder. 'You half-breed-Aussie bastard!'

Dom grinned.

'No bugger wants a scrap,' said Dom, unconvinced of himself, 'but, crikey, I'm glad I'm here outdoors in the reality of it – glad to leave the bloody desk behind me, at last.' War sharpened life's purposefulness, in contrast to years of recycled days bathed in tedium and disappointment, where there was too much time to dwell on a heart full of memories, safest forgotten.

'I hope you do realise it's different now,' said Ben. 'This is *war*. You'll see death. Tonight, or someday soon, people you care about are likely going to die. Maybe me or you. Or maybe you'll do your first killing – that's not fun either, Dom . . . *Max.*'

Yet it appeared less distant from 'fun' than the alternative scenarios, but he didn't reply.

Movement in the bushes. He snapped his head around. An unseen animal scuffled off, disturbing the trail-side shrubbery: one always imagined a snake, but snakes are too wily to be heard.

'I heard you've kept playing along as *Max?* At least, on Saturday nights.'

Dom smiled. Saturday night's ball seemed a lifetime ago. It had been Gwen's idea – no, her *insistence* – that they return to the Pen. *'It will be terribly romantic – a sort of anniversary, celebrated where first we met.'*

Ben spoke in a low voice as they climbed close to the British front line. 'We'll stick with your *nom de guerre* – a good practice for someone in our line. And forget your day job and everything about normal Hong Kong life – it's over. You're a combatant now.'

Dom nodded. As for Ben – who at times sounded rather too mid-Atlantic for a Canadian – well, 'Ben' probably wasn't his real name anyway.

'Ben, did you ever find out anything about Admiral Chan and what I overheard?'

'I initiated discreet inquiries. The Admiral is Chiang Kai-shek's man in Hong Kong. This despite the fact that the Kuomintang is still banned by the British.'

'Is that enough for Madame Sun to have gotten involved and gone to Maltby about him?"

Ben remained stony faced.

He knew more, but he wasn't saying. At least, not yet.

They had climbed through the cool winter air to a familiar point where the view expanded not only south to Hong Kong Island but north, towards China. In recent months, in addition to weekend daytime training, with growing frequency they had spent nights in the hills, navigating routes in the dark.

Ben had taken Dom under his wing but never let on exactly how many operatives he had recruited into other cells. Very few, whispers suggested. Within this shadowy elite Dom saw a mean-ingful role to play. He and his team were better placed than anyone to tip the balance. Holding back the Japanese would give Hong Kong hope of reinforcements and a chance for freedom. And, as a personal bonus, a chance of seeing Gwen again.

'Our superiors believe the closest Japs are way beyond that ridge.' Ben pointed at the moonlit ridge on their horizon.

'And where do *you* think they are, Ben?'

Ben began to shake his head. He pointed ahead. 'I don't believe this.' He motioned for Dom to crouch along as they approached a sentry standing on the crown of the ridge. Ben called the sentry out of the moonlight and over to the shadows. Ben showed their passes and gave the sentry a ticking off.

A little further up, a private on guard outside a pillbox looked Ben and Dom's jungle greens up and down. Unable to spot any insignia of rank or regiment, the private begrudgingly returned a salute.

Ben the Bison sniffed the air and said, 'Someone's been fortifying himself against the cold.'

Inside, the officer in-charge remained seated, his ignorance well-oiled. 'Ah,' he said, 'you must be Captain. . . .' Pinned down by an open tin of jam was a scrap of paper which the Captain picked up. He squinted as he read it, and then he looked up at Ben. 'Captain Benjamin Smith?' Never before had Dom heard Ben called 'Benjamin'. 'Smith' was new, too. 'I'm Captain Edwards. My CO informed me you were coming to sh-show . . . to *sew* your handiwork,' slurred the officer. 'And who's this young whippershhhnapper?'

'This old fella?' asked Ben. 'This is Second Lieutenant Max Holt.' So, in addition to a new name, Dom had gained a rank.

Captain Edwards studied the pair of them in the light of an oil lamp. Ben had streaked blackout grease into his blond fringe, with a tigerish result. 'Good Lord,' said the Captain, 'I shouldn't think you'll be needing your . . . your camouflage makeup. The Japs are twenty *blood-dy* miles away.'

Ben scratched his chin. 'Well, even so, you may wish to do something about the soldiers you've got strolling along the top of the ridge, standing stark against the skyline, visible in the moonlight for miles.' The battalion guarding this stretch of the British line, sent there only days earlier, consisted of pipers, stretcher bearers and others of barebones training.

Captain Edwards' face sobered. 'Look, we may have withdrawn from that . . . that swampland up by the border, but the Nips are still sitting on the blood-dy fren . . . fence . . . on the frontier fence, drowning in sake, celebrating their supposed "success" in prodding a toe over into Hong Kong territory.'

Ben led the way out of the concrete box. Standing waiting in the shadows was the man who had once shot Dom.

'Good evening, Second Lieutenant,' said Ben.

'Good evening, sir,' said Chester Drake. 'Good evening, Second Lieutenant Holt.'

Dom nodded.

That training trip to Malaya had been the second time Dom had met Chester Drake. Their first encounter was at a Z Force selection weekend, where they were buddied up at the shooting range. After what happened that day, Dom had never expected to see him again.

'What a jolly good night for it!' said Drake, his grin as wide as the crescent moon.

The three of them jogged down the grassy hillside, towards the patch of jungle on the valley floor. Dom had roamed this hillside many times, but never before during war – and never before did it lay *ahead* of the British front line. It had been during peacetime daylight hours that they had placed some toys along the valley. Where to lay mines so that whistling Tommies would not step on them but hardened Japanese fighters would, had been a task beyond wishful thinking.

There was one beaten path through the centre of the jungle – too obvious, Ben had argued, for Japanese scouts to use. But, once war had begun, Ben reconsidered: for the mass of troops who would come after the scouts, the hole needed plugging.

The Bison's blinkered penlight gave him an occasional eighteen inches of visibility on the jungle floor. Ben made greater use of his truncated machete, which he waved ahead of himself, forging a route through their own pitch-black, snake-infested jungle minefield – which they had intended to be unnavigable. Ben had pen-dotted the paths marked on his map with potential explosions – pen-dots the three of them now inched around, counting their steps.

The earlier rain made the ground mushy underfoot. As they crept through the jungle a potentially venomous giant centipede fell onto Dom's neck and squirmed inside his collar. 'Shi-i-i—!'

Ben seized Dom's arm as he flicked the centipede to the ground. The Bison clasped his hands around Dom's ear and his whisper funnelled in. 'Forget the arse-wipe nonsense Captain Johnny Walker back there spewed out: the Japs are close. So keep it schtum.' Many officers enjoyed a drink certain in the knowledge that, as the Captain had said before they left the pillbox, 'these slitty-eyed Nips can't see in the dark'. And on such pervasive judgments, battles were fought and lost.

Another distant explosion shuddered through the jungle: to the north, road bridges and railway tunnels were being blown to slow the Japanese advance down from China. Half an hour into their own minefield, Dom was unable to see as far as the ground at his feet, and he wondered if that might be where the next explosion would come from.

Ben led Dom through the heart of the jungle, with Drake sweeping the rear some fifteen yards behind. Clambering through a tangle of roots reminiscent of Cape Tribulation, back in Queensland, Dom and Ben were just a few yards short of intersecting the main path – the *only* path. To plug the gap in their minefield, they would make use of the new arrival they carried in their haversacks: plastic explosive.

Dom squatted down behind a curtain of bamboo that shielded him from the path while Ben stepped out from the cover of the trees. Ahead, the moonlight caught no more than the top of Ben's head before the voice came.

'Hello-hello!' shouted a whisper from ahead of Ben, who had frozen still on the path. Dom glanced back over his shoulder, seeking Drake. But in the blackness of the jungle there was no sign of him.

'Hello-hello!' came the voice again. The voice could have been British, but it sounded more North American.

If Dom had been alone, no doubt he would have bitten back from where he was hidden. If he had spoken up, the odds were that from somewhere in the dark a bullet would have made its way into him, and perhaps a bayonet for Ben. As things were, hidden three yards short of the path, Dom stayed silent. Not because of brains – because of fear.

Then the stranger spoke again from the darkness ahead. 'Howdy!' The jungle on the other side of the path was a wall of black, but Ben saw – or knew – *something*, that much was clear.

Ben had worked in the Shanghai Police before the war, where the streets were lively, seven nights a week. He said a machete, like any blade, was only primitive in primitive hands. So Dom had spent more time than he would care to remember being taught the art of knife-throwing, how to split a single shaft of bamboo from ten yards away. Good preparation for anything bar the circus?

Ben's sized-down machete would not bother a concealed Jap with a bayoneted rifle in his hands. The Bison had a pistol in his haversack, but he did not reach back into his bag while he was standing on that path.

The next thing Dom glimpsed was Ben dropping his knife towards where the voice came from, a visible act of surrender. Ben said, *'Konnichiwa,'* and then a couple of sentences in Japanese which Dom did not understand. He could retrieve his own pistol from the bag on his back, although with all the noise that would make, he might be dead before he could slip the safety off. Was Drake hanging back to maintain silent cover? Sacrifice one – Ben – to save the other two? Or sacrifice two to save himself, more like. Typical Drake.

Then Ben said in English, 'I have no weapon. You can take me to your friends. I'm going to throw you my torch.'

Dom's mouth dropped open. If there was a Jap in there, why, when Ben speaks a fair bit of Japanese, was he telling him this in English?

Then, epiphany. It was not the *Jap* whom Ben was telling – it was Dom.

Dom began to edge around the bamboo to get a clearer line. Ben said something in Japanese and tossed his lit penlight ahead into the bushes. As it began its journey, just a flicker of light caught the Japanese soldier's face. And that was enough for Dom.

A moment after he stood up and threw his knife, a shot rang out from the Jap's rifle.

After a few seconds' delay, Dom crossed over the track, following Ben. Already there, standing over a slumped body, was Drake. And he was holding Dom's bloodied knife.

Drake held up one finger. Ben nodded. One solitary Jap, thought Dom. Maybe.

Before Dom could get a good look, Ben had yanked up the Japanese soldier's tunic to cover his face. He frisked the body.

Blood soaked his tunic, from which grass and twigs protruded from a patchwork of quilted pockets: jungle camouflage. He wore not boots but split-toe rubber sandals, as though fashioned from an old tyre.

They rushed away along the main path, picking a route they knew to be mine-free – from their own side, at least.

Through thinning undergrowth they could see the clearing ahead. Drake hurried a safe distance away with the bags. Dom tied a strip of cloth around Ben's upper arm, where the Jap's bullet had nicked him. Ben told Dom to guard the path while he went over to inspect Drake's work with the detonators and explosive.

Job done, however rudimentary, they continued on through the valley and eventually made it out onto the coastal road. With Drake guarding their rear, they jogged back towards the frontline.

So Japanese commanders trained their men to call out in English? With a 'howdy' or some other connivance lifted from a cowboy movie.

Only as they closed in on their own lines did Ben speak. 'What happened back there . . . don't tell the squaddies. I'll call it in to HQ.' Then he grinned at Dom. 'But, one day, what you did should be one for the history books. Maybe the first Jap killed by any Brit – or Aussie – in this whole damn war.'

'Bugger me! Where did I bloody hit him?'

Ben pointed at his throat.

Ben had trained him to throw knives through darkness, but still Dom could not believe it. The boss had been right: it wasn't fun. It was worthier than mere 'fun'. They were still alive thanks to Dominic Sotherly – or, more probably, *Max Holt.*

'And what was Drake up to all the while?' Dom wondered aloud, unaware his 'comrade' had closed the gap.

'I was there in case you missed,' said Drake.

'Geez, we're not on bloody training anymore, Drake,' said Dom.

Drake grinned. 'Because if we were, I would have shot you again.'

Ben raised his palm. 'Now-now, ladies.'

At the Royal Scots' roadside checkpoint, two sentries were standing outside smoking. Passes shown, Dom scrounged a cigarette. Ben disappeared inside the hut to radio headquarters. Dom stood with the two British sentries and watched Drake take himself away, out of earshot, where he rested on a low wall and rolled up tobacco. It was intriguing how swiftly his exuberance could dissolve.

Following an awkward silence, the senior of the two sentries – a portly sergeant – spoke to Dom. "'Ere, do you nudge nudge wink wink boys know anything about our fleet coming up from Malaya?'

'I've no specifics on ETA,' said Dom, 'but HMS *Repulse* and the *Prince of Wales* are leading a bloody strong fleet. We just need to hold the bloody bastards back a while until they get here. Then we'll be home free.' It was the party line for valid reasons.

'Hmm. Good to hear.' His comrade nodded. 'Deserves a cuppa,' said the sergeant, ostentatiously licking his lips. 'The kettle's full.' He was pulling rank without knowing Dom's, from his unmarked uniform. 'All set for a brew-up.'

Dom could have done with something stronger – shame they were not back in the pillbox with the 'Whisky Captain'.

As Dom dutifully stepped inside the hut, Ben walked out.

'A car's coming. Half an hour.'

Dom grabbed the cord hanging from the unused blackout blinds and closed them. He lit the burner and slumped on a stool while he waited for the kettle to boil.

His first 'kill' of the war, indeed of his life. In fact, he – the Assistant Administrator to the Under-Secretary for Chinese Affairs – had struck the very first blow against the Japanese. What would Emily make of the new man he had become? Disapproval, of course.

Inside the sentry hut, Dom poured tea into two billy cans and a couple of rice bowls and spooned in powdered milk. Rather than pop outside to ask them, he ladled in sugar. Nobody in their right mind had an aversion to sugar in their tea, except – case in point – Emily. Her most recent letters still rambled on as though their separation were temporary, a mere symptom of war. Emily believed love is meant to last in some sort of Austenian sense – or sensibility.

Gwen took three sugars in her tea, as he had witnessed first-hand. Blonde, tall and curvaceous – how Emily would hate her. Yet Gwen only knew the fictitious character Dom had presented to her. What would she make of the *real* him? If this cold killer *was* really him? He barely knew himself anymore.

Chapter 3

Two nights earlier –
Saturday 6th December, 1941

Broad pillars upheld gaudy bronze capitals, a gilded ceiling and sculptured angels hovered above the chandeliers: it was a lobby that announced, if not anointed, itself. Dom rounded the clock-faced central column and whisked a glass of champagne off the tray of an unsuspecting waiter. Clearly the waiter had been commissioned to deliver every one of those glasses elsewhere, for with surprising officiousness he enquired, 'Are you with the Chinese Women's Club, sir?'

There was only one possible answer that 'Max Holt' could give: 'Why, yes, of course,' said Dom, and he spun away, gleefully sipping his quarry.

Gwen had finally consented to a proper evening date, at the venue of her choosing. She called it an 'anniversary', but it hadn't even been a month since they first met. She insisted upon paying – in gratitude for cream teas and companionship.

'Mr Holt?' Dom turned around and nodded. It was the hotel receptionist. 'Sir, we have taken a message for you from a "Mr Ben".'

Max opened the envelope and read the slip of paper:

> *It's your last night of leisure. Expect the big show to start tomorrow. Report in at 6am tomorrow (Sunday 7th) or as soon as the news is announced – whichever comes first.*
> *Ben*

Reality would soon bite.

Under the whirr of ceiling fans, Dom peered over a glossy aspidistra and scanned the lobby lounge tables, looking to avoid anyone he knew. It was the time of day when the chink of China tea sets had given way to the clink of cut glass. Hong Kong's gathering glitterati flaunted their colonial superiority even on the eve of war. Ignorance or strength?

Additional evening and weekend manoeuvres, on top of his weekday job, had conspired to prevent him seeing much of Gwen. They had written to each other with increasing frequency – almost daily – but had met only twice since that first night at the Peninsula, for afternoon teas at a respectable but out-of-the-way restaurant of his choosing. At the first rendezvous Gwen made a bargain with him: they must talk of the future, not the past. She longed to see her parents and to help in Britain's war effort: she had romantic notions of playing a Florence Nightingale role at home. Any suggestion that they prolong an evening beyond tea and cake met with obstruction. 'Mr Holt . . . Max, there is nothing I'd like more than to sail into the night with you. However, as I shall soon be sailing off to the other side of the world, I wouldn't wish to take advantage of your largesse.' *Largesse* was not exactly what he had in mind.

Attended by two starched Englishmen with trimmed moustaches, a banquet of extravagantly dressed Chinese society girls fluttered around the lobby's cocktail bar. Those particular Hooray Henrys were too blinkered by privilege to know the likes of Dominic Sotherly – or Max Holt. But in Hong Kong there was always someone who knew you.

Dom remembered the boredom-driven gossiping he had overheard from the secretaries in the office. He could not blame them for gossiping – despite a high workload and all the promises of war, he somehow remained bored himself. The tittle-tattle of the week had been all about the Saturday night function in the Peninsula ballroom: a 'Chinese Women's Club' fund-raiser for the war effort. *Britain's* war effort, of course.

'Ah, how are you, Mr Sotherly?'

Phyllis Harrop. There cometh the first danger of the evening. Dominic Sotherly may have been low on the imperial ladder, but he was not sufficiently unknown as to be universally accepted as a 'Mr Max Holt'. He hoped that by arriving well before Gwen that he might get many a *'How are you, Mr Sotherly?'* out of the way. Hardly a guarantee of smooth incognito sailing for the rest of the night.

'How delightful to see you,' said Ms Harrop. For that night's shindig, Phyllis Harrop – a cloying champion of all causes Chinese – had apparently mustered everyone who was anyone in Hong Kong, from the Governor downward. No doubt in need of more gentlemen dance partners for her women's club, Ms Harrop had extended the guest list lower still. She need not know that he would be bringing a girl of his own.

'I do hope Emily is well, Mr Sotherly?'

'Quite well, rest assured.' Any sadness at her departure had faded months ago.

'I'm glad you could join us this evening, Mr Sotherly. I'm just sorry we couldn't find you a table in the ballroom for dinner.'

'Not a worry. I look forward to the band later.'

'Jolly good. And have no concern about your attire.'

Dom raised his eyebrow and glanced down at his dinner suit, irked by the implication that he may not be suitably dressed for a function that he had hoped to avoid.

'It's supposed to be fancy dress, but, as you can see, while the girls emphasise the "fancy", most of the chaps regiment into white tie and tails.' She flicked a finger towards the Englishmen at the bar.

He headed up to the restaurant early only to find Gwen already there. She was sitting at *their* table, this time set for two rather than three. She surprised him by wearing the same black gown as the first night they met; surely she was the sort of girl to own a different party dress for each day of the month.

'Max, it's so delightful to see you.'

'Likewise.' Her smile righted the world. Would she still be smiling come tomorrow? 'But it's no good that you'll one day be lost to Hong Kong forever.'

'Oh, Max, let's simply enjoy tonight.'

Each time she said 'Max' he winced inside, the lie picked at like a scab.

She ordered him a bottle of champagne and herself a gin and tonic.

'Is it still your intention to leave?'

'I'm afraid I'm booked on a steamship for Canada, departing Wednesday.'

The smile fell from Dom's face.

'Wednesday? In four days' time?'

Gwen nodded. 'All the more reason to make the most of our last night together. I've come to the conclusion that life's too short to let chances pass.'

She squeezed his hand across the table. 'Do tell me more about your adventures with "Papa".'

His heart sank. He didn't want to keep lying to her. 'I thought we had a deal to look forward, not back?'

'Tonight's different. Everything's on the table.'

Over a shared bowl of mussels, he blustered his way through life in the trenches – not that he knew whether they had trenches in the Spanish Civil War, but surely neither would she. As his confidence, and her cooing, grew, he went on to describe how on one occasion he had protected Hemingway by fighting his way out of a tight situation they were in, against terrible odds. Despite such heroics, the problem with working for somebody famous was that the celebrity relentlessly reclaimed the limelight.

'And yet,' said Gwen, 'I've read from multiple sources that your Mr Hemingway is terribly brave and an accomplished shot, not to mention a mean boxer.'

'Let this go no further,' said Dom, casting his eyes from side to side as if concerned about ear-wigging strangers: 'We take care over Ernest's public image, make it look like he's this fearless battler. But I can tell you he's more bravado than brave.'

Gwen giggled. 'Well, I should say he's brave enough just to go there to war, especially with a wooden leg. Wouldn't that have made things frightfully difficult at times?'

Dom's eyes widened. A wooden leg? Hemingway?

'Or is it just his foot that is wooden? Gwen grinned. 'Do you know, if I met anyone with a wooden leg I should be most likely to pull it. Couldn't possibly resist.'

'Like you're pulling mine now?' asked Dom.

'Like you've been pulling mine for some time,' replied Gwen, her grin deadened.

'Oh, Gwen, I'm so sorry. It was a silly bet with—'

'Chester. I've had my suspicions for some time. So I confronted him.'

Dom nodded.

'We established during that first night that clearly you're no prohibitionist, and I said to Chester I doubt you ever worked for Hemingway. He didn't deny it – he couldn't lie, at least not to me. So I took that as confirmation.'

Dom let out a heavy sigh just as the white-jacketed waiter appeared. 'Is everything to your liking, sir?'

'Be a good mate and bring us a bottle of Sancerre.' There seemed little point in reining in the drinking now.

'Certainly, sir.'

He found her relationship with Chester Drake hard to figure out. She seemed to respect him so much – respect earned during their time in Macao, no doubt. But she would never speak of the past.

'I'm deeply sorry, Gwen.'

'Oh, I can take a bit of fun – an entertaining twist or two on your background. Hence I spared you further probing about your past during our afternoon teas.'

And, quid pro quo, she had spared herself.

'So, tell me, Max, what *do* you do?'

So she didn't doubt that he was called *'Max'* – it was just his supposed temperance and connection to Hemingway that she thought sounded fishy.

'Something far more mundane, I'm afraid. I work for the Governor.' Even that made it sound grander than it was. 'As assistant to the Under-Secretary for Chinese Affairs. *Terribly dull,* wouldn't you say?'

Gwen half-smiled.

Then he saw a possible route to redemption in her eyes. 'Just yesterday I had to trudge up to the New Territories to supervise a delivery of bedding and tucker to a refugee camp.' It had been a rare outing from a grey office. The influx of Chinese had far from abated after the Japanese wrested control of Kwangtung province. 'Provisions are somewhat stretched, as are staff. And the poor refugees can't survive without us.' Fears over the proximity of war had discouraged the supply of coolie labour from venturing so close to the Japanese at the border, hence it was all hands on deck from Dom's office.

'It sounds far from dull, Max. It sounds like you're saving lives!'

'Well, perhaps.' The lowliness of his position had been duly borne through when he found himself personally counting bags of rice off the truck: his Colonial Service 'career' was anything but. A glass ceiling blocked the ladder. The British looked down upon him as an unmitigated Australian – which was only half true.

Phyllis Harrop entered the restaurant. She stood by the maître d', casting her eyes around the room. Max looked away a fraction too late: Ms Harrop spotted him and walked towards their table.

'Someone you know?' asked Gwen.

'Well, yes. She's batty as a broomstick, so pay no attention to what she says.'

Then Harrop stopped, gave Dom a dismissive wave and turned to walk to another table: a bald gentleman with his napkin tucked into his collar was who she had really come to find.

Dom breathed out a deep breath. 'Anyway, I do enjoy getting out of the office and doing something for others. That's why I enjoy my other job.'

'Your weekend soldiering with the reservists? You haven't told me a great deal about that either.'

'Well, I'm in a special advanced unit. Kinda hush-hush.'

'How marvellous. Brave chap. But I do hope the Japs don't cause you any bother.'

'I should hope it would be *us* causing *them* bother!'

'Do you know, your accent has a whiff of English about it?' teased Gwen.

'Don't tell everyone!' Dom smiled. He must concede more ground to truth. 'That's because while my father is from Brissie, my mother is from Sussex.'

'Really?'

And, aged thirteen, he had been sent to boarding school in England before flunking the Oxford entrance exam – reprehensible because both of his parents had passed it. That had sealed his return Down Under, albeit after repeating a year at school. But Gwen need not hear of every failure.

'So how did you end up in Hong Kong?' asked Gwen.

'Boredom,' he replied, truthfully. 'Father, God rest him, retired from the civil service, and my parents uprooted us from Canberra to Brisbane: St Lucia. Mum taught English Literature at the university there – the same one I then studied at. Geography. And so, Brisbane became home – and every youngster bores of their home. I wanted to see the world while I was still young.'

'Yes, life's too short.'

She leaned towards him and grabbed his hand. 'So, Max, will you take me to the ball upstairs?'

'It will be full of *terrible bores,* as you English might say.'

'It won't be a bore if you're there.' She smiled a smile which must have got her what she wanted a million times before. 'I would be eternally grateful. . . .'

'Well,' said Dom, while standing by his seat, 'I did receive an invitation.'

'Take me!' She took a breath and grinned. 'That is, if you don't mind spending the night with me, Max?'

'Why on earth should I mind?'

Despite the wobble in his backstory, Max Holt was proving more of a hit than Dominic Sotherly had thought possible. And, best of all, 'Max Holt' lacked a wife.

Chapter 4

Morning, Friday 12th December, 1941

Max and Ben had been up in the hills, pulling what tricks they could in a vain attempt to hold the enemy beyond the northern fringes of Kowloon. Under a hot winter sun, overladen with rucksacks and holdalls, they beat a hasty retreat south down the hillside, the frontline guns booming at their backs.

Max paused for a moment to light a cigarette. He jogged back to Ben's side, exhaled a rush of smoke and contemplated fate. Moths to a flame? Thousands of Allied troops congregating within Kowloon Peninsula was surely exactly what the Japanese had prepared for.

The previous night, Max had spent a nervy few hours trying to sleep in his central Kowloon apartment – the last time he would lay in the bed he had shared for two years with Emily Sotherly. Through the night, the guns pounded away, rattling the windows and shaking Max's incipient sense of the nobility of war. What would Emily be doing with herself back in Mother England? Nothing except stewing over the child who could not have been saved.

Ben and Max quick-marched past a lone pair of turbaned Indian soldiers on the road.

'You gotta admire them,' said Ben. 'Fighting and perhaps dying in someone else's war, for half a white man's pay.'

'Makes me question their motivation,' said Max.

'Don't you worry about that.' Ben pointed across to the eastern fringes of Kowloon. 'Devil's Peak.' The volcanic-like hill

smouldered, thumped with regular explosions. 'Rajput regiment. Our last stand on Kowloon.'

'So what you mean is, our big stand on the mainland is being
fought by the very people the Japanese have apparently come to
save: oppressed Asians?'

Ben nodded.

Sent on hours ahead of them, Drake – whom Ben protected
as though he were his own son – would already be safely on Hong
Kong Island. Ben had a love for all things Asian, not least his
wife. When Dom had first arrived in the colony, he was warned
by Brits that marrying a Chinese was a sure way to end your
colonial career. But not so for Ben, who was nothing if not a
maverick.

'Hey, tell me,' said Ben, 'what made you sign up as a weekend
warrior in the first place? And don't give me the interview answer
– King and country and all that crap.'

'Crikey.' Max scratched his nose. 'Boredom, I guess. And cash.'
When war threatened Europe, Dom's boss – a greying civil
servant and Great War veteran – suggested he sign up as a
reservist with the Hong Kong Volunteers. There was the promise
of a stipend for each training weekend, plus suggestions of a
promotion at work.

'Not to get away from the wife, then?' asked Ben.

Max felt himself redden. Ben pulled no punches. But in truth
it was more the opposite – an eleventh hour attempt to show
Emily that he was not defined by routine colonial weekends of
leisurely squander. Yet after Emily left Hong Kong he chose to
give up even more weekends and evenings by joining Ben's secret
'Z Force'. Why? The sensible reason might have been to make a
little more money and to lose a little less of it. But the real reason
was to forget, to fill time, to stop the mind from over-thinking.
Twenty-six years old, and there was much to forget.

They passed another group of Indian soldiers, one of whom
tossed a piece of paper onto the road. Max paused to pick it up.
Although he had an understanding of spoken Cantonese, his
ability to read Chinese characters was barely rudimentary.

'Turn it over,' said Ben. 'See – an English translation, aimed squarely at our Indian brothers.'

Max read it aloud: *The British are responsible for this war: they invaded Asia. Kill the British and the fighting will stop. You will be free.'*

They passed the first buildings on the northern outskirts of Kowloon – all abandoned. A familiar landmark, the Central British School, squatted on a hilltop, commanding the surrounding countryside.

'We'll soon be at the Pen,' said Ben, perhaps prematurely. They were aiming to reach the tip of Kowloon's last-ditch command post for the British, encamped within the Peninsula Hotel.

Whereas the hotel had lauded its gauche glory, on Saturday night Gwen had not been the least bit gauche. She had waltzed Dom wildly around the polished dance floor, her flared skirt flying out into a swinging bell. He had had to think quickly that night in the ballroom, as one and then another individual yelled out, 'Hello, Dom,' or, 'Not your usual scene, Dominic!' He told Gwen, truthfully, that his father had recently died. He lied that his father had been named Max. Since then, he said, he himself had preferred to go by his own middle name – Max – rather than Dom. When they were out on the terrace overlooking the harbour and a shout of 'Sotherly!' came calling over, Max ignored it, tugged Gwen close and demonstrably readied to kiss her. Ralph Johnson, the caller of 'Sotherly', promptly about-turned – as though it were a case of mistaken identity.

Ben and Max found themselves amid a war-beaten mix of Empire soldiers who had hauled their kit down from the hills. They funnelled in together on Kowloon's main north-south artery and quick-marched past Sham Shui Po barracks. There, beyond the mesh fence, the few remaining personnel lugged supplies towards the shore in hope of a boat to the Island.

In downtown Kowloon the smell came before the sight. The bombing and shelling of Kowloon itself had – inexplicably – ceased. Swarms of flies had descended upon the town.

Ben slugged a little water from his canteen.

'What *is* that bloody smell?' asked Max.

The Bison was not one of those incessantly cheery Canadians – he had lived too much to play that game. So he replied honestly. 'Death.'

Strewn erratically in front of bombed-out homes and businesses, what had from a distance appeared to be sandbags, were not. The bodies had been dragged out of collapsed buildings and left on the roadside, as if refuse-collecting coolies would continue to do their rounds and pick up some extra corpses along their way.

'And that,' said Ben, pointing at a dark, lumpy liquid seeping out from buildings onto the street, 'is shit.' The vomit-inducing reek of raw sewage fused with decaying remains made Max bury his face in his armpit. Around him, scores of soldiers were doing likewise.

Ben pulled Max's hip flask from the side netting of his haversack and took a nip of rum, before passing it back to Max.

They tempered their march along Kowloon's broad, tree-lined high street, a slow-moving Nathan Road. Word spread that the Japanese were only a mile or two behind now, regrouping to form a line across the top of Kowloon.

'We could be in trouble here,' said Ben. 'Let's jog it.'

The toys inside their haversacks and holdalls jangled as they ran down the outside of the stream of marching soldiers. Below the vertical signage of Chinese characters, shop fronts consisted of broken glass and little else. The British had abandoned the locals to the Japanese, and locals abandoned their sense of peaceful civility and began looting.

The caravan of retreating troops pooled to a halt on the harbour front. Beyond the railway tracks that lined the waterfront, boats from the Island ferried to and fro.

Max pointed at a group of Royal Scots junior officers.

'They've copped it something rotten these last couple of days,' said Ben.

Max approached the officers.

'We've gotta be quick, Max,' Ben called after him.

Max asked around after Captain Edwards.

'The Whisky Captain?' said one chap. 'He stayed, with several of his men. They made a stand at a pillbox.'

'And now?'

The young officer cast his eyes to the ground and shook his head.

Ben tugged Max's arm. 'C'mon.'

'The Japs dug in up the road hours ago,' said Max. 'Why aren't they shelling us?'

'My guess,' said the Bison, 'is that they wish to maintain the façade that they are here to liberate Hong Kong, not destroy it.'

Ben hurried Max through the crowd of soldiers amassing outside Kowloon's solitary tower block, the Peninsula Hotel. There were reasons why Dom, until the previous weekend, had shunned this hotel lobby. Those reasons extended beyond his empty pockets and his disdain for overly fashionable cocktails drunk by overly privileged people.

They squeezed in through a side door. The scene in the lobby even surpassed the first-class flap Dom had witnessed during the previous evacuation here. Then – over a year before the war reached Hong Kong – wives and children were evacuated whether they wanted to go or not. 'Evacuation of the pures' was how people referred to the government decree to send away the 'pure British' – Eurasians or Chinese need not apply, even if they possessed British passports. So here, in possibly the Empire's grandest lobby, was where he had said his final goodbye to Emily. When work called him back to the office that morning – as he had requested them to do – Dom left her standing in a queue to get her ticket stamped. It was four months after Jack had gone, and Emily's ensuing depression had kept her at a desolate distance.

Sixteen months later, Max and Ben witnessed hastily promoted officers chasing their tails around the lobby. Nobody had taken charge. While Ben went off to use a hotel telephone to ascertain further orders, Max lit up a Golden Dragon. The cocktail bar demonstrated an oasis of order, operating as a makeshift first-aid station. The medical staff were shooing away anyone capable of walking in themselves. Once bandaged, injured soldiers were stretchered straight to the Star Ferry Pier.

Forty-five minutes later, Ben returned, shaking his head in frustration. He marched Max towards the exit. 'May as well wait for Shirley-bloody-Temple to come of age, it took me that long to get a telephone line. Then, don't ya'know, the line to Battle Box HQ is down. No one of rank is still here. And the boats will soon stop coming.'

They rushed out of the front of the hotel and into the fading daylight. Just as inside, outside the crowds had dwindled: word had spread that the Japanese had resumed their advance. Loaded with bags and cases, rich and poor bustled by, following the railway lines to the ferry pier, all to a clatter of gongs from the city behind them. Local culture dictated that noise – even a spoon clapping the base of a saucepan – was the best hope of deterring looters.

'Geez, we should've just bloody well sorted ourselves out!' said Max, as they broke into a run, carrying their hefty kitbags.

'I found out one thing, though,' yelled Ben. 'All talk of the British fleet coming up from Malaya is now, not to put too fine a point on it, bullshit.'

'What do you mean?' asked Max.

'The Japs bagged *Repulse* and the *Prince of Wales* off Singapore,' replied Ben as he ran. 'And the rest of the fleet turned back, naturally.' And so hopes of relief by British forces sank along with their only modern warships in the region.

They arrived at the pier just in time to witness the remnants of the Punjabi regiment slip away on a Star Ferry. An angry throng of Chinese civilians were left on the pier, shouting after the boat. At the back of the crowd an older Chinese man spotted Max and Ben in their jungle greens. 'Hey, you help us! They say that last boat. No more.' He grabbed the arm of the woman next to him and pointed at Ben. 'We go with you?'

'I'm sorry,' said Ben. 'We've got no way to get to the Island ourselves.' There they were, stuck – experts in covert warfare, soon to be captured because they had missed the boat.

Max and Ben drifted away and scoured the neighbouring jetties in hope. The crashing of gongs and saucepans had thronged into a constant din.

'Ben, the boats are long gone. But it's only 1,200 yards to Hong Kong Island.'

'Swim it?'

'We've gotta give it a burl!'

'No – we're not leaving HMS,' said Ben, gesturing at their two haversacks and two holdalls.

'So we're gonna let ourselves get captured because of His Majesty's Stationery?'

'I'm going to sort us out,' said Ben. 'Don't stray far from here.' He left Max, and all four bags, three jetties away from the crowd on the Star Ferry pier. Max sat down on his haversack. As darkness drew in, across the water the blackout on Hong Kong Island was observed patchily.

An engine whirred beyond the tip of the nearest jetty. Max sprang up and shouted at an overladen wallah-wallah thirty yards offshore. But his calls were lost to a clamour of voices on board and the thunder of distant shelling. The boat motored on into Victoria Harbour. A Japanese aircraft circled above but made no swoop down to shoot up the ferry. It was as though it wanted to do nothing to deter evacuation. Corral all remaining combatants onto Hong Kong Island, and – at eight miles wide, three miles deep – it would make a neat target for shelling practice.

Max stepped away from the water and peered down a side street, towards the gathering roar. There were no lights around Nathan Road – just fires. The sporadic small-arms fire had thickened in consistency: the Japanese were closing in. A commando 'spy' would expect to face summary execution, decapitation by a samurai sword.

Some distance down the street a number of Chinese came fleeing towards Max, wielding bats or machetes. Several dropped their weapons and darted down any one of several side alleys behind the Peninsula Hotel. Then, in the distant flickering firelight along Nathan Road, Max caught a glimpse that confirmed his fears: the bobbing march of Japanese soldiers with bayonets fixed.

He ran back to the waterfront as the remaining locals scattered. A conspicuous lone Caucasian in uniform, Max lugged the first two bags of 'HMS' to the end of the jetty and down the wooden staircase which descended into the sea. Then he climbed back up to retrieve the remaining two bags. A glance down the side street revealed a detachment of Japanese troops beating a running march towards him, their rifles drawn.

Where the bloody hell had Ben got to?

Max grabbed the two bags from the wharf, bounded down the steps and sat tight. His last thoughts as a free man were not of his wife or even his lost son, but a girl he had met but a handful of times, most recently over an evening truncated by the cry of war.

Outside the doors which opened onto the Peninsula's terrace, Max had leaned in for a kiss. But Gwen had pulled back – just as the orchestra spluttered to a halt midway through *The Best Things in Life are Free*. It was as though the musicians had stopped playing out of disgust for such amorous behaviour. But then an echoing voice started up and party guests rushed in to hear him. A uniformed naval officer had appeared on the balcony with a funnel megaphone. He called upon personnel to report to their stations with immediate effect. Military men and civil servants drained out of the ballroom. The party was over. As was a night with Gwen.

The waves splashed up over his boots. Max removed both revolvers from the haversacks. Then he popped his head back up above the steps. The jogging soldiers came to a halt, raised their rifles and began firing, splintering the wooden post a foot from Max's head. Bullets whizzed by as he ducked back down the steps. He focused on taking a breath. First, deal with the kitbags. Then take out some of those bastards.

He rummaged around the holdall of detonators, found a pencil fuse and grabbed a pack of plastic explosive from a haversack. Suddenly an engine roared up from behind: a Royal Navy motor boat.

But what about Ben?

Max knelt upright to wave frantically at the 60-foot motor boat, and a rifle shot thumped into the wooden decking just above his head. He ducked his head but raised his hands above the parapet and fired the two pistols to slow the Japanese advance.

The motor boat was arriving at both too great a height and too great a pace for Max to jump aboard – until it suddenly reversed its propellers and the bow lowered back into the sea.

There was Ben, a figurehead near the tip of the prow, Bren gun in hand. The bow thumped against the huge tyres lining the jetty. A machine gun fixed high amidships sent the approaching Japanese tumbling to the ground. Max picked up a bag of detonators and threw it to up to Ben. More shots came from the Japanese. The three bags of explosives and ammunition would stay where they were, at the foot of the staircase.

Max climbed aboard, grabbed hold of one of the vessel's fender tyres. A second after he climbed aboard, the motor boat pulled away.

The first Japanese soldiers bounded onto the jetty. Max grabbed Ben's Bren gun and blasted it towards the jetty. The acrid smell of cordite filled his nostrils. He aimed at the bags by the steps. As their motor boat roared away, the staircase, jetty and several Japanese soldiers disappeared in an almighty explosion.

Chapter 5

Evening, Friday 12th December, 1941

Through the cool of the evening, Max and Ben's rickshaw trundled along the praya, the runner's head bobbing indefatigably. The moon lit up Victoria Harbour, where shadowed, bombed out vessels keeled over at drunken angles. The rickshaw slowed to a halt at a makeshift checkpoint. A pair of turbaned policemen squinted a look at the passengers under the canopy. Max and Ben turned to face the sea as they listened to the cries of innocent civilians, the breeze carrying the caterwauling across the water from Kowloon. Neither spoke.

The rickshaw was ushered onward. Minutes later, Ben pointed ahead. 'There's *Tamar* – scuttled!' HMS *Tamar,* the depot ship permanently berthed along the shore from the city of Victoria and used as the Royal Navy's headquarters for generations, had settled in a languid slump deeper into the water, propped up by the seabed below. How long could Hong Kong Island take it, with no air force and all naval ships sunk, withdrawn or scuttled?

Across the water in Kowloon, back-lit by blazing fires, the eight-storey Peninsula Hotel stood tall. From party zone to battle zone in a matter of days. When Max thought of their night-time haunt, it was not only the scenes in which Gwen starred that replayed through his mind.

He tugged Ben's elbow. 'D'you know, Ben, when I told you what I overheard from that pair of Hong Kong royalty on my first visit to the Pen, you never said much.'

'Well, maybe I didn't know much, then.' Ben hesitated, as though weighing what to divulge.

The rickshaw runner turned them inland towards the heart of Victoria, bumping the wheels over tramlines.

'But I asked around. Nothing more came back to me until recently.'

How recently? wondered Max.

'It seems the Japs have put a price on Admiral Chan Chak's head. There's a lot he could tell them . . . I imagine that's what Madame Sun fears. He knows everyone in Chiang Kai-shek's inner circle.' Ben ran a finger across his stubbled chin. 'And the Japs would love to get hold of the Admiral's unparalleled knowledge of the Chinese navy – which he built.'

'So he's looking for British protection?'

Ben paused, as he so often did before he spoke.

'Something like that. Although with the Admiral it could just as easily be the other way around. I've been told he's making a name for himself here on the Island. He's been soliciting local "special forces" – to take on a swarm of fifth columnists.'

The city bore both the scars of war and revealed a sense of distance from it. Sandbags blighted the grand colonial edifices along the seafront, and the occasional smoking ruin served as a warning of worse to come. Yet the trams still ran along the streets, Caucasians in white naval uniforms or ashen suits were hauled along in rickshaws and coolies clad in blue linen carried their loads hither and dither.

'What do you mean by *special-bloody-forces?*' asked Max.

'I mean he's getting to know the "loyal and righteous brotherhood",' said Ben.

A tram rattled by, interrupting the conversation.

'Are those bludgers helping the Japs?' asked Max. 'Or might they help us?' Hong Kong's triad gangs were estimated to number somewhere between 30,000 and 60,000 – far larger than the British, Canadian and Indian armed forces combined.

'That's the question,' replied Ben. 'But my experience up in Shanghai tells me to expect triads to be best at helping themselves.'

'That said,' called Ben, 'there are times when your enemy can be your friend.'

The rickshaw runner slowed his legs to let a mother rush across the street, with her baby slung tight across her chest. This was neither the time nor place to bring up a child, but that fact failed to ameliorate Max's pain. He often thought of teaching young Jack how to sail, around the quiet islands off Sai Kung; of teaching him to ride and, when he was older still, to shoot.

'I'll drop you up on Queen's Road,' said Ben. 'I have to report in at the Battle Box' – the headquarters concealed somewhere under the city.

The rickshaw trundled on just another thirty yards before the runner pulled their carriage to a halt and lowered its front arms down to the ground. Max stepped down onto the road, and Ben paid the ten cents. Under the gaze of ever-present street hawkers, a Chinese lady resplendent in her *cheongsam* glanced at Max and hurried along the street and into the sheltered arches of a long arcade.

Max waved Ben goodbye. There was no mistaking the city was standing amid a warzone, for on the outskirts of town the night's shelling had just begun. But, better *here* than *there,* in ransacked Kowloon.

Max took a swig of rum from his hip flask. It was a short walk to the South China Tea House and then a lengthy climb up a dozen flights of stairs. The lift was still not working. He unlocked door 64 and entered the small windowless office which constituted Z Force's entire floor space.

Max switched the light on, and the first thing to catch his eye was the marvellous misuse of a Japanese propaganda leaflet he had earlier seen trampled into the dirt. Pinned on the drawer of a filing cabinet was a poster of a fat white man, sitting utterly naked with his feet on a pile of gold coins and a nude Chinese girl on each knee. This picture would be the pin-up of choice in pillboxes and barrack blocks across the colony.

He dragged aside two double-locked trunks of TNT – a new arrival from the storage depot – to create space for a bed of cardboard. Max rested his head on his haversack pillow, and his mind leaped around, prompted by the thunder of shelling outside and the proximity of enough TNT to blow the whole building up. Even without the TNT he'd be dead if a shell hit this part of the building; at least it would be quick. But what on God's green earth was that amount of explosive doing in the office?

It would be a long night in Kowloon as the victors claimed their spoils and the locals screamed their pain. Max's home would have been looted by now. Thankfully, he had sent his housemaid, Ah Mei, away to her own family when hostilities began. Although it would be of no surprise if she had sneaked back to check up on the apartment. Everything in it was replaceable, except for the photograph albums. He pulled from his wallet the three baby photographs which travelled with him always. Even in war – perhaps *especially* during war – he thought of his son every day, of all the things they would have done together, if only Jack had lived. 'Cot death', they called it. But he fought against the temptation to dwell, for there lay the descent into madness.

He flicked off the light. The shelling continued, but he tried to get some sleep.

He was soon roused by the creak of the door opening. The darkness was still complete, but he thrust a hand into his haversack and grabbled in vain for a pistol.

Torchlight flashed into the room. 'Evening, Max.'

'Shove it up your blot!' Max sat up. 'Ever thought of knocking?'

Ben flicked his torchlight across Max's face to the filing cabinet. He unlocked it and lifted out a Tommy gun, plus several boxes of ammunition.

'Get up, Max – we've got a major problem to deal with. And this time it's not the Japs.'

Three minutes later, they reached Ben's Sunbeam-Talbot.

'So, this problem,' said Max, 'is it bloody bigger than the Imperial Japanese Army?'

'More barbaric. Even more immediate.' Ben talked in staccato as he raced the car across town. 'Trouble with the triads. They're picking a winner.'

Ben turned onto a now-deserted Queen's Road. Behind them, another explosion burst through the night air.

'So where are we going?' asked Max.

'To see if new friends and an old enemy can help us out,' replied Ben.

Underdressed in jungle greens, Max lit up in the corridor, all the while being eyed up by a dozen weather-beaten but well-dressed Chinese. The gang of smoking Chinese men parted to allow a tall, white-suited gentleman to step forward out of the doorway to the police commissioner's office.

'Deadset – it's Two-Gun!' Max's body stiffened under the big man's handshake. Broad shoulders, squashed nose and with any number of nicks and marks, Two-Gun Cohen was the heavyweight who never retired.

''Ere, what's a little limey-loving-drongo-Aussie like you doin' down the cop shop at a time like this?' queried Two-Gun.

'Same as a big Cockney-Canuck-loving-Jew!' Transcontinental split personalities was one of several things they both held in common.

Cohen, a Polish Jew from east London whose formative years had been spent in Canada's Wild West, steered Max further away from the Chinese men and leaned in close. 'I know you're with Ben's secret Cub Scouts ... Don't look so bleedin' shocked – aren't you supposed to be trained to hide your true feelings?'

Max closed his mouth and said nothing.

'Some bleedin' poker face you've got!' said Two-Gun. 'Thought I'd taught you better.' Corralled into making up a four, for a no-stakes round of bridge at the Hong Kong Club one evening, the silver lining was being introduced to the legendary General Morris 'Two-Gun' Cohen. Cohen, on one of his R&R breaks from China-proper, told Max – or 'Dom', as he knew him then – how he saw his younger self in him. Once their respective partners had retired for the night, Two-Gun dealt poker cards and presented a master class in how to chisel 'producers' – the suckers who played cards for fun and produced a healthy supply of cash.

'Don't worry, mate. I'm doin' a little "consultancy" work for Ben, too. He said you're going by the name of "Max" these days.'

Max relaxed into a smile – Two-Gun Cohen was too good a cheat and too proud an Englishman not to trust.

'Yeah,' said Max, 'for a bet that's never bloody stopped!'

'As long as it was one you won, then it was a bleedin' good bet!'

Max grinned and nodded.

'Anyway,' continued Two-Gun, adjusting both his tie and his facial expression, 'we've got trouble.' He glanced left and right before lowering his voice. 'A ton of trouble we never saw coming with these here triads. It's un-bleedin'-believable what they got planned.'

Max wondered whether he should ask. 'It's hard to know what's going on behind that door. . . .'

'Ben's in there with all the British bigwigs, trying to sort this mess out, mate. Chucked the Chinese mob out into the corridor, they did, after getting nowhere fast.'

Max sighed.

'I just wish we'd focus on the fight,' continued Two-Gun. 'My VIP friend tells me good things are brewing over the border, mate. If we could just hold out here on the Island for a while. . . .' Across the harbour, the Japs were regrouping, preparing to launch an invasion of Hong Kong Island.

'But there's me jabbering on when I expect you're here to see the Admiral – he's in the interview room.' Two-Gun pointed his finger down the corridor.

At that moment, Ben emerged from the Chief's office and nodded at Cohen. He led Max down the corridor, through a cloud of cigarette smoke, and Two-Gun followed a few steps behind.

Max thrust a thumb back towards the gang leaders in the corridor. 'These drongos are a bunch of bloody crims! Lock 'em up and melt the key.'

'Keep your voice down, Max,' Ben whispered. 'It's not simply those six dragonheads in the corridor that we need to worry about. They argued that although they themselves are "the most reasonable of men" and seek to avoid violence, they can't speak for all – there's two hundred sub-heads alone.'

Ben gripped the door knob, stopped for a moment and gazed at Max. 'Over the course of the last two hours, the British brass have failed to come up with a proposal worth listening to – from the triads' point of view. Now we've been given ten minutes to do better.'

Ben opened the door, and Max followed him into the interview room. Two-Gun parked himself on guard outside in the corridor. Max closed the door and remained standing.

'Admiral, I believe you're well acquainted with Zhang Zilian,' said Ben. Introductions were conducted as though Max, the Admiral's adjutant and Zhang's Chinese interpreter were not in the room. The Admiral and Ben took seats on one side of the oval table, Zhang and his balding interpreter at the other. The Admiral appeared tiny even when sitting. Ben had described Zhang as a triad chief in Shanghai, a city that attracted more than its fair share.

'He my friend,' replied the Admiral. 'He come holiday to Hong Kong just to see me.' The Admiral broke into a beaming smile, like a child making a joke of his lie; Zhang had given up Shanghai when the Japanese moved in. 'Zhang help us,' continued the Admiral.

Zhang Zilian, swarthy skinned and steely eyed, soaked up the overtures his interpreter muttered into his ear.

'Yes, Admiral,' said Ben. 'Zhang also helped me, once upon a time.' The Admiral's adjutant distributed three bowls of tea and then remained standing behind his boss. 'Gentlemen,' continued Ben, 'we have been asked to convene this crisis meeting because of the cataclysmic direction the triad gangs are taking us in. Incredible though it is – the history books will never believe it – the triad's all-too specific threat now supersedes even the Japanese in our priorities. The very idea of it is too tawdry for a horror movie and too outrageous for a fifty cent novel. If they carry this out as planned tomorrow night, there will be no battle for British Hong Kong. There will be no British. And that means there will be no Hong Kong.'

'Zhang, this is *wery* bad.' The Admiral pointed his finger across the table, slipping from self-satisfied child to schoolteacher. 'You help us.' Whether he meant it as a question or a statement, it just hung in the air.

'Zhang, there was a time when we managed to work together in Shanghai, for the benefit of all.' Ben had told Max of a deal made where, for a price, Zhang gave up his most trigger-happy henchman – a menace not simply to rival gangs and police officers, but to civilians, too.

'Frankly,' said Ben, 'I can't imagine how you can be planning such a thing.'

Zhang conferred with his interpreter. Then the interpreter turned to Ben. 'Mr Zhang says, "Do not accuse *me* – I have planned nothing. I do not control the brothers of Hong Kong."'

Ben sighed. 'You have influence, Zhang. And you can't deny that you fraternise with all those crim . . . *dragonheads*. Every one of them counts you as an ally.'

Zhang tilted his head, a Chinese version of a shrug. Since arriving in Hong Kong he seemed keen to be viewed as a threat to no one and everyone.

'Do you agree with the massacre they've got planned for tomorrow?' asked Ben.

'Agree or not, it makes no difference,' came the reply through the interpreter. 'But do the British understand *why* the brother-hood have planned this "celebration"?'

'*Celebration?* Is that what you call it?'

'It's what *they* call it,' came Zhang's reply.

Ben leaned his elbows on the table. 'Enlighten me.'

'They want to save Hong Kong Chinese.'

Ben grimaced at the interpreter and then Zhang. 'By murder-ing every last European, man, woman and child?'

Zhang avoided Ben's gaze, his eyes momentarily resting on Max. 'Yes.'

'Barbaric!' Ben lifted up two sheets of paper where Chinese characters filled both sides of each page. 'A list of targets where Europeans will be found in large numbers. Not just barracks and police stations,' Ben pushed the sheet of paper across the desktop, 'look, it includes banks, clubs and even Hong Kong University, and – look – QMH.' Anywhere where the triads would find a glut of Europeans all in one place. 'They are going to kill every Caucasian in Hong Kong. They draw no line. Even Queen Mary Hospital? – which, by the way, serves not only Europeans but also Chinese. And you would do that? All for what?'

Zhang chewed the inside of his mouth. 'They believe that, currently, it is the British who could embark upon a new course of action that would stop the Japanese from bombing and killing Chinese.'

'Then the *loyal and righteous* brothers should join us and fight the Japanese to stop those bombs,' said Ben.

Zhang sipped his bowl of tea. "The brothers see a different solution. Indeed, they see a different problem. You may see Hong Kong as British, but the people living here – and dying here – are mostly Chinese—'

'And most of them fled here from China – because British Hong Kong offered them sanctuary!'

'Perhaps it *did,* but not now. The shells and bombs are falling on Chinese homes and killing Chinese families. And the bombardment continues because the British refuse to surrender. Killing the British would end a battle which is already lost, and it would end the bombing.'

Ben clenched his fist on the table. 'And how do we persuade the triads to alter their logic?'

Max pursed his lips. There was always the machine gun Ben had locked away in the trunk of his car.

On Ben's order, Max stepped out into the corridor, accompanied by the Admiral's adjutant, who set off to find a lavatory. Clearly, Ben believed he could get something more out of Zhang without superfluous witnesses present.

Max sat down on the bench seat in the now-empty corridor and lit a cigarette. The rumble of shelling came and went in waves, designed to unnerve as much as destroy.

Moments later, the outside door swung open.

'Well, hello old chap! Golly, it's been quite a week, *Max.*'

Max refused to engage.

Drake, dressed not in combat fatigues but in a lounge suit, lowered his voice. 'So, Dom, how do you like "Max" now you must be used to it? Straight off the bat, Ben loved the little *nom de guerre* I chose for you!' They had all been in Ben's car, returning from the shooting range, when Drake had first blurted out the idea that Dom should adopt a cover name. 'Although, at the time, you weren't too keen on "Max Holt", were you? You said it sounded too much like some Great War fighter ace – who was it?'

'I believe I said, "Biggles with a temper".'

Max's disdain for the sound of Drake's voice subdued his desire to ask when he had last heard from Gwen.

'We're in a bit of a jam, I'd say,' said Drake.

'Would you now?' What was it to him? *He* didn't need to worry about being butchered by triads – or perhaps he simply wasn't in the know. If the triads and Japs overran the place, Drake could probably work for the Japs – Eurasians would be just the sort of underclass they may like to elevate to do the work of running Hong Kong.

'I'd jolly well say so.'

Max turned away.

Drake sidled up to him on the bench. 'Regarding Saturday night, old chap, whatever happened between you and Gwen—'

He put a hand on Drake's arm. 'Is none of your bloody business, Drake.'

Drake poked a finger towards Max. 'That's exactly what I was about to say. She's a splendid girl, but I knew her in Macao only through business. Although she has become something of a friend. Have you seen her this week?'

'I've been a bit bloody busy this week, Chester, *old boy* – you know, fighting a world war and wotnot.'

'So you haven't seen her?'

Max turned his head away. That was what Drake was fishing for – whether Gwen had fallen into bed with Max Holt.

'Look,' continued Drake, 'if they take the Island, Gwen would be quite a prize for any number of lascivious Japanese soldiers.

She hasn't been in Hong Kong long enough to make trustworthy connections. We need to look out for her.'

Perhaps reassurance that Max had the matter in hand would throw Drake off the hunt. 'Look, I'm going to call in at her hotel first chance I get.' He had a plan to protect her. 'I've sent a message ahead. I've told her to move out of the Hong Kong Hotel and into a low-key Chinese hotel, where I've booked her a room.' Drake didn't need to know *which* Chinese hotel.

'And have you received a reply?'

'No, not yet. But I only sent it last night.'

'I called in at the Hong Kong Hotel yesterday evening.'

Max stared into Drake. 'And?'

'The receptionist told me she's checked out.'

'Shot through? Strewth! Any idea where to?'

'Yes, as a matter of fact, I do,' said Drake. 'She's near Aberdeen. Moved into billets at QMH.'

The rumble of war boomed louder.

'You alright, Max?'

Max bit his lip: Queen Mary Hospital.

Ben stepped out of the office, carefully closing the door behind him.

'Ben, tell me we're ignoring police orders and we're gonna secure the hospitals in case the triad militia *does* go as mad as a cut snake?' He could not help but still want Gwen, which was probably why he hadn't yet told Ben of his suspicions about her.

Ben blanked him. 'Chester, I've called you in because I've got a two-man job for you pair. Get over to our office and grab the TNT. And don't forget the tins of barium nitrate in the cupboard.'

'How much of it?' asked Drake.

'All of it. Get it to the Cecil Hotel by 1am.'

Chapter 6

Early hours,
Saturday 13th December, 1941

Max had been sitting on the desk for five minutes, waiting on the line, while Chester was already in the car with the explosives. He was pleased the office telephone worked at all – it was doing better than the lift.

He was staring at the nude Chinese girls on the filing cabinet when her voice cut in: 'Hello?'

'It's me,' said Max. 'How are you doing?'

'Excuse me, to whom am I speaking?'

It's me was a daft thing to say. A trolley clattered by at the other end of the line.

'It's me, M—'

'Max Holt! Somehow I knew I'd hear from you again!'

He closed his eyes, wrapped his arms around Gwen and pulled her tight. The very thought brought water to his eyes.

'Are you okay? I've been worried sick about you, Gwen.'

The line crackled. 'I'm just fine, Max. And you?'

'I've been desperate to call in on you . . . but. . . .' He threw his hand open, as though she could see him.

'I know. It's okay, Max – there's a war on.'

Max smiled at the telephone.

'It's awfully late – you were lucky to catch me at all.'

'Well, hospitals don't stop at night.'

'You know, you do sound so much less Australian now.'

'You mean when I'm sober!'

They both tried to laugh.

'Gwen, I heard that bombers have been targeting Aberdeen. Has the hospital been hit?' Their real target – at least one would have hoped – would have been the Royal Navy Dockyard at Aberdeen. But nearby, isolated on a hilltop overlooking Aberdeen Harbour, Queen Mary Hospital had not escaped unscathed.

'A few bumps and bruises. We've closed the upper two floors – the wards were deemed unsafe. So it's rather crowded on the lower floors – and we're receiving about a hundred new patients each day now. But we'll cope.'

Max wanted to blurt out there and then what was coming.

'Meet me later—'

'Max, I'd positively love to, but that's simply not possible.' She must have thought it a ridiculous idea, during the middle of the night, in the midst of a battle, the enemy's ground forces only a river's width away. He had a job to do, and a secret to keep, but he was desperate to get her away from what was coming – especially because Queen Mary Hospital was a named target of the triads. Even if those fanciful suspicions about her proved to be more than paranoia, and she was actually spying for the Japanese, she may soon face the same fate as every other Caucasian. So young, naïve, beautiful. What a waste.

'I mustn't leave here, Max. It's simply dreadful. They're all piling in, shredded to pieces. It's a ghastly affair, but someone's got to help those boys.' Gwen sniffed down the phone line. 'What about you? Which regiment are you attached to?'

'Oh, the Volunteers,' he said, tempted though he was to show off about Z Force.

'So they accept Australians?'

'Only good-looking ones.'

She managed to snort a laugh. 'Well, in one sense, I'm glad – we could certainly use the help.'

Incongruously, jazz music came down the line.

'That's Sister Jeffries. She puts the gramophone on to cheer up the patients.'

'Benny Goodman?'

'You've got a good ear,' said Gwen. 'Do you know, I came into town earlier, when the shelling had died down, to buy supplies, and I could hear singing, from down on the waterfront. *Swanee River*, I believe it was. Apparently the Japs were belting it out of Kowloon – or maybe from boats in the harbour. Interspersed with exhortations to the Chinese and Indians to turn against us.'

'*Swanee River* would be aimed at the Winnipeg Grenadiers and the Royal Rifles.'

'Why?' asked Gwen.

'Because they're Canucks,' replied Max. 'It's a misplaced attempt to make them homesick. I've met many Canadians, yet I've never met one who'd desert his regiment because of a song. Let alone an *American* song.'

'At least they stop the shelling whilst they play their music.'

Max plucked a pencil off the desk and twirled it in his right hand. 'Gwen, something terrible is going to happen. It—'

'Something terrible *is* happening,' said Gwen. 'Rightio, Max. It's simply wonderful to hear your voice. . . .'

'But you've really got to go?' He worried not only whether he would see her again, but whether *anyone* would.

'Yes.'

'But first there's something you need to—'

Exploding shellfire outside thundered into their conversation.

'Max! Are you alright?'

'I'm fine. It's you I'm worried about. You can't stay there. Not tonight.'

'Why on earth not?'

'Just believe me. I'm going to take you somewhere safe.'

'There's nowhere safe. Goodbye, Max.'

'Wait!' He snapped the pencil in his hand. 'I've got to ask you something.' He was buying time. She said nothing, but she hadn't hung up. 'Why are you here, Gwen?' She breathed heavily. 'Why do you have to be in Hong Kong at a time like this? Why did you wait to come here so long after the war started in Europe? And why didn't you leave Macao when the British wives were evacuated?' She should have taken the chance to get out whilst the going was good.

'Well, that's certainly blunt, isn't it?'

'I'm Aussie, remember: I'm built to be blunt.'

'You deserve an answer to your final question. I didn't leave when the British wives left because I'm not a British wife.'

'Well, I know you're not a wife, but—'

Footfalls – outside the office door.

'I *am* a wife. But my husband's not British – he's German.' The telephone receiver clicked dead.

'Gwen? . . . Gwen?'

The office door opened. 'Come on, old boy!' said Drake. 'We've got work to do.'

Another hotel bus pulled up outside. 'That's it,' said Max. 'Last one.'

First off the bus was Admiral Chan, all five foot of him. He planted his crutches onto the road alongside one shiny shoe and the flapping trouser leg of his shoeless wooden leg. The Admiral's contacts in the Hong Kong underworld had made this unlikely meeting possible.

Max had once taken Emily for tea and dancing in the Cecil Hotel. If she had known who would later occupy the same ballroom, she never would have set foot in the place.

'Right,' said Ben. 'Just look at this place. . . .' He swept his palm open. 'A hotel thick with thieves and cutthroats. No offence, Zhang.' Zhang's interpreter pretended not to hear against the hubbub of two hundred triad sub-heads and their superiors filtering through the lobby. Zhang's team of bodyguards wore long, baggy tunics – suitable for hiding a machete underneath.

It was an unlikely arrangement: policemen driving the branded buses of a luxury hotel to politely collect – amid a Japanese bombardment – a couple of hundred known criminals and deliver them to a grand ballroom to meet senior officers of the Hong Kong Police.

'Right,' said Max, 'we've got them all in there. Let's hope we can make this happen.'

Ben shot Max a sneering glance, as if to say, *Let's not show our weakness.*

They entered the ballroom, passing by a guard of British police officers. Zhang stepped onto the orchestra's stage, and the clatter of Cantonese voices lowered to a whisper. It was an astounding piece of work by Admiral Chan and Zhang Zilian just to get this far. Sitting on stage, to Zhang's left was Admiral Chan Chak. To his right, four senior Special Branch officers sweated in their uniforms, facing the very people who intended to massacre them and their brethren in a few hours' time.

Ben and Max positioned themselves in front of the closed doors at the rear of the hall. They were not to show disrespect to any of the triad leaders, nor should they allow anyone to leave the building. If no deal could be struck . . . well, Ben's team had not been invited along to serve tea.

There had been little time to think through Gwen's revelation. She had been playing a mysterious game from the outset, but why did she choose that telephone call to reveal the existence of a German husband? Max glanced at Ben. Should his boss be told about her relationship with a German?

CID Director, Superintendent Frank Shaftain, stood up, moved to the lectern and hastily dispensed with minimal pleasantries.

'It is clear to us all why we are gathered here in—'

At that moment a shell exploded somewhere nearby.

'We are here,' continued Shaftain, 'to save every European woman and child from murder, and perhaps save some of your souls while we are about it. I want you all to know, no record shall be kept of what is said here today. Indeed, my staff have already been told that this meeting never happened. Indeed, us merely being in the same room together is readily deniable, for it is too farfetched for fiction.'

Zhang listened to his interpreter and then shouted a Cantonese translation at the assembly. A grumble of low voices gathered momentum around the hall.

Shaftain soon returned to his seat, leaving the stage to Zhang. Max could make out little of his Shanghainese dialect, but he did catch several mentions of *'gweilo'* – Cantonese for 'foreign devil'. An interpreter stepped forward to mutter a commentary in the ear of Shaftain.

'Ben,' whispered Max, 'if someone tries to leave, what the bloody hell do we do?'

Movement on the balcony caught Max's eye: Chester Drake, an explosives zealot, when given the chance.

'Politely ask them to stay,' smiled Ben.

Ben had spent much of his working life fighting against criminal gangs: Triads in Shanghai were responsible for the death of several of his friends and colleagues. There had to be limits to how far his politeness would extend.

'Ben, *if* we remove these couple of hundred triads from the picture – and that's a big bloody *if*, because bolting the doors and blowing the whole bloody place seems too cartoonish for words – but *if* we did manage to take them out, there's still Buckley's chance for us. We would just be making enemies of the other 60,000 triads. We'd be giving them every reason to kill us all!'

One, then another, of the young triad foot soldiers sitting on the back row turned around to clock the faces of the two whispering *gweilos*.

'Yes, there is an inherent problem with that sort of plan,' answered Ben. 'It's bullshit.'

Max sighed out cigarette smoke. 'Then what the—'

'Shhh,' said Ben. 'We have our orders. Now let's hear the Admiral speak.'

The Admiral limped to the lectern. The crowd clapped enthusiastically. The Admiral waved them into silence and then spoke calmly, in Cantonese, of duty to their people and to the Motherland. He spoke of traitors who slipped the location coordinates of anti-aircraft batteries through a network of fifth columnists working for the Japanese. Some of those spies, he said, were closer than were once thought: 'Everybody knows somebody who is working for the Japanese'.

The audience broke into murmured denunciations and sideways glances, before the Admiral waved for quiet and moved matters along. At one point, he mentioned 20,000 of something

– Max didn't catch what – and the crowd jeered. The children in assembly were expressing disapproval of the invited speaker.

A man near the front of the crowd stood and spoke his mind, out of earshot from the rear of the hall. Then a stocky man on the second to last row stood up and said in Cantonese, 'If we deal with the British now, and welcome in the invading army, the Japanese will reward us. We could expect to be blessed with some fine Japanese hardware. And we would have a stake in the new system, and they would know it. We'd do better than the old gambling rackets.'

The floor muttered and nodded their agreement. The British representatives on stage were not even pretending to have the situation under control.

The man near the back took hold of his own paunch and yelled, 'You'll all grow fat with me!' The audience broke into chuckles. 'All for just a little work for them now.'

Scores of men rose to their feet and clapped. Max could not help but think they had a point. And perhaps that was it with Gwen. She believed her side had already won, so it barely mattered anymore – that was why she had told the truth – or at least some of it. Yet it was still possible that she felt something for her would-be Australian admirer, despite her marital allegiance to the Axis powers.

The Admiral waved for quiet and said, 'My friends, who do you expect to win this war? General Yu, a lover of China and of the Chinese Nationalists – just as I know you are, my friends – he has telephoned through good news for us. The General has a huge army fighting its way through the Japanese rear and towards Hong Kong. They will be here within weeks, perhaps days, my friends.'

Again, chatter swept the room. The Admiral let it play out for a minute before he resumed. 'Your duty, my friends, is to your families and brothers in China. Loving your people entails fighting *against* the Japanese, not for them.'

A hush took the crowd.

'Is that deadset, Ben? – about the Chinese Army?'

Ben pursed his lips.

The Admiral waved his arm from side to side, and the room quietened. 'Does anyone expect Japan to be ruling Hong Kong in five or ten years' time?' He paused for a moment. 'So, I ask again: who do you believe will win?'

'China!' yelled one man from the floor.

'America!' yelled another.

'And who are China and America allied with?' The answer didn't need to be stated. Admiral Chan sat down.

The audience conferred amongst itself. Max looked at Ben, in hope of reassurance. Was the Admiral convincing the crowd? Surely, if the British did come back, they could not contain a triad network fattened in the interim under Japanese rule?

'Twenty thousand is not enough!' shouted the man who had paraded his paunch. 'Not for all of us!' The crowd cheered their approval. Sitting on stage, Zhang Zilian tapped CID chief Shaftain on the shoulder and muttered something in his ear, shielding his mouth with his hand. Shaftain remained impassive.

'Now we're getting to it,' muttered Ben.

Chapter 7

Dusk, Saturday 13th December, 1941

'Right, you lock up, Max.' Ben dragged the holdall of clunk-ing metal out through the office door. 'I've got what we need. Let's go.'

When they stepped out into the dusk Max grabbed hold of one of the twin straps so that they carried the holdall between them.

'So what *did* it cost, last night?'

'Last night's deal's done, Max,' said Ben. 'It wasn't without cost, but it's over. Tonight we fight a different battle.'

Ben's racing green Sunbeam-Talbot was just down the street, with its top down. Cars were being stolen or sabotaged by pro-Japanese fifth columnists as a matter of course. As they approached the car, a heavily tattooed and lightly vested Chinese lad stopped tapping his toes on the running board and opened the trunk for the holdall. The young man, whose background was publicised by dragon tattoos snaked down each arm, closed the trunk. Ben slipped him some dollars and off he sauntered.

Max stared after him, and Ben read his mind. 'Don't worry, Max – they're helping us now.' Ben started the engine. 'The Admiral's turned them – he's employing them by the thousand.'

'And the gang leaders get to bludge a big fat gratuity courtesy of His Majesty's purse?'

'It's not exactly from His Majesty's purse – he can't afford it, currently.' Ben turned the car around. 'But money talks in Hong Kong – even during war.'

Ben drove slowly. Darkness was descending upon Queen's Road, where streams of Chinese used the calm between air raids to go about their business, despite intermittent shelling.

'Geez, that's why you paid protection money to that lad back there!' said Max.

'We're learning from the Japs,' said Ben. 'Damn it, they knew they couldn't take Hong Kong – let alone *run* it – on their own. They knew the limits of their own supposed racial superiority. You may think the Imperial Japanese Army is the bull's bollocks, but even they appease the triads.'

They drove past the Hongkong Bank building, its central tower a head flanked by the pockmarked shoulders of a twin tower on each side. With the army barracks and artillery batteries coming up on the hill to their right, and the naval yard of HMS *Tamar* off to the left, this area caught its fair share of bombardment. As if on cue, a whir came from the skies: a Japanese bomber flew low overhead.

A sentry stopped them for ID at the gates to Victoria Barracks, its glass-topped walls in good shape for such a primary target. Air raid sirens across the city leaped into life. At least they were headed to perhaps the safest place of all. But the timing of the air-raid warning alarm tended to bear little relation to the timing of the raid itself, the later often preceding the former.

'So last night,' said Max, 'if the British only came up with twenty thousand dollars – and that wasn't enough – who came up with the rest?'

'That, my friend, we shall never know.' said Ben. 'Officially.'

'Either the Admiral' – Ben frowned as Max spoke – 'or Zhang?' Ben dropped his frown. *'Zhang* stumped up the extra cash!'

Ben said nothing, but the corners of his mouth turned up.

'Why would Zhang do that?'

Ben hesitated. 'As an investment.'

'You mean he bludges himself repayment plus a handsome gratuity from the British?'

'Only if we win the war.'

'Well, that's a loyalty of sorts,' said Max. 'Sometimes I wish I had as much faith.'

He parked up just inside the gates. An open-backed army truck, laden with stores and armaments, swerved around a banyan tree, an oriental stalwart which hunched over and held its ground within Britain's colonial military headquarters.

Ben walked Max across the grounds. The four barrack blocks, rising one behind the other up the slope, had stood firm under bombardment.

They hurried towards the first block, where three tiers of broad colonnades overlooked a flurry of serviceman who scurried to and fro. They rounded a store building, and standing before them was a familiar suit.

'Two-Gun? What you doing here?' Cohen had emerged from a sunken entrance guarded by two soldiers.

'That's *General* Two-Gun to you, kid.'

'Nice general's uniform,' quipped Max, nodding at Cohen's white suit and panama hat.

Ben shook the hand of the recent recruit to the Z Force payroll.

Two-Gun pointed at the door behind him. 'I hope you lads get some good news down there,' he said in a hushed voice.

'Good news?' exclaimed Max. 'We've not got a cat's chance in hell of holding Hong Kong Island!'

Ben stared at Max. 'No, not on our own. But if we do our jobs right, then we've got a chance of holding out long enough.'

'We're not done yet,' said Two-Gun. He shouted to one of the guards to unlock the iron door and then turned back to Max. 'You know where you're going, kid?

'I believe I do, mate,' said Max.

'Things are 'appening,' said Two-Gun. 'Me old Chinese mates are getting their act together – and you need 'em. And I need to collect my two babies.' He flashed open the lapels of his suit to reveal the brown leather of a pair of empty shoulder holsters. 'I'll see you boys later!'

Max followed Ben down a steep concrete staircase lined with pipes and the occasional electric lamp.

'He's been in China that long he's gone native,' said Ben.

'But what's he doing here, anyway?' asked Max.

'It's not just us he works for,' replied Ben.

'I came across Two-Gun up in Shanghai,' said Ben. 'Not that he had acquired that nickname then. But he *was* an arms dealer. Although I don't know whether he made more from that or from playing poker at Short-Time Susan's.'

The descending steps were coming to an end where they met a passageway, forming a 'T' junction.

'Is he a real general?'

'Well, he went from arms dealer to bodyguard for the president of China, so I guess President Sun gave him that rank. And because Two-Gun worked for Sun Yat-sen – Admiral Chan's mentor – the Admiral trusts him like one of his own. And that's good enough for me.'

Metal scraped against metal as an unseen soldier slid the barrel of a rifle along a fire slit in the door ahead, lest they be foe not friend. A duty sergeant stepped out. Max presented his Webley. The sergeant removed the magazine and then fired the pistol into a bucket of sand, emptying the chamber.

Max whispered to Ben, 'Are you sure they want me in there?'

'Yes – it's time you know what's going on. If something ever happens to me, you may find yourself CO of Z Force.'

Ben and Max were shown along the passage and then descended further, following the lurid glare of a string of lights.

'That would give Drake something else to whinge about,' said Max.

'Chester's a fine operative, and he's got at least as much experience as you,' Ben sighed. 'But, politically, a Eurasian would never fit the job requirements – from our superiors' perspective, that is.'

A guard bade Ben a 'Good morning, sir', and opened another iron door leading to the nerve centre of Britain's China Command. Through a narrow passageway and thick air, alternate left then right turns led Ben and Max past doors marked 'RAF Signals' and 'RN Briefing Room'.

They reached the Battle Box's 'Operations Room', knocked and entered. Inside, the air was somewhat less musty, cooled by air conditioning. Service chiefs, decorated with military ribbons, milled around a table of maps that held the centre of the room. A giant sheet of vertical glass mapped out Hong Kong and its environs. Naval ships, airstrips and fixed artillery batteries were among the more obvious markings. Up half a dozen steps at the back of the room, young women worked a communications switchboard.

A lean looking Major-General Maltby turned away from his conversation at the table.

'Ah, Randall. Good to see you.' Ben stepped forward and saluted, leaving Max just inside the doorway. 'Benjamin, how are your boys doing?'

'Morale is high with us, sir.'

'Jolly good. Wish I could say the same here. If it wasn't for the Admiral, it would be nothing but bad news. The Japs have taken Lamma Island, so they can get at us from the south, too. Our MTBs have stirred up a hornet's nest.' Half-a-dozen of these 60-foot armoured speedboats was all that remained of the Royal Navy in Hong Kong. 'They've just shot up some junk boats we thought were up to no good, but it seems that on-board those junks were Chinese fishermen. So, now, even our own Chinese cooks and drivers are striking in protest. To top it all, we've accidentally blown up one of our own barges in the harbour – loaded with ammunition and more than a few good soldiers.'

'A rough—' As soon as Ben spoke the room shivered in tandem with a rumble from above.

'Don't worry about that – happens regularly down here,' said Maltby. He appeared older than he did that night at the Peninsula. Spending your days and nights making life-and-death decisions from a virtual tomb would age any man. The many yards of earth and reinforced concrete may or may not protect its inhabitants from a direct hit, but terra firma belonged under your feet rather than over your head.

'Sir, I've taken the liberty of bringing my trusty lieutenant – well, second lieutenant – with me.' Ben motioned his hand towards Max. 'Should anything happen to me, Second Lieutenant Holt here needs to be in the picture.' Priceless: Ben had just introduced the fictitious 'Max Holt' to Major-General Maltby, the military commander of Hong Kong.

'Quite. Step forward, young man.' Max did as ordered and saluted. 'Stand easy,' said Maltby. 'We haven't met before?'

'No, sir. But we did pass each other in the corridor at the Peninsula Hotel last month.'

'Well, there it is. Anyway, I was just talking about Z Force with the Admiral here.' Only now did Max see the short man standing behind Maltby's two British adjutants. Admiral Chan Chak greeted them with a grin that belied his forty-six years. 'You know what to do, Benjamin,' continued Maltby. 'Should – God forbid – the worst ever come to the worst.'

'Yes, sir.'

'But enough of that – the Admiral has arrived with good news,' said Maltby.

'*Ja-pan-ez-ey* . . . how you say . . . *tip cart of apples?*' said the Admiral.

He shuffled up to the table on his wooden leg and walking stick. 'British work with Chinese now. British need Chinese now.'

'Well, quite. Fortunately, London does now appear to grasp the realities of the situation: we have been given the green light to pursue cooperation,' said Maltby.

Standing a yard behind Ben, Max chewed on his gums. London had reversed its position: before the battle they believed working with the Nationalists would further nothing other than Chinese designs on Hong Kong.

'Let's cut to the chase,' said Maltby, 'as you colonials say. You see, we sent a chap up to Chungking on the last flight from the airport, together with Mrs Sun Yat-sen, to seek some assistance for Hong Kong from the Chinese.' He opened his palm towards the Admiral. 'A reply has just been telegraphed through from Chungking, via Admiral Chan.'

Leaning over the table, the Admiral said, 'Kuomintang China Army come here. From Waichow – Canton. Will defeat *Japan-ez-ey.*'

'So relief forces *are* fighting their way towards us?' queried Ben.

'Not ten or twenty thousand,' said the Admiral. 'An army – 220,000 men!'

'Two hundred and twenty thousand? That *is* good news,' said Ben.

Max smiled. The rumours of an army fighting through the Japanese forces in southern Canton had sounded too good to be true.

But Hong Kong *did* have a chance.

Chapter 8

Sunday 14th December, 1941

'We work now,' said the Admiral. He limped ahead to Ben's car, his artificial leg covered by navy-blue trousers, but he moved fast.

Ben held Max by the elbow and spoke softly. 'Things can get a bit lively with the Admiral.' There was more to Admiral Chan than rousing speeches.

'A night out with a one-legged, slightly mad, heavily armed, Chinese Nationalist admiral,' said Max. 'What could possibly go wrong?'

The Admiral paused by the car door, which his adjutant held open. 'Tonight,' said the Admiral from behind an intent gaze, 'shoot first, talk later.'

'That,' Ben muttered to Max under his breath as the pair of them sat down in the front of the car, 'is the Admiral's modus operandi.'

The Admiral clambered in the rear, joined by his right-hand man, the six-foot-three Lieutenant Commander Henry Lee, whose advanced rank seemed at odds with his youth.

When Max swung his feet inside the car he clunked them against something solid. He shot a bemused smile at Ben: a 't' shape of metal and walnut lay in the foot well.

'You're not special,' said Ben, lifting up his Thompson sub-machine gun from under the steering wheel. 'We've all got one.'

'Mate, who, exactly, are we looking for?' asked Max. 'Some local larrikins?'

'The Admiral and our new friends from the brotherhood have already put an end to most of the more mundane crimes – looting of homes, stealing of cars. He's got at least 5,000 men of dubious repute keeping order on our streets. But we've got bigger problems than that now.'

'Spies,' announced the Admiral.

With no street lighting, Ben drove at a careful pace. The headlamps, blacked out with a ring of paint, left only a spot of light on the road. A pair of nurses hurried along Queen's Road. Not much more than their silhouettes were discernible through the darkness, but the taller one might easily have been Gwen. Max felt that sense of grievance that comes with regret. And to think that she too had been playing games that evening at the Pen: her selected account of her life had made no mention of a husband – Germanic or otherwise.

Henry Lee directed Ben up the steep Peak Road, where homes were scattered among the trees. A pedestrian scurried into the road – Ben swerved around him only at the last moment. They drove around an artillery battery, a den of activity over-lit in ill consideration of the blackout. The initial British reluctance to shell Kowloon, for fear bombarding the Chinese population would incite a mass uprising, including on Hong Kong Island, had dissolved.

Ben threw the car around a deceptively sharp bend.

'Stop!' yelled the Admiral. He pointed up the darkened hillside. They stared and waited.

Suddenly, halfway up the mountain, a flash of light came and went three times. Then darkness fell for a moment, before the pattern repeated itself.

They drove a little closer, passing many of the mansions of the colonial haves. Lee directed Ben to pull in to some trees at the side of the road. Ben switched the engine off, and the Admiral and Henry got out of the back. The Admiral left his Tommy gun in the car but drew a six-inch knife from inside his double-breasted blazer. He was an odd mix of a fella.

'We'll just sit here for now, while the Admiral sorts things out,' said Ben. The Admiral and Henry hurried off down the hillside.

After a few minutes of waiting in the car, Max turned to face Ben. 'What the bloody hell's going on? Who're we after?'

'Fifth columnists – with bright lights.'

Five minutes later, footsteps came through the blackness towards the car; Henry and the Admiral reappeared. He wiped his blade with a rag.

'Crikey,' said Max.

'And there was I thinking you might bring us a prisoner we could interrogate,' said Ben from the driver's seat.

Henry Lee avoided eye contact. 'We did interrogate one of them.'

'We askey questions.' The Admiral pointed down the road. 'He tell me he got friends.'

Ben drove further up Peak Road. They wound around the mountainside and then forked onto a side lane. Ben slowed the car, and they passed a bungalow masked from the road by an extensive hedgerow.

'That's the place,' said Henry. They parked 150 yards further up the lane. Henry stepped around to the trunk and lifted a crate onto the tailgate. He removed the lid slowly to reveal what might have been apples, nestled as they were among scrunched-up newspaper. Max filled the pockets of his combat jacket and clipped a magazine stick into his Tommy gun.

'No questions askey,' the Admiral said quietly.

Lee saw a need to explain. 'He means—'

Then came the distant thunder of artillery fire, followed by an explosion only a little way back down the mountainside. Max ran twenty yards down the road, to a break in the trees that afforded him an unobstructed view of the fireball leaping up from below. The accuracy was scarcely believable: just one salvo and it appeared to be a direct hit on the artillery battery.

Ben arrived alongside Max just as he said, 'Our battery! Blown to hell!'

'We got here too late to save those boys,' said Ben. 'But let's go get the rest of the gang who targeted them.'

'We got job to do,' said Admiral Chan, pointing back down the lane.

They walked on, Ben and the Admiral in whispering conference. Short of the bungalow's hedgerow, Ben stopped and turned to Max and Henry. 'We've got to get in without warning them,' he whispered. 'No talking from here on. If a watchman sees us or they hear us coming, we withdraw.'

Light seeped out of the edges of the shuttered windows at the front and side of the bungalow. The garden was broad but the home was small for the Peak, the most exclusive of locations.

The Admiral and Henry paused before the hedge that ran to the front gate; they would allow the Z Force men a minute to scout ahead. Ben and Max crouched down below bushes at the near side of the front garden. Ben spotted something: a pen-top-sized orange glow. Max's eyes adjusted to the dark, and he could make out a shadowy outline sitting near the front gate, perhaps on a log or tree stump. Max gestured for Ben to continue on down the side of the bungalow to clear the rear, as planned.

Max put down his machete. He squeezed between the bungalow and a spiky bush and raised the barrel of his machine gun. It was impossible to tell in the dark if the man near the gate was armed, but it was safe to assume he had at least a machete.

The man let out a sigh as he exhaled his cigarette. Max had crept to within two yards of his back when a figure appeared from around the hedge: the Admiral, impatient for a frontal attack. Max expected the man to leap up from his seat on the tree stump, but first his right hand rose – attached to a revolver. As the man stood up, Max made up the ground in two leaping steps. He wrapped his forearm around the man's throat while seizing his right arm and jerking it back. The gun dropped to the ground, and the man emitted the beginnings of a squeal, which Max muted with a tighter squeeze to the man's neck. The Admiral lunged with a stab into the man's stomach.

The man slumped down in Max's arms, wheezing and croaking as he was lowered to the ground. Then silence. This was different to the soldier he had killed through the darkness in the jungle that night. Even though it was the Admiral who dealt the deadly blow, this felt worse. Max had been pressed against this man – an ordinary-looking Chinese fellow, not a Japanese soldier in uniform – and he both felt and heard the life gasp out of him.

Chapter 8

Henry and the Admiral had hurried to the front door with their Tommy guns while Max was standing over the body. Max was running on adrenaline and on the silent killing training he had never invoked until last week. The collapsed man was young, probably not out of his teens. His pulse was hard to find, and once found, it soon disappeared.

The Admiral stepped between two pillars of an open-sided porch and pointed his machine gun at the lock of the wooden door. He blew it away and yanked the door open. Light poured out and Henry rushed in firing, with the Admiral hurrying behind him. By the time Max entered behind those two, a sprawl of bleeding men lay across the living-dining area. Their machetes rested on the floor next to their corpses.

Ben entered through the back kitchen. Henry and the Admiral went to check a bedroom each, leaving Max a bathroom. All clear. Max began to check for pulses, but once again the Admiral used the quicker and surer method of approaching each bloodied body and slitting its throat. The pooling blood made the wooden floor slippery under foot.

'Six,' said Henry. His shirt, covered in sweat and blood, had opened at the throat to reveal a silver cross on a chain around his neck.

'Plus the one on the gate,' said Max.

'Eight. There was one in the back garden, taking a piss,' said Ben.

'They *all* take piss,' chuckled the Admiral.

They switched off the house lights and walked back to the car.

'So, who the hell were they? They didn't look Japanese,' said Max.

Almost imperceptibly in the darkness, the Admiral nodded at Henry, to give him permission to speak.

'Chinese,' said Henry. 'Spies from the Jap-backed puppet regime in Nanking.'

They got inside the car and Ben drove off. Max spun his head around to face Henry. 'So, you knew that bastard back at our first stop tonight was flashing to Kowloon side to show the Japs exactly where to fire?'

'Yes, we had seen his signals.'

'Buggers. That's why that artillery post was wiped out before our bloody eyes. And that bastard "volunteered" where the rest of his gang was?'

'There's no time to put them on trial,' said Henry, the plaintive tone of his voice conceding guilt.

'Same-same,' said the Admiral. 'Here or Blood Alley. Same-same.' A dead-end lane off the neoclassical arches of Pedder Street – jammed between Victoria's finest hotels and Hong Kong's most expensive department store – had become the execution zone of choice. Corpses were left lying in the open, bearing placards as warnings to other looters or spies, all within yards of the Christmassy window displays of Lane Crawford. Framed by colourful paper chains, mannequins wrapped in toggled coats and tartan scarves looked away.

'We askey questions and cut off one finger, then one finger more. Then he say where his friends are,' said the Admiral, pointing over his shoulder, back towards the bungalow. 'Then. . . .' The Admiral drew his forefinger across his throat. There would be no more signalling across the harbour by that fellow or his associates.

If the Chinese forces heading to Hong Kong were full of Admiral Chan types, it was almost possible to feel sympathy for the Imperial Japanese Army.

Chapter 9

Monday 15th December, 1941

'Let's go,' said Ben. 'It's late enough.' After an early evening callout for more trouble-shooting, they had dropped Henry and the Admiral back in town and returned their guns to the Z Force office.

Ben pad-locked the bolt on the outside of the door. Max led the way out along the corridor. 'There's someone I need to see. Before it's too late.'

'At this hour?' queried Ben. 'Why not come bed down at our place – the shelling's not so bad on the south side.'

'Thanks mate, but, if you don't mind, could you drop me on your way?'

Ben drove them past the back of an imposing red stone building, home to Western Market. Traders cleared out empty boxes, closing up after another day of business – even on a Sunday evening during wartime. Rickshaws ferried to and fro: whereas mass transport systems were by then grinding to a halt, in Hong Kong private enterprise was the fish that never stopped swimming.

Max spotted a familiar shop, front open, wares out on display on fold-out tables.

'Wouldya pull in for a minute, mate?'

Hong Kong's shops were nothing if not eclectic. They existed to make money, not to fulfil some Westerner's sense of orderliness. This 'medicine' shop always made Max smile: in addition to pharmaceutical goods, it displayed ladies' stockings, spanner and socket sets and, shelved behind the counter, bottles of liquor. The colony's whisky supply had withdrawn more quickly than

British forces, but a half bottle of Filipino 'gin' – if loosely defined – was still available. Max asked for two bottles and paid for four: the costs of war.

Winding up the hill behind Victoria, at one point a bomb crater sucked away almost the entire width of Pokfulam Road. What was just four miles of town-to-country driving became forty-minutes, riding through a darkness sporadically lit up by shell fire, dodging rocks and swerving around potholes. They say that during Britain's Blitz the whistle of an individual bomb could be heard on the ground as it dropped. That evening, over Victoria Harbour, the flashes and bangs aggregated into one atonal pyrotechnic symphony.

Ben drove Max around the sweeping hairpin driveway that approached Queen Mary Hospital.

'I'll leave you with a bottle of this for company, mate,' said Max, before getting out of the car.

A nurse shuffled through the darkness towards an outbuilding, carrying a basket of linen bundled so high it obscured all but her legs.

The moonlight exposed darkened pockmarks on the once-shining-white face of this new hospital. The big guns, placed irresponsibly just outside the hospital grounds, vindicated the targeting of the area. While Max walked across the green nestled between the legs of the H-shaped block, a Bedford van, daubed with a large red cross, pulled up in front of the entrance. Stretcher bearers carried in one half-dead soldier then returned to the van to fetch another. The open double doors to the lobby framed a dimly-lit scene of groaning chaos. Short on chairs and beds, patients filled every inch of floor space.

Max recalled the pair of legs he had seen below the bundle of linen and turned back across the green. He walked towards the nurses' quarters, and there, pegging bedsheets to a line at a quarter-to-ten in the evening, was Gwen. She dropped a sheet to the ground and rushed towards him. They hugged, and Max kissed her cheek. Their cheeks rubbed past each other as their lips neared. Gwen tilted her head back to look into his eyes for a moment, before plunging back to his lips and into a vigorous snog. A nurse and later a porter hurried by as they were kissing, pretending not to see them.

'Gosh, it's wonderful to see you, Max.' He held her in a firm embrace. 'I didn't know if you were still alive. I must look bloody awful. I work until I fall asleep here, rarely on a bed. We have too many patients.'

He loosened his hold on her. 'I've brought you something to buoy your spirits.'

She smiled as the gin bottle was slipped into her hands.

'Is there someone who can look after you when . . . if the Japs get here? Your husband, maybe – where's he?'

'Departed,' she sighed. 'Gone to meet his maker, I should hope.' Her eyes darted aside.

'I'm sorry,' he said.

'I doubt that very much. But maybe I should have told you about him earlier.'

'You and I have both had our secrets.'

'You think you could make do with a very ordinary mongrel Anglo-Australian?'

She smiled and gave a faint nod.

He held her hands. 'Gwen, I know you're busy. But take a break, come out with me.'

'There's nothing I'd like more.' She had this way of averting her eyes when she was about to say something the listener might not like. 'If only there were not a war on.'

He sighed. If she were a spy, what purpose did she serve the Japanese working day and night at a hospital? It was too preposterous.

'You've got to eat. Restaurants are still open, despite the war. . . .' A grimacing sister walked by. 'And so are the hotels, Gwen.' Was her look one of mock surprise or derisory sneer? 'I mean, you deserve a good night in a bed. A good night's sleep, that is.' English girls hated the truth to be said out loud – he should have learned that from his wife. They didn't like inevitability, or at least the appearance of it.

'Look, I might not be alive by tomorrow night,' he said.

'Don't say that!' She tilted her head and placed her fingertips onto his cheek for a moment. Yet she said nothing.

An ambulance screeched by, the first traditional hospital vehicle he had seen that day.

He hesitated before he spoke. 'If I'm, uh, indisposed when the Japs come, call Chester Drake.' Sometimes Max surprised himself. 'He may know a way to get you out of here.'

'I don't know how you think Chester could do that – he's just an accountant . . . isn't he?'

Was she fishing, as a spy would? 'Trust me. Just ask him.'

She looked like she wanted to ask more but didn't. 'Max, I'd best get back to work.' They hugged cheek-to-cheek. 'Max, I know we'll meet again.'

'In the meantime, remember me each time you swig a gin.' He slipped the hip flask out of his pocket. 'It's an old family keepsake. Been with me everywhere. And through the Somme with Dad.' She clasped the flask with both hands.

He kissed her and worked her lips apart with his tongue. After a minute or two, she pulled away. If she was a spy, he didn't care.

'Goodbye, Gwen.'

Chapter 10

Wednesday 17th December, 1941

A quarter moon and a sweep of stars, invited to shine by the city's blackout, hung over the harbour. From a barge moored on the Kowloon side, wailing across a calm sea came the saccharine lyrics of *Home, Sweet Home.* This was the curtain call for the evening's propaganda lectures, boomed across the harbour in English, Hindi and Chinese, with sporadic interruptions by a shuddering double-bass of explosions from either shore. But that particular boat was not Ben and Max's target.

They had waited for the tide to turn before launching the dinghy from the north-east of Hong Kong Island. The nick in the shoulder Ben the Bison had received the previous week did little to slow his stroke. Behind him, Max shovelled at the water with a sawn-off paddle.

The Bison tapped Max on the thigh and they upped oars for a moment. Ben brought the binoculars to his eyes to survey the anchored ship ahead.

Then they assumed a kneeling position and stabbed the water dragon-boat style. 'Steady and silent wins the race,' Ben had said before they set off. 'Less haste equals less noise,' which was their best hope for sneaking up on a Japanese-held ship in the dead of night. But as they cut through the moonlit sea, stirring up great rushes of phosphorescent light with every slash of a blade, Max felt far from stealthy.

Earlier in the day, Admiral Chan had expressed his concern for this abandoned merchant ship, anchored halfway between the eastern reaches of Kowloon and Hong Kong Island. There, the harbour channelled into its narrowest point. 'No good,' the

Admiral had said. 'Bloody Jap ship now.' The Japanese would be using it as an advanced position from which to conduct reconnaissance ahead of their invasion of Hong Kong Island.

The Chinese *sampans*, which for so many decades had hopped around the harbour's coastline like flies on a cow's back, had by now abandoned the scene. What remained was a scattering of bombed-out hulks of metal, listing painfully. On several of these flames still glimmered, spreading a lurid glow over the water. The breeze brought acrid gases which gnawed at their throats.

'Paddle wide to starboard,' whispered Ben. They glided away from the nearest fiery hulk and on towards their target.

They had closed to within a hundred yards of the merchant ship's stern when Max spotted the silhouette of a nightwatchman. The dinghy's slow progress and considerable splash would alert the Japanese on board sooner or later.

The sudden commencement, from the British-held side of the water, of clapping gunfire and streaking tracer gave both the Japanese and Max plenty to consider. The machine-gun fire belting over his head might soon stray towards himself: that the gunfire was coming from his own side was of little comfort when the man pulling the trigger was Chester Drake.

Bullets clanged into the superstructure of the freight ship and zipped into the water just yards away from the little dinghy as its two crewmen uneasily paddled towards the stern. The Japanese guard scurried out of sight, lacking suitable armament with which to return fire at Drake's machine gun post on shore, situated on the rooftop of Taikoo sugar refinery.

Max shook his head. Drake believed he knew it all, yet from the first weekend they had met – on live ammunition training – he had shown his true colours. When Drake thumped his Webley down onto the marksman's bench at the range, the revolver fired a round off which might have killed anyone. As it was, it hit Max's thigh. Was Drake able to avoid sanction because he was genuinely of such high value to Ben? Or was his mild reprimand of the kind that only money could buy?

They paddled furiously over the final few yards, until Max reached out and grabbed the sternpost above the rudder. When the firing paused, they froze. Faint Japanese voices came and went. Rather than targeting the upper deck, the gunfire which recommenced from Drake's Vickers seemed aimed more towards where Max and Ben were headed, at the stern. They paddled frantically ahead of the stream of bullets, around to the sheltered side of the vessel.

Ben held the dinghy close to the stern, courtesy of a rope which dangled from a lifeboat above. Max slipped into the sea. The water chilled through his battle fatigues. Ben passed him the first toy, its weight pulling Max fully under the water. He felt his way down the side of the hull, where barnacles ripped the skin on his fingertips.

'You give me toys,' the Admiral had said, 'and I play a game.' Oddly, Ben *had* let the Admiral take away a couple of limpet mines from the stores for his own unspecified purposes. And then Ben had grabbed two for himself – the first of which Max now slapped against the ship with an unavoidable thud. He flicked on the fuse switch – supposedly good for up to an hour, but one should never set one's clock by the accuracy of a time fuse.

Max came up for air and swam back towards Ben in the dinghy. Concerned the barnacles would deaden the magnetic attraction, after he secured the second mine he gave the handle a yank: the limpet proved worthy of its name.

Once back in the dinghy, they began to paddle away, again under Drake's wavering gunfire. Inward relief arrived when the gunfire stopped – but then came the realisation that this made it easier for the Japanese to hear their strokes. So, oars up, Ben and Max let the current drift the dinghy fifty yards before they recommenced paddling. Max anticipated a shot in the back from the enemy's guns at any moment, however, Drake regained their attention with irregular bursts of fire. From then on, it was a shot in the *front* that Max most feared.

The current drew them forward, doubling the gain of each stroke. When they were about 200 yards from the merchant ship, an explosion roared from behind them. But it wasn't *their* ship. Flames leaped up from a boat close to Kowloon waterfront. Was another Z Force team out on the water? Surely to sidle up to a ship wharfed on the Japanese-controlled Kowloon waterfront would be too suicidal, even for Z Force?

Halfway to shore, a pause from Chester's Vickers allowed small-arms fire from the merchant ship they had mined to follow after them. Max and Ben paddled madly. This time there was no burst of fire from Chester to fend off the Japanese gunfire. But the darkness was saving them, the enemy fire proving wildly inaccurate.

As they closed in on Taikoo wharf, Max gazed across the water, where a small *sampan* was homing in from an easterly trajectory. Traditional lampshade-shaped straw hats topped each of the two figures who paddled towards shore.

Ben secured their dinghy ashore while Max ran up onto the flat roof of the waterfront warehouse. 'What the bloody hell was that about?' Drake was sitting on a box, yards behind his sandbagged machine gun post.

He stood up. 'My dear chap, what on God's earth do you mean?'

'Stop pissing around, Drake – your line of fire came within inches of blowing our heads off!'

Drake stepped down from his firing step and fronted up to Max. 'Steady on, old chap, I just did my job.'

'You've got a lot of front, you bastard. You bloody well shot me once before, and now you bloody well tried to shoot me again!'

'Gosh, can you not accept that was a training ground accident? The bullet barely scratched your thigh. How many times must I apologise?'

'Bloody bullshit.' Max searched desperately for a lengthier comeback. 'Well, I hope you enjoy the thought of me rooting Gwen tonight.' It was weak and quite possibly groundless, but somehow saying it made him feel a little better.

Drake flew a fist at Max who ducked but still received a scuff to his temple. Max clenched his fist and pulled it back. Primed to release his full force forward, an extraneous pair of arms hoisted him up from behind and dragged him away.

'You're on the same bloody side!' shouted Ben. 'Calm down, and come and have a drink.'

Max shook himself free of Ben's grasp and walked away, further annoyed by Ben's behaviour: had he not felt threatened out there by Drake's bullets?

Behind a tower of empty boxes, Max changed out of his wet clothes. He returned to where Ben and Drake perched on crates, just inside the open front of the warehouse. Ben seated himself between the two sparring rivals and passed around a bottle of rice wine. Chinese stevedores, under the direction of a chippy British naval officer, hauled crates back and forth through the night. Max took a double swig of what would have been unpalatable in ordinary circumstances. Drake would get what was coming to him, the only questions were how and when.

Within minutes, a double explosion in the middle of the harbour smashed their merchant ship and all aboard her to smithereens. The three of them stepped a yard out of the warehouse. Ben raised the bottle in honour of their handiwork and offered the last drop to Max. As the fireballs in the harbour tempered to a steady blaze, two familiar faces sidled into the warehouse.

'Good job, ah,' said Admiral Chan, with Henry Lee at his side. Henry's clothes were soaking wet. Ben, Max and Drake stood up, and the Admiral presented a large bottle of rum to pass around between the five of them.

'So your evening cruise went well, Admiral?' enquired Ben.

'*Wery* good.'

'You didn't like those propaganda lectures coming across the water?' asked Max, ushering the Admiral to a wooden box to sit on.

'I'm afraid it was more the music,' Lee said with a smile.

'Yeah, I no like American music.' The Admiral gazed at Max. 'Sorry, ah.'

'It's okay – I'm Australian.'

'Oh – *wery* sorry, ah!' the Admiral guffawed.

The bottle came back to him, and the Admiral polished it off. 'Gone now.' It was unclear whether he was referring to the rum or the propaganda boat that he and Lee had blown up.

Henry, standing tall and earnest despite the water dripping onto the floor, was itching to speak to Ben. 'We must return to our office shortly,' he said, 'but first the Admiral wishes to know if we may speak openly regarding the Chinese Army?'

'We're all friends here,' said Ben. 'Speak away, sir.'

The Admiral allowed Henry, with his faultless English, to continue. 'If the Army reaches the Hong Kong border, we will need a joint Anglo-Chinese delegation to dash around enemy lines to meet General Yu.'

'Sounds like our line of work,' said Drake, managing a grin.

Ben looked at Henry and scratched his chin. '*Around* enemy lines – not through?'

Henry smiled.

'You got fast boat?' asked the Admiral.

Max sipped his tea. Ben had stripped the room of everything important or incriminating. A few hundred yards away, Henry and the Admiral would be doing likewise at their own office. Outside, the remnants of documents burned in the gutter, a paper offering to the gods.

'We won't use this place again,' said Ben. The rest of the floor – if not the whole building – had already cleared out.

'This shelling's got to. . . .' Max waited for another thunderclap to fade. Since their adventure in the harbour, daylight hours had brought unceasing bombardment. 'Got to end sometime!'

'It won't stop until the Japanese cross the water – maybe tomorrow.' Ben shuffled through a file of papers inside his briefcase. 'Cast your eye.' He handed Max a single sheet. 'This is going out to all battle forces tomorrow.'

Max shook his head. 'Strewth, it's all bloody fine urging Hong Kong to "advance against the enemy" when you're cosied up in London. Old Winnie hasn't got a pissing clue what's going on out here. Look at this crap: "the time has come to advance against the enemy – the eyes of the empire are upon us." Jap-bloody-eyes are upon *us,* not him.'

'Churchill's not a complete idiot.' Ben was standing still for a moment. 'Listen, this goes no further than these four walls.' Max nodded. 'Before the war reached Hong Kong, one of our sister agencies procured some of Churchill's private correspondence.'

'You mean the old goat's spy agencies spy on him?'

Ben's pursed lips dodged that one. 'The point is this was his estimate of Hong Kong's prospects: in the event of a possible Japanese attack, Churchill said there was "not the slightest chance" for Hong Kong.'

'Not the slightest chance? Then why the bloody hell are we here?'

'Shh,' mouthed Ben, placing his finger to his lips.

They both looked at the door: uneven footsteps stuttered down the corridor and grew louder. Ben peered through the spy hole before opening the door.

'Good evening, sir,' said Ben. 'Your first trip to our little hideaway and I'm afraid we're all packed up to leave.'

'I come see your office,' said the Admiral, stepping inside. 'First time and last time. It's shit.'

The Admiral leaned heavily on his stick. His face turned unusually grave.

'Is your man with you?' enquired Ben.

'Outside. In car.'

'Would you care to sit down, Admiral?' Ben pointed at the only chair in the room not occupied by boxes or stacks of paper.

'I no stay.' The Admiral shook his head. 'I tell you news.'

He waited for the next explosion to fade.

'Of the Chinese Army coming to save us?' queried Max.

'Um, no.' said the Admiral. 'No yet.'

Max sighed, audibly. 'Do we even know how close the Chinese are at present?'

The Admiral said nothing.

Max looked at Ben. 'Can we last long enough for the Chinese to get here?'

'Maybe,' answered Ben, 'if we can prevent the buggers from landing on shore in the first place.'

'That my bad news,' said the Admiral. 'First Japs crossed water.'

Max thumped his fist on the desk. 'Deadset? They're here already?'

Ben exhaled audibly.

'East,' said the Admiral. 'At Lye Mun.'

'Then we have to move,' said Ben. 'What's your plan, sir?'

The Admiral stared at Ben and said, 'I fight on.'

'But you mustn't get caught!' Max blurted out. The Admiral was too important, too knowledgeable.

'While there is fighting, I fight,' said the Admiral. He held his hand up by way of farewell and turned to go.

Max closed the door behind him.

'Ben, what the bloody hell's our next move?'

'I'm working on something.' If an ordinary man had said he was 'working on something', you would know better than to hope.

Chapter 11

Tuesday 23rd December, 1941

Max and Ben shared a cigarette on the foredeck of the gunboat. Max raised his palm to shield the sun from his eyes. Amid the stevedores working just yards away on Aberdeen's wharf, Chinese children played in and around a wicker basket. The calm could not last. He had overheard Ben mention a 'Plan B' to the boat's captain, Lieutenant Ashford. What Plan B entailed – including whom it involved – was as yet unclear.

On deck, a caged duck – invited on board for the festive season – began flapping around violently. Suddenly, a muffled explosion shuddered the motor torpedo boat, and Ben and Max went to ground. Max held his oversized tin helmet in place and looked up. Ashford was standing over them, tapping his fingertips against the long-empty torpedo storage tube. 'That's simply the minefields, gentlemen, which protect the southern approaches to Hong Kong. We are blowing them before the Japs get hold of the mine-control stations.'

Lieutenant Jack Ashford was the sort of square-shouldered officer who commanded respect by his physical presence and surety of purpose. One weekend last summer, Max had crewed on Ashford's four-sail gaff cutter. Afterward, they enjoyed drinks on the terrace of the Royal Hong Kong Yacht Club. Max had fallen back into sailing soon after he married Emily, not least because she hated the club. She disliked one thing he had loved about it – its isolation, on a rocky outcrop of an island a hundred yards or more offshore. And she considered the members, 'a haughty, starched-collar hive of Henrys and Randolphs, with wives who stretched the first syllable of "darling" beyond credibility' – but he could only admire her for that.

Max and Ben were standing together with Ashford near the prow of the motor torpedo boat. Onshore, the heads of the two smallest children popped up from the basket. Periodically, when an aircraft roared overhead or mortar shells dropped from the hills towards Aberdeen dockyard, the youngest kids would disappear under the rattan lid of the basket.

A hammering noise resonated from below decks. 'How are the running repairs going?' Ben asked Ashford. With the slipway bombed to smithereens and the Japanese likely to appear in Aberdeen dockyard before long, dry-dock repair work was not an option.

'Oh, we've plugged the holes in the hull,' said Ashford. 'Not without challenges while she's sitting in water. Now, we're just finishing off the fuel tanks.'

Ashford left them for a few minutes.

Upon his return, Ashford's demeanour had lost its perkiness. 'I managed to get through to HQ, and the news is not very festive, I'm afraid.'

How could it be? The Japanese were already driving a line from north to south down Hong Kong Island's heart.

'The Japs,' said Ashford, 'have now secured the eastern sector of the Island, as well as the centre and pockets to the northwest. Aberdeen and Stanley are pretty much all that remain of the British Empire in China. We've still got a mishmash of pongos – Middlesex, Indians and Canadians – up in the hills between us and the Japs, but don't hold your breath.'

Max edged closer to his boss. 'Shouldn't we be doing something, rather than simply waiting for them to sweep us off the Island?' Over the previous days, the naval ratings had offered a mix of perfunctory nods and distant stares: the presence of two jungle-camouflaged, well-supplied commandos no doubt incited feverish speculation.

Ben frowned. 'We've given the Japs plenty to think about.' They had spent two days mining the hills and several nights blowing up Japanese ammunition stores and gasoline depots.

'I may not know the half of it,' said Ashford, 'but I know you secret handshake boys have earned your places aboard my ship.'

'Now,' Ben said to Max, 'we have other priorities.'

'Motoring this holey bucket around Hong Kong to rendezvous with the Chinese Army?'

'*This bucket* has already saved your life once, young man,' said Ashford. That much was true – Max and Ben would not have made it off Kowloon Peninsula otherwise.

'Sorry, sir. It's just that the Admiral's gone walkabout, and we've no idea where the Chinese Army is. . . . You still think there's a chance, Ben?'

Ben hesitated.

'I know this much,' answered Ashford, 'a fighting ship has a fighting chance.'

For once, Max held his tongue. This "ship" – crewed by a complement of eleven – was only 60-foot long and all out of torpedoes.

Ashford began to walk away.

'Max,' said Ben, 'the Admiral's not gone walkabout. He simply refuses to leave the city as long as the battle is still being fought.'

'Stubborn bastard. And what if the Chinese don't even get close to reaching the border in time? What's Plan B? Other than us all getting killed or locked up?'

Ben looked skyward for a few seconds, and then at Max. 'Other parts of Z Force will stay behind – they've already gone to ground.'

'Including Drake? Have you heard from him?'

Ben simply continued as though Max had not said a word. 'But going to ground is not something our one-legged Admiral would take kindly to, so it's not an option for us.'

An engine roared out from beyond the nearest hillside, and the duck began flapping and squawking once again. Air raid sirens had fallen out of use over previous days on the grounds that a few seconds warning is no warning at all. On the dockside men scattered for cover. A Mitsubishi Zero fighter careered towards them, low over the forest of masts in the harbour. Its guns gave a short burst of fire, splintering the wooden decking just yards away.

Max had crouched down but kept his eye on the aircraft. He clicked the safety catch off, raised the Bren gun and fired skyward, spitting brass cartridges to the ground. The noise, in tandem with the smell of cordite, suddenly thickened: Jackson – a naval rating – had joined in with a fixed Vickers yards behind Max. After so many days of punishment, there was pleasure in having a crack back, even if the Japanese pilot failed to notice. In seconds, the aircraft was gone, harried away from the Aberdeen-to-Stanley coastline by Britain's remaining anti-aircraft batteries.

Ashford surveyed his ship and crew. All personnel appeared unharmed, but he ordered the first officer to report back any damage.

Minutes later, Ashford called over to Ben and Max. 'Just one casualty! Tomorrow's Christmas lunch may be less fresh than planned.' He called them over to the cage where blood pooled from the dead duck.

The comings and goings of men and equipment resumed on the wharf.

'Let's hope that flyby wasn't reconnaissance for later. We could do without a full-blown raid.'

'Are we preparing to evacuate, sir?' asked Max.

'We are the Royal Navy, and the Royal Navy *never* absconds during battle,' said Ashford, narrowing his eyes.

'And, Max, you and I will be going nowhere without our precious cargo,' said Ben.

The first officer hurried back up the bow. 'Sir, we've just received orders.'

Ashford took the note and read it to himself before reading aloud, 'We are ordered to block the sea approaches to Aberdeen by scuttling all ships here in the harbour.'

Ben winced. 'Does that mean the end of play, Lieutenant?'

'Bugger that,' said Ashford. 'You never heard or saw that order, gentlemen. Our little flotilla has still got a contribution to give to the war effort.' Max frowned. There were still four other motor torpedo boats. They skulked offshore when they were not being used to ferry VIPs to and from Stanley Peninsula on the far southeast of Hong Kong Island. Perhaps that would be as much of a 'contribution' as the navy could manage – an evacuation to five miles away to be at the party for Hong Kong's last stand?

'We'll need to cast off,' said Ashford.

Ben looked at Max. 'The Admiral?' asked Max.

Ben nodded. 'When the time is right.'

'But by the time the battle's over, the city of Victoria will be in Japanese hands – with the Admiral inside it.' And so would Queen Mary Hospital, sooner or later. What would the Japanese do to Gwen? He almost hoped she was on their side, for her own safety.

Chapter 12

Thursday 25th December, 1941

Hong Kong crafted another winter's day of unhindered sunshine and never-ending sky. Sheltered beside the uninhabited islet of Aplichau at the mouth of Aberdeen Harbour, five motor torpedo boats, strewn close to the shore, nestled out of sight from Hong Kong Island. Aboard Ashford's lead boat, under a fresh camouflage of camphor tree branches, Max's watch duty astern would finish at noon. He shook his head in disbelief at Ben's playbook. By waiting for the Admiral to waltz out of the centre of a warzone and swan up to their boat, the risk of capture or death for all aboard increased by the minute. A malaise of inactivity had set in on deck – men sprawled across the deck dressed in shorts and perhaps a singlet, impotent and bored. But the day was destined to be anything but tranquil.

Jackson arrived on time and with cigarettes. ''Ere we are, mate. 'Appy Christmas to ya!'

'And to you, me old cobber!'

Max finished his cigarette and left Jackson on watch. He climbed down through the hatch to the wardroom. His hands were still splattered with grey and brown paint after the previous day's efforts to camouflage the boat against the rocky shore.

In the small but rigorously varnished officer's room, Max picked up his Christmas double whack of rum, sharply followed by a double pink gin.

'You enjoy your Nelson's Blood, boy,' Ashford remarked as he poked his head down. 'The sun is over the yardarm.' The navy had rules about no drinking before noon, although shouldn't a drink be permissible anytime on Christmas Day, even in the midst of a losing battle? But the British were sticklers for rules.

Protocol did go out of the porthole for Christmas lunch, when officers crammed in with the ratings where their quarters narrowed into the bow. Max got in on the first sitting of roast duck – the ship's cook had insisted there was no lead poisoning. The duck's premature execution had come in the form of a lethal splinter rather than a bullet.

It was all washed down with claret, the first wine Max had tasted since the battle began. No port or brandy was in the offing, but after dinner they were back on the Plymouth. It may have been a decent gin, but sitting on a bench, squashed between the bulkhead and a sweaty sailor, a tin mug of the 'water of life' was not quite drinks at the Peninsula Hotel with Gwen. What, or more to the point, *who,* he wanted for Christmas was out of reach. What sort of Christmas would she be having? Would the Japanese have taken the hospital by now? Would they have taken Gwen? Unless he were to leave Ben and Z Force – and, indeed, absconded from Britain's armed forces altogether – there was nothing to be done.

Each blast of mortar fire was a door slammed in Max's ear. The Hong Kong Volunteer Defence Corps manned a battery on one of the hills protecting Aberdeen Harbour, and they were no doubt attracting Japanese firepower. Small-arms fire soon peppered the din. Max longed to be either out of this war or in it.

He was sitting on deck when some of the crew jumped overboard for a swim. Moments later, the first of them climbed up the ladder. It was young Jackson with sea water puddling around his feet onto the deck. His slicked torso shimmered in the bright sun.

'That were 'orrible. Someone must'ar dun poured a ton of grease into that there wa'er!' The young naval rating was wet behind the ears more than literally.

'Jackson, it's oil that's in the water,' said Max. 'From damaged boats. Don't worry, mate – it's good for keeping the mozzies away!'

Max began to shuffle the pack of playing cards he kept in his pocket. 'Now, sit down here and let's have a little game of poker.'

After Max deliberately lost the first hand, Jackson upped his stakes and Max won the next four. Ben walked over and dropped a newspaper onto his lap.

'And the Governor's special Christmas message is in there,' said Ben, before he left them for a moment to spit over the side.

'The *South China Morning Post* is as relevant as ever.' Max held up the front page to Jackson: DAY OF GOOD CHEER, ran the main headline. 'And here we go: "Fight on. Hold fast for King and Empire. God bless you all in this your finest hour."' Max sniggered. 'He's got no idea how fine an hour you can get upstairs at Short-Time Susan's.' Not that Max had ever been to Shanghai.

Max smiled. Then he thought of Gwen.

Ben drifted back towards them. 'Have you heard from Drake today?

'Yes,' said Ben, 'but—'

'Sir!' The first officer rushed over to Ben. 'Sir, you'd best come. It's naval headquarters.'

'In your own good time, Jackson.' Max got up to follow Ben. 'That's twelve bucks you owe me.'

He followed Ben past the bridge and down the rear hatch. Max stopped in the doorway of the tiny wireless transmission office. Pencil in hand, headphones on ears, the young telegraphist focused his frown at the transmitter dial. Ashford was standing with his arms folded above the telegraphist's head.

'Ben,' whispered Ashford, 'It's done. Maltby and the Governor are to take a boat over to Kowloon. But it's best not to know when the official surrender is signed. Surrender involves a promise to hand all military hardware over to the enemy. We are just awaiting confirmation of our orders. The line's crackling, but our man thought he heard an order to V2 – that's me, flotilla commander.'

Ben appeared worried, a rare sight indeed. 'We can't leave without—'

The telegraphist hooked out one headphone and proclaimed, 'V2: Go! Repeat: Go!'

Chapter 12

'Right,' said Ashford, 'we're under strict orders to get away at all costs. Now.'

'We've got to wait for the Admiral,' said Ben. 'He's essential to our mission and to our future.'

Ashford's gaze moved from Ben to the scuttled wrecks in Aberdeen harbour and the hillsides beyond. 'I'll send the other four MTBs away first, but then—'

'Look!' yelled Max. He pointed at a nearby hillside where a British position had just announced its presence by raising a white flag.

It was 3:15pm. Hong Kong had fallen.

Max repeatedly shook his head from behind the wheel of Ben's Sunbeam-Talbot and yelled with only himself to hear. 'Shouldda done this hours ago, Ben-bloody-Bison!' He slipped his tin helmet onto his head: the canvas car roof offered little protection. Splinters of metal and clods of rock shot through the air as the shells rained down around Aberdeen – surrender or no surrender. What had been the dry docks had become smouldering rubble scattered with dead bodies.

He zigzagged the car around craters and bounced it over debris. One jolt up off his seat made him wince – he had run over a corpse lying under a straw sleeping mat. The road block the Canadians had set up outside of Aberdeen village had been abandoned, but even with a set of wire cutters from the glove compartment it cost Max precious minutes.

Gwen needed him more than the Admiral. He thought about telling Ben – not without merit – that the road into Victoria was unpassable. Then could Gwen be saved?

Instead of continuing into the city, he swung off the main road, swept up the long driveway and hit the brakes hard by the green grass cupped within the hospital's 'H' block.

All six storeys of the Queen Mary's main building had by now been blackened by war. He ran past a sentry and in through the open double doors. The smell hit home first. Ostensibly a civilian hospital, the lobby was packed more with patched-up soldiers than shell-hit citizens. A stretcher bearing little more than fragments of a human being – a forearm and a foot were recognisable – lay ignored on the floor of the lobby-cum-ward.

'Gwen Harmison?' he approached the first nurse he saw. 'Do you know where she might be?'

He asked three more hospital staff before he found her in a first floor ward, changing the dressing on some poor wretch's amputated stump. The patient stared straight up at the ceiling, lost in misery.

'Max?' she smiled and frowned together. 'You're alright?'

Max nodded. She turned back to her patient and placed a cloth across his eyes.

'Wait in the corridor. It'll be a few minutes before I can chat.'

'No, there's no time, Gwen.' She unravelled the last of the bandage around the bloodied stump. Max saw enough to understand why she had covered the patient's eyes.

'It's over, Gwen. We've surrendered.'

He heard a groan from the patient.

'What?!' exclaimed Gwen. 'It's all over? Are you sure?'

'Yes. We received a call. Maltby and the Governor are on their way to sign the official documents.'

'On their way where?' enquired Gwen.

'The Peninsula Hotel – that's where the Japs wish to mark the occasion.'

'In *our* hotel. . . .'

She sponged the wound, and the patient writhed his torso. 'It's alright, Corporal Patten, we're almost done.'

'So everyone's surrendered, as quick as that?'

Max felt himself redden. 'Well, my crew haven't surrendered, but the regular forces have.'

'Aren't you in the Hong Kong Volunteer Regiment?'

He stared at her for a couple of seconds. 'I am a Volunteer, just of a more specialised kind. I've sworn an oath of secrecy to the King – otherwise I would tell you more.'

She tilted her head at him and then returned her focus to her patient.

'I'm sure the wounded will be looked after, but the nurses – a young, Caucasian nurse ... Gwen, you've no idea what beasts these Japs can be. You've got to get ready to leave. Now.'

She wrapped a new dressing around the stump. 'Wait in the corridor, Max. I promise I'll just be one minute.'

Twelve minutes later, Max ran out into the fresh air and vomited on the entrance steps.

He got back into the car with a heavy heart and continued north on the coastal road, rounding the western tip of Hong Kong Island, still talking alone to himself. 'You'd better be easy to find, Admiral Chan Chak – or the Japs can have you.'

Slinking downhill, the roots of banyan trees twisted up the roadside wall ringing Hong Kong University, where he had once attended Chinese classes. The roof had been blown off the students' union building, the redbrick Great Hall was pock-marked by shellfire and a gaping hole had replaced the clock face of the grand tower.

Despite Gwen's resolve to stay at the hospital come what may, when Max told her to get a bag together and be ready in thirty minutes, she had put up negligible resistance. He had asked whether she kept valuables somewhere in a vault in town? But she had emptied her bank account at the first opportunity and kept both cash and jewellery in a place she considered safer than a vault: under her mattress.

Something infuriating – whether conscience or pragmatism – had forced him to attempt to fulfil his mission. In avoiding the city centre and waterfront, Max found an easier stretch of road by skirting across the hillside at the back of town. Glancing further up the hill to his right, he caught sight of a squad of Japanese soldiers, perhaps receiving final instructions before crashing down into town.

Victoria Barracks came into view. Hurrying out through the open gates, officers straggled behind their men. Some stared lustfully at the Sunbeam-Talbot.

In the courtyard beyond the gate, an orderly fed another pile of papers onto the fire.

Max wound down the window and called out to the solitary sentry. 'Hey, can you tell me if the most senior officers have left?'

'I'm not at liberty to say, sir.'

'Strewth.' Max shook his head. 'Mind my car, wouldya?' He flashed his pass and ran towards the sunken entrance leading to the Battle Box.

Two orderlies emerged from behind the iron door, one carrying a cypher machine, the other a sledgehammer. The sentry closed the door on Max. He raised his papers to the spy slit but was refused both entry and explanation.

Max ran back after the two orderlies who were walking towards the fire.

'Hey, you need to bury that!' he shouted.

The first orderly dropped the cypher machine next to the fire and turned to face Max. 'Excuse me?'

'It won't burn, and if you break it up the Japs will soon piece it back together. Check with your senior officers, if you don't believe me.'

'Ha! *Senior officers?* You think they're still here?!'

'Apparently not. Thanks for the intel.' Max ran back to his car.

Sitting at the wheel, engine running, he hesitated. Where would Hong Kong's great and good go to at a time of great peril?

He pulled away down Queen's Road and into Victoria proper, where Union flags still projected from grand façades. A smattering of British uniforms and Chinese civilians darted hither and thither. He raced past neoclassical arches and screeched to a halt in front of the stone columns of the Gloucester Hotel.

There, standing on the steps, was Two-Gun Cohen. Find Cohen, Ben had said, and their man should be close by. And Two-Gun was living up to his name. His towering frame commanded the front of the hotel. Shorn of jacket, empty shoulder holsters clinging to his braces, he brandished a revolver in each hand.

'Ain't it good to see ya, Max.' Two-Gun had been expecting him. 'He's on the fourth floor. The Japs are already seeping in to Victoria, so don't hang about.'

Max left his helmet in the car: making himself less visible to snipers was preferable to the wafer thin protection the helmet would provide against a high-calibre rifle.

'Which room on the fourth floor?' enquired Max.

'All of them,' replied Two-Gun.

He asked Cohen to keep an eye on the car and ran into the hotel.

Guarded by a lone Indian soldier, the lobby held a host of homeless humanity lounging in armchairs or spread across the floor, putting their hopes in the inviolable civility of a prestigious hotel. There, before the invasion, the elite would saunter in for afternoon tea in the lobby or cocktails with a view on the eighth floor.

The fourth floor was a Chinese stronghold. A series of armed Chinese – each trying to outdo the other with the number of tears in their shirts and the menace of their tattoos – escorted Max out of the elevator. They hurried him along the corridor to the end room. The door opened from the inside, and Max stepped into the lounge room of a modest suite. There, standing behind his desk, tall and angular, Henry Lee gazed on as Chan Chak addressed a gang of ruffians hunched around the room.

'Ah, *Lieu-ten-ant* Max – you come too?' asked the Admiral.

'Bin doh?' replied Max.

'Come kill Japanese.' The Admiral held up a string of hand grenades and his loyal and righteous friends projected their newly-acquired revolvers into the air. 'We got tools, we do job.' The Admiral had been asking the British for weapons for his gangland recruits, but it never crossed Max's mind that the authorities would actually cede to such demands.

'Crikey, Admiral, it doesn't sound like much of a plan.' Max dodged through the crowd to reach Chan's desk.

'We got weapons now.' The Admiral raised his walking stick and swept it around the room. 'We use them. You go holiday?'

'Funny.' Max scrunched his face. 'Think of the reprisals, Admiral.'

'You want surrender? British no surrender!' It was true that the British Empire had not surrendered any possession for 170 years, since American Independence.

'Sir, if you take a Chinese gang to kill Japs at this late stage, the Japs will take it out on all Chinese.'

'All Chinese must fight.'

'Well, I've got my orders, Admiral – we have promised Chiang Kai-shek we'll keep you safe. Besides, we're going to need you to secure a rendezvous with the Chinese Army.'

'Japs use big army to stop Chinese. Chinese gov'ment say they need one month . . . one month to get here. But Hong Kong no fight – so no army come.'

'The Chinese Army aren't close?'

'Not close enough,' said Henry.

Plan B would have to be implemented.

'Well, Chiang Kai-shek still needs you, Admiral,' said Max. 'China needs you.'

The Admiral conferred with Henry in rapid Cantonese.

'General Cohen,' shouted Max, as he opened the rear door for Henry, the Admiral and Cheung, his stocky bodyguard, 'now is the time to join us.'

'And miss the bleedin' fighting? Hell no!' came the reply, in his cockney-Canadian drawl. Two-Gun was an adventurer who didn't know when to quit. And that was something to be admired.

Max swung the car westwards down Queen's Road, where hawkers still held their ground. An unnerving calm brewed anticipation. Squeezed together on the back seat, the three Chinese passengers had dressed down in the loose tunics of Chinese workers. Henry and the Admiral debated what would become of the men they had just left behind. The front passenger seat of the Sunbeam-Talbot lay empty, specially reserved.

He slowed for an old man as he crossed the street towards Jimmy's Kitchen. From a lane off to the right, in between the restaurant and the Queen's Theatre, the front rows of a column of troops – led by an officer, denoted by the samurai sword swinging from his belt – jogged onto the main road just yards away. Max kicked down the accelerator and didn't look back. On the back seat, Admiral Chan Chak yelled in colourful Chinese and pulled out his pistol. Henry managed to calm the Admiral and persuade him to find his holster.

The roads around Western Market were clear of Japanese, and the shelling had, of course, ceased. Max dropped down a gear to climb the hill and pass Hong Kong University. He had doubts about his own plan. Would Ben and Ashford allow a civilian woman to join them? Maybe they could use a nurse?

Across the green from the hum of the car, at the doors into Queen Mary Hospital, there were no longer British sentries on duty.

'Why we stop here?' asked Admiral Chan, leaning forward from the rear seat.

'There's someone else we need to rescue.' As he said the words, doubt reared in his mind: would Gwen, as the wife of a member of the Axis powers, be safer left alone rather than on the run with Allied forces?

He was about to cut the engine when a pair of Japanese soldiers ran out of the double doors. One pointed at the car and shouted. From the back seat, Henry yelled something which sounded Japanese. Placated, the two soldiers lowered their rifles. Max put the car into gear and eased forward. Shots rang out at the back of Max's head: Admiral Chan had poked his head out of the rear side-window, together with one pistol in each hand. He thrust his foot to the floor and the car screeched out of the hospital grounds.

Gwen was now on her own. He felt his stomach fall away.

Aberdeen was just down the hill, and the shellfire had thinned, but he was preoccupied by what he was leaving behind. Ben had said the Japanese may let European women leave the colony unharmed. That seemed unlikely.

'Max,' said the Admiral, 'you know what Henry say to Japanese?'

Max said nothing. He didn't give a damn what Henry had said.

'Long live the Emperor!' said Henry.

'Traitor,' muttered the Admiral. It was impossible to tell if he was being serious.

'I didn't specify *whose* emperor,' Henry said. 'Maybe I meant King George VI!'

Artillery fire shook the car as Max weaved around shell holes on the main road into Aberdeen. The sun was beginning to lower over the harbour. Max pulled in on the praya, pointing the car to the sea. The stench of rotten fish mingled with the whiff of raw sewage. Henry, Max and the Admiral's bodyguard shoved the car off the wharf. The green bonnet splashed into the sea, and the rear of the car fell back against the harbour wall.

Something pinged off the cobblestones just two yards away. 'Get inside!' cried Max. Then another: sniper fire. The four of them dashed into the relative shelter of the fish market building, under the half of the roof which had not yet collapsed.

Max stared out of the open-fronted warehouse, looking for the MTB or a launch to pick them up. Beyond the dockyard wasteland, countless boats lay half-submerged in the harbour. Splashes exploded from the sea as shells searched in vain for any ship not yet wrecked. Beyond the firing line of shelling, an array of junks and *sampans* anchored out close to Aplichau Island. But there was no sign of a motor torpedo boat, unsurprisingly – why would Ashford want to leave the sheltered spot which had kept them safe? Max remembered what the first officer had said earlier: 'We cannot prejudice the safety of our crew to save a Chinaman, however distinguished he may be.'

Max had followed procedure and ditched the car – so they were stuck there, just waiting to be killed or captured. Was there any hope of seeing Gwen in captivity? 'Don't be stupid,' he said to himself.

Then the shelling stopped.

'Looky here!' The Admiral pointed towards the far end of the waterfront.

'Let's go,' said Max. They hurried along the wharf, sticking to the shadows. Then he persuaded the three Chinese men to wait inside a warehouse while he dashed across the promenade.

Max crept along a jetty. Alongside the jetty, two Caucasian men sitting in a motor launch were working at its helm, mumbling in a Germanic-sounding language.

'British officer,' announced Max, brandishing his pistol. 'Who the hell are you two?'

A crag-faced man rested his spanner on his knee and looked up. 'Captain Damsgaard. And this is Cadet Olsen.' He spoke near-perfect English. 'Danish merchant navy. When the battle started, we joined the dockyard staff, working for the British.'

The whirr of an engine – a motorcar – prompted Max to jump down into the boat and join the two seamen in cowering under the hood of the small cabin. Up on the quayside, the motorcar came to a halt. He had to hope the Admiral would be hiding out of sight. A smaller engine – a motorcycle – pulled up alongside. Men shouted to each other in Japanese over the hum of their engines.

A minute later, the engines motored away. Max poked his head up: no sign of the Japanese.

'That's why the shelling's stopped,' he said to Damsgaard, 'to allow Japanese patrols in safely. We gotta get outta here.'

'We're almost done,' said Damsgaard. 'But we could do with more fuel.'

Olsen and Max ran over to the warehouse, found the others and took them off to the naval depot. Ten minutes later – laden with kerosene cans full of diesel plus bags of rice, tins of food, water, rifles and ammunition – the wooden motor launch set off, sitting low in the water. Max scoured land and sea with his Bren gun at the bow, while young Olsen scurried around the deck attending to this and that. Ben, Admiral Chan, Henry and Cheung were sitting inside the cabin as Damsgaard jinked the boat port and then starboard, chopping through the shipwrecks littering Aberdeen Harbour.

Leaving land behind heightened the reality of leaving Gwen behind, too. What apparent madness, sailing out of the harbour in broad daylight when the cover of dusk was just an hour away. But Ashford wouldn't wait any longer than dusk before making his own move – 'Don't expect us to still be here come six o'clock,' had been his parting words.

Shelling had recommenced in an irregular beat on the waves on the west side of the harbour, forcing Damsgaard to chart a course eastwards, where Aplichau narrowed the sea into a channel. Clustered junks nudged the island's shore, their tatterdemalion latticework sails patched and torn. As the throbbing hum of the engine approached, faces aboard the floating village peeked under their canvas canopies to inspect the passersby.

Beyond the moored junks, an eerie tranquility ensued. Within a couple of hundred yards, on both the port and starboard sides, shorelines weaved below jungled hillsides. Max had beat the wind up this channel many a time, although on his most recent sail there he was more passenger than crew, on a luxurious gaff-rigged sloop.

He stared into the trees backing the shoreline. The guns of war fired an on-going percussion, several miles away. He glanced back towards Aberdeen and beyond. Would Gwen still be waiting with her bags packed? Husband or no husband, he had let her down. She had been bursting with both tears and apologies when he had last seen her. 'Max, I *had* thought it was all none of your business – but now I simply want to be straight with you, as I should have been from the beginning.' They held each other close, standing in the dispensary as nurses busied in and out. 'My husband – Klaus – he probably isn't dead, but he may as well be. He's dead to me. I think he's working for the German government. I don't know where he is – perhaps he's where I left him, in Macao.' He told her it didn't matter now. He told her to forget Klaus and to think of a different future. He told her he would look after her. And he told her he would be back to pick her up.

Theirs was the only moving vessel in the channel. *Barely* moving. A spluttering top speed of five or six knots confirmed that the motor launch would never carry them to freedom. And the fading light would soon both help shield them from predators and hinder their search for freedom.

Young Olsen left Damsgaard at the tiller and appeared at Max's side. 'Where do we head?' asked Olsen. 'Stanley?' Ahead, the channel widened into open waters.

'We could. Our men should be holding the ground all along here, down to Stanley Peninsula,' said Max, convincing himself. 'But we'll be safer hugging the Aplichau shoreline. Then we could—'

Crack! A single rifle shot rang out from the north shore. He shot an eye across the hillside as he ducked down with Olsen behind the roof of the trunk cabin. He dropped the safety on his Bren, got to his knees and gave a two-second burst of fire at the pillbox he had glimpsed through the trees. Silence. For a moment.

More incoming rifle fire followed, joined by machine guns with tracer fire which splashed through the water and into the boat. Max ducked out of sight. The smell of petrol gathered strength, so it was fair to assume the hull had been perforated. Tracer fire could blow the whole craft at any moment.

Olsen tried to run round for the cabin – but he was cut down before he reached the threshold to the cabin. He lay prostrate, his head in, his body out of the hatchway, blood pooling onto the deck. Then another burst of gunfire floored Captain Damsgaard. Both bodies lay still.

Max waited for the enemy machine gun which had proven most accurate to pause for reloading, and then he darted past Olsen and jumped off the top step into the cabin.

Admiral Chan had taken command: 'We swim.' He pointed through the porthole, towards Aplichau. 'One *li.*' The small island was a good 600 yards away. 'Ev'ry man for self.' The Admiral turned to Henry. 'No help me.'

Henry shook his head in frustration. He held the New Testament he always kept about his person and muttered a quick prayer. 'Only God can save us!'

'If he does, I'm all his!' yelled the Admiral. Bullets ripped through the deck and smashed around the cabin. 'Abandon ship!'

Henry hurled off his jacket. The Admiral unstrapped his wooden leg and stripped down to his underwear. He ordered Cheung to help him strap his pistol and passport around his waist. Max kept his pockets full and his clothes on – should he live for another day, he figured he was going to need his gun, some cash, and his walking boots.

Max, Henry and the Admiral were ready to leave, but Cheung blocked their way. In Cantonese, he said, 'It's too dangerous. We'll die out there.'

The Admiral shrugged. 'You make your own choice, but I'm not going to surrender like a slave.' The Admiral pushed his way past.

Cheung followed him up the steps. 'But, sir – we're gonna—'

'What's your problem, Cheung?' the Admiral yelled over his shoulder.

They raced out of the hatchway and over to the starboard side, keeping the cabin between themselves and the onslaught of gunfire coming from the hillside.

'Cheung, you'll need this.' The Admiral reached up to grab a life-ring hanging from the cabin roof. Then the Admiral winced in pain – blood poured from his wrist. He leaped into the dark chill of the sea, quickly followed by Max and Henry. Bullets rained into the water all around. A non-swimmer, Cheung and the life-ring stayed on board.

The time would be recorded on Max's wristwatch: it stopped working as soon as it hit the water. It was 5:30pm.

Chapter 13

Evening, Thursday 25th December, 1941

Sniper fire followed Max out of the water and onto a rocky islet. He kept low as he scrambled across the causeway, a rocky sand bar which bridged the islet to Aplichau. Barnacles stabbed his palms and knees. Ahead, the Aplichau hillside of grass and shrubs would offer some camouflage. But before he could get there, suddenly firebombs lit up the scrub-covered hillside. Within seconds, he was beaten back to the rocks by roaring flames. The Japanese had known where he would head before he did.

Wet, cold, hungry, thirsty, blood seeping out of his hands and knees, he prostrated himself on a patch of sand amid the rocks and waited for a sniper to find its mark. Or, if they failed, they would have to go to the trouble of sending a boat out to pick him up. And then he would cause as much trouble as possible – he still had his pistol.

Minutes later, he caught a movement edging from the water onto the sand of the causeway. He propped up on an elbow for a better view. Slithering along, his white underclothes clinging to his torso, with one leg and one good arm, was Admiral Chan Chak. A bullet zinged off the stones nearby and Max slapped his face back down against the sand. He considered his next move.

He had crawled halfway back along the spit when the Admiral spotted him and called ahead, 'Me okay. You stay there. Makee cuppa tea.'

Max was unsure whether to ignore the Admiral's refusal of help. But he did what he was told – aside from making tea.

The Admiral crawled over, his vest and long johns dripping wet. The saltwater had cleaned the Admiral's wound, but the bleeding would not stop. Max tore off his shirt sleeve and tied it around the Admiral's shattered wrist. Another sniper's shot pinged off a rock some yards away.

They lay still, largely covered from the line of fire by jags of rock, their minds egging on the gathering dusk. Ahead, the fires started by the incendiary shells had died down, although swathes of hillside still held an embering glow.

Max had plenty of time to plan a sentence in his best Cantonese. 'Admiral, shall we wait a while and then walk up the hill together?'

As usual, the Admiral replied in English. 'I run ahead. Max, you stay.' Max twisted his face. The Admiral chuckled. 'I no run! I no walk! No wooden leg. See?' Max reddened in the darkness.

The Admiral's breathing sawed as he loosened off a chunky gold ring. 'For Auntie Chak,' he said.

'Who? What?' asked Max.

'You go. One day maybe you find my wife.' The Admiral gulped in air. 'Give this her. Ev'rybody know her. My wife. *Auntie Chak.*'

Crouching in the darkness, Max plucked his pistol from his hip pocket and handed it to the Admiral.

'Stay here, sir. I'll be back in a jiffy.' It was one of those pretentious words he generally eschewed, but in these circumstances English sophistry seemed more appropriate that honest Australianisms.

After a slothful and uncomfortable crawl over the rocks, Max ran up the singed hillside, the heat shimmering off the ground. He was already thankful for his boots. They had dragged in the water, but he was experienced at swimming in full training kit.

He reached the trees and then withdrew a miniature machete out of his left boot. The difference compared to three weeks earlier was that Max now knew that he knew how to kill.

He would avoid mounting the crest of the hill and projecting his silhouette. At fifty feet short of Aplichau's summit, stooping low, he rounded the hilltop. Facing south, he surveyed the bay where some of the MTBs had settled in that morning. Hilly islets hunched up out of the sea, confusing his eyes in the low light. But close to the west shore of Aplichau, squatting down in the water, what appeared as a craggy shadow of rocks presented fresh hope.

He sensed movement in the darkness behind him. He crouched down, but there was little cover. Thirty yards away, a large man was ambling up towards the crest of the hill. The outline of his humped back appeared comically exaggerated, worse than amateur dramatics. Whether friend or foe, if he made it to the top of the hill, the man would be liable to be seen and shot at from Hong Kong Island, and that may be in nobody's interests. Max crept up from behind. As he began to close the gap, the image distilled. The tall man was carrying on his back a distinctly smaller man.

'Henry? It's Max. Come down this way.' He led Henry around the summit and then helped him set down the Admiral. Henry wasn't just six-foot-three, he was athletic to boot: a volleyball and football player, and a medalist at the last Far East Games.

'How are you doing, sir?' enquired Max.

'I okay. Want to kill Japs!' Not an uncommon feeling in Max's circles, but one which obsessed the Admiral more than most.

'The bleeding has stopped,' said Henry. 'But he's angry with me for picking him up.' Max was surprised how plainly Henry spoke in front of his boss. 'He thinks he'd rather have stayed sitting on those rocks waiting for the Japanese and his own painful death.' Henry Lee appeared unusually ruffled.

Max pointed down across the bay, to about 500 yards offshore. 'Is that what I think it is, Admiral?'

'I see boat. Do boat see us?'

'Let's find out.' Max took a shift with the Admiral on his back – there must have been all of six stone of him – and led the way down a slope blessed with clutches of bamboo.

'If boat see us,' said the Admiral, 'we have trouble!' Max frowned as he jogged along. Something must be lost in translation: *if boat see us, we're home free!*

He set the Admiral down with Henry and clambered ahead over the rocks. He waved and shouted in hope that his voice would carry across the water and be recognised. 'We're here! Can you see us?'

He did not have to wait long for an answer.

The reply came in the form of a burst of tracer fire and the rattle of a Lewis gun. Max threw himself down on the rocks and edged backwards for cover. Henry and the Admiral were safely behind the rocks. Did the MTB crew believe they were firing at the enemy?

Max thought back over his Christmas Day. He had come face-to-face with a Japanese patrol column in Victoria; driven a car through treacherous shelling; been shot off a motor launch; was machine gunned while swimming, sniped at on the rocks and generally fired upon more times than he cared to remember. And still the odds gathered against him.

'Max!' Henry called out from a thicket of bamboo.

'Stay covered!' said Max, who was crawling back to join them.

The Admiral was sitting on the ground behind Henry. 'I tell you. You no listen!'

Max pursed his lips.

'Max,' said Henry, 'I could swim out to them.'

'Crikey, are you crazy?' asked Max, searching for a way out of this. 'If our boys are still holding the boat, they're gonna leave Aplichau. Why would they stay after they locate what they thought were Japanese forces – us – on the island? More likely, the boat has been taken over by the Japs. Next, they'll land forces here on Aplichau.'

'No choice,' said the Admiral. 'We stay here.'

Half an hour passed. Nothing happened. No more shooting. No artillery was called in, no landing forces. And the MTB had not budged. Why wouldn't the boat have moved? And why did the firing stop as suddenly as it began? Ben the Bison was the only answer that came to mind.

'Henry,' said Max, 'you can't swim up to that boat – Brits can't tell a Chinese from a Jap in broad daylight, let alone in the sea at night. I'll go, mate.'

There were two ways to approach it. One, swim the straightest route, waving and shouting. That would involve complete faith in the theory that Ben had put a permanent end to all shooting and assured the sailors that the figure they had seen on the rocks was probably their long-lost buddy. Max chose the second way.

He crawled along the rocky foreshore for about a hundred yards. Then he took off his boots and slipped into the black sea. He swam an arc that would lead him to approach the MTB from its rear. A steady breast stroke rather than a frantic freestyle. He thrust his hand down through the water to check that his knife was still fastened safely inside his pocket.

His eyes penetrated the darkness better by the time he neared the MTB. A naval rating paced back and forth on watch at the stern. A chatter of voices – distinctly British voices – heralded a den of activity near the bow. 'Easy does it' . . . 'Put some muscle into it' . . . 'Up she comes': weighing anchor.

If Max yelled out or startled them, the first reaction may well be a stream of fire from a Bren gun. He covered some good yards with front crawl before easing to the stern using the stealth of breast stroke. As he reached the boat, he kept an eye on the watchman standing aft on the portside. A stream of liquid splashed into the sea.

'It's Max. Don't poke your long Tom at me.'

'Eh? Wha' the bobbery's goin' on 'ere?' That Cornish-meets-the-East-End accent could only be Jackson's. The rating buttoned up his trousers and peered over the stern.

'I mean, don't bail out your piss on my face!' Max grabbed hold of a strut above the rudder. 'Dammit, Jackson, would you gimme a hand up?'

As the MTB's skiff motored to shore to pick up Henry and the Admiral, Max stripped off his wet clothes. He was sitting in the wardroom wrapped in a wool blanket, drinking a mug of 'gunfire' – black tea and rum – to warm his insides.

Ben stepped down the ladder from above decks. 'You lucky bastard! Bet you thought you were scuppered?'

'Crikey, when you were bloody shooting me up on the beach, I did think I was about to cark it!'

'Jackson was on the Lewis – got a bit trigger happy until I slapped him one.' Ben clamped his hand onto Max's shoulder, a gesture some would mistake for affection. 'But, from a distance, you do look like a Jap.' Ben grinned.

'Bugger off.'

Ten minutes later, a wet Henry and Admiral Chan Chak had clambered from a launch onto the deck.

Under the dim glow of the wardroom's oil lamps, the Admiral was sitting with a Royal Navy blazer thrown over his shoulders and a blanket cocooning him from the waist down. Max could make out the bullet embedded inside Admiral Chan's wrist.

'I'm no doctor, but do you want it taken out, Admiral?'

'You leave in, is good. I okay.'

Max cleaned up the wound with Dettol.

Ben and Ashford pored over a map at the pull-down desk.

'These boats could make it there,' said Ashford. 'We can do 400 miles without stopping. We could hop all the way to Singapore.' Max didn't like the sound of that – the Japanese were swarming all over the coast from Hong Kong to the Malay Peninsula.

Ben slowly shook his head. 'We'd need to stop for fuel, and lots of it. Diesel's hard enough to come by, never mind in occupied territory.'

Henry Lee entered the room bearing clean linen. Max began to bandage the Admiral's arm.

'Go north,' said the Admiral. 'China. To Mirs Bay, walk to Waichow, then Kukong. My Kuomintang friends in Waichow, British in Kukong. I know way.'

'Overland?' asked Ashford. 'The Japs have an army in southern China.'

Max failed to understand what the Admiral then muttered to his right-hand man, but a troubled expression took hold of Henry's face. He coughed demonstrably. Ben and Ashford looked up from their map. The eyes of the room fell upon Henry, who smiled awkwardly.

'The Admiral knows a secret army that will help us,' said Henry.

Max stopped his attempts to fix up a sling. The Admiral always seemed to *know an army.*

'East River,' said the Admiral. 'East River Reds. No more Japanese patrols there. East River shoot Japanese. No more patrols. East River rule Mirs Bay.' Lying between the northeast of Hong Kong and occupied China, Mirs Bay was the size of a large lake.

Ben inclined his head and looked to Ashford.

'Going further east and going red were two things I had hoped to avoid,' said Ashford. The communist guerrillas were known to be ferocious fighters, and their regard of the British was as yet untested.

'Let's get up to the bridge,' added Ashford.

Max found a mariner's sweater to guard against the chill and climbed up the ladder.

The motor torpedo boat had throbbed away from Aplichau. On the starboard yardarm the red St George's Cross, with Union Jack in the top-left corner, fluttered in the night breeze. On Hong Kong Island, fires burned through the darkness. Max was relieved at the prospect of avoiding the prison camps that presumably awaited the surrendering troops – but not this motley crew. As for Gwen, would the Japanese forces intern foreign nurses? Would they rape them? Or worse?

Admiral Chan, standing proud in the gold-braided peak cap, shoulder-striped jacket and pressed trousers of a Royal Navy lieutenant commander, had taken charge at the open-sided bridge. Ashford's spare uniform hung loose about the Admiral, with the folded-up left trouser leg dangling below the knee, but he still had a swagger about him. A novice swimmer, shot in the wrist and short of a leg, earlier in the day he could not have expected to live long. But here he was alert and upbeat, speeding them on to freedom. He slapped one hand down onto the roof of the wheelhouse in front of the bridge and pointed at the shore of Hong Kong Island, maybe less than a thousand yards away.

Ashford took the hint. 'Starboard five,' he called down to the helmsman in the wheelhouse.

'Five of starboard, wheel on, sir,' came the reply. The boat jinked a little away from land, lest the Japanese lacked sufficient shooting practice for one day.

Bren gun in hand, Max was standing next to Jackson manning the pair of Lewis guns in the foredeck's swivel turret. Edging out of the darkness one, then another, then all four of the other MTBs formed up behind their leader. They had been out there all along, an unseen rearguard. The flotilla – a great escape of around seventy-five men in all – followed along in single file.

Ashford barked 'Full ahead' down the voicepipe which ran down to the stoker below. The engines bellowed and the MTB thrust up in the water.

A quarter moon had appeared and lit the white wash of the boats as they rounded Stanley Peninsula. Despite holding back from full speed – and therefore, full *roar* – the five motor boats were hardly inconspicuous.

Muffled explosions echoed from on shore. Between Stanley village and the fortress at the southern tip, flames glimmered and volleys of small-arms fire showed no let-up: there, the fight was still on. Perhaps word of the official surrender had failed to make it through? Either way, Brigadier Wallis' men were holding a suicidal last stand.

Max had sailed yachts off Stanley many times, usually followed by a slow gin on the shoreline lawn of the Lucas' weekend cottage. *That* was what was being left behind, if not destroyed – not only people and place, but a way of life. A privileged, overly entitled, glorious way of living.

The boat bobbed more violently as they headed out to sea. Max sat down on a capstan. A coastal battery searchlight flicked around the sea between the MTBs and the shore. Perhaps they had been heard, but they were too far off shore to be seen.

Ramping up their speed, the Admiral continued on an eastward bearing, before turning northward, rounding Hong Kong Island. Behind, the flotilla snaked along through the darkness.

Max caught final glimpses of grey land and isolated lights to the west, on Kowloon-side, then the straggly peninsulas and islands of the New Territories. If life had played out differently, he would have taken Gwen away there for weekend sailing, off to a secluded beach.

They motored across Mirs Bay, no land in sight.

Off the starboard bow a sabre of light swept up into the sky: it had to be from an enemy ship. The searchlight scoured the sky not the sea – the Japs must have heard the engines and assumed they were aircraft. A red flare lit up the sky. Then a starburst of fireworks floated down upon the silhouette of a Japanese destroyer heading in the opposite direction. The enemy's flares had exposed nothing other than themselves, and the motor torpedo boat veered away.

Free of any would-be pursuer, they cut deeper into Mirs Bay than Max had ever sailed. It was five past midnight and already Boxing Day was proving better than Christmas.

And yet what he had left behind seared his joy. Gwen had not had the opportunity to get to know him. She knew him primarily as a party-going charmer; admittedly, at times that was how he knew himself. Since Emily had left he had had every reason to swan around town. Some evenings he set out alone to see what the night would bring. But Gwen Harmison was different. He barely knew her, but she was the one who got away, the missed chance.

PART II

Gwen

December 1941–March 1942

Chapter 14

Laying there on a cot bed in the corridor, the soldier looked so peaceful, so still, so very young. Yesterday's animated countenance had turned to wax. Gwen pulled the bedsheet over the face of another victim of a battle lost and sighed a deep sigh. Had Max been killed too?

Logic dictated that that was the most likely explanation as to why he had failed to return on Christmas Day. Suitcase swiftly packed, she had waited on the hospital steps for an hour before retreating at the sight of Japanese soldiers approaching. Later on Christmas Day afternoon, an officer and two lackeys had prowled around the wards. The thought of Max dying worried her beyond all rationality. She hardly knew the man, but his mystery intrigued her. A soldier who acted more like a spy – and her would-be protector. So different to her husband.

A man of a thousand moods, Klaus was Prussian from his knee-high boots up to his proud moustache. He had initially derided the Nazis, but then, however much he may have tried to hide it, she viewed his pride as growing with Germany's. Good times were lived, initially in Shanghai – so different to the garrison colony of Hong Kong, whose *raison d'être* had always been militarism. The Paris of the Orient, the most cosmopolitan of cities, Shanghai matched Klaus's cosmopolitan aspirations. But within a couple of months of a heady engagement, the war arrived in Shanghai and the expats left. She had hoped the move to Macao would result in a smaller-than-planned wedding, but Klaus used it as an opportunity to announce himself in the colony. He sent invitations to a host of society people he had never met. After the wedding, her role centred upon furnishing their three-storey home, a pillared Portuguese-style villa. Soon, a routine of consular dinners and society balls established itself. She encountered more German, Italian and Spanish couples than she did British. Initially, this seemed like a broadening of the Anglo-French circles she had moved in in Shanghai before she had met Klaus. Later – too late – she realised that she had crossed the lines drawn by European politics. It transpired that Klaus had based their social future upon whomever happened to accept their wedding invitation. The British consul, followed by a swathe of British entrepreneurs and merchants, had politely declined. She put this down to the fact that where she came from people simply do not attend the weddings of individuals whom they have never met. Klaus took it as British snobbishness and an unwillingness to do business with a German.

Gwen set off down the gloomy corridor to find Matron. The electricity wasn't working, and most of the oil lamps were needed elsewhere, such as the operating theatre. As she passed by, several of the bed-ridden patients lining the corridor raised a palm and a 'Good evening, Sister'. Most patients tried to sleep or just stared at the ceiling.

The shadow of a figure – tall, almost certainly a man – approached from the far end of the corridor. Her heartbeat raced. Should she turn and run, or would that solicit a shot in the back from a Japanese soldier? After their initial inspection, Japanese soldiers had thus far remained outside of the wards.

Last week, at the Race Course Hospital, soldiers had come by during the day. The closest girlfriend Gwen had in Hong Kong had been there: Arabel Jenkins, whom she had first met through the tennis club in Macao. The Race Course nurses had considered themselves immune, as if the red cross on their chests would keep the devils away. Arabel had moved to Hong Kong ahead of Gwen, and they roomed together at the Queen Mary until Arabel was moved to the Race Course Hospital during the last week of the battle. After scouting around the hospital that afternoon, the Japanese devils did go away. But they came back at night. They must have been sizing up their bounty during daylight hours, making mental notes. After dark, they returned to seize every nurse on shift.

Violated, battered and broken, Arabel had somehow stumbled her way through the night to the Queen Mary, to be

Chapter 14

admitted as a patient. Since witnessing Arabel arrive that night, Gwen had taken certain precautions, although she doubted they would save her.

As the man came closer, Gwen sighed in relief. There was no rifle, no dangling samurai sword, just the hanging lab coat of Doctor Swinton. She smiled at him as they passed each other. Pre-war, he worked in trauma care – a department she had once experienced in Macao from the patient's perspective.

Shortly after their second wedding anniversary, Gwen was hospitalised. There remained the trace of a scar above her left eyebrow. Nobody else appeared to notice it, but it was always there. She had been fooled by an older man's apparent sophistication, but at twenty years young wouldn't any girl have fallen for a wealthy rising star with rugged looks and a lustful glint in his eye?

She turned a corner and approached the office door. After the Japanese had arrived at the Queen Mary, Matron Lofthouse – whose first name was a matter of speculation – had increasingly retreated from the wards to her office. Matron's depressed state had begun before the battle was officially lost, and coincided with the unexplained loss of painkillers from the drug cupboard – a locked cupboard for which only Matron and the doctors had the key. A lonely office was the last place Gwen would want to be when a gang of off-duty Japanese soldiers might sweep through the hospital. Matron could not rely on her age and her size to deter them.

Gwen knocked on the wooden door and entered. Matron looked up with a start, before lowering her face back to the papers on her desk.

She stepped forward. 'Excuse me, Matron. Private Havers has died.' The last image he would have seen through the dim light was that of a 'veiled angel' – that's what he had called each nurse. 'And the mortuary say they can't take one more body.'

Matron didn't respond.

Gwen coughed. 'It's ghastly to simply leave him in the corridor alongside the other, living patients. . . .'

'They are all dying,' said Matron, raising her head from the desk. 'We are all dying.'

Behind the blinds beyond the desk, darkness was falling. Gwen imagined sitting on the verandah that ran along the back of this row of offices, sipping a gin and surveying the sweeping lawns and the sea beyond. Hospital staff and patients were now forbidden from even stepping onto that first floor verandah because the Japanese sentries outside objected to Europeans looking down on them.

'Matron, I'm sure. . . .' Gwen wasn't sure what she was sure about, but she did not need to complete the sentence. Matron bounded to her feet, a cat alerted to something beyond human hearing. She rushed to the open door to poke her head, swiftly retracted it and screamed.

Clicking heels and yelling in Japanese came barking down the corridor. Matron slammed the door shut and backed away to her desk. Gwen stepped towards the door, but there was no key in the lock. Matron began shaking and whimpering. Gwen seized the ring of keys clipped to Matron's waist and thrust a likely candidate into the lock. Too large. Shouting Japanese soldiers, just yards away.

The next key she tried turned in the lock. She peered over her shoulder to where Matron cowered under her desk. 'Matron, we must get out of here!' But she showed no recognition nor inclination to move.

The soldiers were banging hard on the door now with rifle butts. Gwen left Matron and leaped towards the door to the veranda. She pulled up the blind, which had been hastily fitted in deference to Japanese sensibilities, wrenched back the bolt and darted outside.

Darkness might hide her from the view of sentries in the grounds below. She looked along the verandah, which ran the length of the building without interruption. The sound of wood being thumped and splintered rang out from the door to Matron's office. Gwen slipped her shoes off and ran.

At the far end of the verandah, she reached for the handle of the last door back into the building.

'Stop!' called a voice behind her.

The metal door rattled its frame but wouldn't budge.

One, and then another, and then a third Japanese soldier came running along the verandah, two with bayoneted rifles in hand. Then a torrent of Japanese words came spitting out in between cackling laughter. She backed up to the low wall at the end of the verandah and risked a glance to the terrain below. She would give them something to laugh about. She would risk the jump rather than succumb.

But the first man, an officer – without a rifle – rushed at her before she could make a move. He grabbed her round her ribcage and threw her backwards onto the rough stone floor. She immediately propped herself up on her hands. Before she could get up, a hand slapped her right cheek, then a blow landed on her chin, sending her back to the floor. She wheezed in a breath and whacked both clenched fists up together onto the sides of the soldier's face, as if clashing cymbals.

He paused in shock, before pummelling punches into her throat. All went dark.

She could hardly breathe and pain crushed both her arms. She flickered open her eyes: the other two soldiers were standing one on each arm. The first soldier ripped off her outer apron and examined her grey cotton uniform for a way in. He soon gave up and pulled up the skirt. He tore her stockings down to her ankles – and then looked up in alarm. Screwing his face up in disgust, he spat at her blood-stained knickers. The eager grins on the other two soldiers' faces dropped.

The soldiers backed away, off in search of another, cleaner victim. The precautions had worked. If he had removed the knickers that she had stained with blood from a hospital vial, underneath, the soldier would have found another pair of knickers – an inner pair, devoid of blood. She then realised the risk she had run in wearing two pairs of knickers – all because she could not abide the thought of a stranger's blood rubbing up against her genitalia.

Chapter 15

In these days after the battle, during daylight hours on the city's streets an ill-defined, hazardous freedom of movement appeared to be tolerated for Europeans. A Japanese soldier might let a nurse pass – although one lugging a suitcase would have attracted greater attention.

Gwen felt a measure of protection inside the hospital car, its bonnet daubed with a large red cross. Holding back tears, her suitcase on the backseat beside her, she set out for the Gloucester Hotel intent on meeting the one friend who perhaps might save her. An hour earlier, she had donated most of her books to the hospital amid uncomfortable farewells. Her case contained little of weight, for she had left Macao hurriedly. But she had liberated her beloved pearl necklace – a parental wedding present – and the more valuable pendants and earrings, gifts from Klaus.

The hospital car turned into Pedder Street. The arcades lining the hotel had seen the demise of every single pane of glass, the empty windows heavily sandbagged. At the top of the steps to the hotel, Japanese sentries were standing in place of the Gloucester's footmen.

She held her breath, avoided eye-contact and walked inside. Instead of the chink of fine China echoing across a tranquil lobby, a clamour of European and Indian languages filled the air. Toddlers ran wild, their mothers' energy spent. Civilian men, unshaven and unslept, guarded their patch of carpet, their fate thus far preferable to that of their uniformed counterparts. Britain's defeated military had suffered a forced 'March of Humiliation' – as the now Japanese-run English newspaper read – to a prisoner of war camp in Kowloon.

The Gloucester hosted not only the well-to-do, to whom it was accustomed. Most populous were Indian and Chinese police officers – the 'mezzanine' classes within the colonial hierarchy –

who had likely never set foot in the hotel before the battle. Gwen ducked into the ladies' room, where there was little in the way of light and less in the way of water. She smoothed her palms down the dress she had whipped out of her case. She had worn nothing other than her nurses' uniform for some time. Unwilling to let her looks retreat in defeat, she dabbed on some rouge and lipstick and she tucked a loose wave of hair back up under her hat.

The hike up six flights of stairs was laborious, especially with no bell-boy and one heavy suitcase. She passed several open doors along the corridor; the hotel bedrooms thronged with more people than may feasibly find space to bed down on the floor.

She reached the closed door of room number 58 and sighed. She knocked and immediately the door opened a sliver on its chain. An eye squinted through the crack.

The door opened a few inches, still latched.

'My goodness, are you going to let me in?'

'Shh,' was the only reply. Dressed down to an undershirt, slacks and braces, he set about tidying up the room. Only once satisfied did he throw on a shirt and open the door.

He took her suitcase and closed the door gently behind her. 'Gosh, Gwen, it is truly wonderful to see you.' Chester Drake clasped her shoulders in his hands. 'But what brings you here?'

'Max said if the Japanese came, you would protect me.'

Just three weeks ago, she had slipped away from the protective presence of old friend Chester Drake in favour of the affections of new acquaintance Max Holt. And then, with his parting advice, the latter had thrown her back to the former. While Chester was diffident beyond all measure, Max was the other type – he had made his desires terribly clear from that first evening. Was there something instinctively attractive about the more aggressive type of man? Or had Klaus taught an unforgettable lesson on that score?

She stared at the bottle on the desktop.

'Would you care for one, my dear?' Everything was spoken quietly. She nodded.

He poured and enquired, 'And where is Max?'

'Dead, presumably. He came to the hospital on Christmas Day. He said he would return within half an hour to take me somewhere safe, but I never saw him again.'

She slumped in a wing-backed armchair, gin in hand. That it was only 9:30am seemed of little relevance. She gazed, through the glass of the verandah doors, across city rooftops. Some buildings had been blown away, others half collapsed, rearranged like a cubist painting.

Each sip cooled her mouth and warmed her spirits. Chester Drake fixed a darn good gin. How he had a supply of ice in a time of much war and negligible electricity was a magician's act to behold. And it was a prescient sign of resourcefulness for what lay ahead.

'Chester, how on earth did you get this lovely room?'

'It was, erm . . . pre-arranged for me.' She raised her eyebrows. Chester dropped into the other armchair. 'By my company.'

'How do you manage to keep it all to yourself?'

'Primarily by being selfish. I'm probably good at that.' He stared straight through her, and she failed to discern if he was in earnest. But then he managed a half smile.

She glanced around the room. When she was out in the corridor peering through the crack of the latched door she had spotted him hide away a map that had been on the desk.

'Gwen, how on earth did you get here?'

'By ambulance car, darling – seemed the safest way.'

'Did you run out of food at the hospital?'

'No. They're hoarding a tremendous amount of supplies in the basement. Although it's only a matter of time before the Japs take it all. Any day now, they're expected to formally requisition the hospital – and the nurses.' Abandoning both the staff and the patients wracked her with guilt, although Doctor Swinton had advised her to leave.

Chester raised an eyebrow. 'And what of the patients?'

The rumour mill churned continuously. 'The Europeans will no doubt be sent to hospitals behind barbed wire. But perhaps you know better than me where that might be for civilians?'

'Well, I've heard rumours – as have you, I'm sure.' Whereas news through official channels was not forthcoming, the bamboo telegraph had delivered whispers to the Chinese nurses.

'First,' she said, 'we heard that all civilians are to be interned in Kowloon. Then Stanley. No, shipped to Formosa. Or to Japan itself. Terrifying!' She thought of her husband. When he was a young child, Klaus's family were living in Tokyo when the Great War broke out and Japan and Germany had found themselves on opposite sides. Klaus's childhood shattered – memories, from before the war, of a jovial father and a happy home, disintegrated. During four years of internment for the whole family, his father barely spoke. The humiliation of defeat had an effect but so did the deprived living conditions. Both his father and mother would suffer the permanent loss of both teeth and hair. And the psychological scars ran deep. His father remained virtually mute even after the end of the war. Both parents died in their fifties.

Chester stared into her eyes. 'You've made a mistake in coming here, old girl. The hotel has run out of food. We'll have to fend for ourselves from now on.'

'Can't Eurasians come and go freely?' she said. 'I gather nurses – even European nurses – can.' But he didn't bite. Did he fail to see the asset before his eyes?

She sipped her drink. 'Chester, Max Holt said something about you—'

'Max Holt talks rot.'

'Right,' she sighed. 'Well, that's a fine way to speak of the dead. He simply said that you're more than an accountant, hence I should seek you out for help, should the time come. That's all.'

Chester pursed his lips.

'Upon my word, I do believe you're more resourceful than your average dull accountant!'

He demurred through silence. She then told him enough of her ordeal at the hospital to elicit a softening of his face and tone. He stood up and rested a hand on her shoulder. Perhaps he did still have feelings beyond friendship, despite her alcohol-fuelled flirtation with Max at the Peninsula.

'I fear for the future,' she said. 'I fear for all of our futures in a prison camp, but a young *gweipo* has fears of a particular kind, a kind that a man need not worry about.'

'I do worry. You're twenty-five, blonde and beautiful: you cannot go unnoticed.'

He fixed another drink for her and water for himself. Then he delivered the line she had been waiting for. 'If there's anything I can do. . . .'

'You speak Cantonese, and clearly you're equipped with at least one map. I've got money, enough to bribe whomever we need to.' Although she had long anticipated each month being the last, Klaus still paid her allowance into her bank account. 'I'm going to find a way out, by one means or another. I plan to get off this island and get to Macao while its neutrality is still respected. My goodness, Chester – you don't want to end up in that camp, and I don't think you want me to.'

He sat down again. 'It's not much of a plan. The Japanese are all over Macao.'

'Then I'll go north instead,' she said. 'Through the New Territories.'

'Where to?'

'Chungking.' Chiang Kai-shek's capital was about the only Chinese city she could name that she knew to be free from Japanese invasion.

'Only 800 miles to walk.'

She sighed. 'Chester, stop playing games. Those maps you've got there – that's not you planning a weekend away.' She had nothing to lose, save embarrassment. 'And "only 800 miles to walk"? What sort of resigned-to-internment accountant would know the walking distance between Hong Kong and the current capital of Free China? I don't know what your game is, all I know is you've got one. I'm getting out of here, you're getting out of here: let's do it together.' She smiled, remembering too late that she had come here to charm – rather than berate – him into action.

A full minute passed in thought. 'Gwen, have you got a pair of trousers in your case?'

'Yes, why?'

'A dress is awfully impractical to hike in,' he smiled.

She beamed alive with hope. 'I knew you'd be my man.' They clinked glasses.

'We'll need some large stockings, too,' he said. Hardly her priority, but he had his reasons.

A thump on the door stopped her mid sip. 'Open up, please! I know you are in there!'

She dropped her glass and the ice tumbled onto the carpet. She would know the owner of that accent anywhere.

Her eyes met Chester's.

'It's my husband.'

Klaus Stern introduced himself to Drake, smiled at Gwen and grinned as he took in the room. His moustache had greyed, and his hair had begun to recede. But he had if not a joy then a purpose in his eyes – just like when they had first met in Shanghai – which took years off him. He kissed Gwen's hand and then disquieted her by opening his mouth. 'Is it not customary to get a divorce before . . . before this?' He pointed at Drake. 'You do know she is married?'

Gwen, standing with her hands on her hips, broke into a smirk. Klaus had once mocked Britain's mission to 'civilise' other races. She wondered if his disgust at this apparent liaison felt all the worse because of Drake's ethnicity.

'It's not what you think,' said Chester. 'She—'

'Yes it bloody well is!' announced Gwen, to poke one in the eye of the 'master race'. Chester stared at her, his mouth sinking open.

'Never mind, Mr Drake.' Klaus had that shared Anglo-Teutonic male inclination to disengage his emotions. 'I have come to help Gwen.' He stepped forward and took hold of her hand. 'I would have come after you arrived in Hong Kong last year, my dear, but as the British interned all Germans who were here, I would not have been pleasantly received. But I bring you good news. Perhaps there is some place to talk?' He spoke to Gwen but cast a glance to Drake.

'I can wait outside, Gwen. Leave you two to talk – if that's what you want? If you'll be okay?'

She nodded.

After he had accompanied Klaus down to the lobby, Chester returned to the hotel room and locked the door behind him.

She stared out of the window at the grand and barely blemished Pedder Building across the street.

'Would you like to tell me what Klaus had to say?' he asked.

She turned to face him. 'Would *you* like to tell *me* what he said to you? You took an age to walk him out.'

Chester set about shifting the double bed towards the window. 'I ran into Flat Face down there – that's what people have nicknamed the Jap officer who appears in the lobby from time to time. He has suspicions about me. He wonders why a Eurasian accountant needs to be holed up alone in a plush hotel. After telling me days ago that I shouldn't be here, he flipped the party line: if I attempt to leave the hotel, they'll shoot me.'

He jammed a kitchen knife between the floorboards. 'They've searched the room twice. But not very well.' She hoped what lay inside would be a passport out of Hong Kong. Instead, she got tins of bully beef and a packet of raisins: an enticing combination for lunch. At least it would be eaten off the Gloucester's fine China.

They took their seats in front of the window.

'Look, my dear, you've got a German husband: You can avoid internment!'

'Not on my own terms, I can't. I'm not a German, nor do I wish to be counted as one. I'd have to give up my British passport – then how on earth could I ever get to England? I'm British and plan to remain so.'

'Spare me the imperial superiority and think pragmatically.'

She rolled her eyes. 'My goodness, your concerns are terribly touching. But Klaus doesn't want me free – he wants me back.'

'He's come to Hong Kong for that purpose?' He handed Gwen tinned beef on a saucer.

'Oh, he'll be here for business, I'm sure. When I first met him, he supplied metal for train tracks. Now, he supplies all manner of materials – presumably for armaments, for Germany or the Japanese. Probably both. But he *says* he's here in Hong Kong for one reason only: me. But I'm sure he's here to try to bolster his status and his market share with the Japs.'

'So are you going to tell me what else your husband had to say?'

'Oh, stop calling him that,' she said, suddenly aware that she too had referred to Klaus as her 'husband'. 'It makes me sound like I'm part of him, owned by him. And I will be again, if he gets his way.'

She examined the slab of sticky beef on her plate and, in the absence of an offer, got up to fix another drink. 'In any event, I heard you two muttering down the corridor. What on earth do you two have in common? And don't say *me* – that would be terribly trite.' She tutted: there was nothing but water in the ice bucket.

'Well, if not you, what else could there possibly be to talk about during the maelstrom of war?' He grinned at her. 'No man would converse about the future of Hong Kong or of Britain and its empire when there's a blonde woman to talk about instead.'

'Fine.' Rather than offer Chester a shot of his own drink, she took her glass back to her chair by the window. She sipped her gin, but it didn't taste so appealing, iceless and with a measure of guilt.

'Klaus says – and I've no idea if he's lying – that all American, Dutch and British civilians are to be herded behind wire in Stanley – some sort of "concentration camp".'

'When?'

'The day after tomorrow.'

Chester nodded.

'And he offered to save me. Said he could keep me out of the camp, by playing "the German husband" card. All I'd have to do, he said, is go back to Macao with him.' She sighed.

He nodded again. 'And will you?'

She stuck her fork into a splodge of beef and put it in her mouth.

Chapter 16

It had been wondrous to sleep in a bed with a proper mattress. She had wanted to offer half of the bed to Chester, but propriety won out and he slept on the floor. The relative oasis of calm the hotel room provided could only last another twenty-four hours – until they would be turfed out and interned.

She smoothed loose strands of hair back under her veil and ran through her plan with Chester one final time. Then she ran down the stairs and out past the sentry atop the hotel steps.

Along Queen's Road, in front of the boarded-up shops, street hawkers – their tiny stalls, three or four deep in places – began piling up all manner of loot for sale: pots and pans, silk dresses, brassieres, half-full bottles of perfume. The hawker's eyes met hers when she overpaid for an item of clothing by offering a silver bracelet in exchange. Gwen shoved the large pair of stockings into her duffle bag and hurried away.

The smell of roasting chestnuts – a winter favourite among the street kitchens of Hong Kong – filled the air. She hurried by, attracting curious looks from the Chinese hawkers. Ahead, a group of Japanese soldiers was standing on the street outside Jimmy's Kitchen, talking at each other all at once. The simplest matter – walking along a street – was now trouble-fuelled. Would crossing to the other side be safer? Or would that attract greater attention? She kept her head down, strode on and prayed to God they would not stop her.

She passed the soldiers and let go a deep breath. In Western District, she turned right, towards the waterfront godowns. Chester had taught her the Cantonese phrases she would need and told her how much to offer, at least as an opening gambit. The warehouses along the waterfront, some punctured by bullets or charred by shellfire, stood abandoned. All except for the fish market – there, there was life. The Japanese would not want the boats to stop bringing in their catches. Cages of crabs and baskets of bream cluttered the wharf, some within a fish's leap of their natural home in the sea below. The fishermen went about their business, not raising an eyebrow as a white nurse wandered in, looking to engage in conversation.

Two hours later, Gwen mounted the steps of the Gloucester reflecting that she had achieved her day's objective. But she was not yet safely back in their room.

She passed through the double doors and was brought to an abrupt halt as two Japanese soldiers dragged an Indian policeman across the lobby. The Indian's trailing foot clipped her ankle. The doors were cast open and he was thrown down the steps. A pistol was drawn, but she looked away before the gunshot.

She hurried on towards the staircase, at the foot of which the Japanese officer in charge had commandeered a desk. His eyes followed her up the stairs. As she reached the first floor, footsteps – and the jangle of the officer's sword – echoed up the staircase from behind her. Then came a bark of something in Japanese. She ran up the next two flights and onto the floor itself. She rounded a corner and smacked into the uniformed chest of a Chinese police officer.

'Help me!' she whispered. Behind him, a hotel room door was standing ajar. She didn't wait for a response but sidestepped into the room, and the officer followed. She closed the door behind him and turned to face a card circle of Chinese policemen staring at her. She dived under the bed: not the most original of hiding places, but beggars could not choose.

After fifteen minutes, the policemen coaxed her out, gave her a chair and pressed a bowl of jasmine tea into her hand. Two bowls later, three of the officers escorted her down the corridor. 'I don't much want to go back to that staircase,' she said to Inspector Hong, the officer whom she had ran into.

'Don't worry, no need.' He steered her to the lift. Somehow she had failed to notice that the corridors were lit up: the electricity was working again.

The fifth floor hotel room door was locked, and Chester Drake wasn't answering.

'You can come back with us for more tea,' said Hong.

Seconds later, Chester appeared, walking towards them from the end of the corridor.

She thanked the police officer and slipped inside. Soon, a gin glass – with ice – was shaking in her hand.

'I'm glad you're safe, old girl. Everything okay?'

She nodded. A minute later, her second gin in hand, she was ready to tell Chester what she had arranged. 'Eight pm tonight, just where you said. I followed your suggestions.' She deliberately avoided the word 'orders' lest he gain the wrong idea: if they were going to spend the next few weeks together, he had best get used to the idea that she was no subordinate.

Chester nodded. 'How much?'

'A hundred and twenty-five. Plus I had to promise him a generous *cumshaw* if all goes well. He said if the Japs catch him they'll cut off his head and massacre his family.'

'The best tip we can give him is: *don't get caught*. We'd better pack.'

She was not going to get as much as a 'well done' out of him. Wouldn't Max have been more encouraging? Even Klaus, for that matter.

The two nurses left the hotel as daylight began to drain from the city. The sentry saw only the back of them, one shapelier than the other. Shorn of moustache and legs clad in seasonally heavy stockings, Chester Drake had passed the first test. They hailed over a rickshaw and, following a startled look from its runner, disappeared under its canopy. Gwen had been pleased with her accomplishments with a little mascara and ruby red lipstick: Chester almost appeared pretty. The rickshaw runner was on to them, concerned at possible aspersions regarding his own role in the conspiracy. But he didn't refuse the fare, and he certainly ran them along at double pace.

The next day, all Europeans would be corralled behind barbed wire. But Gwen and Drake sought to forge their own fate.

As dusk fell, hawkers set about disbanding their stalls. Off-duty Japanese soldiers gutteralled away, leered and gesticulated. She held her breath as the rickshaw passed one group then another.

They trundled out of the city. Twice, on dispiriting inclines, the two apparent nurses got out, and Chester helped haul the empty rickshaw up the hill. Gwen listened and looked for Japanese as they walked along the coastal road towards their target village on the eastern tip of Hong Kong Island. Each time a car engine could be heard, they jumped back up and sat down under the canopy of the rickshaw.

By the time they got to Siu Sai Wan Village, darkness had fallen – welcome cover for two nurses who would struggle to justify their presence there. Aside from rickshaw runners – whom the Japanese made use of – all locals were under curfew from after sunset. There was no sign of people bar the odd glow behind shuttered windows. Gwen was relying on the one fisherman who had spoken to her earlier that day – Mah Sam, he called himself.

And there he was, in the shadows next to the temple, as promised. She dropped her duffle bag, grabbed his hands and thanked him just for being there. The kind eyes she had met in daylight now jittered. 'We go,' he said. Mah Sam led them down the alley next to the temple and along a path behind a row of houses.

Were they confronted, nothing could explain why a man was dressed as a nurse: the disguise would have to see them safely onto the boat. The boat would take them beyond the east side of Kowloon to the New Territories' hills. Onboard, they would take off their veils and change into trousers, for the mountain hike ahead.

They took what cover they could behind the sprinkling of trees which led down a slope to the inlet. Anchored some way beyond the rocky beach, a wallah-wallah bobbed nonchalantly. They stepped towards the water. Unnerved by the feeling of eyes upon her, Gwen scanned around the shoreline and back towards the path and the trees. She sighed relief: there was no rock big enough to hide even a single Japanese soldier and the trees offered only wispish cover in the bright moonlight.

Mah Sam stepped into the shallows and reached a rope out of the water. Chester soon joined him in hauling the wooden boat towards them. It was larger than they needed – more a floating shack than a boat – but at least they would be well hidden inside. Thigh deep in water, she tossed her bag up and then clambered up a tyre which buffered the hull of the foredeck. Mah Sam was standing by the boat while Chester returned to the beach to grab his backpack. At the bow, Gwen sat down on the damp skirt of her dress. She smiled at Mah Sam, only to see his face turn ashen. 'Missy!'

A figure appeared from inside the cabin.

'My dear, the game you are playing is a dangerous one. I could help you, if only you allow me.' Klaus offered his hand to help her up. She slapped it away. 'Otherwise I'll have no choice but to throw you in with the other enemy civilians – you'll be safer there. One day you'll see that I have saved your life: the Japanese would have tortured and killed you for trying to escape.'

'How on God's earth did you know I was here?' she said after she sprung to her feet. By the look on Mah Sam's face, *he* hadn't betrayed them.

Klaus glanced to the beach.

Chester Drake: the double-crossing bastard.

Chapter 17

Queen Victoria's profile struck a defiant yet uncomfortable pose: she was anything but amused. Hundreds of Europeans milled around, stacks of suitcases, trunks and even mattresses clumped all over the square. Gwen was standing in the sunshine, staring up at the Queen. Behind the statue's back, the head and shoulders of the pockmarked Hongkong and Shanghai Bank building loomed above. Ahead of Victoria's throne and backdropped by the harbour, the Great War's Cenotaph was now tainted by the flag of the rising sun.

Two well-dressed older women kiss-cheeked each other as though meeting at a garden party. 'Davina, how lovely to see you, despite it all!'

'How the goodness are you, darling? Is Frank here to look after you?'

'He's over there, undermining the occupation, I should hope!' She pointed to a scrum of Caucasian men huddled around a desk in the nearest corner of the square. Gwen wandered over.

She kept her back to Klaus, a lurking presence on the outside edge of the cordoned area. He had said he would oversee things to ensure fair treatment. However, after she had again refused to be spirited out of Hong Kong by him, she suspected he was present that day out of pure spite.

A pair of Japanese soldiers wielded their bayonets in an effort to form an orderly queue of the thirty or so well-dressed civilian men haranguing the officer at the desk. Standing next to the seated Japanese officer an East Asian civilian yelled out, 'One man at a time. You're first. Do you have identity papers?'

A white-haired man leaning on his walking stick replied, 'Sorry, old chap, but we had to leave in such a hurry one simply forgot.' Then he smiled. Or smirked.

'How old you are?' asked the interpreter.

'Well, that depends.'

The interpreter looked blank.

Gwen had drifted as close as she dare. To avoid staring at the commotion around the desk, she opened her diary and pretended to read it.

'It depends upon whether you mean last birthday or next birthday,' said the old man. 'And it depends upon whom is doing the asking. I know some nationalities prefer to age a person by their next birthday, some by their previous birthday. And I'm not entirely sure what race you are, so I'm unsure how to proceed.'

The seated officer glared at his interpreter.

'So,' said the old man, 'are you Japanese or Korean or something else altogether?'

Gwen smiled. This man – with the bearing of a Great War veteran – was turning the registration process on its head. If others followed his example, the Japanese would fail to complete an accurate record of their captives.

'I'm Chinese,' said the interpreter.

A furore of gasps and groans broke out from the crowd of queuing European men.

The seated officer duly barked something at the interpreter, whose facial expression turned grave.

'What are you called?' asked the interpreter.

'Bunny,' replied the old man.

'B-U-N-N-Y?' enquired the interpreter.

'Yes.'

'Bunny?' queried the interpreter, 'That's not your surname?'

'No, don't be silly,' replied the old man. 'A man can't go around being called "Mr Bunny"!'

'So it's year Christian name?'

'No, that would be an equally daft Christian name, now wouldn't it! But you asked me what I'm called, and that's what people call me. You see, it goes back to my childhood. . . .'

Gwen grinned, turning her face away from the desk. She gazed around the square. There were no other desks, almost certainly no other interpreters, and no other attempts to begin to register the one or two thousand civilians milling around: the old man was almost single-handedly obstructing the entire registration process.

A lorry was let inside the line of Japanese bayonets ringing the square before it squeaked to a halt nearby. A string of Caucasians jumped out from the open back of the lorry. Gwen turned away in guilt and melted into the crowd. The nurses who clambered down from the lorry wore the uniform that had been her identity – albeit for a mere matter of weeks – before she had abandoned them. The 'uniform' she wore that day felt distinctly less worthy yet rather more honest: a civilian's grey wool dress.

While she waited alone with her suitcase she began to think over the decisions made and unmade, the ifs and buts that had brought her to the point of imprisonment. Suddenly at Gwen's side appeared another one of the men in her life who just would not let her go. Why did men need to be so controlling?

'I thought I might have lost you, old girl.' Impeccably dressed from trilby to brogues, he parked his suitcase, haversack and incongruously effeminate handbag at her feet.

'I was talking to an Austrian woman – like you, she's going in voluntarily. But there's a difference, Gwen.' Chester Drake just didn't know when to give up. She had once seen that as an appealing quality, but it soon became infuriating.

'You've got a nerve talking to me, Mr Drake.' She spat out the words. How could he betray her to Klaus? What had the war come to when a British-Chinese Anglophile betrays an English-woman to a German. 'What on Earth are you doing here? Eurasians are not being interned.'

'The Austrian woman's husband is a British civil servant, and so the wife is choosing to be interned with him.' He had a way of both dismissing a question and answering it at the same time.

'Well, that's terribly wonderful for them.'

He grabbed her by the elbow. 'Gwen, old girl, it's not too late. You could remain free.'

'So could you: Eurasians are free to pick sides. And clearly *you* have a special relationship with the enemy.' She would not look directly at him. 'Whereas, the Japanese won't let me leave Hong Kong on a British passport, and Klaus would make damn sure I don't get a German one unless I give up my British one and go and live with him. Even then he'd probably requisition *any* passport I held.'

'Did he say that?'

'He didn't need to.' She cast her eyes aside.

'Good grief, Gwen, I don't think he harbours any ill-intent towards you. Ask yourself, is Klaus an out-and-out liar? If the man you married is fundamentally an honest person, he is your best way out of here.'

She stepped away. Streams of people herded onto the square. Men pinned down by cases of clothing and food, women projecting an air of indifference. At least one young woman endeavoured to paint on a brave face – literally. The girl held a vanity case and set to work with mascara and lipstick. Gwen pulled out her own lipstick and did likewise. They may be standing amid a ruined British Empire, but that simply gave more reason not to look ruined oneself.

'Gwen' – he appeared at her side once again – 'if you're resigned to this, I wonder whether you would be so kind as to carry this handbag for me?'

She hesitated and then slipped it onto her shoulder despite herself. He must have felt her scowl clawing at his face.

'I know you're angry with me, old girl, and to an extent I can understand why. But I didn't tell Klaus our half-baked plan.'

She stopped herself from snapping back at him while half a dozen soldiers strutted by, just yards away.

'So what *were* you speaking to Klaus about in the hotel corridor?'

'Well, he simply asked whether we might endeavour to stay in touch, concerning your well-being.'

'And you cut some sort of deal?' Her eyes bored into him.

'No, we did not.'

Japanese soldiers were moving from one group of refugees to the next, searching through suitcases and bags.

'So how did he know our plan, Chester?' She spoke with an intensity that demanded attention.

Drake glanced left and then right out of the corner of his eyes. 'He must have had someone follow you when you went out of the hotel the previous day to arrange things.'

She stared Drake in the eye.

He lowered his voice further. 'If you won't take the easy ticket out of here, well ... there may be another way. I just can't tell you much now.'

A British man climbed up the steps at the foot of Victoria's statue as a podium from which he called out. 'Binoculars, cameras and guns! If you've got any of those, please give them up to the Japanese at once.'

She instinctively held the heavy handbag tighter and stared at Chester. The look he gave her made it clear he had packed neither a camera nor binoculars in that handbag.

She stepped close to him and spoke quietly. 'Chester, what were you thinking?'

'The battle's over, Gwen. Their proper troops are already on leave. These layabouts aren't the same sort of soldiers.'

'But they aren't simply going to let you smuggle arms into a prisoner of war camp!'

She walked the few steps back to her suitcases and he followed.

'*Internment* camp – security is slacker than for military prisoners. Look, I've been watching them: they're not even searching all the bags. Can't you see how chaotic the whole show is today? Did they even take your name?'

She answered by not answering.

'No, me neither,' said Drake. 'The Japs had not the slightest plan for what to do with enemy civilians. They don't even know how many there are, let alone *who* they are. Civilians, especially female ones, are not seen as a threat.'

'But we're not *all* civilians, are we Chester?'

He lowered his head and stared into her eyes. 'It will be useful, Gwen. We'll need it later.'

'I—'

'Stop talking about it.' Japanese soldiers were now scrutinising the group of Americans next to them. Three soldiers moved on and approached Gwen and Chester. Two opened up the suitcases, while the third delved into Drake's rucksack. 'Why you here? You no British,' said one soldier.

'I am half British.'

The Japanese soldier appeared unconvinced. 'Eurasians no go prison.'

'I have a British passport, and,' said Chester, casting his eyes onto Gwen, 'a British fiancée.'

The Japanese scowled his disgust.

The young soldier with Drake's rucksack performed the only diligent search of the three. When he had eventually finished with the rucksack, he started on Gwen's duffle bag. His two colleagues, having piled clothes and tinned food besides the open suitcases, called their colleague to follow them. The third man put down Gwen's duffle back and pointed at the handbag.

'Bin-o-clar? Cam-ra?'

She shook her head.

The soldier followed his colleagues on to the next family. But suddenly he about-faced and said, *'Gun?'*

She didn't know what to say.

The soldier crowed out laughter as he turned away to return to his work.

A Japanese cavalry officer, samurai sword swinging against his horse's ribcage, clomped over and barked instructions to his men to herd the crowd seaward.

Soon Gwen and Chester had been shouted into a line, four abreast. They marched along the praya, where bayoneted rifles threatened on the inland side and barbed wire penned the procession back from the drop-off into the sea

Beyond the soldiers, clinging close to the buildings rimming the praya, Chinese civilians queued in silent wonder. The lack of jeering suggested sympathy. The queue snaked along to a godown used as an impromptu rice distribution point. The Japanese had announced their intention to reduce the population from 1.7 million to half a million, and what better way than through starvation? A wail from one man in the queue shattered the wall of Chinese stoicism. A Japanese soldier leaped away from his position alongside the marching Europeans and jabbed his bayonet into the Chinese man's ribs. He collapsed to the ground.

The rubber-necking Europeans were prodded along. They pooled to a halt by Queen's Pier, where the nearest of a queue of Star Ferries swayed gently. Nearby, the body of some other unfortunate Chinese lay slumped over the barbed wire. Fifty yards further on lay another.

Most of the children had been evacuated long ago, but ahead of Gwen in the queue a fair-haired boy of four or five toddled along beside his mother. He was weighed down by an overcoat, and from its belt hung an enamel mug, two saucepans, spoons and forks. His mother carried two suitcases. Glued to the outside of each case were several portrait photographs of a man and a handwritten note. In one photograph, he was dressed in an army uniform. The note read: 'Please tell me if you have knowledge of Sergeant Henry (Harry) Perkins of the Royal Scots'. Gwen found herself sucking in her lips. Personal tragedies were everywhere. So many wives who would not know whether their husbands had been killed or were now incarcerated in the military camps across the harbour in Kowloon.

She edged her feet forward alongside Drake's and leaned into him. 'Chester, whatever you're up to better work.'

'Trust me.'

A Japanese soldier scythed the air with his bayonet, splitting each row of four prisoners into pairs to funnel into the gangway ahead. People stumbled, swayed and crowded aboard the ferry.

Gwen and Chester kept to the rail inside the boat and set their backs to the crowded deck. At least the sea was calm.

The ferry eased away from the wharf.

'What you should have done, my good man, is told me about these "other plans" – plans which you still haven't clarified. I will not be kept prisoner!' Her initially hushed tones rose into something of a yell. The sun screwed her eyes into a squint as she stared into the inviting water. She placed a foot on the lower rail and stepped up onto it, only to be yanked back down by her waist.

'Don't be daft,' said Drake. 'And please keep your voice down.'

She stared at him and blushed. 'This whole business is damned degrading.' To jump overboard was tempting but pointless. 'But, Chester, if not now, then when?'

The ferry chugged westward through the harbour, circumventing one jagged shipwreck then another.

'There are one or two things I have to do inside Stanley first. Perhaps you'll help me.'

'And then what chance is there we can make it out?'

'We're not going to know for sure until we get there.'

Chapter 18

Stop staring at it, Gwen. Focus on the distance. Not here, but there.

She was sitting on the grassy hillside. Below her, an industrious nest of Europeans and Americans darted hither and thither, their desperation deceived by hope. She set her back to the fence that barricaded the northern perimeter of the camp and swept her eyes around the sea-bound sides of the camp. The view down to Stanley's main beach and across the bay made for a picture postcard.

The foreground was a horror movie. Chester Drake had walked down the slope to scout out a bungalow on her behalf. A row of earth mounds rimmed the garden of the bungalow. Primitive crosses loomed over four of these hastily fashioned graves, although one was marked simply by a Tommy's steel helmet where the jagged hole told the story. Completing the tableau was a mattress flung over a body and weighed down by a few shovel loads of soil; the pair of feet protruding from underneath the mattress drew her eye and brought on nausea. *Focus on the distance, Gwen. Not here, but there. Not now, but then.*

The ocean glistened in the sunlight. A large junk, its sail ravaged with holes and its deck crowded with Chinese, bobbed out to sea, led by a small, open craft carrying Japanese soldiers.

'Gwen, is that you?' Nurse Arabel Jenkins left the mêlée below and came bounding up the hillside. 'I thought you might be dead!'

Gwen stood up and hugged her friend. 'Arabel, how on earth are you now? When did you get here?'

'I'm okay.' Arabel beamed a smile from another era – in Macao, and a friendship based around lawn tennis, cream teas and inattentive husbands. 'We arrived yesterday. We're staying in this bungalow. We missed the prime real estate – the Americans got there first.'

'Bloody yanks,' said Gwen. 'Where are the Australians?'

'Scattered around,' said Arabel. 'A few are in the school building.'

Gwen pursed her lips. Was there any chance Max was among them? No, how could he be a live civilian rather than a dead soldier?

Arabel kept a hold of her friend's hand. 'Gwen, there's good news – have you heard? America has flattened Tokyo! Bombed it to smithereens, apparently. Not long for us to go now.' Arabel was still Arabel: buoyant despite all she had been through.

'That's marvelous news. How did you hear that?' Clearly the Japanese would never mention it in their new English paper, *The Hongkong News.*

'Well, George Baxter has a chum called Blowers who is rooming with a chap who's smuggled in a wireless. He's picked up a station broadcasting from goodness only knows. But it seems some chap speaks enough Chinese to give us the news! Anyway, there's more: Churchill has promised to retake Hong Kong within ninety days.'

Chester hurried up the slope. Gwen introduced Arabel, and Chester removed his hat.

'Arabel was just telling me the good news.'

'Do you mean the one about Tokyo being bombed into submission? Or the one about Churchill marching in here next month? All poppycock, I'm afraid.'

Arabel gaped. Gwen glanced at her and then looked skyward. From far out to sea, a muffled cheering rumbled up the hillside. The junk which had passed earlier had become an orange glint on the ocean.

She squinted at the boat. 'Chester, is that—'

His face froze. 'Good Lord – it's on fire!' It wasn't *cheering* they had heard, but *screaming.*

'God save them!' cried Arabel.

Motoring away from the junk, the smaller craft carried the Japanese back towards Stanley. 'There's nothing that can save them,' said Drake. 'Beasts, absolute beasts.'

The junk was a floating fireball.

Chester took a few steps down the slope and beckoned with his hand. 'Ladies, come down to the bungalow with me.'

'But someone must help them!' said Gwen. 'I saw that junk pass earlier. It looked like just ordinary Chinese people on board. How can the Japanese. . . .'

'The Japs want to reduce the local population,' he said. 'And this seems to be one way they're setting about it. It's too barbaric to watch.'

'This is the best of what's left,' said Drake.

'Oh yes, Gwen, you must join us here! There are forty-eight of us. We've got two rooms for single females and two for males.'

'Four rooms and there's only forty-eight of you,' said Gwen. 'You'll get terribly lonely.'

'It's a little cramped, but we can squeeze in another body on the floor.' It was Arabel's use of the word 'body' that pierced Gwen's thoughts. 'It won't be for long.'

Gwen aimed to make sure of that. Arabel had conspired with Drake to take their minds away from what they had witnessed offshore. Gwen's mind was not so easily moved, but there seemed more reason than ever to find a way out of the hands of the Japanese.

In the shade of the skinny pine trees ringing the bungalow's garden, three older men were wiring together two tin cartridge cases with a shell case on top, fashioned as a chimney: a stove, of sorts.

'There's no electricity, yet,' explained Arabel, 'so we need fuel.' She pointed at a flat-capped man making little headway sawing a bread knife into the trunk of a pine tree.

'No!' A turbaned camp guard came jogging across the garden. 'No, you must not, sir.' Gwen could not decide which was stranger – being ordered what to do by an Indian policeman who had, until just weeks ago, worked for the British? Or the fact that one of their captors addressed a prisoner as 'sir'? 'No cut down trees. Japanese say so, sir.' The man with the bread knife stepped back from his assault on the pine tree.

The bungalow's windows were glassless and bullets had chipped holes in the surrounding stonework. Inside, the smell was oddly familiar. The lounge room was strewn with rolled-up blankets, cotton quilts and a conspicuous lack of furniture. Gwen was introduced to two women who were washing red splotches off the walls. But lacking a step-ladder, streaks of blood were still present high up and splattered across the ceiling. Then the odour found its place – it was just like the hospital morgue.

'We're doing our best to clean the place,' said Arabel. 'And people sleep anywhere and everywhere. There are six chaps in the garage – well, it's more of a shed than a garage. There are four more in the storeroom and a fellow the others call 'Toothpick' sleeps curled around the cistern in the cupboard in the hall. Everyone's jealous of the privacy he's nabbed for himself!'

The stench at the back of the bungalow was strong as they passed the bathroom. 'The toilet doesn't flush properly,' said Arabel, 'but we've got a bucket of water in there now. I'm glad you didn't see the state of it when we arrived – no water supply and the toilets were blocked to overflowing. Disgusting.'

Arabel led Gwen through to the small back bedroom. 'We can't claim it's well appointed – there's not a single piece of furniture. There are seven – well, eight of us now – who sleep in here.'

Gwen stopped in the doorway and stared open-mouthed. The room was less than ten-foot square with an added feature that even an estate agent could not gloss over: the centre of the bare floorboards gave way to a two-foot wide hole.

Drake had squeezed past Gwen and was standing over the charred hole. 'Hand grenade. There was some frantic room-to-room fighting here at the end.'

She turned to face Chester. 'This is the best of what's left? What about the school buildings? A chemistry lab would be positively luxuriant compared to this.'

'Our dear police have taken the last of those.'

She sighed. 'So this is home.'

'You had a handbag outside,' said Arabel. 'I'll go get it for you.' Then Gwen remembered what she had left inside that bag.

She stared up at the sky through the small window. *Not here, but there. Not now, but then.*

She sidled up to Drake. 'Might Max—'

'He's not in Stanley, Gwen.'

Then neither should she be. 'What shall I help you do, Chester?'

'Excuse me?'

'You asked me to help you,' she whispered. 'Before we break out of here.' Perhaps he needed reminding that it was *we*. 'I smuggled your gun in here – in the bag Arabel is now fetching – and I will be with you when the time comes. But before we break out, you said there were "things" you have to do here in the camp. You wanted my help – to do what?'

Chester squeezed her elbow. 'I must glean some information, make some lists,' he whispered. 'But this is not the time and place, old girl. If anyone hears us, it could put not just our plans in jeopardy, but our lives, too. From now on, there can be no more talk of it.'

Chester could be as bossy as any Englishman. 'You're not your typical submissive, place-knowing Eurasian!'

'And you're not your typical submissive, place-knowing woman.'

'Touché. You make your lists,' she said, turning away. 'I'm going to find a way out of here.'

Arabel appeared at the bedroom door. 'Here's your bag. And I found you some blankets. I'll make you a space on the floor.'

'Give the bag to Chester, please. It's got something of his inside.' Gwen strode past her. 'I'm going to explore this camp.'

'Hold on a mo' and I'll come with you,' said Arabel.

'No, it's okay – I'll escort her,' said Drake. He grabbed the bag but handed it back to Gwen outside.

She led the way out through the garden, where, despite it all, the grass was green, and red and white flowers bloomed.

Drake appeared beside her. 'That was rather rude, wasn't it?' she said. 'Not letting Arabel come along.'

'Probably. But for good reason.'

They walked towards the western seaboard of the camp. The hillside rolled down to the little pier where they had arrived earlier.

'Chester, we can do this.' The main obstacle on the hillside was the roll of barbed wire just yards below. There was no wall or fence or watch towers, just shrubbery and then shoreline rocks to negotiate. Nothing insurmountable.

Drake led them away through a scattering of imported pine trees. 'Getting out of the camp is possible, but we need to plan what we would do next. We can't expect to stroll across Hong Kong Island, swim the harbour and march through Kowloon and the New Territories and onto Chungking.' The thing was, as a Eurasian, Chester probably could do just that. It was easy to see why he had been reluctant to take a woman – at least, a white woman – into his plans and harder to see why he had relented.

Nevertheless, she resented his patronising manner.

'Tell me exactly what "information" you're looking for. Perhaps I can help?'

Drake stopped her amid the trees, away from the scurry of internees on the path ahead.

'You must be careful where and how you speak, Gwen, or I'm out of our scheme for good. But whilst it's quiet here, I'll tell you what you may soon hear from others. Something ghastly occurred here, and I need to find out the horrid details. We need reliable witnesses. We need to make a record to show the world, to help people outside to know exactly what they're fighting for. And we need to make detailed lists of everybody who's survived and those who perished. So we need to know everyone who's within the barbed wire of this camp – dead or alive. The Japs count numbers not names. The families of the prisoners – whether they're in England, America, Australia or wherever – will have no idea whether their loved ones are alive or dead. Even if we hand the Japs lists of who's here, we can rely on them *not* to pass the information on to the outside world.'

She looked at him like a knowing parent looks at their child.

'Gwen, don't you think your parents want to know you're here? There'll be desperate with worry.'

There was too much to explain to him, too much pain. But, yes, she nodded, she knew all too well about the anguish of not knowing.

They meandered clockwise along footpaths of hard mud that passed the two storeys of St Stephen's College. She smiled at a group of children playing hopscotch in the dirt. Surely the Japanese would repatriate mothers and children with some haste?

Outside the school's main H-block, an Indian policeman was standing on guard, unmoved by the Britishers coming and going with bedclothes and luggage. Through the window, internees rolled out their bedding in between the raised workstations of a science classroom.

'What happened in there is what I want to find out about,' said Chester. Vague rumours had reached Gwen at the Queen Mary, but then so did rumours of a Chinese army coming to the rescue.

Chester glanced through the arched entrance to the school and promptly about-turned. 'Should we enter in and look for clues?' she said.

'No, Miss Marple. Let's keep going. I took a peek in there earlier. There's nothing to see except blood stains – and we don't need to leave our bungalow for that, old girl.'

A man with a thick moustache and a baggy white shirt, half undone, walked out of the school and stopped.

'Well, good day, Drake. I'm surprised to see you end up here.'

'Good day, Captain Chattey.'

'Less of the "Captain", if you don't mind.'

'Of course. Sorry. This is Miss Gwen Harmison.'

'I'm sure it is,' said Chattey.

Well, you shouldn't be so bloody sure, thought Gwen. Legally, it was still Mrs Klaus Stern.

'I'm glad to see you looking so well,' said Chester. 'I heard things got rather sticky here during the battle, and you were in the thick of it. I was hoping you might tell me about it some time.'

'*Rather sticky?* Well, you could say that. No doubt you've had a nice time of it.'

'Well, I can tell now is not the time. We had best be on our way.'

Drake and Gwen wound through the trees, catching sparkling views of the South China Sea. 'So who was that man?' she asked.

'Crumb Chattey. And I've no idea why everyone calls him "Crumb". As a teenager I used to work as a weekend waiter at the United Services' club, and Captain Chattey – he was in the Middlesex – was one of the few who didn't treat me and my kind like an inferior species.'

'He doesn't seem to like you much now.' The sun disappeared behind a cloud and she overlapped her cardigan across her chest. 'I suppose,' she continued, 'many will question what a Eurasian man is doing in here by his own free will. Perhaps people like Chattey fear you're here to spy on them for the Japanese?'

'Well, maybe. I believe it's more because he ran into a spot of bother last year, and I – I'm ashamed to say – made no effort to see him after he was arrested for . . . well, the most humiliating of charges.'

'Arrested?'

'That's not a story for me to tell.' From west to east, they crossed the neck of the peninsula in just a few minutes. 'What's important,' continued Chester, 'is that he was here when horrible things happened after the surrender on Christmas Day. He's someone who can help me find out what really happened here.'

They halted their walk to gaze down upon Tytam Bay.

'But he hardly seems likely to talk to you.'

'I believe he finds it rather difficult to like anyone, these days. I'm not sure how much he's ashamed and how much he's angry. His friends rather let him down, I'm afraid. Although others would take a more scathing view – he is a convict, after all. But nobody doubts he was a brave soldier.'

Gwen breathed out slowly. 'Don't you mean he *was* a convict?'

'Well, that's debatable.' He sat down on the grass, retrieved a notebook and pencil from his blazer pocket and motioned for her to sit. 'I'd not been out this side of the camp yet,' said Chester. Beyond the barbed wire, the bank that ran down to the tip of Stanley's main beach appeared invitingly negotiable. But Gwen said nothing. The long sandy beach lay resplendent in the sunshine. She had bathed at that beach soon after arriving in Hong Kong, when the autumn warmth had cast the colony as a South Pacific idyll. The sun still shone but the temperatures had dropped, and old hands said the cloud and cool of winter would take up residence any day.

He glanced all around and then bowed his head to return to writing furiously, using coded shorthand.

'I wonder what's in those godowns?' asked Gwen, pointing down at the two warehouses between the wire and the shore.

Chester's silence suggested he knew the answer to that.

'What are you writing?'

'Now that we're out of sight from any guards, I'm jotting down some things we've learned today.'

A few minutes later, they recommenced their tour of the peninsula. Around the rear of St Stephen's College, and some way ahead of them, lay what first appeared as rubble on a darkened patch of ashen ground.

'Perhaps the Japs burned some evidence?' suggested Gwen. Chester grabbed her elbow and steered her sharply away. She peered back over her shoulder. Among what was now clear were charred remains, a human skull stared out.

She refused to accept the silence. 'Do the Japanese cremate their war dead? Or. . . .'

Chester did not reply.

She contemplated who those poor people may once have been. British soldiers? Chinese civilians? She thought again of the pain of their loved ones, the pain of not knowing, the pain that had pushed her to Asia in the first place.

People carried suitcases or dragged trunks between buildings. They passed the Dutch block, complete with bowling lawn, and came upon the three blocks of flats occupied by the Americans. 'The best billets in the camp,' repeated Chester.

She managed a nod. They passed another block. Amid a flurry of cursing, one young man was ejected from the doorway. 'No room here,' was a cry heard as many times as in Bethlehem 1941 years or so previously.

Around the other side of the blocks of flats, the hillside dropped away suddenly, giving an unlikely view down into the main building near the tip of the peninsula.

'The prison within the prison,' said Chester. 'The Japs seem to be using that as we did – for the real criminals.'

'Keep away!' a guard yelled. 'No look in the prison!'

They walked on down a slope and skirted around Stanley Prison.

'I heard the inmates were set free during the battle. Is that right?' she asked.

'Near the end of the battle, one or two with a proven military record were brought out to fight to defend Stanley. But, ironically, the violent criminals were kept behind bars.'

Minutes later, they caught a glimpse of 'Crumb' Chattey, who had taken a different path. He marched ahead of them and stared across at the barbed wire topping the prison wall.

'I wonder where he's going, with such purpose?'

Chester shrugged his shoulders.

'Crumb! Your Captain Chattey was imprisoned in here and yet was let out to fight?'

Chester nodded in affirmation.

'So he never completed his sentence? He should still be a convict? What's his crime?'

Chester again gave that blank stare. 'That's not for me to say.' He sighed a deep sigh. 'Look, old girl, we'll head back now.'

'Not I.' Nothing determined her mind more readily than a man ordering her around. She gazed through the trees for another sight of Chattey but failed to see him.

'Come on, Gwen. Let's go. I've got a sumptuous tin of tomatoes we could split.'

The oddest things made her think of Max. Being half English and half Australian, would he say to-*mah*-toes or to-*may*-toes? She didn't know if he *liked* tomatoes. She didn't know if he lived or died. It was the same when her parents went missing: there comes a certain guilty point where to hear they are dead would be better than to hear nothing at all.

'Let's go back to the bungalow,' said Drake in more of a pleading tone. 'Home' was within sight, but her attention was diverted by the green grass of a cemetery. There were only three other people present, the quietest area within the camp's grounds. There was no bedding to acquire or food to prepare there. A young couple were sitting in the shade of a tree talking quietly but intently. Beyond them, crouching, inspecting a gravestone, was 'Crumb' Chattey, his capacious white shirt flapping in the breeze.

'I'm heading back,' said Chester, glancing into the cemetery. 'If you talk to anyone, be careful not to say anything of our intentions. Word can spread, and before you know it a guard hears something, and then the Japanese will—'

'Trust me.'

Chester gazed at her and she braced herself for a further ticking off. But he simply ripped some pages out of his notebook, handed it to her and walked away.

She cast her eyes across one gravestone then another as she edged towards Chattey. There was the odd European tombstone engraved with nineteenth-century dates, but most of the stones were rough-cut blocks daubed with Chinese characters.

'Plague victims, in the main,' said Chattey, as he stood up from beside a gravestone. 'But there's a few unlucky pirates to boot.' He stepped towards her. 'Chattey, Walter Chattey, at your service. I'm terribly sorry about earlier.' He took Gwen's hand and shook it.

She peered into his tired eyes. She had an idea as to what Chattey's great 'crime' may be.

They sat down on the grassy bank above the headstones.

'So what's a nice English girl like you doing here? Shouldn't you have been evacuated?'

'Well, when the war broke out in '39 I happened to be married to a German.'

'Could happen to anyone, I s'pose!' Chattey grinned.

'Well, quite,' she said. 'However, plenty of my own people – the English, that is – still snub me for that apparent crime. And those who now grudgingly accept me assume I left him because of the war. Anyway, I left him in Macao and came to Hong Kong, looking for a boat home.'

Chattey began to roll a cigarette. 'Bad timing, my dear. Must have been difficult being married to the enemy. Although there are good Germans.'

'Yes, I know. It wasn't really the war that divided us. . . .' Although, as she said it, she began to wonder.

'So you found yourself alone, halfway round the world,' said Chattey, encouraging her with a braced smile.

'I discovered that in British society one thing worse than having a German husband is being separated from one's German husband. I don't really fit in on either side.' She pursed her lips and paused her apparent stream of consciousness, designed to entice Chattey on-board. 'The wives seem to think I'm some sort of prostitute, and I suppose the men can't abide the thought of an English woman sleeping with the enemy.'

'Not fitting in is something I can relate to,' he said. 'You may be the only Britisher in Hong Kong who doesn't know about me – or perhaps you do?'

'I'll know only what you're willing to tell me,' she lied.

'People don't say anything to me, but I know they talk. You'll hear soon enough that I was, until recently, imprisoned in the gaol over there. I shouldn't much care if the Japanese find out – what could they do except throw me from one prison into another. Or maybe they'd put me out of my misery?'

The young couple who had been cuddling on the grass upped and left, to wander back into camp reality. Gwen and Chattey were alone in the cemetery.

'I won't tell a soul,' she said.

'It matters not, my dear. Do you know for what great crime I was sentenced to two years' incarceration?' The scandal, if it was the same one, had made headline news across in Macao when it broke the previous summer.

'It's frightfully shocking to some. I was an officer in the Middlesex, you see, and that sort of thing just isn't done in the British Army. Except it is, I can tell you. But perhaps I'm the only one to be caught *in flagrante delicto.*' Chattey clocked the impassivity on her face and then stared ahead.

'You see, I was born – and I remain – a homosexual.'

She remained expressionless but allowed her head to nod.

'And so all my friends melted away. Now the lot of them find themselves prisoner here with me. And, what do you know, in here too is Sir Athol MacGregor – the chief justice who put me in prison in the first place.'

She tilted her head in surprise. She would hold her silence for as long as he was speaking and she was accumulating his trust.

'So I went from being an army officer, to convict, to fighting Hong Kong's last stand, to now being a prisoner in Stanley once again. There wasn't time to find me a uniform, but they gave me command of Stanley Platoon. Oddly, I had three prison wardens – my former jailers – under my command. One was killed, poor sod.

'Anyway, I took a couple of nicks on Christmas Eve and the CO was on to me. He disarmed me before the Japs could and made it clear he considered me a civilian. A wounded one at that. Perhaps he thought I'd be better treated as a civilian than a military POW, or perhaps he thought the likes of me didn't deserve military recognition. Anyway, early on Christmas morning he sent me down to St Stephen's College – which was a makeshift hospital and was, by now, ahead of our front line. Anyway, my own wounds were minor, so I reported to the hospital to volunteer my services as an orderly. Just before the Japs got there.' He glanced at Gwen and then up to the heavens. Perhaps he felt he had already said too much. Chattey produced a box of matches, lit his waif of a cigarette and lay back flat on the grass.

'Mr Chattey, it's an incredible experience you've had. You must have witnessed a great deal.'

'And what of you, my dear. You look about twenty-three. Why aren't you cosseted away by your parents in a country house in England?'

'Twenty-five. And I've never been asked that before. My parents were always torn between caging me up or letting me fly. The latter, in a roundabout way, came to be my father's preference. So I chose to take my cue from him.'

'And did this upset your mother?'

'It couldn't. I'm afraid it's quite a story.'

'Imprisoned here, time is on the side of the storyteller, my dear.'

Gwen smiled. 'Well, I was nineteen when my parents went on their first holiday without me. Dad had just received a golden handshake – he retired as assistant branch manager for Lloyds in Sunningdon. They spent it on a once-in-a-lifetime trip. Dad had always wanted to see America. He sent me a letter – posted in Madeira, where they stopped on the way. His letter told me he had been giving some thought to a proposal Uncle Charlie had put to him some time earlier – but my parents had kept it from me until that letter. Uncle Charlie was out in Shanghai then. I had terribly fond childhood memories of him. He had been living in Asia since I was twelve, investing in this or that and trading something or other – even opium crossed my youthful mind! Uncle Charlie had offered to put me up, to give me an opportunity to get to know the world a bit – and get to know myself, I suppose. And then, of all people it was *Dad* who told me, in this letter, that it was time to live a little – just as he was beginning to do himself, I suppose. I had always lived with my parents and Vi – Violet, my little sister. She was still at school. I used to help her with her homework. She was lousy at Latin.

'But she blossomed into a beauty, and the boys came calling. Her blue eyes sparkled, and her vibrant blonde bob trumped my straw-like hair. Anyway, I had completed a basic nursing course and practised part-time in a home for retired soldiers near Kingston-upon-Thames. At first when Dad told me to do something with my life I felt offended. But then I saw opportunity and freedom – freedom from boredom, most of all.'

Perhaps boredom had also played a role in the marriage break-down, but was that not Klaus's fault?

'I *was* very young,' she continued. 'In fact, it's only in these last few months that I believe perhaps I've begun to grow up.'

'So you took your old man's advice and jumped on a liner to China?' asked Chattey.

'Almost. Unfortunately this freedom I then felt soon disap-peared.' Her eyes swelled with tears. 'It was the not knowing. The not knowing tore right through me. And as for my sister. . . .'

An older man appeared through the trees. He stopped walking when he caught sight of Chattey and Gwen and about-turned, as though it were correct that the cemetery should only hold two living people at a time. Once again, they shared the space only with the beat of unseen cicadas.

'Not knowing what?' Chattey held out a handkerchief. 'Or is it impertinent of me to ask?'

'No, it's okay.' She had to carry on. 'You may remember *The Duchess*?'

'The liner that went missing?' enquired Chattey. 'Caribbean, wasn't it?'

Tears streamed down her cheeks. 'I had received that letter from Dad on the Tuesday and wrote immediately to Uncle Charlie saying I'd love to come to China. But then on the Friday I heard news of a cruise liner disappearing in the Atlantic. It was the following Monday before they named the liner as *The Duchess*.

'And then, nothing. Just the waiting. The worry drove Vi mad. Nothing I said got through to her, she was inconsolable. The doctors prescribed drugs so that she slept nearly all day and all night—'

'Hold on a moment,' said Chattey. 'I thought they found the ship, did they not?'

She dabbed her cheeks with the handkerchief. 'Not in time. We were waiting for news that didn't come – at least, not in time.'

'Oh, I am terribly sorry.'

'The prospect of losing both parents at once. . . . It was the not knowing that was the worst of it. Things would have been so different . . . if only we had been informed . . . if we'd heard they had found the ship, found our parents' bodies, we both would have got through it, together. I believe that in some sense, some quick, definite news, sad as it would have been. . . . Just to know anything would, dare I say, have come as something of a relief to Vi.' And not only to Vi.

'I had to go back to work. One Wednesday – and I've hated Wednesdays ever since – the police visited me at work and delivered the most extraordinary news. I rushed home after my shift at the nursing home. But when I got home Vi was out. She hadn't been out of the house – well, not beyond the garden – since we first heard that *The Duchess* had gone missing. I'd tried to take her for a walk many times. She left a note which said she was going to meet the London express train at Halsey Halt. So I rushed out to catch her, myself invigorated by the news I had to tell her. I marched apace along the old canal path. When I heard and then saw the train – or more its mane of smoke – steam across the bridge before Halsey, I froze, my feet clamped to the ground. I knew what was about to happen. I ran for my life up to the bridge and then straight down the train tracks towards Halsey Halt. All because she didn't know whether our parents were alive or dead.'

She wiped at her stream of tears. 'At least I'd been able to follow the news reports and talk to the police. But Vi hadn't, she was so out of it. In any event, by the time I got there the police were holding back a small crowd. And yet the ship had been found. Taken by pirates, diverted way off-course through thick fog and grounded on a remote, uninhabited island. . . .'

She took a breath. 'Of course, everyone in the Halsey area knows fine well that express trains do not stop at Halsey Halt. . . .'

A sea eagle swooped down and skimmed the tops of a line of casuarina trees.

'Vi,' she continued, 'had killed herself. For all that time when we thought our parents were dead, they were alive – and they still are.'

Chattey sat upright, and, lacking the social awkwardness of so many an Englishman, he put his arm around her shoulder. 'A tragedy indeed. I'm so sorry.'

'After Vi died, I found myself sinking into a depression. Vi's death felt like it was my fault, and every time my parents so much as looked at me I felt their glances betray their feelings – they were asking themselves, "Wasn't there something Gwen could have done to look after Vi better?" And of course there was – I should have stayed at home with her every minute of every day until our parents returned.'

'You mustn't blame yourself, my dear.' Chattey rubbed his hand on her shoulder.

'I don't know if I do. In any event, Dad became insistent that I go and live a little, go and see a bit of the world. He probably thought I'd find a husband, too. I'm sure Mum found it odd that he wanted to send me away on a passenger liner after their experience. But off I went, to stay with Uncle Charlie in Shanghai, fell in love with one of his younger friends, got married, separated and here I am. My parents couldn't face sailing out to Asia for the wedding, so they never met my husband. Not that it really matters now. Anyway, I came to Hong Kong to get away from my husband and book a passage back to England. I suppose I'll be one of those old maids – "returned empty", people say – should I ever make it home.'

'But then the battle broke out and here you are.'

'Yes,' she replied, 'here I am.'

'Something of a misfit,' said Chattey. 'Like me.'

'Do you know I've never told anyone all that before, about my parents and sister,' lied Gwen.

Chattey offered her a cigarette and lit it as it hung between her lips.

'I've heard something about what happened here at St Stephen's College on Christmas Day, Captain Chattey.'

'Call me Walter. Everybody seems to think they know what happened, but it's all Chinese whispers. The only people who knew were those who were here.'

'You were here, Walter. You know what happened.'

'That's true, my dear, but what good would come of telling everybody about it? People in this camp are already fraught enough.'

She rested her finger tips on his arm. 'It's not the people *inside* the camp who need to know. It's the wives and parents *outside* the camp – scattered around the world – who need to know if their loved ones are alive or dead. What if there were a way to get word out of the camp to—'

'How do you intend to get information out?' Chattey took a drag and then gushed out cigarette smoke. 'Drake? You're spying for Drake!'

Gwen smiled. 'I'm going to help him form lists of who's alive in here and who was killed and how they were killed. Contrary to the Geneva Convention, the Japanese won't tell foreign governments or the International Red Cross such things. We have to do it for ourselves. I know what it's like not to know. There will be another Violet out there somewhere now, and if they don't hear, for better or worse, what happened to their loved ones. . . .'

'Okay,' said Chattey. 'Of course.'

He took his time before he spoke again. 'I understand. I can tell you what I saw, I can give you some names.'

'Thank you.'

'But it's not pretty. In fact, it's rather horrific.'

'I was a nurse during the battle: I've seen horrific. And three Japanese soldiers tried to rape me.' She opened her notebook. 'Captain . . . *Walter,* I know you won't treat me like a *pathetic* woman, as so many men do.'

Chattey rubbed blades of grass between his fingers and released them into the breeze. 'The college was used as a hospital, as you may know. A large Red Cross flag fluttered from the roof. The patients were all casualties of the battle. Men scarred by shrapnel, some with half their face missing, and amputees with bloodied stumps. We had patients from the Indian, Canadian and British regiments, all ending up in this last-ditch hospital, side by side.'

She began writing.

'And even Wilkinson was there – one of the warders who ordered me around in prison and then fought under me in the battle for Stanley.'

'On the staff side, there were two medical corps doctors. Old Doctor Black – or should I say Lieutenant-Colonel Black – and Captain Witney. Oh, and there was Father Barrett. And—'

'Do you know any Christian names?'

'George Black, a gallant man, and a Hong Kong institution. But, of course, you've not been here long. And Peter Witney. Not sure what Wilko's first name was. I was only there a few hours so I don't know everyone else's full name. Once I had got a decent dressing on my scratch, I mucked in with the Chinese orderlies. I didn't catch their Christian names; there was a Chan and a Wong, but then there usually is!'

She bit her lip. 'Right. Do carry on Mr Chattey.'

'There were half a dozen nurses. Sister Begg I knew from before the war. And then there were the Chinese nurses from St John's Ambulance. Nurse Leung had a particularly lovely bedside manner, God rest her. She would hold a chap's hand and just listen to him witter on, or moan and groan.'

'Do you know any more names?' She tried to hide the frustration from her voice.

'Look, leave it with me, my dear. I'll check with one or two others in here – fellow survivors. I'll get back to you with a full list.'

'Thanks,' she said.

'Well, anyway, that night going into Christmas Day, as the Japanese advanced, There wasn't much sleeping going on. Bullets flew in through the windows, shattering the glass to the floor. I was on duty in the main ward in the school hall, lit by the low light of three or four hurricane lamps. Around 5:30am, Father Barrett was preparing Christmas communion as if there was nothing to worry about. We – the orderlies – began helping the nurses distribute cups of tea to all the patients.

'Then the first blasted Jap came crashing through the front door. Doctor Black rushed towards the leading officer shouting, "Stop! Stop! This is a hospital." Before you knew it a bullet had flown into Doctor Black's head, and he dropped dead.' Chattey stared into the distance and shook his head.

'Then came the battle cry, "*Banzai!*" Hordes of soldiers jostled forward, wielding bayoneted rifles. Captain Witney was right behind where Doctor Black had slumped to the floor. He drew his revolver and shot down the first Jap. And then Witney was gunned down, too. As he collapsed to the ground, a press of soldiers bore down on him and scythed him to pieces. And that was just the start of it. It beggars belief, really. These Japs, drunk on both alcohol and victory, rushed to each bed and thrust their bayonets into the wounded patients. The wailing shrieks of the dying is a sound I'll never forget. Then rifle shots shut them up forevermore.

'I was unarmed, standing at the back of the hall where I'd been chatting to a Private Smithers in the end bed. I turned off the nearest hurricane lamp, grabbed Smithers out of his bed and hauled him underneath it. I draped the bedsheet down towards the floor, but not quite so it touched the ground – that might have looked too suspicious. I planned to leave Smithers and front up to the Japs. But Smithers clasped my arm tight and pressed his finger over my lips. I don't know if he acted out of fear for himself or concern for me, but I don't suppose I'd be here were it not for his actions.'

'I'm sure he would say the same of you,' said Gwen.

'Well, perhaps.'

Chattey rolled another cigarette.

'So we took our chances under the bed. It was still dark, and the Japs were drunk enough. Two or three of them vomited on the floor. Suddenly we saw muddy boots beside us. You could sense him raise his rifle, then he shrieked as he thrust the bayonet down into the bedcovers. The blade went through both the mattress and the slats underneath and came within inches of my head. We ducked down, then came the shriek again as the blade sliced through the empty bed for a second time, then a third.'

Chattey stretched his legs forward across the grass and leaned back on his hands.

'Then they just stopped. Two doctors, seven nurses and over fifty soldiers were killed in five minutes. The bastard animals. . . . What makes men do that, I can't comprehend. . . . The remaining nurses were taken away. . . . We could hear their screams. . . .

'Later, they rounded up all the remaining men – about fifty of us – and crammed us all into a dorm room. From there, until news of our surrender came through, one by one, men were taken outside. We could hear what those bastards were doing to them. Not just killing them, but torturing them, slicing off ears, splitting open their guts, cutting out tongues. . . .'

Chattey's eyes were wet. She handed back his handkerchief.

'Oh, I shouldn't be telling a nice girl like you all this. Father Barrett and one or two of the nurses are here in the camp. I'll talk to them, I'll get you your names. But we have to get the details on something else, too. There are people in here who witnessed the murder of surrendered British soldiers, thrown off the cliff near Repulse Bay, two days before Christmas. I'll get you lists for that, too. You get the lists out. You're right: people out there need to know.'

'Thank you,' said Gwen. She glanced at her wrist – again forgetting she had stopped wearing a watch since the Japanese came to town, for fear of losing it.

'Yes,' he said, 'we should move along shortly. But first, do you know why I came to the cemetery this afternoon?'

She shook her head.

'To plan where to put the graves of all those poor wretches whose remains have been left out in the open. To hell with the Japanese orders. On Christmas Day we were forced to break up school desks for firewood, and under the duress of thumping rifle butts and pricking bayonets, we carried dozens of bodies outside to cremate them. But – as you may have seen – we were ordered to leave various remains in the open, as some sort of macabre warning, I believe.'

She nodded. The charred bones outside the school would live long in her mind.

They rose to their feet.

'Mr Chattey – *Walter* – you've been awfully helpful.'

'Don't mention it, my dear.'

She dusted grass off her skirt. 'Walter, may I ask you something?'

'Of course, my dear. I feel like you're my closest friend here, and I've not known you an hour.'

She smiled. 'Well, friend, do you know where a prisoner might find a drink around here?'

Chattey raised his eyebrows.

Chapter 19

Swelling around the ankles: the first sign, apparently.

Sitting on the grass in the cemetery, awaiting her rendez-vous, Gwen loosened her cashmere cardigan, and examined herself. Five weeks as an internee and already the diet was taking its toll. Two meals a day, the best of which consisted of a spoonful of rice and soggy lettuce. And so, as her body waned, her ankles swelled – the first sign of the dreaded beriberi. Untreated, the expected prognosis involved vomiting, limb pain, difficulty in walking, and, ultimately, cardiac arrest and death.

She worked relief shifts in the camp hospital, so she was fully aware of the lack of assistance available. Ignoring an international convention Tokyo had never signed, the Japanese authorities – ensconced within their camp headquarters on 'the Hill' – prevented medical supplies from entering Stanley. The number of cases of beriberi and dysentery were mounting up, and she was logging every one on paper.

The air was so fresh and the sky so grey, that staring up beyond the tops of the casuarina trees took her back to Britain. When Hitler had obliterated Europe in 1940, her parents' letters implored her to stay away in the 'safe' part of the world. A certain peace of mind might have been achievable amid the tranquility of the cemetery, were it not for the unrelenting hunger pains.

Initially, everyone in the camp bet hope on a swift Allied reconquest of Hong Kong. But as reality stepped out of the shadows, a new hope had to be found. So talk of repatriation soon filled the void. The Japanese cared greatly for their own: could a swap with Japanese internees – from America, Australia, Canada and Britain – bring freedom?

He arrived dressed, as every day, like an accountant on holiday: cream blazer, tie and trilby.

'Chester, do you think there's real hope of repatriation?' She had sat back down on the grass after rising to meet him, but he was still standing over her.

'Wishful thinking. There are hardly any Japanese interned in Britain, so why would the Japs let a couple of thousand Brits go for nothing in return?' He was glancing all around the cemetery, looking everywhere except at her when he spoke. 'There's a message for you from the Hill. Your presence is requested there at two o'clock. Are you feeling up to it, old girl?'

'I can guess what that's about.' Although, in fact, she had two very different guesses.

'And tell me, what did the doctors say?'

'You needn't worry about my strength of body for our trip,' she said. 'I don't need the doctors to tell me I'm down on thiamine. It's nothing a little fish or even some good old bread wouldn't fix.'

'Neither of which are on offer here,' he said.

'Don't worry, I've found a solution to that problem.'

'What sort of *solution?* You talk in more mysterious tones than any spy I know of!'

'I found a friend on the outside who can help me – and us.' Smut Medley was a banker she had known in Macao before his employers, the doubly-oxymoronically-named American National City Bank, moved him to Hong Kong. The authorities had kept Smut, like most of the bankers, out of Stanley and jammed into a cheap city hotel, formerly a brothel. Smut was marched to and from his bank each day. In Hong Kong, nothing – not even war – has ever stopped the banks.

Standing over her, Chester lowered both his head and his voice. 'I've no doubt your friends outside can get hold of what you need. The tricky bit will be getting it into camp, past the Japs – they open every package and simply take the food and medicines for themselves.'

'Tricky, but not impossible. I've just received the goods this morning! All in order. A dozen tins of salmon and sardines, silk stockings, this cashmere cardigan, lipstick and mascara – I do so love a spot of Liz Arden. And – tell no one – a half bottle of gin! My only regret was not asking for more.'

'How on earth did that pass the pilfering censors?' he asked.

'I've made a useful contact – a most unlikely figure – when we had to file into Japanese HQ to register last week.' Block by block, bungalow by bungalow, the Japanese had ordered the internees to present themselves and their details. Indeed, should Gwen and Chester eventually escape, their absence at roll call would now be missed. 'In fact, I want to tell you about the chap I've found – Watty – he's—'

'No – on second thoughts, don't tell me,' said Chester. 'I don't need to know. Gwen, just be careful. If you get thrown into solitary for weeks or months for smuggling in contraband – like Hutchison just has – your spring vacation is not going to be what you hoped it would be.'

'On, and I've been saving up specially for our little cruise.'

'More of a walking holiday, I expect.' Chester sat down on the grass next to her. 'We need small denominations,' he said. 'Your cash is in large notes, is it not? See if you can work your charms on your contacts and get that broken up.' Drake scoffed at her flimsy sandals. 'Then you'd do well to barter or buy a decent pair of shoes.'

And then, as was his habit, he reeled her back in. 'You've done well, Gwen, interviewing witnesses and collecting evidence. What you've got from Crumb Chattey alone is more than I could have hoped for. I believe what we now have is close to an accurate list of who was killed and who is in the camp.'

'So we're ready to go?' she asked.

'No. First, you need to eat well. But also, I'd like to gather a little more intelligence. For one thing, I'd like to see the records the Japanese have just made of who's in here, to cross reference with our own information.'

A bird swooped down out of the trees to rest on a nearby gravestone. Chester caught her staring at the bird. 'A red whiskered bulbul,' he said.

She licked her lips: it could taste good in a broth.

'My contact may just be able to help us get a copy of that list,' she said.

'That, my girl, would be tremendous. But I want to hold on a little while anyway. The Japs are still constructing aspects of this camp, not least for securing the perimeter. I want to report back specs of the camp as complete as can be.'

'Really?' she said. 'You wish to wait for the Japs to further tighten the camp's security and *then* attempt a breakout? That's positively barmy!'

Chester lifted his hands off the grass and wiped them on his handkerchief. 'It's not me who is baying for tighter security – it's the Brits.'

'What on earth do you mean?'

'The Camp Committee – they've just petitioned the Japanese up the Hill to do something about the slack security.'

Her mouth fell open. But then she twigged. 'Because of the locals?'

'Indeed. Those poor villagers are ravenous. But the committee's first duty is to the internees. The Indian guards are the ones left on night patrol – not the Japanese – and the Indians, perhaps sympathetically, do nothing to stop Chinese villagers from sneaking into the camp to scavenge food. And then when you bear in mind the nationality of our so-called "commandant" it's little wonder the committee have gone directly to the puppet masters.'

'So we can expect more guards and more barbed wire between us and freedom?! That's just bloody marvellous! And then you'll wait another six months for them to build a twenty-foot wall and a machine gun tower every thirty yards?!'

Visibly irritated, Chester glanced around the cemetery before he spoke. 'No, we will go soon. Trust me.'

She sighed. 'Are we not finished until we have documented each and every atrocity?'

'That would not be possible. For one thing, would the British, or anyone else, care about the rape and murder of what probably amounts to many thousands of Chinese?'

Gwen closed her eyes for a moment. There was nothing she could say. The creak of the cicadas stole the air.

Minutes passed before she spoke again. 'Well, what do you expect the authorities to *do* with the information we give them? Do you really think that once they know about the Stanley massacre and all, Britain and China will redouble their efforts to liberate Hong Kong?'

'Maybe, maybe not. But exposing the Japanese internationally is the best hope for improving conditions in Stanley for the likes of Arabel and Crumb Chattey. If not to shame the Japanese, then to imply the threat of similar treatment for Jap internees in America, Canada, Britain, Australia.'

'However,' he continued, 'as for liberating Hong Kong. . . . At worst, nothing will change in terms of the course of the war. But it will affect the *history* of the war. Imperial Japan would have it that they are liberating Hong Kong and Asia from colonial tyranny. Britain's track record may not be great – our Indian friends will remember Amritsar, for example – but bayoneting injured soldiers and raping and killing nurses as a matter of course? . . . as an unspoken policy? Why, that's beyond barbarity.'

Gwen nodded slowly.

'Anyway, it's 1:40pm,' said Chester. 'Are you not curious about why the Japs are requesting your presence on the Hill?'

'I believe I can guess that – can't you?'

She went into the bungalow's bathroom and put her new contraband directly to use. She did not look forward to letching stares from Japanese officers, who rarely left their headquarters. But there was no better person to fortify a girl's confidence than Elizabeth Arden. Summoned to the Hill to be accused of smuggling? Or was it instead due to a not-entirely-unexpected visitor? Either way, survive the encounter and – if allowed to return to the bungalow – a large measure of gin would be in order, mixer or no mixer.

She smiled her way past the card circle sitting on the lounge room floor. Outside in the garden, Larry and Geoff called out 'good afternoon' from the hammocks they had fashioned: their latest project. She smiled at the pair of them; she still had no idea which was Larry and which was Geoff.

Within a minute of leaving the garden she caught sight of a pair of Japanese officers striding up the path ahead of her. The Japanese generally only left their headquarters on the Hill to instigate room searches for contraband or to cart off suspects for interrogation in the prison block. An Indian guard held a long, low bow as the officers walked by.

An elderly internee was standing on a kerbstone watching the two officers strutting up the centre of the lane towards him. Gwen knew what was about to happen. She quickened her pace in hope of signalling to the old man before it was too late. Then one officer began barking in Japanese. The white-haired man remained unmoved, no glimmer of a bow. Gwen, just twenty yards behind the two Japanese, had to do something. Suddenly, the officer ran up to the gentleman and swung his rifle butt, thumping the old man into the gutter: the conquered must not assume a higher position than their mighty conquerors.

The officer leaned over the old man's crumpled body and spat into his bloodied face. A small crowd of internees had gathered behind her.

A man dashed forward and grabbed her arm. 'I know you wanna help, Miss,' he said softly, 'but let's leave it a tick.' This big chap, not so young himself, took a firm grip on her arm. The Japanese officer shot them a glare, sizing up potential trouble.

The big Englishman pulled her away. 'We're just going to pretend we're two friends who've just met 'ere in the street, Miss. So keep your eyes on me, and we'll help the old fella once the Japs move on.'

She gazed up at the man with the cockney accent. 'Why, aren't you Two—

'The people who call me that tend to be the same people who say I used to be a general fighting with the Chinese. And you can imagine how much I'd like the Japs to hear about that.' He doffed his panama. 'Pleased to meet you, Miss.'

The two Japanese had marched away up the slope. Gwen rushed over to the man in the gutter and dabbed his lips with her handkerchief. 'Are you okay, sir?'

'*Yeth,*' was all he could manage to say.

The big cockney helped the man sit up on his backside. 'Okay, I'll take you to Dr Peterson – he's just down the lane.' With that, General 'Two-Gun' Cohen picked up the wiry old man and cradled him in his arms. 'He'll be alright, Miss.'

She was standing in silence as Cohen carried him away. Then she collected herself. It was time to walk on up 'the Hill' and not let the nerves show.

She climbed up the outside steps and allowed her eyes to wander through the window to a Japanese officer who stared out from his desk. The outside door to the building swung open. The pungent aroma of pickled radish, a Japanese delicacy, wafted out. She stifled a smile when she recognised the officer who held the door open for her. This one was different, a civilian cloaked in military garb.

She stopped and bowed and whispered, 'I don't mind bowing to you, Watty.'

'And yet you do not need to,' he replied. His full lips brought softness to his feline bone structure.

'You never know who is watching,' she said. She stepped into the narrow waiting room and sat down on a wooden bench, facing an unflattering portrait of Emperor Hirohito.

Kiyoshi Watanabe closed the door and then handed her a glass of water. 'Well, you do look better than when we first met. But how are you *feeling* now?' He remained standing, his eyes set on the window, his ears close to the door.

'Stronger. Thanks to you, Watty, I've greatly improved my diet.' It was possible another officer could be listening in at the door, but Watanabe was the only Japanese in the camp able to understand fluent English, because that was his job. 'And thank you for that list you—'

'Don't mention it,' he said.

She understood that he wanted nothing further said on the matter, whether or not his colleagues could listen in. 'I hope your family are safe and well?'

'Perfectly well, thank you. And perfectly safe. The Americans pose no threat.'

No, not *yet,* thought Gwen.

'Miss Harmison, how are things more generally?'

When she had interviewed Father Barrett about the Christmas Day massacre at Stanley, he had used Watanabe to make the point that not all Japanese men in uniform were bad sorts. 'Well, our camp hospital ... the staff are doing tremendous work in difficult conditions. But worst of all is the lack of medicines for our patients.'

'I see,' said Watanabe.

She opened her purse. 'I've taken the liberty of writing a list of basic medicines which would be of great benefit, and would help save lives.'

'I'll take the list and work with my colleagues to improve matters.' She knew that was half a lie – the other Japanese officers shunned Watanabe, no doubt for being too friendly with the prisoners. He too regularly joined Father Barrett for mass, which was where the latter had discovered that this particular Japanese officer was a Lutheran pastor from Hiroshima. Years earlier, Kiyoshi Watanabe had lived in a seminary in the United States, known there simply as 'John'. More recently, he had been conscripted into the Imperial Japanese Army, which took him away from his family to Hong Kong, to work as an interpreter.

She stood up and passed him the list. 'Thank you. And there's one more thing. . . .' She delicately brought up the matter of the official registration list of internees. He nodded reassurance.

She smiled into his eyes. 'Watty, do you know why I've been summoned here?'

'No, but it's by the commandant's order. I shall find out if he is ready for you.'

The one thing about the Japanese headquarters known to be conspicuously un-Japanese was the commandant himself.

Watanabe took her to a seat into an anteroom adjacent to the commandant's office. Aware of the scouring eyes of the commandant's secretary, Watanabe smiled farewell.

If she were to be questioned and tortured, Gwen expected to be taken immediately by the Kempeitai. The Japanese equivalent of the Gestapo were irregularly brought in from town to deal with suspected smugglers of contraband or harbourers of wireless sets.

When the secretary opened the door to his office, Gwen caught a glimpse of the decidedly *Chinese* commandant, Mr Cheng Kwok-leung. The real power lay above him: his Japanese superiors who would visit the camp almost daily. Cheng's pre-war role as a travel agent for Thomas Cook & Sons may not have given him the necessary credentials to lead an internee camp, but apparently the nationality of his Japanese wife did. With Indian camp guards and a Chinaman as puppet leader, the Japanese clearly wanted as little contact as possible with Western civilians. Cheng was free enough to run his own racket – even the commandant was laundering loot, which was why he clamped down so hard on rival looters in the camp.

Cheng called her in, yet, apparently absorbed in paperwork, he did not look up for a silent thirty seconds. She remained standing in front of his desk, endeavouring to detect whether the two Rolex watches he wore showed a different time on each wrist.

Eventually the commandant said, 'He not come, Missy. Go home.' With that she was dismissed. Whether to feel pleased or slighted was a moot point.

She walked back to the bungalow and hoped that Arabel wasn't there. For what Gwen planned to do she could not have managed if her friend was in or around the building.

Larry and Geoff were still swinging in their garden hammocks, having a smoke. Inside, card games, sewing or general fussing with one's belongings occupied every room. The bedroom would have been safely empty were it not for Jenny Somerville. Gwen managed to eke a smile of 'hello' from Ms Somerville. What on earth she was doing anywhere outside of a mental institution was a matter Gwen's mind never settled. Ms Somerville was sitting on *her* mattress – the only mattress to speak of in the bedroom – and counted her stock of tins of tomatoes and pineapples. In itself, not so strange – but she did this repeatedly. Scores of times each morning and afternoon, and yet she had no more than six tins to count. She would form at first two small pyramids, and then one larger one – which she would knock down in order to repeat the process. Presumably, like all of the internees, Ms Somerville daydreamed of scoffing her entire stock in one al-mighty feast. Well, Gwen would now live a parallel dream. She rummaged through her haversack, careful not to reveal her own stash of tinned food, which had cost her several items of pawned jewellery. She removed Max's hipflask, and when Ms Somerville was preoccupied rebuilding a pyramid, Gwen swished the flask under her cardigan.

Two of the chaps were toing-and-froing from the kitchen to the bathroom, where they were working on the plumbing: she would have to find somewhere else. She had to idle around the hallway for several minutes, swallowing each pill of passing small talk with feigned patience, before the coast was clear. When nobody was in sight, she opened the cistern cupboard where Toothpick slept each night. He had fashioned a latch of sorts, so she locked herself in the dark, with just a crack of light seeping in along the top of the door. Sitting upright, she stretched her legs almost straight, the cistern bulging across her thigh. She unscrewed the top to the flask. The first sip of neat gin caused her nose to twitch.

Getting hideously drunk was the sort of behaviour she had never felt free to do when she lived with Klaus. Max was clearly very different – he would no doubt actively try to get her tight as a tick at the earliest opportunity. But would he need to? Perhaps a healthy dose of loveless sex would have been in order? Never mind that lovelessness was one thing she had run away from. After a wondrous couple of years with Klaus, ever since he raised a hand to her, sleeping with him swiftly became just that.

She sipped her gin. Her throat was burning. In the absence of any water to hand, she took another nip of gin. At least ten minutes passed before she heard her name.

'Gwen?' Arabel's voice called through the house. 'Gwen, where are you?'

Stay silent or confess and share? Hang it, Arabel did not much like gin.

'Has anyone seen Gwen?'

She stayed quiet.

Then she drank some more. Arabel's voice faded. So Gwen glugged back the flask.

Some minutes later, she swayed forth. She tossed the empty flask to the floor, demonstrably close to Jenny Somerville's latest pyramid. Jenny gasped in shock.

'Jenny . . . *Jenn-i-fer,*' slurred Gwen, '*doeshh* being stark, raving mad somewhat dull the pain of imprisonment?' Before Jenny could pick up her jaw and even think of forming an answer, Gwen continued. 'And are you aware that you snore like a damn train? Now, do trains snore? Well, if they did snore, we now know what they'd sound like! And another thing – or is it 'things'. . . ? I can't remember the *first* bloody thing!'

'Gwen, are you alright?' Arabel was standing in the doorway.

'Wonderful, darling. I was just telling Jenny here . . . just telling her . . . something.'

'I was looking for you earlier to see how you got on up the Hill?'

While she endeavoured to remember how, indeed, she had got on, Larry *or* Geoff came scurrying in.

'Gwen,' said one of them, 'there's a guard outside waiting for you. You're to report up the Hill forthwith.'

She was standing facing Cheng's desk for the second time that afternoon. A loud burp erupted through her, followed by a metronome of hiccups. Cheng didn't flinch, his head buried in a flimsy cardboard folder. A mug of pine-needle tea on the walk up performed little sobering, but at least all nerves had dissolved in the alcohol.

Cheng raised his head with the look of a man who wanted to be somewhere else. 'Missy, you lucky-lucky.' A man stepped through the open doorway behind her. She did not turn around: she knew whom it was.

'I go inspect now,' said Chen. He left them alone.

'My darling, how are you? I'm told you may be unwell? The diet may be troubling you?' He pointed at her swollen feet.

Gwen cast her eyes to the floor.

'Klaus, you weren't a damn Nazi when I married you, so why are you a damn Nazi now?'

He closed the office door. 'Ah, you've been drinking. Okay, firstly, it is good to see you, my darling. Secondly, I'm not a Nazi, but I am a German – I'm afraid there is not a thing I can do about that. Unlike you, I have only one passport to choose from.'

'You speak bollocks.' Gin was mighty empowering. No wonder important colonial men, from civil servants to military commanders – the ruling class – put so much time into drinks on the verandah.

She stepped closer and stabbed her finger at him, inches from his chest. 'What jumped up position of power are those Jap buggers giving you?'

'None. You think I like to stay here and work for the Japanese? You really don't know me. And I am thinking you are a little tipsy, my dearest. Maybe prison is more fun than I thought.'

'Bloody well sod off, Klaus. Today I drowned my sorrows on the only sniff of alcohol I've had since I entered this sadistic holiday camp.' She took a step back. 'What are you really doing here? In fact, what are you really doing in Hong Kong?'

'Pretending to buy rubber.' His tone softened. 'The only thing preventing my recall to the Reich are my trade negotiations. I have to be at least *seen* to be securing materials of use to Germany. Rubber is my current excuse. I am about the last German left in Hong Kong. Whenever I leave the hotel I have to be driven by a Japanese stooge ... my movements are closely guarded, my papers regularly checked. The Japanese do not want Germans interfering. And, of course, they will not allow Germany to plunder Asia and swipe raw materials from their own back yard. If my German superiors knew my real motivations for being here – and especially if they knew that the Japanese will simply extend rubber negotiations indefinitely and never allow significant quantities of it to be shipped to Germany – then I would be dragged back to Berlin. Or, more likely, the Eastern Front.'

She was sitting on the commandant's desk, swinging her legs like a cheeky school kid.

'My darling,' said Klaus, 'I desire to leave here as much as you do. The difference is I cannot leave you behind.'

'And if I did come with you, where would we go?'

'A neutral place.'

'Switzerland?'

Klaus walked over to her and placed a hand on her shoulder. 'Do you know the only place in the world that rubber is native to?'

'Clapham Common.'

'Erm, no – South America.'

'You want us to swan over to Rio-bloody-de-Janiero, never mind the war?'

She shrugged his hand off her shoulder. 'Look, can't you use your German influence to repatriate all the prisoners here?'

'Gwen, believe me – I have no influence here.'

'Well, how many *could* you get out?'

Klaus just stared at her.

'Surely you could get *one* friend out with me?'

'Ah, your one special friend, Mr Drake?'

'You don't approve of him because he's half-Chinese.'

'I don't approve of any man who gets to see more of you than I do.'

He had placed both hands onto her shoulders. 'I can get you out for the same reason you could get yourself out – because you are married to a man from a country that is not at war with Japan. My connections in shipping could take you – *us* – to South America. We would live as separately, or together, as you wish.'

She sighed. 'Why do you still want me, Klaus? I ran out on you. You should hate me.'

'And yet it is you who hates me. I have come to understand you no longer loving me, but I don't understand what I've done that makes you hate me so.'

She had nothing to say. He offered her a cigarette. She half-smiled and accepted. He put his arm around her, and, for a moment, it felt like their early days.

Within moments of her leaving Cheng's office, Arabel came rushing up the hill. 'Gwen, what's happening? Are you okay?'

'Rarely been better, darling. I do so love a damned fine bottle of gin – for which I can only apologise to you.'

'What happened on the Hill?'

'I've got a free pass out of here.'

'Klaus? He's getting you out?'

Gwen nodded, and Arabel gave her friend a hug.

'When?'

'Day after tomorrow.' She hated to do this to a friend.

'Oh Gwen, that's wonderful!'

Would she say that if she knew the *true* plan? It was infuriatingly typical of Arabel to appear to put others first.

'Isn't it just?' said Gwen, putting on a broad smile.

They jaunted down the hill arm in arm.

'Probably best for Chester, too' said Arabel.

'And what is that supposed to mean?'

'Well, just that you two seem to have become unduly close, if you don't mind me saying so.'

Gwen inclined her head. *Unduly.*

'I expect,' continued Arabel, 'the poor boy will be sad.'

'Yes, I expect he will.'

'You must be aware that it's the talk of the gossips. After all, the only other Eurasians who have opted to put themselves into Stanley are married to Europeans. But Chester isn't married – unless. . . . Is he married, Gwen?'

'Who's to say?' She turned away and walked down the path.

After eating a measly spoonful of rice-à-la-fish-bones that evening, she spent a noticeable amount of time in the bathroom. Upon returning to the bedroom, Jenny hissed at her. Gwen blanked her and gathered a list of belongings into a haversack – ostensibly an overnight bag.

Arabel appeared in time for Gwen to explain – within hearing of other housemates – that she was feeling rotten.

'I think I'll go down to the hospital.'

And that was her 'goodbye'.

Chapter 20

'What on earth—'
'Shhh,' whispered Gwen.

'But you can't walk around like that!' He had never hidden his intention to give the orders.

Woollen pants, socks, stockings, flannel trousers, three vests, three sweaters, two cardigans, woollen gloves and an old captain's cap, plus a haversack crammed with biscuits and tinned food: some people might call that travelling light.

The winter night air was fresh, even in the sub-tropics. 'If I'm going to sleep on a hillside, at least I won't be cold.' She peered around the darkness. 'Let's get on with it.

She slithered down the rain-slicked grass of the bank. It was 8:45pm: after dark but before lights out. The guards would patrol just feet above their heads. Cheng had been promising the power outage would be over any day. It had felt more like a threat, but at least it had proved empty: there was no floodlit perimeter or searching spotlight.

Gwen worried about Klaus as much as the Japanese: it would be nothing other than foolish to trust him. And she held out little hope that he would trust her. 'Don't fret about him,' Chester had said. He had assured her that she had performed well enough to convince Klaus, and everyone else, that she had, indeed, acquiesced: she would be leaving Stanley with her husband two days later.

But she was not so sure.

They crept across the path and then clambered cautiously down another bank. Below them, before the barbed wire, was the perimeter road. An exposed spot but only patrolled every twelve minutes, if Chester's reconnaissance work proved reliable.

Separately, the previous evening, both Gwen and Chester had checked into the camp hospital – to buy time, so that they would not be missed at morning roll call. Furthermore, upon a dona-tion of one pair of gold earrings to 'hospital funds', her colleagues in the hospital had burnished her escape kit: iodine-zinc oint-ment, quinine tablets and two mosquito nets materialised, with no questions asked.

Along the perimeter road a flashlight and the jingle of metal disturbed the still night air. A guard? Or could it be Klaus? She ducked into the shrubbery alongside Chester.

He let a minute pass and then signalled to her to crawl to the barbed wire. They had scrutinised this in daylight through a contraband pair of field glasses borrowed from Two-Gun Cohen. It had surprised them how slack the wire appeared: the Japanese did not expect escapees, for where would they escape *to?* Chester stood out inside the camp, whereas, outside, Gwen would be easily identifiable as a Caucasian – whose movements and papers would now be scrutinised.

Chester wriggled through the barbed wire, carefully negotiat-ing the passage of both of their haversacks without a snag. Inevitably, when Gwen followed, her outer cardigan caught on the barbs. Then muffled voices came from behind. Chester was only a few yards ahead but to call out would alert the sentries behind.

No one had yet escaped from Stanley, but they had heard chilling reports from the military camps in Kowloon. One British officer had escaped but was hunted down and returned to camp. The next morning, during roll call, he was brought forward and beheaded.

Her fingertips patted the bottle of sleeping pills in one pocket and Max's hip flask in the other: she was not going to be taken alive. Thanks to one particular hospital orderly and his broad views on 'medicinal' supplies, she possessed something worth-while with which to wash down the sleeping pills. There were worse ways to go.

The voices faded. She slipped off her cardigan, leaving it caught on the wire. Chester looked back open mouthed. He scurried back past her to retrieve it.

The pair of them hurried onwards a few yards and rolled into the next ditch. There, they listened for the next patrol and, after it passed, they counted to twenty. Chester edged forwards and glanced up the bank. He motioned for her to come: all clear. They slipped down the final bank and through a thin line of trees, emerging onto the sandy beach. There, the moonlight shone brighter and freedom tasted perilously real.

'*Brains but no application . . . spirited but directionless*': In recent days, she had chewed over these words from an old school report. She would have to get further than a Stanley beach to prove her teachers wrong.

She followed Chester alongside a four-foot-high sandbag wall which ran along the back of the beach. They paused by a squatter's shack which punctuated the beach. Behind the shack, a desolate village street ran away from them and towards the sanctuary of the hills. They pulled themselves over the sandbags, and Chester's water bottle jingled against his hip. Her heart pounded through her sweaty layers as she followed him onto the road.

They stuck to the walls on the side of the street shadowed from the moonlight. The front doors of shuttered houses opened directly onto the road. Gwen heard movement and paused, halfway between two doorways. Chester, oblivious, jogged on, past the next house.

A flash of curfew-breaking light shot out of the doorway and out onto the street between him and her. She held her breath. Klaus? Somehow he must have known.

Chester stopped. He looked back to see the wavering light that separated them.

Footsteps shuffled around just inside the open front door.

Slowly, she crept back to the previous doorway. But the locked door was inset only a few inches. There was nowhere to hide among the terrace of houses.

She was standing still, trapped in the shadows of moonlight on the street, awaiting fate. Would Chester use his pistol? If it was Klaus, she wanted him stopped but not killed.

More footsteps. The creak of a door. The light swept away, darkness resumed.

She sighed. Chester began to step back towards her, and she jogged on to him. In the blackness, her shoe kicked a stone. A dog barked. They hurried onward down the street.

After they left the village behind them, a narrow track forked off the road and out into open countryside. Chester paused but opted to lead them onto the track. Fields and then a wooded hillside lay before them. The earlier footsteps and light from the village house doorway were almost certainly, he explained, due to a resident preparing for bed – perhaps sweeping out the cockroaches first.

She sweated under her layers as she panted up the hill, several paces behind him. She caught him up after they passed a farmer's hut where there was little sign of humanity.

'I can smell it you know,' he whispered with some force.

'Smell what?'

'Alcohol.'

'Oh, sorry, how rude of me. Here you go.' She held out the hip flask.

He shoved the flask away and stopped walking. 'Gosh, you know that's not what I mean, old girl. If you wish to jeopardise the escape by getting drunk again, I'll be pouring this away.'

She squared up to him. 'Getting drunk? I'm not drunk . . . I've had one tot! You're just ticked off that you – despite your terribly significant "commando" training – haven't got the foggiest idea where we are!'

'Keep your voice down,' was his only retort.

She sighed and walked on ahead, along a raised path which bisected paddy fields. The hill seemed never ending, and the straps of her pack were cutting through her layers, deadening her shoulders.

Suddenly her foot slipped off the path. As she fell, she threw an arm out and grabbed a bush which pricked through her glove and into her skin.

She lay on her back, her haversack flattening a bush underneath her, and wriggled her arms and legs like an upturned tortoise. Chester leaned over her, pulled her to her feet and they exchanged smiles.

She brushed herself off.

'Listen, old girl, you're right – I don't know these paths around Stanley, but I do know the hills across the water, if we can get there.'

If.

They stumbled on to something more akin to a proper footpath and wandered on and up. Cloud hid the moon and stars.

Time slipped by.

'Chester, we've been messing about on this hill for so long . . . aren't we just crashing around in circles?' He did not reply. But he did not pretend to know where they were. The sky was still black yet tinged with a suggestion of morn. Soon they would be exposed by daylight.

Around a corner, just visible through the foliage, was a squat concrete pillbox. Chester motioned for her to stay back. He crept to the entrance and listened. Between two glassless windows – gun ports – an iron door hung ragged, as though drawn on by a young child. He eased the door open and again listened, and then looked, for signs of life.

Inside, the air was cool and the smell was not that of corpses but of grass – the floor was covered with dried grass. She slung her pack down. Under the aperture of each gun port lay swivel mountings bare of machine guns but laden with grease. She sat down on a wooden shelf seat and took a drink from her canteen. A pair of vests hung on a washing line across the back wall. Birds sang outside. Back in the camp, the hospital staff would have noticed her absence last night – she had left before nine o'clock – but they should have assumed she returned to her billet. In her room, the girls would soon start rising. By the 8am roll call her absence would be apparent. But, if questioned, the girls would inform the guards that Gwen had gone into the hospital. Yet all it would take was one inquisitive guard to traipse down to the hospital – or a visit, or even just a telephone call, from Klaus –

and search parties would be out. Would tracking dogs have much trouble following her scent?

Chester hauled a sandbag to his chest and thrust it into one of the square gun ports. Then he did the same with the second port.

'We'll sleep here,' he said. If found sleeping inside, there would be no escape. He wiped down his Colt .45. She hung some of her damp sweaters on the line, wrapped herself in a mackintosh and bedded down on the hay.

'Should the Japs come, be a darling and save a bullet for me, won't you?'

'Good night, old girl.'

Chapter 21

Cream cheese and cucumber sandwiches. A rolling hillside with wild brambles and, incongruously, grass clipped like a bowling green. She was having a picnic with her sister and parents. The location was non-specific countryside, but it was undoubtedly *English* countryside.

Gwen awoke to the edifying scent of dried grass. Light sabred in where the door failed to fit its frame. She took a deep breath in through her nose and smiled: they were free.

Chester was sitting on the bench, chiselling mud from the tread of his hiking boots.

'Good morning,' she whispered. Then she glanced at her watch: 12:45pm.

He would not raise his head to meet her eyes. 'Not sure there's much good about it.'

She smiled a tight smile. 'I beg to differ. I—'

'Look outside,' he said.

She got up, put on her blue sweater and eased the door open. The sky was clear and the sun bright. She raised her hand to shield the sun and rued her former sunglasses, bartered for a canteen the previous week. The breeze whipped along the hilltop. She stepped across the trail, leaned over a bush and peered down. Despair clawed at her throat.

Chester appeared beside her. 'Rather pathetic, isn't it, old girl?' he said. Laid out in mockery before them was Stanley Internment Camp. 'We're sixteen hours into our escape and we haven't made it off Stanley Peninsula.'

He handed her the binoculars. This was too much. She could see people milling around the camp. She could even see the roof of her bungalow. What she could not know was whether the authorities had detected their escape.

Inside the pillbox, they divided a tin of tuna and half a dozen hard biscuits. They boosted their Vitamin C levels by flavouring their remaining quart of water with a spoonful of pine needles.

The roar of an engine came careering overhead. Gwen moved to the doorway and squinted up through the gap between the door and frame. A red-balled plane swept low over the hill.

After the roar had faded, shellfire and explosions filled the air. She grabbed the binoculars and stepped outside. Down in the bay at Stanley, the Imperial Japanese Army were up to their old tricks. A patrol boat was shelling a junk within easy range. The fishing junk burst into flames. Crewmen leaped into the water, losing their conical rattan hats as they jumped, arms flailing in the sea.

She gasped as Japanese machine gun fire erupted into life. Seconds later, there were no fishermen, just blue-clad corpses bobbing with the waves. If that was how they treated the innocent Chinese people they were 'liberating', what would they do with a pair of escaped enemy prisoners? And if escaping were not sufficient to warrant torturous execution, she could rely on damnation thanks to the lists she was smuggling – of over 2,500 British internees, plus close to five hundred Dutch and Americans. Not to mention the witness accounts of Japanese atrocities. Female spies may first expect additional horrors.

She laid out the lists, written in three columns on paper so thin it was almost transparent, and unravelled the single roll of toilet paper the pair of them possessed. She used Chester's penknife to cut the lists into their columns and the interviews into strips and fed them into the toilet roll, close to its cardboard core.

The remainder of the afternoon passed hunched over Chester's map of Hong Kong.

'If we don't get off the Island tonight, we never will,' he remarked. They speculated where they might find more drinking water, perhaps in the concrete drainage ditches lower down the hillside. They planned a route which they talked through again and again until neither of them needed to view the map to know where they were going.

Chester closed the iron door behind him and wandered down the path, intent on recceing the beginnings of their planned journey. Gwen packed up and then scrubbed: she wanted no biscuit crumbs to tell of their presence.

Dusk began to descend and still he had not returned.

She froze: footsteps came close, before they faded into silence. Her immediate thought was neither of Chester nor even the Japanese, but, once again, of Klaus. Not that hill walking was typical of Klaus. When they were together, she had once suggested they go hiking. Klaus had responded by saying, 'What could I learn from a mountaintop that I can't learn better from my library?' What came back to her now was something Klaus had said when he found her in the Gloucester Hotel. 'I prepared myself for the long-haul. I expected it to take a long time to find you and even longer to win you back.' He had then said, 'I would climb every mountain to bring you back.'

Slowly, she had learned to take him literally. 'I will stay by your side always,' he had once said to her. Such earnestness may be unattractive in a lover yet essential in a husband. They had argued aplenty in their final weeks together, after Klaus lost control. He may have done so only once in twenty-five months of living together as man and wife, but once was enough for her. Of course, that fit of anger – or 'one raised hand' as Klaus later referred to it – had put her in hospital. Prior to that, his preoccupation with himself and his work had grown, widening the distance between them. After the raised hand, the next thing she would remember that night was waking up in a hospital bed with Klaus sitting at her side. He was stroking her hand, apologising unreservedly and promising to do 'all she needed and all she desired' forevermore. He may even have said then that he would 'climb every mountain' for her. But she never wore her wedding ring again. It was impossible to say whether leaving Klaus was more due to fear or boredom.

Now, he troubled her, but he certainly did not bore her.

Soft footfalls approached the door to the bunker.

The door opened. Chester slinked in.

Trekking around the eastern hills on Hong Kong Island afforded a view across the harbour to Kowloon, where stabs of light perforated the curfew.

Gwen tried to stick close to Chester as they scurried down the hillside, nipping from tree to bush in what must have looked like Laurel and Hardy fashion. Packs bouncing on their shoulders, they bobbed through a sloping glade, cast in the light of a sliver of moon. They slowed to make their way through discarded shell cases which covered the ground like hailstones.

'Down there – maybe that's it,' she whispered. Was that nullah the catchwater they hoped for? His silence blanked her through the darkness. It had barely rained in weeks.

She stumbled over something and gazed down to see the hilt of a curved sword. She took a breath and then hurried on to close the gap on Chester. At least he finally seemed to know where he was heading.

He pointed ahead with one hand and held one arm back to stop her continuing. 'The catchwater.' They stepped forward to the edge and peered down into the nullah. It was dry at the near end, but where it widened was barely visible through the darkness. He led her down a ladder of iron rungs.

They walked the length of the concreted basin and beyond without seeing anything more than tiny stagnant pools amongst patches of mud.

'Listen!' said Gwen. She led him out towards a scratching noise which came and went with the breeze. She rushed forward towards the sound, pushing aside tree branches.

She stopped. A stream trickled down the hillside onto some rocks. She grabbed her canteen and scrambled down.

'No!' said Chester with vigour. 'Wait.' He beamed a cone of light around the rocks. She dropped the water bottle. Upstream, two gashed and mangled bodies lay sprawled on the bank, their feet in the water. She scrunched her eyes shut and turned away. He returned her empty canteen, and they walked away.

An hour later, they were walking alongside a slope which had been concreted to prevent mudslides. At knee height in the banking, a piped hole dripped water to the ground with ponderous rhythm. They took it in turns to hold Gwen's canteen under the drip: in fifteen minutes they accumulated half a bottle to share.

They trekked along a dirt road. It was leading them down towards a rural hamlet overlooking a seaside village. There was enough moonlight to catch movement on the water. Through the field glasses, she spotted a *sampan* being rowed into the little jetty. A man stepped aboard to be *yu-lo*'d away into the darkness.

Encouraged, they sneaked past a shack whose line of damp washing suggested somebody was at home. They came upon a wooden hut of the type thrown up by the Japanese as an individual sentry post. They bent low under the open window as they passed. A whiff of pickled radish hit Gwen at the same time as the rising stutter of a snore.

Once they were well clear of smell, sound and sight of the sentry post, Chester tugged her to a halt against a tree, for a whispered conference. The glimmer of daylight exposed abandoned helmets and army tunics along the roadside.

'We'll never make it tonight, my dear,' he said. As if to strengthen his argument, rain began to spit down through the branches above them.

'But we must,' she said, like the sort of well-meaning but brainless heroine she so despised.

'Soon it will be light, old girl. A sentry or a patrol will spot us.' He led her back along the road a few yards and then cut up the hillside.

A hundred yards away from the road a shuttered bungalow ringed with barbed wire invoked reminiscence of 'Camp Stanley'. Chester cut a gateway through the wire and made her wait in the rain behind some bushes.

He completed a circuit of the bungalow. The shutters were padlocked. So Chester crept towards the front door. Without awaiting an invitation, she followed him. The stench of sewage wafted by.

A roll of paper plastered with Chinese characters sealed the door to its frame. 'Property of the Emperor of Japan: No entry', Chester later translated. She looked beyond him, at the lock: shot away. He bent down to peer through the hole. Gwen stared back at the road. Any passerby might spot the pair of them on the verandah.

Then they froze.

A scratching noise wisped by behind the door. The whole scene was like something out of the sort of novel she would never read.

Chester drew his pistol. 'Probably just a rat,' he whispered.

She braced herself. If this were a bad novel, Klaus would be sitting inside smoking a cigar.

Chapter 22

The smell was all too familiar, with a pungency that gnawed at the throat and reached into the stomach. Gwen eased the front door closed behind her. Chester's pistol led the way.

The front door opened onto the living area, but a tall Chinese screen prevented any clear view into the room. Chester stepped forward and beamed his flashlight around armchairs and bookcases. Topped with joss sticks held in China vases, a sideboard hugged the centre of the long wall. It was the normality of the room that seemed strange: pictures hung, porcelain remained, furniture stood its ground.

A rat scurried by the skirting board, making the scratching sound heard earlier. Chester motioned for her to stay back near the front door while he approached the first of two doors near the end of the room. But she simply followed him.

She peered into the gloom of the next room. Chester edged his torchlight across the bed: empty. The mosquito net was hanging down, not twisted away above the bed.

They returned to the living room and Chester approached the other door. He eased it open a couple of inches and an odour of sewage wafted out. He offered Gwen a handkerchief and pointed at the armchair behind her. She obeyed him this time, not driven by his orders as much as by the stench.

She caught a glimpse of what must be the kitchen, before Chester closed the door behind him, leaving her alone. She flicked on her torch. On the wall were framed photographs covering at least three generations. Expensive-looking frames. Why had this place not been looted?

Chester returned some minutes later.

'Almost set,' he said in a low voice. He told her to remove her toothbrush and water canteen, and then he carried the haversacks away through the kitchen door. 'Stay here,' he ordered.

Oddly, when he returned he deliberately spilled the joss sticks across the top of the sideboard and swiped away the two small China vases. He disappeared into the kitchen and then came back again to ransack the sideboard of an ornate boxset of chopsticks, among other things. She remained seated, an armchair spectator. After taking his time over depositing the latest goods beyond the kitchen door, he reentered the living room with a bucket in hand.

'You're not to go in there,' he said, pointing a thumb at the closed kitchen door.

Her eyes quizzed his words. 'Why—'

'Just do what I say, old girl. This place is empty. I know the smell's bad, but we've no choice but to stay here through the daylight hours. You sleep in the bed, I'll take the first watch.'

She stood up to re-enter the bedroom. Chester had said the tap was dry, so the grime would have to stay where it was on her face.

'Oh,' he said, 'and the bathroom is also out of bounds. Perhaps you could make use of this?' He handed her the empty bucket.

'It's eleven o'clock. Your turn, old girl' said Chester, his hand shaking her shoulder. She reapplied the scented mosquito cream along her upper lip to stave off the full force of the stink from the kitchen. She added a jumper and shoes to the sweater and trousers she had slept in and joined him in the living room. He positioned her in a wooden chair next to the window, shutters open a fraction.

'Just come and get me the second anyone approaches from the road. And please don't enter the kitchen . . . it's not safe.'

'What sort of "not safe"? Unexploded mines?'

'Exactly,' he said.

Exactly? She wondered what military scenario had required the mining of a kitchen.

'Wake me at 2:30pm, would you?'

She nodded. 'Sleep well.'

Gwen gazed through the crack between the shutters, across a garden which grew wilder with every yard it stretched away from the bungalow. There was barely a path, no garden gate and no fencing – just an arbitrary demarcation where wild undergrowth spilled onto the road. A car whizzed by. The odd pedestrian came into view. Baskets swinging on either end of their bamboo pole, villagers lumbered towards town to sell the contents – perhaps the catch of the day.

A headache was pegging itself down in her temple. She unlocked the window and nudged it open against the shutter. It only opened an inch, but the sliver of fresh air was welcome. To inhale the foul air inside the house hour after hour would not be good for anyone. What was causing that smell? Surely it could not be unsafe to merely open the kitchen door and take a peek?

But Chester would see it as her duty to remain by the window.

None of the reading material on the bookshelf tempted her, for none was in English. To sit at length with no book to keep oneself company was an unwanted experience at the best of times.

Her mind strayed through Max – and whether any man would want her, a runaway wife, for keeps – and then back to Klaus and the night that ended everything. They had argued and she had ended up at the bottom of the stairs, but she could never recall precisely what happened in between. He had raised his hand as if to strike her, but what had followed was less clear. Klaus swore he never touched her: she simply stepped back and fell. The doctors would not confirm whether one of the bruises on her face might have been a blow suffered before she fell. But, of course, Klaus paid the doctors' bill.

Thinking the worst of Klaus had become a habit. Sitting behind the shutters, pondering the possibility of a truckload of Japanese soldiers returning to claim their property, she sought – perhaps for the first time – to understand his version of events. Just like it was *possible* that Klaus was not then tracking her every move, plotting her re-incarceration of one kind or another, it was just possible – *possible* – that her supposition of events of that night was less than proven. He was, after all, the only one of them to maintain consciousness throughout proceedings. However, *that* – said the nagging voice inside in her head – had simply given him the opportunity to lie. In any event, how much high ground would this moral distinction afford Klaus? Rather than receive a blow from her husband – for he had conceded that a hand had been raised – she stepped back and fell down the stairs.

Gwen had been sitting still for two hours. She heard the rumble of the truck before it trundled across her view through the slit between the shutters. At the time, nothing alarmed her. She was only subconsciously aware of the doors of the truck clunking shut down the road. She stared at a desolate stretch of road in front of the house – not a human being in sight.

Standing tall at the window, she stretched her palms towards the ceiling. She tried to train her mind to block out images of what may possibly lay behind the kitchen door. A self-censoring thought process of self-preservation: so many of her thoughts fitted that prescription. She sighed as she collapsed her arms. To wait until Chester was on watch to sneak a peek into the kitchen would only provoke his ire.

Facing the window, she took three steps backwards and squinted at the bright slit between the shutters. She told herself she would still be able to detect movement outside after another few steps backwards. The kitchen door beckoned her away from the window. The other side of the living room, the bedroom door was standing ajar. At that moment, her dread of Chester catching her disobeying his orders was greater than any other fear.

No doubt locked, she thought as she stretched out her hand to reach the handle of the kitchen door. Suddenly, voices rang out in a foreign tongue. She swung around. Outside the front of the house: shuffling boots, the jingle of military apparel and guttural shouts in Japanese. They would soon notice that the paper seal they had left across the front door was broken.

She darted towards the bedroom door. Chester was already sitting up in bed. He grabbed layers of clothing from a chair and whisked away the water bottle she had left by the bedside. He had made a mess, with the wardrobe door and most of the drawers left open, but there was no time to put things back together.

Beyond the Chinese screen at the far corner of the living room, the front door shimmied in its frame and scraped open. Chester opened the kitchen door and grabbed her hand.

'Don't look!' he whispered as he tugged her into the room and gently closed the door behind them.

A horrifying few seconds later the pair of them were standing in the dark behind the door of the kitchen broom cupboard, tucked around a corner next to the exit to the back garden. Chester had thrown out an arm to pull the dustbin across the kitchen floor and up against the cupboard door as he closed it from the inside. She preferred to focus her mind on the thumping movements of the enemy soldiers rather than on the sight she had just seen in the kitchen.

Chester's pistol clicked to the ready. She held her spare jumpers across her chest and wept silent tears.

Boots clouted the wooden floor of the bungalow in all directions. It was impossible to tell how many soldiers were rushing around the home. She put her hand into her trouser pocket and removed the phial of sleeping pills: sufficient to do the job, if the cupboard door opened from the outside.

'My toothbrush!' whispered Gwen. Chester placed a finger over her lips. Her toothbrush was still out there as evidence, sitting on the bedside table. Then there was the matter of the window ajar in the living room, not to mention those various drawers Chester had, for reasons unspoken, left open.

The kitchen door crashed in. Laughter followed: that was how they reacted to the horrific sight they or their colleagues had created. They wrenched open kitchen cupboards. It would only be a matter of time before they made their way towards the storage cupboard near the back door.

In the distance, a whistle shrieked. The boots thundered all at once. And then quiet.

It was only after several sweaty minutes of hush outside the cupboard door that she considered that the soldiers may not have been searching for people but loot. Perhaps they were very much used to seeing a paper seal broken by any number of looters. Perhaps they were hoping to find food in the kitchen. Or booze.

After perhaps three minutes, Chester spoke. 'That whistle would have been their officer calling an end to the looting party. Stay here.'

As he opened the cupboard door and slipped out, she avoided looking into the kitchen. The last time she had been alone in a cupboard at least she had had a bottle of gin for company. At the back of the cupboard paint pots lined up on the shelves. She questioned the cupboard's neatness . . . no, not the neatness but the sense of space – odd in a small home where every other cupboard had been jammed full. Other than an empty can of kerosene on the floor, there was nothing in the way . . . just enough space for two people to stand and hide there. It was as though a space had been cleared just for them. . . .

It was then that she made sense of Chester's actions: the removal of the China vases (while leaving the joss sticks strewn behind); the rummaging through the sideboard; the open wardrobe and drawers in the bedroom.

'It's all clear,' he said, before opening the cupboard door. 'Except for the odd rat.'

'Are you sure?'

'Yes, don't worry. It's over.' Chester wrapped his arm around her shoulder and led her out of the cupboard. 'Are you alright, old girl?'

Gwen nodded, as one does. He rushed her towards the door to the living room. She should not have even glanced at the mess on the floor, but she couldn't help herself. The smell of emptied bowels and decaying flesh was one that had become all too familiar at the hospital. The two decomposing bodies slumped back-to-back on the kitchen floor had their hands and feet bound together. Both were dark haired, but their battered faces were so mutilated that it was impossible to confirm that they were Chinese.

In the living room, cigarette smoke hung in the air. Chester walked over to the window: the Japanese may soon be back. Not wishing to feel alone, she sat down on the armchair nearest to him.

'They've an odd way of doing business, these Japs,' he said, as British as ever. 'You would think, if only in clear self-interest – if this is to be some Jap's home – they would not leave bodies here to rot and stench.'

'They're unhinged,' she said. 'Senseless.'

'We look for reason where sometimes there is none.' He rested a hand on her shoulder. 'Look, it will be dark soon. We need to get ready to get out of here.'

'Upon my word! You made it *appear* that someone – whoever had broken the seal, the Japanese were meant to think – had got in here before them. Looted the place, been and gone.'

He smiled.

'Chester, why was there a nice space in that cupboard just our size? And where have our haversacks disappeared to?'

He turned from the window and put his hand on her shoulder. 'I cleared a space in that broom cupboard so we could use it to hide in, if needed. And I hid the haversacks among some prickly bushes at the back of the house to lessen the odds of them giving us away. Looters tend not to search the undergrowth. And that's where I put the loot from the sideboard – just to make the place appear like it was missing some things. I'll head outside now and get our things.'

She had considered herself the sort of girl who could look after herself, but without Chester Drake she would have had no chance.

Chapter 23

Gwen peeked out from under the *sampan's* bamboo and tarpaulin hood, before slumping her head back down onto Chester's lap. She gazed up at him and her tongue circled her mouth as he shielded her from the breeze. He would soon have to protect her from more than just the wind.

The *sampan* owner and his son were standing tall, oriental gondoliers. The craft edged across the east end of the channel, far from the hub of Victoria Harbour. The stars were out and all was quiet, bar the slosh of paddles and the lapping of inky water.

In making prior arrangements, the boatman had sent his son – his second son – on an errand, to rustle up spare sets of Chinese peasant clothes. In faded blue shapeless trousers and loose tunics, topped with Chinese straw hats, Chester and Gwen spoiled the local dress code only by retaining their sturdy walking boots.

The boatman and his son *yu-lo'd* the craft slowly clear of the listed bow of a shipwreck. Hong Kong Island behind them, they set a course eastwards, towards a headland on the mainland. Gwen sat up when the boatman's son handed out chopsticks and a bowl of cold rice with vegetables.

'*M'goi,*' she muttered with a nod of her head. Things were going too well.

It was all too extraordinary, bobbing along peacefully under the stars, detached from the war. For a little while, there in the strangest of circumstances, it was possible to enjoy the moment – something she had failed to do for a quite some time before the war. Since she had left Klaus – indeed, even *before* she left – her recurring thoughts were of being somewhere else, often being some-one else. Walking out on Klaus had been to truly *live-in-the-moment.* Since then, reminiscing of an unfathomable past and dreaming of an unreachable future tended to squeeze out the here-and-now. Yet the here-and-now was very much what Max had offered.

They had paddled around the headland and out of view from Victoria Harbour.

While scouring the night sea with his eyes, Chester had been listening to the boatman's whispers.

'Would you believe it?' Chester whispered to Gwen. 'He just casually mentioned that a few minutes ago he spotted another *sampan!* I'll be damned if I could see it.'

'No!' said Gwen. 'Klaus? The Japanese?'

'Well, my dear, I can't see the Imperial Japanese Navy setting off in a *sampan*. No, apparently, the Japanese have forbidden fishing boats to go beyond certain markers. But they forgot to order the fish to swim within those waters.'

'So *sampans* sneak around at night following the fish?'

'So it would seem.'

She smiled. 'The Chinese are more spirited than I'd given them credit for!'

'*Spirited* is one word for it. *Hungry* is another. Do you know, the old man told me earlier that he had another son.'

Gwen sat up. '*Had* another son?'

'Yes, my dear. The Japanese took him away, I'm afraid.'

'What's become of him?'

Chester shrugged. 'His father hopes he's been taken as slave labour. But he fears that it's more likely that he's dead.'

She tried not to feel grateful: such heartbreak surely encouraged the boatman to risk ferrying two of Japan's enemies across the channel.

They had entered a tiny horseshoe bay and were closing in on a moonlit beach. The father left his son to guide them in while he came over to speak to Chester.

'He says that if we make it into the hills there are Chinese robbers – bandits – who cause more trouble than the Japanese.'

'Jolly good job you've got a gun,' she said.

'Yes. And, like the man says, the bandits are lazy people – they don't like climbing high in the mountains, so we should be safe up the top.'

She gazed across the water: a bay backed by hills – pretty much a summary of Hong Kong.

'It's Clear Water Bay,' said Chester. 'Only a night or two's walk to Sai Kung.'

The slosh of oars ceased and the *sampan* grated onto the shingle, at the foot of a hill several miles east of the city of Kowloon. Chester held out a roll of Hong Kong dollars, but the boatman demurred. Gwen shooed the money away, rummaged around her haversack and placed two tins of bully beef on the gunwale. She thanked them with *'m'goi'* upon *'m'goi'*.

The pair of oarsman smiled and bowed. It was typically Chinese to brush off such a service – a service which may have cost them their lives. The father and son pushed the *sampan* back afloat and slipped away in the darkness.

It was a starry night, and the warm spring air was still. Chester and Gwen were standing on the beach securing their packs and contemplating the hill-trek ahead.

'Gwen, the trickiest part is over. I've done training in this area, I know the routes through the hills. Out here in the New Territories, the Japanese only visit the market towns – they're too scared of the bandits to patrol the countryside. But you mustn't worry about bandits – I can reason with them in Chinese. Or shoot them.'

She liked his smile – a smile that said, *'We've just about made it'.* Never mind the remaining fifty-mile walk across occupied Hong Kong and China.

'We've gone days without washing,' she said. 'And there's not a soul around.' She swivelled her shoulders to face the sea. 'Dare we. . . ?'

He said nothing.

She removed her layers, one by one.

'I should turn away,' he said.

'It's dark,' said Gwen, with deliberate ambiguity. She began to undo her blouse but changed her mind and removed her trousers first. The epiphany, which arrived just minutes earlier, had dissolved angst and lubricated self-assurance like a navy strength double measure. Here, in the middle of nowhere, in the middle of war, European snobbery offered nothing to fear.

Chester had slowly removed his jacket and boots without concealing his desire to gaze at the girl who had stolen his attention once before, all too briefly one evening in Macao.

She turned away, removed her blouse, dropped it on the beach and waded into the water. The sea was cool but warmer than Brighton in August. She was thigh deep in the water and remembered she had no spare bra. Chester, stripped down to his briefs, stepped into the water behind her. Before it could get wet, she unclipped her bra and tossed it beyond him onto the beach. She splashed her chest down through the surface and swam.

When she had thought of Max, she had questioned for how long she could enjoy a man without love or security, without the probability of a future. But love, security and a future were not a bundle of goods that one acquires en masse like a dinner service. Sometimes one simply wants a new whisky glass – even if one barely drinks the stuff.

She swam further, out of her depth. Chester pursued her with front-crawl vigour. He swam up close, if only to whisper, 'Gwen, we must stay closer to the shore. If we see a fishing boat or anything, we will need to make an awfully quick getaway up into hills.'

'Yes, of course,' she said. Perhaps she had been too forward.

He led them into shallower water. Treading water where their feet could touch the bottom, their arms waved circles underwater, not a yard apart from each other.

'What would your British friends make of this?' he asked.

'Well, the men would want you flogged, and the women – those who are decent and honest – would be positively jealous of me.'

His knee brushed her thigh. That was enough: she let a wave surge her forward, and her chest bumped into his. His arm wrapped around her side to the small of her back. Their bare bodies bumped together.

All of a sudden, he broke away and placed his forefinger across his lips.

'Listen.'

A distant whir whir was growing louder.

'That's a motor boat,' he said. 'And it's moving fast. Fishermen usually have *sampans* or sailing junks – not speedboats.' He stood tall and rushed out of the water.

The boat darted into their bay as they yanked dry clothes onto wet bodies. 'It's either bandits – smugglers – or it's the Japanese,' he said. 'This was a damn stupid idea.'

That was too obviously true – but why did he have to say it aloud?

By the time the haversacks were on their backs, the boat was drawing into the shallows amid a chattering of Chinese voices. Chester and Gwen would have to climb a fair way up the hill before sufficient foliage would offer cover; with heavy packs, they had little hope of outrunning their foes.

The first of the bandits, brandishing a club or machete, splashed into the water. Chester dropped his pack onto the sand and drew his pistol. If he fired it, then they might all be joined by the Japanese to boot.

'Gwen, walk up the beach. *Walk.*' He held the gun aloft and shouted at the three Chinese men in the water to halt. But they waded on energetically. He fired a single shot just over their heads.

The men froze.

They muttered to each other and then yelled something back to their mates on their boat. Chester turned and ran after Gwen. They clambered up the grassy hillside, scrambling for greater cover than the low shrubs provided. Two of the bandits were tearing up the beach after them, while the other had returned to the boat, perhaps to summon the rest of the hunting party.

The two bandits were gaining fast. Chester stopped running, took aim and fired. The foremost bandit clutched his thigh and dropped onto the sand, still holding his knife skyward. The other man rushed to his aid.

'We should be okay now, Gwen. But let's get over this ridge before it gets light.'

In petering darkness, the track they rushed along took them towards a run of hills. The sea stayed reliably on their right side and Kowloon flicked in and out of view to the west.

They rounded a hilltop and paused to survey the terrain ahead. The beach was ninety minutes of speedy hiking behind them now. Gwen caught her breath.

'We're marching at a good pace, old girl. You coping okay?'

'Yes. You think women can't hike?'

'No. I know Europeans who need extra care when hiking at pace. It seems you're not one of them.'

She nodded her satisfaction and then sipped some water.

'The guy you shot – will he die?'

'I just hit his leg. He should survive.' He met her steady gaze. 'Would you rather I let them steal all our food and kit? And maybe you too?'

She shook her head.

'We need to find somewhere to rest, out of view,' he said. 'It will soon be light.' He led them off the track, through the scrub.

'Do you know a hideout around here?'

'No, not here,' he said. 'We used to train further north. We'll head that way when it gets dark again later.' He led them into a grassy hollow where they cast down their haversacks. A steep bank cupped them on the hillside and thick bushes hid them from the track above.

'It's not ideal,' he said, 'but it will do.'

A blood-drop sun edged up out of the ocean. They spread out their ground sheet. 'You may get chilly,' he said with a hint of a smile. He spread his jacket and jumper as a 'mattress' adjoining the bed she was arranging out of her spare clothes. He cut open a tin of beef, she used the biscuits to make bovine finger sandwiches.

A rustling sound swooshed through bushes, somewhere up near the track. Chester drew his pistol and, crouching low, made his way up the slope. He disappeared out of sight, once again leaving her alone and unnerved. What would she do if, on one of these reconnaissance forays, he simply did not return? The salty flavour of bully beef dried in her mouth.

Minutes later, Chester did return. 'It was nothing,' he whispered unconvincingly.

'I hope there's not a tiger round here,' she said.

'Ha! More likely a wild boar. Would make a decent feast!'

He glanced back up the slope every few seconds. 'We had better keep watch today and sleep in shifts again.' He showed her how to release the safety catch on the gun – 'Just in case'.

He shuffled closer to her and rested his pistol on top of his half-empty haversack. 'You look worried,' he said – the perfect excuse to put his arm around her. 'You'll jolly well be fine with me, old girl. Tomorrow night we'll stay in one of our hideaways. It's too high in the hills for bandits to find, too well hidden for the Japs to stumble upon. It should still be stocked with water and tins of food. Best of all, we'll then be within easy reach of the red guerrillas.'

'*Guerrillas?*'

'Friendly locals. Well, some are local. Others, from what I hear, have moved down from Kwangtung.'

'Reds? Communists? Are we allowed. . . .' She let the nonsensical remark fade into the dawn.

'Resistance fighters. They're on our side.' He swigged from his canteen. 'Local politics was something the British never—'

'*You* seem rather British, to me.' It was conceived as a compliment but discharged as an accusation.

'I am, when I need to be, Gwen. I'm half one thing, half another – not unlike Max.'

She tensed her shoulder under the grip of his arm. 'Max? He's half English, half Australian, is he not?'

'There's more to it than that. He's been hiding rather a lot from you. Your man is not the person you seem to think he is.'

'He's not *my man!*' Perhaps Chester simply needed reassuring. 'Nothing happened that night at the Peninsula.' She rested her hand on his chest. 'You don't much like him, do you?'

'I've known him longer than you have. Just to give you one example: I imagine he hasn't told you he's married?'

Her jaw dropped open. 'Um, no. He didn't.' But then, who was she to throw stones? She had misled Max about her own marital status. 'Where's his wife?'

'Emily's in England. Evacuated in 1940. I've no idea what state their relationship is in, but it wouldn't surprise me if she was expecting him back.'

She sighed.

'Do you see, Gwen? There's more to him than meets the eye.'

'That may be, but what does it matter now? He's probably either dead or in one of the POW camps in Kowloon.'

'Oh, he's very much alive, I'd say. From what I've heard, they made it out of Hong Kong and through Japanese lines.'

She pulled away and Chester's arm fell from her shoulder. 'You mean you've had contact from Free China? From the British?'

He said nothing.

'Why didn't you tell me?'

He turned his head away. 'Well . . . I know only that the group made it. I have no news on Max specifically.' It was an unconvincing excuse. 'Anyway, I'm sworn to secrecy. I should not even have told you now.'

He looked at her and brought his face close to hers.

'But what you must now be thinking is correct, Gwen – I've loved you since Macao, since you first came into my life. And you didn't seem to notice me.' That was both the truth and yet not entirely true.

'I noticed you!'

'For one alcohol-fuelled, instantly regretted moment, perhaps. But I was nothing more than a friend to you. As was proper when you had a husband at home.'

'My husband was never at home! Anyway, Macao was a different lifetime.' She placed her hand on his lap. 'And I don't regret that moment now.'

'Well, in any event, then you met Max – and it just took one evening for you to become besotted.'

She withdrew her hand. 'Perhaps I behaved foolishly at the Pen that evening. But nothing happened that night or any night. And it's not Max I notice now.'

He sighed and then held his palm open on her knee. She placed her hand on top.

'That's because there's only me to notice,' he said with a smile.

He cast his eyes around the scrap of hillside upon which they were huddled.

'Even if Max was here, I know better now, Chester.'

'Do you, my girl? You know, after all this, who knows where I'll be, where you'll be. But it may well not be on the same continent. You may even run into Max again.'

'Oh Chester, let's stop talking about Max and let's—'

'My final word on him, I promise: he's not who you think he is, in any sense. And I don't just mean in his work, I mean his character. He's a cad. I can tell you that he's not—'

Crack!

Chester Drake stared ahead and wheezed in air through his teeth, before his bloodied head thumped back and hit the ground.

His eyes gazed up at the sky.

This was what death looked like.

A movement came from some bushes thirty yards away, up near the track. A man stood up amid a bush with a rifle in his hands. Gwen grabbed Chester's pistol, flicked off the safety catch and pointed it at the man. Before she could decide, the Colt decided for her: just by resting her finger against the trigger, it fired. The man turned and ran.

Blood seeped from the back of Chester's head and soaked the cream jumper he had laid down for his bed. She rested her hand on his heart. A heart she had only so recently appreciated was hers.

'Chester! No! No! No!' she sobbed over his body. 'Chester, what the hell do I do?'

Chapter 24

It was a humid, misty day that threatened to soak her in rain at any moment. Glimpses back to Kowloon were no more, but recurring views of a grey sea gave some sense of direction. Gwen had run and then walked across hillsides all morning. Her desire to distance herself from Chester's killers outweighed any sense of fear of the Japanese.

A curtain of bamboo alongside the track offered cover for a brief rest. Ahead, the hillside tapered down into a shallow valley. A huge staircase of a rice terrace rose up from the other side of the valley.

There were half a dozen biscuits plus two tins of fruit left. She rolled her eyes in disgust at her inability to think straight earlier. There was no need to bolt away quite so sprightly. The pirate had run away first; with hindsight, a search through Chester's pack, if not his pockets, would have increased both food rations and the odds for survival. Not to mention the map and compass. But two key items *were* rescued: Chester's gun and the precious loo roll.

Chester was dead and these were her primary thoughts? He was her loyal protector, her advocate from the beginning in Macao, such a good man – and so much more than that. And then there was that moment in Macao, that forbidden touch. And yet she had distanced him long after she had become a free woman. Swayed by the prejudice of 'society'?

She was sitting still on a tangle of grass on the bank behind the bamboo. If the pirates were in pursuit, would she hear them coming? She ate a little, each bite louder than the step of a sure-footed pirate. Perhaps the man who had popped up out of the bush was content with his revenge: shooting Chester after Chester had shot his fellow bandit.

Crumbs of biscuits and sinews of beef lingered around her gums and under her tongue. Trekking on through the trees on blistered feet, her backache deepening, she swigged the last of her drinking water. A plan was needed – or, at least, the illusion of a plan – to keep despair at bay.

Below her, a road cut around a hillside. It emanated from the direction of Kowloon and was the first tarmac seen since arriving on the mainland side of the water. The options were to hide in the undergrowth on the hillside until darkness fell – some four or five hours away – or to cross the road in broad daylight. How to survive without water and food? She could not decide if she was hoping to avoid humanity or find it.

As she walked down the hillside not a single vehicle came into view. Despite the mud she had rubbed into her hair, the Japanese would hardly mistake a tall, hatless streaky blonde for a Chinese.

Gwen stepped out from the cover of bushes and ran onto the road. Almost immediately her fate was determined by two sights, one even more terrifying than the other.

Firstly, as soon as she reached the middle of the road she saw a pair of cone-hatted Chinese walk into view from around the blind bend coming from Kowloon. They stopped in their tracks and stared at this foreign apparition. She ran on across the road, sizing up whether to jump the drainage trench and scramble up the muddy bank ahead of her. The couple walked on, and then the woman pointed ahead. At first, Gwen felt the finger centre on her, but on closer examination, it pointed beyond her. She turned and looked down the hill. A couple of hundred yards away, parked on the roadside, several Japanese soldiers were standing around the front of an army truck. Gwen instinctively placed her hand onto the pistol, tied onto a string belt hidden under her untucked tunic. She was tempted not to use the gun but to ditch it.

The soldiers focused on their job at hand – changing a wheel – but to walk on down the hill towards them would be suicidal.

She wrenched open her haversack and plucked out the prized toilet roll. Her next move was one she made no conscious decision over: she threw the haversack – which the Japanese would view as a suspicious-looking item for a Chinese peasant – into the trench. Then she kicked her shoes off into the ditch and strolled barefoot towards the Chinese couple.

They appeared older from close quarters. Each carried an empty straw basket, and the man walked with a bamboo pole too long for a walking stick. The man made no attempt to disguise the shock on his face. The woman muttered something to her husband.

Gwen still did not have a plan. Chinese peasants had plenty of reason to resent a Britisher and much reward to gain for turning one over to the Japanese. Indeed, some – like the Chinese commandant at Stanley – must have been hankering for their day to upturn colonialism and have their former masters at their mercy. Ignore the couple, walk past them, hide around the corner and hope to return later for the haversack? It dawned on her that embedded inside a pair of socks in the ditched haversack were a string of pearls tied around a roll of Japanese military yen mixed with Hong Kong dollars.

The engine of the truck cranked into life, the noise carried up the hill by the breeze. In one easy movement the Chinese woman removed her hat and hugged Gwen. As she withdrew she placed her hat onto Gwen's head. The man, who had stood up after wiping his hands in the dirt, placed two muddy hands onto her cheeks. From a distance, it was a reunion of family members. Behind Gwen, the truck was chugging closer up the hill.

The old man gave her his basket and placed himself and his wife between Gwen and the upcoming truck. The three of them walked downhill, leaving the haversack in the ditch. Now dressed as a Chinese from conical hat down to rolled up linen trousers and bare feet, and her face muddied dark, she was grateful that the couple had taken control.

The truck hogged the middle of the road. As she walked she stared at her bare feet and their contrast to the sandals of her supposed Chinese parents. The truck slowed as it approached. The Japanese soldiers must be suspicious. Even if they failed to spot her as a Westerner, they would be sizing up her slender femininity for vile designs.

The old man, and then his wife, held out the empty baskets, wide open. The truck crunched into gear and pulled away. Those particular soldiers had been after food, or fuel, or other saleable goods – but not muddy peasant women.

By the roadside, the old man began to hurl Gwen's clothes from her haversack into the two baskets. Concealed in a jumper, the pistol thumped to the bottom of the first basket. On top of a pile of clothes in the second basket, the bundle of pearl-wrapped cash tumbled out of a sock and into view. The old woman's eyes lit up, before she shoved the valuables back into the sock and thrust them under a sweater. Gwen could make a grab for the pearls and cash and run away – but run to where? For the time being, she had to be content that she was not being tortured or raped in a Japanese prison cell.

However, the couple could still hand over their captive *gweipo* for whatever reward the Japanese promised, plus her five hundred dollars and pearl necklace. Then the guilt set in. She was alive and well: Chester had saved her from the pirates and paid the price for her freedom.

The old man rigged up the baskets, one on each end of the bamboo pole. The couple considered it prudent to leave the distinctly *gweilo* haversack in the ditch, covered with grass – after looting its entire contents.

They led Gwen off the road and onto a track that snaked up through the lower rice terraces where patches of water glistened. The ground was dry and the rice crops stripped bare, harvested before they could ripen. The old lady produced a paper packet from under the layers of linen she wore. She unwrapped a sort of patty or dumpling. Gwen was pleased to bite into it. Perhaps some looters played fair?

They hiked through and beyond the rice terraces. Conversation with the couple was limited to Gwen's *m'goi's* and their gesticulations. Up ahead sloped the oddest-looking hillside, scorched by brushfire. Blanketed around charred tree stumps, growing out of the ashes, wild lilies shone as white as snow.

The old man put down the basket, and the couple began to pick lily flowers. After some hesitation, Gwen joined in. She put it down to cultural differences: for herself, a tot or two of gin would help take the edge off the depravities of war; for the Chinese, perhaps a roomful of lilies hit the spot. (This was not so strange: the perennial singles champion at the tennis club in Macao was a Dutchman who swore a glass of milk had the same intoxicating effect on him as a double-gin and soda did for her.)

When a village came into view ahead, the old man pointed and said, 'Ho Chung.' Gwen nodded, but the old lady scowled at her husband and rattled off something in Chinese.

The people starved, yet amid the burning incense sticks outside the village temple, the shrivelled skin of yellow fruit honoured the gods. Womenfolk greeted the Chinese couple and then backed away upon seeing the *gweipo*. The bamboo wireless could rapidly transmit news of her presence far and wide.

A few minutes later, she was left on a low stool in the white-washed main room of the couple's home, just her and Buddha. The paint was flaking off the statue, undermining the smug expression on Buddha's face. The old man had made lighting the incense sticks his first priority. There was a certain logic to appeasing the gods when harbouring a fugitive.

The old lady gave Gwen a cup of water. She drank quickly. The lady bustled around her cupboard of a kitchen. The man disappeared behind a bamboo partition – the bedroom area. He then walked out of the front door, perhaps to tell who-knows-who of the *gweipo's* presence.

Through sign language, Gwen offered to help in the kitchen. The lady was preparing the lilies, covering them with salt and a grey, sooty powder: so they were to be cooked, after basking in an ash-infused marinade. She waved Gwen away and set about heaping piles of dried grass to supplement the remnants of charcoal within the small earthenware fireplace.

Gwen rummaged through the basket and located the cash and slipped it into her pocket. But the pearl necklace was too large, so she left it in the sock. Upon inspection, it was clear that her blistered feet would have benefitted from the Vaseline she had left in the first-aid kit with Chester. She half-expected him to walk into the room at any moment. Then came tears of guilt: she was missing a mere first-aid kit whereas poor Chester had lost his life. She rested her soles onto the cold stone floor and wept in muffled sniffles.

Minutes later, the old lady returned with a teapot, steam smoking from the spout. That great Anglo-Chinese panacea: although the British had simply looted the Chinese remedy for the worst of life's ills. She set four small bowls down onto the low table and poured tea into two of them. An aroma like cocoa tinted with tobacco filled the room. The lady repeatedly glanced expectantly at the front door, anticipating her husband's return. But there were *four* teacups. She brought a cloth towel and a large bowl of hot water to Gwen. Never had a face wash felt better.

Somewhat outwardly refreshed, she joined the lady in drinking Chinese tea. A bowl of rice cakes and salty fish also lay in front of her. The old lady refrained from eating, perhaps waiting for her husband. But who was the fourth teacup for?

Gwen plucked from the basket the hairbrush she had kept hidden from Chester for fear of his disapproval of carrying extraneous items. But the brush barely penetrated her mud-matted hair. The lady refilled the bowl with clean, warm water and found a sliver of soap. It took a good deal of hacking out clumps of mud with the hairbrush and several refills of the bowl to enable progress. Gwen was still kneeling on the floor, her hair dipped into the bowl, when the front door scraped open.

She wrapped a cloth around her head as a towel and rose to face the visitor the old man had brought into his home.

The wiry young man stepped forward and said, 'I speak little English.'

'I speak even less Chinese.'

'You speak Chinese?' asked the youth.

She shook her head. 'No. My name is—'

'No!' shouted the youth. 'No tell name.' That the old couple had not disclosed their own names was perhaps far from accidental.

The pot refreshed, the four of them sat down on stools and sipped black tea.

After much babbling between the three Chinese, the young man again addressed Gwen, reading certain English phrases from a notepad. 'We give you a pirate.' Her mouth dropped opened. 'I mean,' continued the youth, 'we give you *to* a pirate.' The pirates from the beach, the murderers of Chester – this young man was here to deliver her to them. 'The pirate, he helps—'

She slipped her hand under her tunic, rose to her feet and brandished the pistol at the young man.

'Listen, boy, if you try to take me back to the pirates I shall shoot you and then as many of those bastard pirates as I've got bullets for.' She was going to have to make her exit. To sleep there for the night would be to surrender. The callow lad would bring the pirates here and they would sell her on to the Japanese.

She backed over to the baskets. Keeping the gun trained on the youth, she rummaged through her belongings.

'Missy, you no understand. Least Bad is a good pirate – like, ah, Robert Hood. Same-same.'

'*Robin Hood?*' queried Gwen. '*Least Bad?* He steals from the rich and gives to the poor, does he?'

'No. He steal from Japanese and kill them. Okay, maybe not same-same as Robert Hood.'

She was not sure what to make of this young man. Was he hoping to joke his way out of trouble? She grabbed the sock with the pearls from the basket, on her guard lest he lunged for her pistol.

'It okay. Least Bad, he live near here. In the hills. He can take you to the Reds in Sai Kung. They take you to British in China.' It sounded too easy. 'No worry, Missy. Least Bad only kill people he no like. And it no true, what people say – he not eat people. Not many.'

Another night, another hike. She had jettisoned half of her Western clothes in Ho Chung village and carried just one basket of belongings. The pistol lay near the top, under a blouse, within easy reach should Least Bad live up only to part of his name. He did not look like a pirate from a children's book. He was simply an ageless Chinese man, albeit with a knife in his hand and worse in his pockets. At one point Gwen had flashed her torch onto his face – somewhat rude and unnecessary, with hindsight – and saw that Least Bad did have one piratical feature: a fearful scar. It seethed red, not yet fully healed, and ran high up his cheek to an ear short of an earlobe.

The moonlight shone off the water and helped to give a reassuring sense of direction. He held a torch, but he barely used it along tracks he knew well. Walking up lonely paths in a winding valley, she stayed five yards behind him at all times. Her Lane Crawford raincoat destroyed the Chinese peasant *de rigueur* apparel, but she wore the conical straw hat regardless. The night breeze swept a chill off the sea and up the hillside as they climbed.

There had been little choice: how far would she have got on her own? The deal struck in the Chinese couple's living room was that Least Bad would come alone, which he did, and unarmed, which he did not. Least Bad apparently would not be able to endure his pirate friends' laughter were he seen unarmed and prodded along by a *gweipo* with a pistol. The shame would have ended his career.

After an hour of hauling the basket up through the hills, Gwen relented and let Least Bad act like the gentleman pirate he claimed to be: she let him carry her basket, having placed the pistol in her coat pocket.

They were mounting a steep hill when Least Bad stopped dead in his tracks and sniffed the air. He motioned for her to stay back while he crept forward. He soon faded out of view further up the hill, and she waited alone on the path.

A few minutes later he returned and led Gwen silently back down the path. After they had retraced their steps back several hundred yards, Least Bad pulled Gwen off the path and whispered something to her. She regretted insisting Least Bad alone should escort her: they needed an interpreter. Squatting down amid the dark undergrowth, they listened. Once he was satisfied that they had not been followed, without a word of English – and only one word of Cantonese – Least Bad conveyed to Gwen the cause of his concern. He touched her arm, sniffed the air and said, *'Gweilo.'*

Europeans? In the mountains surrounding Sai Kung? It seemed as improbable as Least Bad's detection methods. In the unlikely event of there being any truth in it, it would surely be good news.

But then Klaus came to mind, and she had second thoughts.

Least Bad was so very certain that trouble lay ahead that he led her a mile or more back down the muddy track. Then a hint of an opening emerged between some bushes and he tugged her through dense foliage onto what, in daylight, may have feasibly been describable as a 'path'.

Their detour dragged them down a valley, alongside a creek. They filled their water bottles and then began another climb through thick woodland, where even Least Bad switched on his torch to throw forth a thin circle of light. She stumbled through bushes and over roots, all sense of direction long lost. They could be headed back to where they had started in Ho Chung, or off to Least Bad's hideaway lair, perhaps. She was grateful for the gun and that Chester had shown her how to use it.

After half an hour, the trees thinned. Least Bad stopped and pointed down the slope ahead. An unsealed road curved around the hillside. A mile or so away the grey sea brooded under a waning moon and a rising hint of daylight. Least Bad pointed at a village set back a little from the roadside. They trekked down and were met by a pair of scraggy wild dogs, who provided a snarling escort into the village.

Least Bad led them to a shack tucked away at the rear of several dozen houses in varying states of health. After he whispered a greeting through a crack in the door, a shuffling movement inside came towards them. Least Bad sniffed the air with concern.

The door opened. A gaunt-looking woman stepped back to let them in to the unlit room and closed the door behind them. Gwen was standing near the door, her eyes raking for familiarity within the darkness, when a voice came from the other side of the room. 'Well, you took your time. We were expecting you hours ago.'

Least Bad took a step back, recoiling at the sound of that voice.

Gwen stepped forward. She did not need to see his face to know who it was.

'Max?'

'The very same.' He had the presence of a soldier even in the dark and out of uniform. He pulled her in close. His smell – a sweaty mix of tobacco and metal polish – invoked the deepest of sighs in her. She was safe now.

'Crikey, it's bloody wonderful to see you,' he said. 'Or not see you – they won't let me light a lamp in here. They're probably less worried about attracting Jap patrols than they are about wasting kerosene.' His wittering – no doubt designed to reassure her – brought tears to her eyes.

'Max, I just can't believe it's you. I'm so awfully pleased . . . just so pleased.'

'Well, pleasing you is something I'd like to do a great deal more of, my girl.' He caressed her cheek with his fingertips.

In the darkness of the shuttered hut Least Bad had departed surreptitiously. She had never even thanked him: Least Bad had more than lived up to his name.

PART III

Max and Gwen

March–April 1942

Chapter 25

Sunlight attacked the cracks in the window shutters and door. He watched Gwen's eyelids flicker and then open. Max was sitting at the end of the single mattress, his back against the wall. He put down his notepad and pencil.

'Good morning.' She pulled the blanket back up to cover her body. 'So it wasn't a dream?'

'G'day, beautiful.' He leaned over, slid the blanket aside and kissed her naked hip. 'No, it wasn't.' It was hard to believe that he had once wondered whether she was a spy for the Japanese.

'What are you writing?'

'A report on the package I'm duty-bound to deliver unharmed to British authorities: *Five-foot-eight, blonde hair, blue eyes, frightfully attractive – too beautiful to trust.*'

She snorted through her grin.

'Oh, you don't mind being a "package", do you?

'"Too beautiful to trust?"'

'Ah, that's what you take exception to. I have to put something negative in there – otherwise they'll think I'm in love with my escapee, and that *wouldn't do at all.* Against regulations.'

'Max, tell me what happened to you after you left me at the hospital on Christmas Day?'

'Long story. It can wait.'

She sighed. And sadness hijacked her eyes. A tear fell onto her cheek. 'He meant a lot to you, didn't he?' Max put both arms around her naked torso and hugged her tight.

He got up and disappeared behind the wooden screen, into the hut's kitchen area. The place was barely furnished, but it served its purpose. Aside from the low single bed, which also served as a settee, the only furniture was a bamboo side table and two stools.

She pulled on a tunic and a pair of knickers, and he returned with a plate of rice cakes.

'Brekkie.' He glanced at his watch. 'Or afternoon tea.'

Sitting on the stools, they munched through the sticky rice.

'Does somebody live here?' asked Gwen.

'Only sometimes.' The villagers had decided that pointing fugitives or resistance fighters to a disused shack was safer than welcoming them into their own homes.

'Tell me what happened, Max.'

'You'll find these rice cakes have an unusual taste,' he said. 'Certainly unlike anything I would have eaten before the war.'

'I think I know the secret ingredient,' she said. 'Lily flowers!'

'Yes, well done. Least Bad delivered some—'

'You know Least Bad?'

'Oh yes,' he said.

'I was under the impression he has some sort of aversion to *gweilos*?'

'Well, that's a recent development – all my fault. The first I time I met him was one night a few weeks ago, up on the big hill you would have climbed last night. He jumped me from behind, no doubt to rob me. His accomplice was a weedy fellow who did nothing more than wave a baby knife in front of me – which I kicked out of his hand, into the undergrowth. Least Bad had his arm around my neck, but he didn't think to disarm me first. So I was able to draw my machete and nick him on the side of his face – hence his missing earlobe. So I'm not his favourite person. I'm glad he's a better guide for you than he was robber of me. He's not the most menacing bandit in the world, poor fellow. But at least I've helped him to look the part!'

Her grimace edged into a smile.

Max handed over his canteen for her to wash down her food.

'Do you know,' he said, 'last night I ventured up that hill again, guessing the route Least Bad would be taking you. I told myself I needed to hike up anyway to check on a supply dump. At one point, I thought I heard movement along the track. I was hoping it might be you.'

'Oh, I rather think it was. You see, all of a sudden Least Bad turned us around. He seemed to feel frightfully concerned that someone was ahead of us on the path: "*Gweilo*", he whispered to me.'

'He's smarter than he looks.'

She smiled. 'Where are we now?'

'We're a couple of miles north and a little east of Sai Kung town, in an area called Tai Mong Tsai. We need to hike over ten miles to get to the eastern tip of the wild peninsula which lies before us.'

She squared her shoulders to face him. 'And, Max, what are you doing here? Tell me everything.'

He grinned. 'How was Stanley holiday camp?' He immediately regretted what he had just said. 'Sorry, it must have been hard there – and then bloody horrid for you to witness Chester's death. That fella was such a good mate to you in life. I'm sure he'd been looking after you well? *Don't* tell me quite everything.'

She sighed. 'There was never anything between us.' Her eyes darted away. 'But Chester was a dear friend to me. I wouldn't have made it without him. It's terribly sad.' Her voice trembled. 'And what about his family? They will have to be found and told.'

'Leave that to me. We are building a network across Hong Kong, with the Chinese.'

'Who's "we"?'

'Certain contacts. Tell me about what happened to you since I saw you on Christmas Day.'

She finished her rice cakes and talked Max through her ordeal, from when they last met at the hospital through to Chester's murder and beyond.

As her narrative came up to date, he got up to tidy away their bedding.

'Do we have to leave now, Max?'

'No. It will take a good few hours to get you to . . . to get you to the next place. And it's daylight now, so we'll have to bunker down here through today.'

'In that case, there's time for you to tell me what happened to you?'

He nodded and walked back to the table, sat down and placed his hands on hers. 'Well, you know there were Japs at the hospital?'

'Yes, I understand why you couldn't return on Christmas Day. But how did you end up here?'

'Oh, I've been a lot further than here.' He would tell her the truth – nearly all of it. 'We got our motor boats out of Hong Kong, and on the other side of Mirs Bay we met up with some local guerrillas Admiral Chan knows. Then it was a long hike through Jap territory up to Waichow. The Japs barely hold much of that area – not in the way they occupy Hong Kong. Outside of major towns, they don't *hold* the countryside so much as nervously pass through it from time to time.'

She nodded along.

'Crikey, these East River boys – the guerrillas – they're real battlers. They looked after us, but we couldn't have done it without Admiral Chan. He knew each of these fellas by name. Anyway, sporting Homburg hats and armed with Mausers, those Reds guided us clear of trouble all the way to Waichow – the first town we came to in Free China.'

'Who's "us"?'

'From all five boats, we were seventy-odd strong, British and Hong Kong Chinese, mainly – plus the guerrillas. It was quite something that *Communists* led us through the *Nationalist* front lines, into "Free China". The Admiral couldn't walk a step as he'd lost his wooden leg back in Aberdeen Harbour. So in a colonial reverse, we had the Asian Admiral in a sedan chair, carried aloft by British sailors. Once in Free China, we marched with a couple of standard-bearers flanking the Admiral – waving the Royal Navy white ensign and the blue and red Nationalist Chinese flag. Someone got a mouth organ going to add to the party atmosphere. We met some wide-eyed locals on the road as we approached the city walls. Word clearly spread ahead of us – when we reached the city gate the locals set off fire crackers.

'We got a similar reception in Kukong – that's the new Chinese capital of the province now the Japs have taken Canton city. This time the locals had pre-made banners: *Welcome to the heroic*

Admiral Chan Chak and his men – that sort of thing. They threw flowers, and a sweet little girl handed me a bouquet. Of course, all of the hoopla was for the Admiral—'

'Max, dear Max, I want to know all about *you*. You can regale me with tales of all of the fawning over the Admiral another time. But how on earth did you get back here?'

He shuffled his stool closer and leaned his shoulder against hers. 'Truth is, I couldn't get you out of my mind, Gwen. I made it to Kukong and realised that I had to make a decision. Kukong is a bustling sprawl of a city. It's where the railway lines to west China begin. The others were busy sorting out their travel permits for the next leg of the trip. The future – or, *a* future, was laid out in front of me.

'Arrangements were made for Ben and the rest of my escape party to journey on to where you're headed – Chungking – for tea, cake and debrief at the British embassy. Then a plane to Delhi and a ponderous voyage back to Blighty. England's not all bad, but it was lacking one crucial element – you. So I deemed it necessary to come up with a plan that would keep me in southern China – or, better still, bring me back to Hong Kong.'

'So when the others left, you stayed in Kukong alone?'

'For a while. Without the safety of the large group, things could have gotten a bit sticky in Kukong, had I not had my wits about me. . . .'

Her tilted face asked a silent question.

'Nothing I couldn't handle. I was simply mingling with the locals for a few days. And they can be a little rough around the edges.' He was perhaps telling her more than he should, but there was no denying the nature of the place: she would soon see Kukong for herself, all being well.

'I see,' said Gwen, when clearly she could not.

'Shall I clear these plates?' He took them over to the kitchen area.

When he returned, she stood up and asked, 'And why did your commanders let you come back? For a woman, of all things?'

'Geez, well, I had to be a little economical with the truth. And I got lucky. The British in Kukong were beginning to make moves to formalise an intelligence network with the Chinese in Hong Kong and southern China. The "British Army Aid Group". A banal name chosen for its innocuousness, I s'pose. I've been sent back here to Hong Kong to make contacts and run errands, but that's another story.' With slow purpose, he reached his hand up to her open neck. He ran his fingers over her clavicles and up the side of her neck. Then he turned her cheek so her lips were inches from his and kissed her.

'I've been waiting for you for some time,' he said.

'And what about your wife, Max?'

Chapter 26

They had stayed in the shack not only the whole day but into the next night. An opportunity engineered by Providence or by Max? Not that she had any complaints about spending all day in bed with him: she had never felt so alive. Or, at least, not for a long time. Klaus had managed to excite her with routine efficiency in their first year or two together, before his powers declined and she settled for faking it.

The previous night, Max had reacted to her tragic news of Chester's murder with limited emotion. But then her own emotions – not to mention desires – had also moved on with disconcerting alacrity. Chester dead, her actions clinical. Was the sort of girl who could switch her affections so quickly, the sort of girl worth keeping? Perhaps one indiscretion in Macao had brought Klaus to think not.

Even after darkness fell, Max was in no rush to leave the shack. They waited until six hours before sunrise: the paths they would take towards the end of their night hike were so remote and convoluted, daylight would become a necessary friend at that end of their journey.

Another night, another trek along hillside tracks. He shone his torch ahead of Gwen's feet and carried her belongings – including the gun – in his own haversack. After a couple of hours hiking above isolated villages, they dropped down onto a coastal track.

'Isn't this dangerous, being on the road?' she asked in a whisper.

'We're safer here with our torches switched off than we were trekking through the undergrowth flashing our lights for any bandit to see,' he replied.

Looking southward across the bay, a sprinkle of lights shone across the water.

'Sai Kung town,' he said. 'The Japs have set up their regional headquarters in a school there, but they don't come out here at night. This muddy path is leading us to a sprawling peninsula so wild the Japanese won't venture there.'

He put an arm around her shoulders. 'Your legs must be tired with all the walking you've done since you left Stanley?'

Her soles were so blistered that when they were in bed all day she had connived to deny him any possible glimpse of her feet.

'I'm fine, Max.' She looped her arm through his. It was glorious to feel virtually free of everything – the Japanese, Klaus, bandits.

He had timed their journey perfectly. They were up in the hills, beyond humanity, when daylight crept into consciousness. Just beyond the crest of the highest peak of the day, they sat down and watched the sun rise out of the Pacific Ocean.

'Beautiful,' she whispered.

He leaned in and kissed her.

'That's Tai Long Bay.' He handed her the water canteen. 'I'll take you camping on that beach after the war.'

After the war – he really thought that far ahead? Max had once appeared to be all about *carpe diem* – or seizing the *girl*, at least.

'Then how about living in the Lucky Country?' he said. 'Plenty of gorgeous beaches along the Queensland coast.'

She grinned. There he was offering a future, albeit a distant one.

Northwards, the vista was of a corrugation of hills and sand-fringed inlets, a picture postcard from the west coast of Scotland. They scissored ahead, mercifully downhill. The gurgle of a stream drew them down through a thicket of bamboo.

She was admiring the purplish-blue blossom fifteen yards ahead of them when from behind the tree two armed men stepped out onto the path.

She froze. They were not Japanese soldiers, but Chinese bandits were no better, as had been proved.

But Max walked on regardless. *'Jo san,'* he called, no longer bothering to moderate the volume of his voice. The pair returned the greeting before Max rattled off more Cantonese.

She jogged a little to catch up, which gave the two Chinese guards more cause to gawk and grin.

Max led her onward, following the stream as it ran through a hamlet of stone houses to an inlet of sea water.

'That's the high street,' he said. He pointed across the inlet to where a cluster of stall-fronted homes loomed over the water. 'This village is the last stop east in Hong Kong. The final outpost guarding an eastern seaboard smuggling route which we will make good use of.'

Holding her baby, a local woman flicked up the blue frill hanging around the brim of her straw hat and called out to people inside the house behind her. An elderly couple emerged from the doorway, and soon more villagers mustered to eye up the guests.

'It's you they're staring at, Gwen. Crikey, they've seen me aplenty, but many of them will have never seen blonde hair before. These are Hakka people – fishermen, hunters, farmers. Some of the locals around Sai Kung – especially the fishing families – speak only Hakka, not Cantonese. But there are also fighting men here who've come from all over China, with all manner of backgrounds. There's one particular local character … I recently completed background checks on him and discovered he attended the local equivalent of Eton!'

She chortled. A plump pig rolled in the mud near the shore: the taste of roast pork was but a distant memory.

A boatman *yu-lo*'d a flat-bottomed *sampan* over to Max and Gwen, and they climbed aboard. A few strokes later, they stepped off into a land of plenty. Each home among this row of houses opened on to the street and offered foodstuffs barely seen in the city in recent months, let alone inside Stanley. Eggs, legs of beef and ham and all manner of greens, plus 'My Dear' cigarettes and half a dozen kinds of sweets.

'Let's buy the place out, Max!'

'Wait a while, honey. Trust me.'

She bit her lip as they walked on by.

They meandered up through a maze of paths. Around one corner, a young man sitting on a front step bolted to his feet upon seeing Max. He rapped out a rhythmic knock against the splintering wood of the door, which promptly opened.

The first room was dingy. Straw matting covered the floor and rolled up bedding lined the walls. They were led to a staircase, steep and lacking a banister. Another armed man appeared from the shadows. They were escorted front and back up the wooden stairs, each step creaking underfoot. At the top, an unshaven man was standing in front of a door. With his revolver in one hand, he offered his other hand and took the haversack from Max's back.

They were entering the lion's den. Her mind questioned how much Max knew about such a rough-looking band of men. In the reception room, they sat down on a weathered sofa. Max peered out of the window onto the street below. She stared at the closed door opposite her.

A few minutes later, they were led inside. Bamboo matting hung from the walls, obscuring two of the three windows. Upon a large bed, inside a mosquito net, a *cheongsamed* girl glanced up for a second before resuming reading her book. Beyond the bed, a smooth-skinned Chinese man was sitting at a round table. His features appeared more delicate than the Hakka people, more Cantonese.

He stood up to greet them and bowed.

'Gwen, may I present Number 99,' said Max.

'Won't you please sit down,' Number 99 said in faultless English.

'*This* is the Eton man!'

'Queen's College,' corrected Number 99.

'Chester's school!' said Gwen.

'Yes, although I never knew him then. I'm a bit older,' said Number 99. 'But I was so sorry to hear about his death.'

She pursed her lips. Just how he knew that was mystifying.

They sat down on stools around the table, upon which Number 99's enormous pistol rested unashamedly. The midday sun poured in through the glassless window at Gwen's back. A woman appeared with a teapot, but Number 99 waved her away and barked something in Cantonese.

The woman returned with an English teacup that emitted an unrivalled smell. Number 99 beamed with pride. 'Coffee, my dear. With milk and sugar.' A grand gesture – her first sip of coffee in months and never had it tasted better.

A man appeared with a homemade pipe, fashioned out of bamboo. Number 99 passed it to Max and lit the end of it.

'With special ingredient,' said Number 99. He winked at Max.

Max took a deep drag before holding the pipe. 'Well, Chief, I found her.'

Number 99 looked her up and down. 'Yes. You did.'

A waft of roasted chestnuts streaked ahead of a woman carrying a tray laden with dishes, double stacked.

He passed the pipe back to Max. 'She's pretty. How much?'

Max's eyes widened.

She gasped.

Number 99 snorted, and the snort became a chuckle. 'I do believe you were considering my offer!'

Max broke into a grin. 'Gwen, Chief 99 has the worst bloody sense of humour of any fella I know. But he's the Reds' chief for this sector, so we have to deal with the bludger!'

She summoned a smile. But a worrying thought process had been set in motion.

The covers were removed to reveal bowls of hot soup, a chestnut and beef stew, and an array of salted fish.

'You know, my friend, it's going to cost you.' Number 99 narrowed his eyes on Max. 'We have a junk you can take across Mirs Bay this afternoon, for a contribution to our war chest. And, to get through the Japanese-held territory, you'll need to take an armed escort again—'

'I can remember the way to Kukong. And it's warmer now than when I did it in January, so we'll be right, mate.'

'I don't doubt that, but my brothers won't let you through without payment for an escort, unless you arrange one first. So don't be a hero, Max, let a couple of guerrillas escort you through to Free China. Even with your passable Cantonese, you'll never pass for one!' He guffawed at his one-liner. 'You do have money?'

Max glanced at her. 'Yes, we have money,' she said.

'Which currency?' Number 99 asked Max.

She cleared her throat. 'A hundred in military yen.' The Chief grimaced. 'And four hundred Hong Kong dollars.'

Number 99 still addressed Max. 'The yen is useless. No one wants to bet on the Japs winning the war. It's unpatriotic. We can change Hong Kong dollars into Chinese for you. And we'll take two-fifty in Hong Kong dollars for our expenses.'

'That's half of our money!' she exclaimed.

'Now, now, Gwen,' said Max. 'We mustn't be rude. Chief, we are happy to contribute to the resistance movement, as I promised, just so long as those charges mean that our guerrilla escort covers all costs.'

'You need not worry about food and transport. Bribes are a separate matter.' He picked up an empty bowl and ladled some stew into it. 'Best not to proceed on an empty stomach, my dear.' His girlfriend remained on the bed, uninvited to the table.

He set the bowl down on the table before Gwen. 'I hope you know what you are getting into, my dear. You've a dangerous journey ahead. You can't always tell which side an individual is truly on. Best to trust no one.'

Chapter 27

Two Weeks Earlier

As soon as he stepped inside, Max headed straight for a *sic bo* table and rolled the dice. In Kukong, every bar entailed a game of chance.

'Lieutenant Max! *Guo lai laa!*' The voice boomed in Cantonese. 'You came back? Third time in a week? Don't waste your money there – come and join us.'

Max had little choice but to cut his losses in favour of free cigars and *baiju* – an acquired but addictive taste. He strolled over to General Yu's boothed table. The General pointed his smouldering cigar over the table and yelled to a hostess, 'Bring out your finest rice wine!' – an oxymoron if ever there was one. Slightly built, the young-faced commander of the Nationalists' southern army would keep the five silver buttons of his service jacket fastened to the top throughout even the most excessive of drinking sessions.

'Good evening, sir.' Max saluted the biggest cheese in Kukong, if not southern China. The General's mute adjutant stepped away and Max sat down. Velvet curtains closed off the river and the night sky. Only the gentlest of sways suggested they really were on a boat.

'So, I heard you went back to Hong Kong.' The General spoke in slow, clipped Cantonese, for Max's benefit.

Max half-smiled. 'So much for secrecy.'

'You know, Max, it really should still be ours. . . .' Whether he meant *China's* or *the Allies* was perhaps deliberately unclear. It was General Yu's Kuomintang army which, the previous December, had given the British – whether they fully understood it or not – the possibility of surviving the Japanese onslaught on Hong Kong. A subject the General enjoyed reviewing.

Max sipped his *baiju;* he had learned to do so without wincing.

'*Mot-bee* – he should have fought longer,' the General said.

Max nodded, although he failed to see what else General Maltby could have done once battle had begun.

'We were fighting our way down to save Hong Kong ... if only the British fought on. *Mot-bee* should have called us sooner. Not be scared we take over Hong Kong for keeps.'

As if to make amends for his anti-British slur, General Yu raised his glass and slipped into English. 'To Great Britain!'

'*Gambai!*' chorused a trio of hostesses and a group of officers sitting in the neighbouring booth.

Max emptied his glass. It was swiftly replenished. He knew the routine, so he raised his glass.

'To China!'

'*Gambai!*'

The piercing clink of *mahjong* tiles resumed in the booth behind them: the gambling game at which Max was lousiest. The Chinese had an in-built cultural advantage. But perhaps he would try his luck again later.

On the podium at the far end of the barge, two Chinese girls in short dresses duetted a traditional love song. All the women present in the saloon worked there, in varying capacities. Other than Max, the clientele was strictly Chinese men, from sandalled shopkeepers to uniformed officers. It was hard to imagine a British general spending an evening in such an establishment – the British upper crust would not socialise anywhere that would admit riffraff like him.

'It's a shame the rest of your party has left Kukong.'

He doubted General Yu was missing the Admiral: Yu would not have enjoyed the stolen attention. 'We'll have to drink for them!' added Yu.

They chinked glasses and downed their shots. It was a Chinese custom for a host not only to initiate something of a drinking contest, but also to be seen to win it. But Max hated losing.

'So, what keeps you here in Kukong, Max?'

There were three possible ways to tackle that question: an honest answer; an official but secret reason; or a downright lie.

'Oh, there's been a delay with my travel permits. The British authorities here don't know their arse from their elbow.' Officially but secretly, he would be heading to Hong Kong early in the morning. As to why he had opted not to continue on to Chungking with the others, well the honest truth confused even himself. Was it simply to claim the woman he had come so close to having? And if and when he could find her, save her, have her – and what then? Long lost alter ego Dominic Sotherly had once thought himself to be the marrying kind; Max Holt knew better.

'I've noticed,' said General Yu, 'that there's still not a great deal of British officers in Kukong.'

'None of the top brass want to leave the civility of Chungking – they're too comfortable there.' Free China's capital may have been open to Japanese air raids, but Kukong was closer to the front line. And Kukong – a Wild West sort of a town – attracted all manner of escapees and refugees: problems which the top brass had little time for.

They downed another round.

'You know, you drink like Hemingway.' The General could barely finish a drink without mentioning an infamous session he enjoyed with the American writer a year earlier.

'I'll take that as a compliment,' said Max.

An impeccably dressed Chinese gentleman in a Western three-piece suit and manicured moustache hovered near the General's table.

'Max,' said Yu, 'you got a girl in Hong Kong.'

He half smiled. Was the General posing a question or stating a fact?

'Nice English girl,' Yu continued. He raised his replenished glass, prompting Max to do likewise. 'To English girls!' yelled the General.

'*Gambai!*'

The thin, well-dressed gentleman, stepped up to their table. 'Max, this is our host, Mr Li.'

'Of course, I've seen him here before.'

'Good evening, sir,' Mr Li said in the King's English.

'Do you know, you have looked kinda familiar to me ever since my first visit here,' said Max.

Mr Li smiled. 'Is everything to your satisfaction, sir? More girls perhaps?'

'Look at this young man!' The General pointed at Max while maintaining eye contact with Mr Li. 'He doesn't need to pay to get a girl into bed!'

'Of course, General Yu, sir,' said Mr Li.

'I may not *have* to pay, but it sure could make things less complicated!'

Then the General motioned for Mr Li to lean in, and he lowered his voice in Cantonese. 'When you get some new girls. . . .' The rest of the sentence trailed out of Max's earshot.

'Of course, General, sir.'

The evening wore on with a procession of military and civilian men kowtowing at the table to pay patronage. Max was beginning to consider how to extricate himself when a young officer came rushing across from the doorway. He saluted the General and placed an envelope on the table. He stepped back, and the General opened it and read the message. The General twisted his lips and peered at his watch in deliberation.

'Work calls, Max. I had better see to this.' He waved the folded paper. 'But you make sure Li and the girls look after you. It's all on me.'

The General trailed a wake of officers from the bar who followed him out and across the gangway to shore.

'Another drink, my friend?'

'Strewth . . . the problem with a free bar, mate, is that a fella cannot possibly say "no". Make mine a brandy, Mr . . . um—'

'Mr Li.'

'You're a good bloke, Mr Li. But where did you learn such bloody good English? At school?'

'I didn't go to school – I was tutored at home, in Victoria.'

'Ah, so I have seen you somewhere before?'

Mr Li nodded in a bow. 'My parents invested their hard-earned money in me. They realised that to advance in Hong Kong one must speak better English than the English. It helped me in my career – as a restaurant manager at the Hong Kong Club. Last year, you dined there on at least three occasions, Mr Holt.'

Max nodded slowly. Impressive recall.

A whisky and soda and a fine cigar soon arrived at the table. Only later would he question how on earth Mr Li acquired such luxuries.

The salon room would not stay still. Wherever Max looked, the floor slid up to the ceiling as though the boat were being spun on its axis. He ordered one of the girls to open a window, to drain some of the stuffiness out of the smoke-filled room.

The place emptied out, and he found he had four girls to himself. There was a bedroom curtained off at the far end of the boat. After some fun, he could happily sleep there; walking down the boat appealed more than staggering down the towpath to his billet.

Two of the girls left the table at Mr Li's beckoning. They both returned with a pipe in one hand and a lamp in the other. The first set was delivered to a knowing Chinese gentleman in the booth opposite. The Chinese gentleman reclined.

Moments later, the other girl appeared at Max's booth with Mr Li. The girl placed an oil lamp with a funnelled chimney onto the low table.

'We don't like to embarrass General Yu,' said Mr Li, 'by bringing these out in his presence – it doesn't really fit with the sanctimonious propaganda of the New Life Movement.' Chiang Kai-shek was encouraging clean living and was against such a 'Western-imperialist scourge' – a scourge which refused to go away.

Mr Li removed a pea-sized pill from a clam shell and impaled it with a needle.

'You know there's another general,' continued Mr Li. 'Our benefactor, the Jade General – you must know of him? Well, he is rather partial to a pipe, among other things.'

Chapter 27

Max had heard whispers of a local warlord – a self-proclaimed 'general'. He had, it was said, retreated upriver and quietly consolidated his local empire while the Nationalists fought first with the Communists and then with the Japanese.

Then Mr Li held the needled pill over the heat rising from the lamp's chimney.

'The Jade General owns half of the hospitality boats on this river and taxes the other half. Since the Kuomintang came to town he has kept to the hills. But he was here before Chiang Kai-shek's lot got here, and no doubt he'll be here long after they're gone. He's an incredibly powerful man.'

'So what does General Yu make of this bloody Jade fella?'

'Much of the southern army would turn their guns against General Yu if the Jade General gave the word. So Yu has no choice but to accommodate him.'

'Look mate, I'm not sure why you're telling me all this.'

'He's obscenely wealthy,' Mr Li continued. 'And he treats his women well, showering them with gifts. Do you know, he once told me how much he would pay for an evening with an attractive European girl?'

'*Any* attractive European girl?' enquired Max.

The pill darkened. Max found himself smiling as the creamy odour filled his nostrils.

The girl passed the pipe to her boss. Mr Li affixed what appeared to be an ornate doorknob to the stem of the pipe. He inserted the needled pill into a hole in the metal 'doorknob'.

Max lay down flat on his side, his head resting on a cushion, the top of the pipe in his hand. At the other end, Mr Li positioned the bowl of the pipe over the heat of the flame. Max held the mouth-end as steady as he could.

'It should be ready to taste now, sir. Would you mind if I sit here next to you?'

'Sure. Go ahead.'

Max sank down into the cushions, and Mr Li sat down close behind his head. A waitress brought her boss a handleless cup.

'Would you care for a cup of tea, sir?' enquired Mr Li.

'I'll stick with brandy, thanks.' Max put the pipe to his lips and inhaled. The sweet vapourised opium fumes filled his lungs and buoyed his spirit.

He inclined his head to glimpse at Mr Li and asked, 'How much?'

'The sum that would go to the girl in question – or to the man who brings a young white woman to us – would be one thousand American dollars.'

'Screw me down backwards!' Max propped himself up on his elbows. 'Deadset? Strewth, I'd think about dating the Jade fella *myself* if that was the going rate!'

'Well, that's very open-minded of you. But it must be a lady – a real lady. She would spend just one night of fine dining and champagne with our cultured benefactor—'

'Sure. Fine dining – that's all he'd want!'

'Well, it is quite possible that the young lady in question may relinquish herself to the General's charms. . . .'

'You mean they would strike their own financial arrangement for "extra services"?'

Mr Li smiled and opened his palms.

'And you'd get your cut, I'm sure.' Max drained away the remainder of his brandy and rested his head back down on his cushion. 'Well, he sounds like an interesting bloke, this Jade fella.'

'Another drink, my friend?' suggested Mr Li.

Max nodded with his eyelids.

Chapter 28

Under the mainmast's boom Gwen huddled in close to Max, her eyes buried into his chest, away from the machetes of the marauders whom surrounded them on deck.

Chief 99's final remarks before they had left the hideout stayed with her. He had stretched his arm across the table and held his fingertips on to the side of Gwen's chin for a moment. 'Be careful,' he said. 'You will be entering the wilds of China, my dear. Anything could happen. Don't trust any man.'

Amid the crowd on deck, Gwen and Max huddled under their rattan hats, dodging doubtful stares. Chinese families were sitting on baskets and trunks of their worldly goods. One man was sitting on a cage of live chickens.

She couldn't quite believe they were making the journey in broad daylight – surely the Japanese navy would have something to say?

She rested her head on his shoulder. 'Max, I'm sure it's only a matter of time before some of this lot – most likely our own two guards – make a grab for our cash, what's left of it.'

Positioned a deniable distance away from them on deck were their escorts. This particular pair were dressed as anonymous peasants, ready for the onward trek through the countryside. Their guns were hidden, as perhaps were their true intentions, Gwen feared.

Nearly every man appeared armed and many made an effort to appear piratical, with dirty scarves tied around heads, machetes dangling from their waistbands.

Max avoided following her stare. 'Darling, our pair are good blokes – trust me.'

Their guards did not indulge in dental hygiene, and they did not speak English, but when they had stepped up to the table in the Chief's hideaway, this pair of guerrillas had made one thing clear – through the Chief's translation: they enjoyed nothing better than slitting the throat of a Japanese soldier. This penchant for killing had clearly impressed Max, while adding to her fears. Why should these Chinese warriors wish to kill one colonial oppressor and yet aid another? In the wilds of the Chinese countryside, there would be nothing to stop the pair of them from slitting Max's throat one night and then doing as they wished with her.

They sailed parallel to the shore, passing floating fishing villages and white sandy beaches. Amidships, she lay on Max's lap as the boat bobbed along, trying to fill her mind with anything other than the journey ahead.

'Max, where does your wife live now?' She had asked him about Emily on the first day of their Sai Kung reunion, pointedly – if not conditionally – before they first made love. He presented his estranged spouse as yet one more point of commonality between her and himself.

'I honestly don't know. Probably England. My former wife,' as he referred to Emily, 'lives a continent and a lifetime away, and that's all you or I need to know.'

Despite the fragility of their current situation, she could not help but imagine a future. Indeed, that helped her find the mental strength to face the journey.

'Does your wife know with certainty that you're not going to return to her?'

'Crikey, if you must think of her at all – for I have cut her from my being entirely – you mustn't think of her as a balanced human being. Emily doesn't comprehend *anything* with certainty.'

Then Max handed her the binoculars and pointed out the rubbled remains of a village on a hillside above a bay ahead. 'Good blokes. And sheilas. The Japanese bombed that village not once, but many times. And now those villagers can't do enough to help anyone who's against the Japanese.'

She smiled. 'What goes around, comes around. But where has the Jap navy been while we sailed across a sunlit sea?'

'Keeping their bloody distance.' He explained that the illicit junk across Mirs Bay operated something like a ferry service, departing each day from the eastern reaches of the multi-fingered peninsula above Sai Kung. Many on board had left their homes in China only in the preceding years – when Japanese troops threatened the south – and were determined to return home. 'Escaping' from dependence on Japan's flow of rice into Hong Kong to dependence on relatives in China was a development Hong Kong's Japanese authorities blithely encouraged.

The junk came to ground on the sand, where it would stay until the next tide. Village children, standing on the beach, stared while their fathers splashed forward to help. 'Ah One' and 'Ah Two' – as she, in the absence of named introductions, called their two escorts – wisely preferred not to be taken for a white man's lackeys. They jumped off the boat first and let the two *gweilos* carry their own bags.

As Max and Gwen waded through the sea, a jolly Chinese man with a pistol strung around his neck splashed through the shallows towards them. The man greeted Max with a hearty, *'Jo san!'* and a very un-Chinese bear-hug. He insisted upon carrying both of their backpacks. Once he had seen them onto dry land, the man shook Max's hand and headed back towards the junk to help others.

Max grinned at her. 'And did you recognise that fella?'

'No. Should I have?'

'Kenny, there – *Kin Lok* is his real name – was a porter at the Peninsula Hotel. He was there the night you and I first met.'

'Upon my word! And now he's helping the guerrillas?'

'Told me he quit the Pen because he wants to shoot Jap bastards rather than wait on them. Most bloody commendable!'

She half smiled and pictured Kiyoshi Watanabe – Watty – the kindly interpreter in Stanley. *They're not all bastards,* she wanted to say but failed to.

Chapter 29

Forging ahead through sunlit countryside, picking wild raspberries on the way, their two guerrilla guides seemed far less menacing than Gwen's imagination had earlier decided. They were Hakka people who spoke little Cantonese. Ah One appeared as old as Gwen's own father, with the skin of a dried prune and soft, comforting eyes – once she had pealed preconceptions away from her own eyes. Ah Two was younger, with a baboon's toothy grin and a seal's hearty laugh.

The wild countryside of their first few days' walk gave way to an increasingly cultivated land of stepped, rice-covered slopes. There were times along the route north when it was necessary to meander through the hills to avoid Japanese checkpoints. But Ah One and Ah Two increasingly trusted local roads to provide safe passage.

While wary of strangers, Ah One and Ah Two greeted the various locals they knew with bonhomie. As the days ticked on and Free China beckoned, villagers hosted Gwen and Max for *yum cha* and rice cakes in small but crowded tea houses. Befriending the locals – rather than showing aloofness – reduced the likelihood of betrayal. And villagers would forewarn Ah One and Ah Two of the movements of nearby Japanese patrols. Nights were spent on bundles of hay, at best. Some locals willingly gave up their beds, although without a mattress they were often as hard as the floor.

One afternoon, on a muddy road softened by the previous night's rain, Gwen and Max found themselves striding up behind a father hauling a rickshaw under the weight of a trunk with two children on top and hung with bamboo baskets, clinking with cooking pans and utensils. These refugees, seeking a route out of occupied China, gave not a second glance to the two *gweilos* peering out from under Chinese hats.

Once they had cleared past this family, Gwen said quietly, 'Max, do you think you'll ever see Emily again?' She was determined to get more out of him.

They were in sugar country now, and, in no rush to answer, Max chewed heartily on the sweet cane. Many hands worked the fields, peasants under wide-brimmed hats, hunched at backbreaking angles.

'Well, if I had wanted to be with my former wife, I would have taken that train to Chungking and travelled onward to England.' He announced his English words with liberating volume, confident they were all-but in Free China. 'Do you think you'll see Klaus again?'

'No, not once I'm out of China. At least, not by choice. The last few occasions I saw him were *all* because he hunted me down.'

'Deadset?'

She nodded.

She was still unclear as to why, but Klaus was always the frustratingly loyal sort. He was gallingly steadfast regarding one chap in Macao with whom he had increasingly spent time – or, at least, that's who Klaus had said he was with. It all seemed an overly convenient excuse to spend less time with his wife.

Klaus had spent less time at home and more on his construction materials business. The Japanese march southwards through China threatened Macao and its neutrality, and international businesses began to pull out. His own business apparently in trouble, Klaus was soon in need of some advice about both insurance and investment – the two seemed to go together. Who better to advise him than the accountant son of a construction magnate?

'The last time I saw Klaus was in Stanley, and he tried to persuade me to swan off with him to bloody Brazil. I daresay he's still waiting for me.'

On the other side of the track, a man was pulling along an emaciated cow by a rope threaded through its nose ring.

'Max, what's going on up there?' She pointed ahead down the muddy road. Ah One turned around and smiled at her.

'I believe. . . .' Max began his answer but stopped talking as Ah One and Ah Two began muttering furiously to one another. Then the Chinese pair stopped by the side of the road. Gwen glanced at Max, and he pointed ahead: a column of soldiers, some wearing conical bamboo hats in place of a helmet, were streaming along the road towards them.

She had expected to see the transition from Japanese-occupied territory to Free China demarcated in some way. Her first thought on the matter had been that she would have to crawl a hundred yards across no man's land in the dead of night in the hope of dropping down into friendly trenches unopposed. But in wartime China, the lines were rather more blurred than in Great War France. Max had explained that although few frontier points were marked and manned, troops from both sides knew that straying into a town in no man's land would invite attack.

'Crikey, we've only bloody well made it!' yelled Max. She resisted the urge to dash over and kiss every one of those marching Chinese soldiers; instead, she settled for kissing Max.

Once the column had passed, the four of them walked on as one unit. Even Ah One smiled. The physical process of putting one foot in front of the other may not have changed, but everything else had. Freedom felt official, and legs felt lighter.

Max took a hold of her hand as they walked, and she smiled.

'Now, Gwen, I've been meaning to say something to you. I'm sorry I've shown you so little sympathy . . . I guess I've been distracted by . . . well, escaping and rescuing and all that shenanigans! Over the course of your ordeal in Hong Kong, escaping from Stanley and so on, you and Chester went through a lot together. You must miss him, poor thing.'

'Well, thank you, I—'

'And, of course, you've known him so long – going back to Macao. Although I'm not clear on what brought you two into contact there.'

Was that why he brought up Chester? To dig up more of her past?

'We met through my husband – through his work. The main investor had pulled out of Klaus's business venture – with due cause, given the perilous circumstances – and it was Chester Drake who miraculously managed to find new backers to keep Klaus in business. But, in return, Klaus now had to specialise in supplying materials for war industries. So he began by surreptitiously working with the Chinese – until the Japanese arrived. He always insisted that the whole scheme of sourcing rubber and metals for war machines was Chester's idea, and that Chester had some sort of involvement even after Chinese forces retreated from the province.'

'Sounds suspicious,' said Max.

'Yes. To my mind, it's positively unthinkable that an Anglo-Chinese patriot such as Chester would ever encourage anyone to supply the enemy.'

She gave his hand a squeeze. 'But Macao was a different lifetime for me. Chester was there for me when things became tricky with Klaus. He never did anything a good and proper friend wouldn't do.' Her stomach tightened. 'Whereas Klaus was up to no good. He would arrive home increasingly late, and occasionally not at all. He had apparently abandoned his swish city-centre headquarters for a cubby-hole office at the cargo port. That move made no sense to me – it had to be cover for his infidelity.

'When he was at home,' she continued, 'Klaus would talk in nothing but generalities of the "demands of work". And he tried to pin things onto Chester, curiously saying that, "Drake helped me and now he needs my help – I mustn't let him down."'

'I wonder in what sense the millionaire's son needed help?' said Max.

'Klaus never would explain anything.' Hence other, sleazier, explanations of his extended absences held the more credible ground.

'Perhaps after the war,' said Max, 'we should look up Chester's family, pay them our respects.'

She smiled and kissed him on the cheek.

Another kiss in that other life, in Macao, could have had life-changing consequences – and, in a sense, it did.

The Grand Hotel, a palace of marble steps and internal columns. Klaus had arranged to meet her there but then had the temerity to call through a spurious message – via his secretary. Apparently, a tragedy on the wharf was holding him 'at work'. From past experience of the 'delayed at work' variety, she did not expect to see him for quite some time. It was while leaning against one of the thickset columns in a corner of the ballroom that she had found herself seeing a new friend in a new light. All this, she told herself for a long time afterwards, was due to one too many gins.

Or was it one too few?

In the imperial splendour of the Grand Hotel's ballroom she had found herself chatting with a man whom she had met only in passing when he came to the house for meetings with Klaus. Chester Drake had appeared all the more dashing in white tie – and awfully young and awfully Eurasian for such an influential man. As the pair of them talked with growing flirtatiousness, she slowly side-footed her way, with Chester in tow, around the side of a column. The broad column concealed them from the dancers and general partygoers in the centre of a room far too big for its purpose.

Talking in a faint whisper enticed him to lean closer to hear. She cupped a hand around the back of his head, spreading her fingers through his short, clipped hair. She drew him closer and planted her lips onto his. He did not push her away. Encouraged and emboldened, she grabbed his hip and pulled him in tight.

The draught of the double doors opening some yards behind Chester's back shattered the moment. She shoved away her admirer. A glance back to the doorway revealed the entrant: Klaus.

At the time, she felt unduly persuaded on two points. Firstly, that Klaus would not have seen enough to warrant an argument. And, secondly, his earlier-than-anticipated arrival was most likely a sign that he had been with another woman: the act itself no longer took him anything more than a few minutes.

Chester neither visited nor corresponded for months after that evening. And only later – after falling down the stairs – did news spread that a man had indeed been killed at the wharf that evening, crushed to death by a cargo container when a cable snapped.

Chapter 30

Unlike his previous visit, Kukong failed to provide a special welcome. No banners, no fireworks, no welcoming party whatsoever. But then instead of bringing a Chinese hero through the gateway and into the dusty, ragged city, this time Max was escorting an anonymous *gweipo*. There were the usual incessant stares for a blonde in China, and Gwen was a particularly attractive blonde. He had half a mind to tease one local 'businessman' with a glimpse of the potential booty – if only to discover how high her value might rise.

He would have to reveal his arrival to the toffee noses at HQ, if only to check for any telegram reply from Emily. Surely she could not say 'no' to his request: a wife must stand by her man.

Max pulled out a black and white map to plot a route through town. Fenced in by three rivers, Kukong was roughly triangular in shape. Kukong offered a striking change of atmosphere to weeks spent in the countryside. The local sandstone brought a red tinge to an expanding city under construction and *re*-construction – for bombs fell from the sky daily.

They made their way to the bank of the Western River, where he set down his rain jacket over a patch of sand amid grass tufts. Gwen sat down first. They were sitting shoulder to shoulder, the bustle of humanity around the shanty town at their backs almost outdone by the flurry of activity upon the river. *Sampans* shuttled up and down, interrupted by others ferrying goods from one bank to another.

She raised her hand to turn Max's face towards hers, and they kissed.

'I feel like we've finally made it,' she said, smiling.

'We made swift progress – swifter after our two guides left us!' He chuckled.

'Those two bicycles helped tremendously,' said Gwen.

It was not clear whether Ah One *could* not ride a bike or simply *would* not, but whatever it was ran deep. For each time they so much as walked past a stationary bicycle, resting against a tree or a building, Ah One would stray towards the middle of the street to give it a wide berth.

'But I can't help but miss Ah One and Two!' She giggled.

'You thought they were planning to slit your throat.'

She smirked and looked down in embarrassment.

Once left alone in Free China, Max and Gwen used bicycles at first, but, as the road steepened amid the sheer karst hills on the approach to Kukong, they ditched the bikes in favour of hitching a lift. Max rattled off some Chinese, name-dropping Admiral Chan, which smoothed them on board a truck. In case greater persuasion was needed, he had his pistol handy. The roads were intolerable. With reflection, the only surprise was that the truck's tyre had not been punctured earlier – when it happened, they were in sight of the city gates.

'So where's the British consul, or whomever the King's representative is in this god-forsaken town?' asked Gwen.

'Rest up, then I'll go and see my boss and get the old-timer to book you onto a train to Chungking. It's a front-room outfit, run by some Aussie old-timer with a disconcertingly pukka accent. But the British Army Aid Group is about as high-ranking as we've got in Kukong. There's no consulate here, Gwen, like there's no grand hotel worthy of such a beautiful, well-to-do woman.'

'Despite the fact I've not had a hot bath in weeks, I'll take the "beautiful" – but I'm not well-to-do. Not if you mean well-off. Not anymore.' His arm lifted momentarily, before he re-lowered it onto her shoulder.

He opened a paper-wrapped array of sweetmeats which they had bought from a street hawker during their stroll through the city. He had driven a fierce bargain, berating the old lady in response to her opening price. Their route had taken them through narrow lanes lined with stalls teeming with local wares, punctuated by local produce. Street vendors barked out the merits of their goods with raucous disregard for passing eardrums. Often unable to see the ground ahead through the throng, Gwen's small feet fell between wobbly cobbles. Men, dressed in military khaki, and a good number of women sporting the navy blue of civilian officials, made their way through town on foot, bicycle or rickshaw.

'Well, you might not view yourself as well-off, but people around here certainly would.'

'Well, maybe,' said Gwen, plucking a squidgy, sugary bun from its wrapping paper.

'Anyway, isn't your old man a banker?'

'He's a retired assistant manager from a small town in Surrey. My ability to live the high life in the East was never based upon my father's money – nor my own, for that matter. It was my husband's. And that source of funds, as you may imagine, has somewhat dried up.'

Perhaps she was simply being coy. She certainly spoke with the over-pronounced vowels and clipped consonants of the English upper class. He used to think that the British had a monopoly on class distinctions, but China, too, lived hierarchy with rigid and ancient obedience. Carrying empty buckets to the water, a stream of women passed by on the riverbank, dressed in a variety of rule-breaking colours – unsuitable for their class – that marked them as refugees from Hong Kong. Selling dried fish and river crabs from their *sampans*, local river folk wore the working-class uniform also seen on street hawkers, builders and the like – traditional *samfu* jackets and trousers. Around Kukong's shopping district, local women wore blue *cheongsams,* the uniform of the middle class.

The rare sound of a car engine spluttered behind them. Probably military. Max glanced over his shoulder: only a tall poppy would have access to an open-top car. The chief occupant of the rear seat looked imperious with the metallic gold insignia shining high on his collar. Max turned away, remembering the last time he had spent an evening in Kukong. Although the General had left early, he conflated General Yu with Mr Li and the sticky business discussed on the floating bar that night. Unfinished business?

Max unwrapped a second paper packet, and Gwen dug into the black peanut toffee.

'I've never stayed anywhere with so few European faces,' she said. 'Where are all the Brits?'

'Chungking, of course. The last fellas from my own escape party should have arrived there by now.'

'So *when* will we be able to meet His Majesty's *Man-in-Kukong*?'

He wrapped an arm around her. 'There's no ambassador coming here to greet you.'

'I know that. I'm not longing for cocktails on the lawn, Max.'

'I know. You're—'

'I'm looking for someone who can contact the ambassador, and tell him what I've got for him,' she said. 'Lists of internees for the families back home who won't know if their loved ones are dead or alive. Details of conditions and of food rations that break the Geneva Convention – and of rapes and massacres which must be exposed and condemned. Perhaps then they'll get me on a train – or, better, a *plane* – to Chungking.'

'Don't bank on a sidebar in *The Times* having any effect on the behaviour of the Japanese.'

'Gosh, I know the Japanese will still do whatever on Earth they want, but at least our boys will have a better idea what they're fighting for out east. For a British lad who's never left London or Manchester or Glasgow, being sent to fight in the jungles of Malaya or Burma or – one day – reinvading Hong Kong, must be like being sent to the moon. Why should they care about the Far East if they don't know how people – including people not so different from them, from London, Manchester and Glasgow – are suffering?'

The afternoon sky darkened. Meandering along the towpath a gang of white-shirted schoolchildren shouted and giggled as children do.

He stared up to the heavens. 'Come on, we'd best go find our billet,' he said. 'We've been lucky with the weather so far – but there's no such thing as a dry day at this time of year.'

'Where did you say we are staying?' she asked.

'Um, in a place with character . . . upriver.' They stood up, he dusted sand off the back of her skirt, and they set off for the nearest bridge. The stonework was crumbling under the weight of the shops and stalls.

'Just like the Ponte Vecchio in Florence!' said Gwen. 'It's lovely!'

'Lovelier from a distance,' he replied. He flashed a pass card at the sentry and they entered the throng on the bridge. Parting the way ahead through the crowd, a labourer carried a hefty trunk on his shoulder. On one stall, Szechwan ducks hung from a line of hooks, smoked and sold whole or sliced like ham.

They chanced upon a gap between the shops and took in the view downriver. 'There's nothing these coolies can't shift from A to B,' said Max. 'Just look!' The two straining coolies on the path moved in slow synchronisation with the barge. 'See,' he continued, 'they even pull boats.'

'They may not look much, but I do admire the strength of the Chinese,' she shouted over the hubbub of hawkers and potential customers. 'In so many ways.'

'Oh, they're bred for it, these coolies!' retorted Max. 'Any other country would have mules or horses working this towpath, but why would you when you've got a whole sub-race built wide, short and with enormous calves.'

They walked on, edging closer to the end of the bridge. There on the east bank, beyond the godowns and workshops, Max's current employers had established a headquarters within the compound of the Methodist Medical Mission's hospital. Their new clandestine organisation in southern China: the 'British Army Aid Group'.

The new telegraph line had not been installed in order for personnel to send messages to family in Blighty, but everyone was at it. Emily must realise he was only asking for money that was rightfully his. She had to do the right thing: he was her husband, after all.

But he could do without running into his boss, a fellow Australian miscast by the hero-worship of the other special ops boys who had rushed to join this merry band. What the others all saw in this overly officious, depressingly prudish old colonel mystified him. Surely there should always be a place for a bit of light-hearted, if not light-*headed*, relief to release the strain of war? Perhaps his former self, Dominic Sotherly, would have managed to feign respect for the old goat, but Max had little respect for Dominic Sotherly anymore.

He steered them down onto the towpath and led them in the opposite direction from BAAG HQ. One good reason for arranging one's own billet was to avoid the interminable wait that relying on the authorities would have entailed. Another reason was that the British would divide them into separate male and female unmarried quarters. With the British attitude to sex, it really was a wonder the population of that chilly isle did not dwindle towards nothing with each passing generation. They needed an empire to keep their numbers up.

A couple of hundred yards upriver a second bridge stretched flat on the water, a sequence of wooden rafts tied together.

'Gwen, I wouldn't wish you to have high hopes about the accommodation.' As the words left his mouth he questioned their worth.

She giggled. 'I'm not staying anywhere that fails to match the Peninsula!'

'Ah, that could be a problem. Some people would say this place is not fit for a lady.'

She stopped walking and glanced sidewise at him. 'Then why—'

'Because you've seen the city – it's flattened daily.'

She cast her eyes to the empty grey sky; there was sarcasm in her gesture.

'They're regular, Gwen. You've only been here for an afternoon. You'll find we'll get air raids in the mornings, as routinely as we'll get rain in the evenings. That's why the shops were so busy this afternoon. You may have noticed vendors setting up when we first entered the city this afternoon – like every afternoon – the shops don't open for business until two o'clock, once the Betties – the Jap bombers – are gone.'

They walked on, past the pontoon bridge. Locals scurried across it, unconcerned by the floor wobbling under their feet.

'And it's much safer to stay out here on the river,' he continued. 'I'm taking you to the only safe place I know. It's where they put us up – Admiral Chan Chak's men, Royal Navy officers, the works. If it's good enough for them. . . .'

Moored to a jetty a hundred yards from its nearest neighbour, he spotted their 'hotel': a large blue and white houseboat. And Mr Li's floating bar was nowhere to be seen.

'So, here we are! It may be seaworthy – well, river-worthy – but it doesn't actually move anywhere.'

Gwen paused at the gangplank, sizing the place up.

Max hesitated but figured she was going to work it out anyway. 'Welcome to our very own *flower boat* – emptied of all *flowers*.'

Chapter 31

A bored-looking Chinese teenager led them along the port-side passageway. Gwen considered whether this girl was old enough to be one of the 'flowers'. Max might have been saying sweet *anythings* to the teenager as he chatted away in Cantonese.

The girl knocked on the next door. There was no reply so she shoved it open, and Gwen and Max stepped inside.

'Here we go,' he said. 'It's a cosy little cabin, but so is every room.'

Gwen pushed the wall with the palm of her hand: the sheet of plywood bowed. 'Well, you call them "rooms", but this is more like a cubicle. For "entertainment", I assume?'

He smirked. 'I wouldn't know. I was here with officers of the Royal Navy: they wouldn't know *entertainment* if it poured them a whisky and sat on their lap!'

She hoped her sour face said enough.

'Honestly, darling, there were no girls when I was here, I swear.'

She said nothing.

He set down the bags. 'Well, anyway, this is the cabin that's in best shape. Comes complete with comforts from home.' He pointed at the oil painting above the bed. 'Don't ask me where the "Battle of Trafalgar" came from – it was already here when I arrived with the escape party.'

On the curved wall of the hull the room's single porthole faced the riverbank. It was near dark outside. The cracks in the hull's planking were worse close to the circular window. She put her hand up to the widest crack; a thin breeze chilled her palm.

She flung her raincoat onto the bed but buttoned up her cardigan. 'Are we the only guests?'

'Annie – the girl who showed us in – said—'

'*Annie?*'

'Oh, they often take a Western name. Just for fun.'

'I bet,' she said.

Max hung up Gwen's coat on a hook behind the door. 'Anyway, she said they've been commandeered by the Nationalist authorities. They're expecting a delegation from Chungking to arrive to stay here soon. So they stopped renewing the tenancy of guests. She was complaining about how she's having to clean all the rooms.'

Gwen resisted the temptation to ask why the girl allowed Max on board when she was supposed to be losing guests not gaining them, but he read her face. 'I guess we got lucky,' he said.

Max closed the door and sat down next to her on the bed. He ran his hand up over her thigh. 'Talking of getting lucky. . . .'

'Max, I'm covered in grime and layers of my own perspiration!'

He kissed her neck. 'Hmm, just the way I like you!'

Annie managed to rustle up some warm water in the galley. There were inside latches to lock the kitchen doors, so there amid bags of rice and bottles of cooking oil, arching over a tin bucket, Gwen sponged herself down. And she soaked her underwear and blouse, too.

The next day she would meet the British authorities in Kukong and hoped to send a telegram off to her parents. She would not prolong their pain – the pain of not knowing.

Someone tried the kitchen door handle. Then there was a thump on the door followed by shouting in Chinese. By the time she had dried herself off, put her dirty skirt on and wrapped a towel around her chest, and opened the door, there was nobody there. So she took her time hanging her wet clothes over the sink and strolled back to the cabin.

'That was Annie's uncle, Ah Kei, that fella who came knocking,' said Max. 'He owns the boat.'

She found her dry blouse. Rain splattered against the porthole and dribbled through one of the cracks.

'I was hoping,' he continued, 'that he's here to inform us of what's on offer for dinner tonight. . . .'

'The menu would be plain rice with rice, from what I saw in the kitchen.' Her back to Max, she was sitting on the bed, topless for mere seconds before Max's warm hands slid around each side of her waist and then upwards.

'Max, I'm too hungry for that.' She gently but firmly removed his hands.

'Okay. Well, that was what Ah Kei had come to explain. He said he's got nothing worth bloody eating, but dinner will be brought to us shortly. He used an old form of Cantonese in some of his expressions, which, if you're born this century, is incomprehensible – even to the Chinese, at times. Anyway, I saw him shoot through, off the boat: he must have gone out to buy us dinner and bring it back for us.'

'So we'll just have to wait,' she said. 'Shame we're out of gin.' She had rushed on a blouse without first finding her other bra, an oversight that did not go unnoticed.

'Geez, we'll just have to think of something else to do,' said Max, who began feeling her breasts through the thin cotton of her blouse.'

'You're not getting me all grubby! You'll have to wash first.'

Max sighed, grabbed the damp towel and bolted up from the bed. He opened the wardrobe and removed his clean shirt. He planted one knee onto the bed and kissed her on the lips. 'I'll be back before you know it. In the meantime, don't put any more clothes on.'

She lay back on the bed. As one may expect, the mattress had little spring left in it. A familiar and solitary literary work – in English – had been left on their bedside table. As she plumped her pillow, a distant wail of music came through the crack near the porthole.

Moments later, she lay back down. She would read the book the only way she knew: by chance. She had read parts of it before as a child, and she had heard readings from it when Klaus had dragged her to his Catholic church in Macao. Perhaps he considered himself a godly man, but she just saw Klaus socialising and lining up the next business meeting. He would arrive early and wander among the congregation shaking hands and receiving smiles as though it were *his* flock. At the end of the service, he would linger – more likely to make a deal than make a prayer, although perhaps the two went together. Meanwhile, she would be taken ahead to lunch with some of Klaus's friends. He would arrive late but to popular applause.

She closed her eyes, flicked open the Bible, stuck her finger firmly onto the middle of a page and opened her eyes to Corinthians. Tracking back to the beginning of the sentence, it read: *Love bears all things, believes all things, hopes all things, endures all things.* Was her heart heading that way with Max? Then she admonished her gullible mind: one may as well believe a fortune teller.

A second after she slammed the book shut, the boat jolted violently: something must have rammed into them. The music had grown louder. Then a knock at the door. She opened it and there was Annie, who used her hands to mime eating and then pointed along the passageway. Gwen put on her shoes, grabbed the drawstring handbag she had bought for peanuts in town earlier, and followed Annie up onto deck. The light was fading but the air was warm.

And they had visitors.

'Gwen!' Max called her name with some urgency. His hair wet and his clean shirt half undone, he had hurried up from his wash to witness the cause of the commotion. He gaped as he stared at the sight of their new and very immediate neighbours – the barge that had drawn alongside them.

'Gwen – you'd best go back to the cabin.'

She laughed and ignored him. 'Well, this is a type of catering service I've never seen before! This gives new meaning to the term "restaurant delivery"!'

Two deckhands from the barge roped the two boats together. A Chinese man in an English suit, with a waiter's towel over his arm, beamed a smile from the neighbouring foredeck. Standing behind him, Annie's uncle – who had put a suit jacket on over his white vest – kept his head bowed.

'Ah, Mr Max, how are you, sir?' The well-dressed man spoke perfect English.

'Oh Max, thank you!' said Gwen. 'How tremendously romantic! Not what one expects in a war zone. Oh, Max – you're an absolute delight!'

'Allow me to introduce myself,' said the man in the three-piece suit. 'I'm Mr Li, an old friend of Mr Max. We are normally closed on Mondays, but for you we have opened up specially.' He stepped forward to offer her a hand on-board. 'We have managed to source for you bighead carp. It's so fresh it's still swimming in our tank, but we will have it at your table before you know it.' Ah Kei passed Mr Li a tray with a covered dish. 'But first,' said Mr Li, 'steamed rice vermicelli rolls. Do come aboard.'

Standing on the edge of the deck, she glanced at Max and hesitated.

'I have heard that you enjoy a gin, Miss,' said Mr Li. 'I have kept for you a bottle of Plymouth.' She winked at Max, took Mr Li's hand and boarded the saloon barge. Max was playing dumb, but he must have arranged the whole thing. She gripped the handbag that swung from her shoulder – the contents were too important to risk dropping into the river. Max duly followed her on-board.

'Mr Kei will make you at home.' She followed Annie's uncle down five steps into the salon's reception area. She waited for Max just inside the hatchway and listened to him talking insistently but quietly out on deck.

'Mr Li, I wouldn't wish you to think I was sober last time we met.'

'I quite understand, sir,' said Mr Li.

'Don't bullshit me. Whatever we may have discussed – and I'm not quite sure I remember – there is no deal.' Then Max switched to Cantonese.

Gwen sighed. He was just like Klaus. Men always had to be making – or unmaking – one deal or another.

But Mr Li replied in English. 'Sir, the Jade General and his desires have not gone away.'

Max snapped at him in Cantonese.

'I do understand most clearly, sir.'

She strolled on into the lounge bar. Void as it was of clientele, she picked a booth and sat down. Ah Kei brought over Chinese tea. Gwen carefully tied the drawstring of her bag through a belt loop on her skirt. She had opted to bring the toilet roll with her. *The* toilet roll. This was not so odd, because toilet rolls were hard to come by in China. It had seemed safer to carry the secreted details of internees and massacres with her rather than leave the treasured toilet roll for someone to pinch from their cabin.

Max ducked his head as he came down the steps. He appeared anxious when he should have felt relieved – they had made it to somewhere safe enough and civilised enough to enjoy a romantic dinner.

Gwen slammed another empty glass to the table. 'Damn, that's mighty fine gin!'

'Well, you should bloody well know!' said Max, sitting opposite her in the booth.

'That was the best damn meal I've had in a long time.' She cast her eyes around the vacant saloon: it was odd being the only guests.

'Do you know, you talk like a Yank when you've had a gin or six,' he said.

'That's not all I do when I've had a gin or six.' She shuffled close and kissed up Max's neck. 'It's a warm night. Maybe, after another gin, we could find somewhere outside, under the stars. . . .'

'Everything to your satisfaction?' Mr Li had appeared from nowhere.

'Wonderful, thank you,' said Gwen.

'Did you enjoy the river snails?'

Max handed an empty dish back to Mr Li. 'Look, we're fine, thanks, Mr—'

'I must admit,' interrupted Gwen, 'I wasn't expecting to like snails. But they were sort of . . . fragrant and sweet. Rather delicious.'

Mr Li bowed in gratitude. 'We fry them in vanilla, Miss.' He stacked up the other empty dishes and headed for the kitchen.

Max stood up from the booth. 'I need the loo. Excuse me.'

A minute later, Mr Li reappeared at Gwen's table with a pot of green tea. 'I thought you may be in need of refreshment?' He held the teapot high above the first of the two bowls and poured theatrically. 'May I ask, Missy – are you feeling adventurous?'

'Do you know, I've never felt so daring! Must be the damn fine gin!'

'Then permit me to bring you something you may not have tried before. We Chinese believe *yang* must be balanced with *yin*. *Yang* is found in the tea you drank and in many of the foods you ate. Allow me to bring you a taste of *yin*.'

'You are a darling – a true beacon of kindness – but I'm not sure I could eat another thing.'

'This will take up no room in your stomach, Miss.'

'Upon my word. . . . Are you going to hit us with a bill the size of China?!'

'Everything is paid for, Miss.' She smiled at Max walking back towards the table. Mr Li shuffled away.

'What did he want?' asked Max, as he slipped into her side of the booth.

'Oh, he wants to bring us something else terribly exciting to taste.'

She kissed Max slowly on the lips, flicking the tip of her tongue onto his. Under the table, her hand stroked over his thigh and up his groin.

'It's been such an awfully wonderful evening – thank you so much, Max.'

He smiled.

'What do you believe lies in the future for us?' said Gwen.

'Well, how about if we got married? Would you settle for that?'

'*Settle* for it? I shouldn't say one *settles* for marriage. One settles a debt, not a marriage. You have to build a marriage, every day. If you stop building for just one day. . . .'

'Is that what happened with Klaus?'

'Oh, I didn't know of such things then. I barely know now.'

Mr Li startled them, speaking before Gwen or Max were aware of his presence. 'This is our tradition – something of an aphrodisiac. It's lightly flavoured to suit a delicate lady.' Smoke smouldered from the intricately carved pipe which Mr Li held over a lamp.

Max stared at Mr Li. 'Um, what the hell do you think—'

'Max, don't be such a damn puritan,' said Gwen. 'You admitted all that temperance talk you spouted the first evening we met was utter tripe – as if it wasn't obvious – and you can't honestly tell me you've never tried this before, can you?' He just stared at her. 'Thought so. Well, I'm curious, and I'm not a cat.'

She snatched the pipe from Mr Li.

'Gwen, do you even know what that is?'

'Hmm . . . is it an oboe?'

Her 'oboe' was heavy, but Mr Li retook the other end and held it over a flame. She held the mouthpiece to her lips and sucked gently, barely allowing the taste to reach her throat before she stopped. She leaned back and sighed. Max took the pipe from her hands. After he inhaled, she took hold of the pipe once again.

After a while, she closed her eyes and rested her head on Max's shoulder. The lapping motion of the boat, which must have swayed back and forth all evening, became the dominant sensation. She felt light, lifted into the air. She was in a field, naked, lying almost on the ground but hovering above it with grass tickling her back.

Then the dream shattered.

'Gwen, are you awake.' She opened her eyes. 'You know, I've gotta ask you – did you or did you not have an affair with Chester?'

She sat up from his shoulder. 'Oh, why spoil things with your obsession over Chester? Nothing happened between us. But what if it had? You and I were not together until after Chester died.'

'I have no problem that you've been with other men. I even find it a bit amusing that you married a German.' His eyes bored into hers. 'But with a Chinese? It hardly seems right.'

'What? I bet you've had a damn Chinese girl!' He didn't answer. 'And, Chester is *Eurasian.*'

'I'm not sure that helps much. Surely you admit bludgers like Drake are of a lesser breed?'

'*A lesser breed?* Max, you talk like the old colonials I thought you despised? Chester Drake is . . . *was* clever, resourceful, strong. And he's every bit as much a man as you are.'

'Ah, so you did have him, didn't you?' He stood up from the table. 'Well, you can have them all, Gwen!' He walked up the steps and disappeared out of the hatchway.

She had neither the energy nor the inclination to follow him. How dare he accuse her . . . and how dare he say such things about poor Chester, martyred for her cause.

Mr Li came over carrying a pair of large cushions. 'Anything I can do, my dear?' He placed the cushions next to her on the booth's bench seat.

She managed a smile. 'I'll be okay.' The opium pipe lay invitingly on the table. She brought it to her lips once again.

She sucked on the pipe three more times before she let herself flop down onto the cushions.

An engine rumbled into life. At first, her body swayed gently back and forth, but then she was pulled along with the boat, floating away.

PART IV

Foe and Friend

Chapter 32

August 1942

The evening sun invited drinkers to crowd the street outside, a signature of a London summer, war or no war. Max was happy to have the inside of the pub more or less to himself – a homely atmosphere of polished mahogany and quiet conversation, just right for the occasion.

'Sarah Carlisle' was the name given when the boss had introduced her the previous week. Mr Robertshaw had introduced Max, unforewarned, as a 'Benedict Spratt'. In general, they were discouraged from having any contact with colleagues outside of their section, so Max doubted that their introduction had been a coincidence.

He smiled and gently shook his head as the previous evening's conversation at home ran through his mind:

'Must you work every evening, Dom?' She stacked up their dirty dinner plates next to the sink and then stood behind him at the table. Pressing her chest into the back of his head, she ran her fingers through his closely clipped hair.

'It's not that I don't want to be here, darling. . . .'

Then Mrs Arkwright blustered back into the kitchen. 'Hmm. So you're out again tonight, are you? Seems fair: you never pay us any rent, but then you rarely ever spend the night here.' She withdrew a tumbler from the cupboard and slammed the kitchen door shut behind her.

'I'm sorry about Mother. She'll get used to having you around, just give it a couple of months and you'll be best of friends again.'

He suppressed a smirk. The idea that he had ever been friends with his mother-in-law amused him.

'I missed you desperately when you were stuck in the Far East,' she continued, 'and now I miss you every night at home.'

'I'll make it up to you this weekend. Trust me, Emily.'

It was rather odd, living with Emily at her parents' house in Highgate, yet seeing other women. So it had to be *their* place, of course – or a well-chosen hotel. But 'Sarah' seemed special – or harder work, depending on how one wanted to look at it. Patience would be required.

Max sipped his pint of mild and kept an eye on the open doorway. He was able to live off Emily's contributions – well, her father's, really – enabling him to devote his secret thousand-dollar payoff to other pursuits. 'Blood money' sounded unsavoury, but the reality was it did help take the edge off things.

There would be little point in wasting money on rent. At least he was getting paid again. And old Robertshaw had begun to show a little faith, packing him off for the occasional training course – which helped provide cover for nights away from Emily. Ironically, the one big truth he had told his wife – which was regarding SOE and his role within it – was the one big official secret.

The director forbade colleagues to 'congregate' in the nearest pubs on Baker Street, so they tended to gather a couple of blocks away in the White Stag. Hence, Max had chosen the Crooked Hook, a fair walk in the opposite direction. Arriving early allowed him to secure a strategically positioned window table with an early-warning view of whomever entered the pub. He was only just beginning to get to know 'Sarah'. When she perhaps assumed nobody was paying any attention to her – outside of round-table meetings and her perfunctory 'good morning' greetings – Sarah's countenance appeared sullen, if not sad. But her innocent appearance – her blue misty eyes, her absurd youth – invoked in him a passionate curiosity that he had believed he had lost along with Gwen. How many times had he relived that night in Kukong and agonised over the alternative decisions he could have made? Yet, in his heightened state, had he wanted the money more than he had wanted Gwen that night? His behaviour was, in part, an admission to himself of a barely concealed truth: his future did not lie with Gwen.

On the night itself – or the next morning – he had toyed with the idea of not telling a soul what had happened, but concluded that it would have caught up with him sooner or later. And there was always a glimmer of hope that the British Army Aid Group may actively help. The BAAG's small office consisted, in the main, of escapees from the military prisoner of war camps in Kowloon, so they might have been expected to possess a little understanding?

That proved a vain hope. The officer in-charge displayed no empathy for the trials his fellow Australian had faced journeying to and from Hong Kong, but he was greatly distressed at hearing of the abduction of a British woman. He unsubtly questioned Max's competence in the process. There was nothing he could have done, Max implored: after dinner that evening, she stayed up when he went to bed. And that was no word of a lie.

When pressed to disclose what action he would take, the officer preened his moustache and said curtly, 'other agencies would have to be consulted'. BAAG's meagre resources were aimed south against the Japanese, not north towards some warlord's private army. 'Proper channels' would take too much time, Max had implored, but they insisted a diplomatic approach was the best course of action. In the first instance, at least. There would be no second instance, thought Max.

The episode denigrated his reputation among the British in China and secured him a place on the next plane to Chungking: they simply wanted rid of him. Then it was onward over 'the Hump' to India and a perilous journey home, around Africa, within a steamship convoy flanked by naval escorts. Every night for six weeks Max was consumed by nightmares.

That night on the river would stay with him for the rest of his life. If he could go back, he would conduct himself differently. But he could not change it, only relive it.

Max stormed back to their cabin. He lay awake waiting for Gwen to return, to have it out with her once and for all. He sought to distract his mind, to make the interval of time pass quicker. He looked around the room but saw nothing to read. His mind oscillated between wanting to strike her and wanting to sleep with her, perhaps one last time. The fermented grain and ground poppy seeds caught up with him; he could keep his eyes open no longer. A deep humming sound stirred his slumber, before the noise faded away.

Max awoke at first light. Before his eyes were fully open he flung his arm out to the side where Gwen should be sleeping, and his hand thumped down on the empty mattress. He sprang up. Only then did his head ache and his stomach churn. Still wearing the previous night's clothes, he ran out of the cabin and onto the deck. The sun had not yet risen into sight, but there was light aplenty to see that the barge was not within half a mile up or down river. He stormed back below decks, thumping on doors until Annie's uncle, Ah Kei, appeared in the passageway wearing his ubiquitous white vest.

Max fired questions at him in Cantonese. 'What's happened to her? Where has the barge gone? Where is she now?'

The older man was silent.

Max grabbed him by the ears.

'The Jade General,' the old man muttered. 'He takes any woman he wishes. There is nothing to be done.'

'What do you mean, *nothing to be done*? We have to find her. Now!'

'No, sir. You cannot find her. He has an army that not even the Nationalists interfere with. You would not get to the "House of Happiness". You would not get past the guards. Believe me, I have tried. The Jade General takes all the girls he pleases.'

'What becomes of them?'

The old man stared at Max, perhaps wondering if he was stupid or whether his ability to comprehend even elemental Cantonese was limited. 'He uses them for his personal pleasure, and then discards each one after a few days or weeks. Then they go to the "House of Happiness".'

He had to hear it for himself: 'What is the "House of Happiness"?'

'It is where everyone is happy except for all the girls who are enslaved there. It's a prison-brothel, where, I'm told, the girls are chained up day and night.'

Max took a step backwards and leaned his body against the wooden wall.

'The only way to get a brothel pass to gain access there,' the old man continued,' is to join the Jade Army. Although perhaps the General would keep a *gweipo* somewhere different, somewhere special. Or it might be considered too risky to keep her anywhere at all.'

Max exhaled a deep breath.

'Sir, it simply is not possible. I know it is hard, but there is nothing to be done.'

Max squared up close again, towering over Ah Kei. 'You helped them, didn't you?'

'I believe you helped them more, Mr Max.'

He raised his fist and rammed it into the old man's jaw.

Max walked away but then turned around suddenly. 'What do you mean, *you've tried?*'

The man was sitting on the floor, nursing his chin. He spat out a tooth.

'You said, "You've tried"?'

'I . . . my daughter. . . .' His speech was muffled. 'She was taken . . . last year. I went after her. They shot me in the leg . . . dumped me in the river. But *unfortunately* . . . I survived. I know . . . I will never see her again.'

He helped the man to his feet before returning to the cabin. It was only as Max stepped back into the room that he noticed a thick envelope on the floor. Had it been there earlier?

He read the note inside:

A message from his Excellency the Jade General: The General will take good care of the woman – unless you cause trouble. If you cause trouble, he will dispose of her in a manner where she will never be found. If you come after her, you will be killed and so will she. Go back to England and enjoy this as a token of the General's appreciation.

He counted the money: one thousand American dollars.

Max was on his second pint when Sarah walked in. She wore not her austere angle-length work suit, but a flimsy cotton dress. Her dark bob slid around her jawline as she turned and spotted him standing up to greet her.

'Ah, there you are.' He kissed her on the cheek.

'Mr Spratt, we hardly know each other!' she said with a glint in her eye.

'Oh, crikey, please don't call me that.'

She sat down on a bentwood chair across the table from Max. 'Then, Benedict.'

'Huh! That's even worse!' he chuckled. 'I'm Max.'

'I thought we were not supposed to use our real names.'

Max grinned.

'Ah, I see – it's not your real name. Well, in that case, you had better stick to calling me "Sarah".'

Her accent was European but not French, somewhere further east. 'Okay, Sarah.'

'Max, before I forget, M was talking with your head of section in the corridor as I left. They stopped me to say they want us to return to the firm in half an hour. In fact, your boss seems to particularly want *you* back.'

Presumably, thought Max, for yet another interminable debrief; he had already spent a soporific amount of time in the interview room, recounting his experience of operations in China and Hong Kong. The snoops had spent a couple of months on his case and had nothing to show for it.

'Bet they've finally got another mission for me.' When he would be entrusted to perform any future mission was yet to be determined. 'Miller, in the Southeast Asia section, told me something's brewing.' Although whether that would include him would be subject to the final results of the investigation.

'Actually,' continued Sarah, 'they appeared to know I was going to meet you, so perhaps you should expect a telling off. Anyway, it's just for a few minutes, he said.'

He stood up and shook his head. 'Strewth, is Robertshaw really spitting the dummy about us having a drink?' Could the headmaster's study not wait until Monday?

He returned from the bar with a half for Sarah, plus another pint for himself.

'There you go.'

She smiled her thanks.

'May I say,' said Max, 'it's good to see you looking so cheerful.'

'Do I generally look so miserable?' She sipped her beer. 'Yes, I suppose I do. Well, your invitation to come for a drink got me thinking that I need to pick myself up a bit – there's plenty to be grateful for.'

'You're not long back from a jaunt, are you?' Sarah's blank stare in the face of such a question was standard issue at the firm. 'Neither am I,' he added. 'In fact, this is my first spell in Britain since before the war.' He paused but Sarah was not curious enough to take the bait. The heroic storyline he was eager to share would be close to the truth. Escaping Hong Kong, twice – retold minus the love affair and losing the escapee whom he was supposedly protecting.

'Well, I'm guessing your last mission didn't go so well,' he continued. There were rumours that an operation in France had poisoned a love affair 'Sarah' had been enjoying. 'And neither did mine.' He lifted his pint. 'Cheers!' They clinked glasses.

'Are you single, Max?' She was even more direct than in his fantasies.

'London to a brick, I am!'

She furrowed her brow.

'That means, "yes". Very single.'

'And you?'

'Well, I am now. I was engaged until last month.'

'Dyta!'

She clenched her cheeks.

He could not help himself from blurting out the name – or codename – that he had just recalled. It came out the previous week, one afternoon when the bosses were out and office gossip burst forth. Kate Hatchcock, a secretary who acted with diplomatic immunity – she was having an affair with one of the top bosses – let the name slip. 'Dyta' was apparently a young Polish woman whose mission had somehow resulted in her breaking off her engagement to an English pilot.

'Sorry, I just figured out who you are,' said Max. 'I am sorry I spoke it aloud. I can see you'd rather I stick with Sarah.'

'Yes, but it's okay. I guess people know about me. It's a good story for the gossips.'

Sarah was ready for another half, so he fetched more drinks from the bar.

'There we go, my dear. Cures all manner of ills, does this stuff. Cheers!'

They clinked glasses once again.

'May I ask what happened last month?' enquired Max.

'I killed my fiancé's brother.'

'Strewth!' She did not have the look of a highly trained killer, but nobody was what they seemed in the firm. 'That's rough. Well, you're not in prison, so it must have been in the line of duty,' he continued. 'But it must be upsetting. A tragic accident. . . ?'

'Well, I didn't mean to kill my brother-in-law-to-be,' she said.

'No, of course not. May I ask how he died?'

She finished her drink and set the empty glass down. She gesticulated with her hands as she said, 'I grabbed hold of his head and wrenched it so hard that his neck broke.'

Max gulped down his pint.

'Ah, Mr Spratt, do join us!' said Robertshaw in between coughing. 'And you can join us, if you wish, Miss Carlisle.'

He waved them into his oversized office. 'Eden's about to make a statement in the House of Commons, based upon information *we* secured in the East.'

A coterie of office workers from the Southeast Asia Section huddled around a wireless set, in a scene of excitement far removed from the scolding Max had anticipated.

'You've not been with us long, Spratt, but I thought you might want to hear this more than anyone. Now, everyone, shush!' Robertshaw bent over his considerable girth to twiddle the volume knob, inadvertently decreasing it before ramping up the voice of the Secretary of State for Foreign Affairs:

> Out of regard for the feelings of the many relations of
> the victims, His Majesty's Government have been un-
> willing to publish any accounts of Japanese atrocities at
> Hong Kong until these had been confirmed beyond
> any possibility of doubt. Unfortunately, there is no
> longer room for doubt. His Majesty's Government are
> now in possession of statements by reliable eye-wit-
> nesses who succeeded in escaping from Hong Kong. . . .

Incredible, thought Max. The work of *his* labour. All those debriefs – not to mention the troubles of escaping – came to mean, something, at least.

> Their testimony establishes the fact that the Japanese
> army at Hong Kong perpetrated against their helpless
> . . . prisoners . . . without distinction of race or colour,
> the same kind of barbarities which aroused the horror
> of the . . . world at the time of the Nanking massacre of
> 1937.

The crackling interruptions to Eden's speech and the attention-seeking roars of Robertshaw's cough frustrated Max's attempts to catch every word.

> . . . It is known that fifty officers and men of the British
> Army were bound hand and foot and then bayoneted
> to death.

Stanley: he had told his interviewers at SOE HQ all about the massacre, best as he could remember it without Gwen's notes, which had been lost with her.

> It is known that ten days after the capitulation,
> wounded were still being collected from the hills and
> the Japanese were refusing permission to bury the dead.
> It is known that women, both Asiatic and European,
> were raped and murdered and that one entire Chinese
> district was declared a brothel.

That would be Wan Chai. Max half-smiled. He made eye contact with Dyta and at once cast his eyes to the floor.

Robertshaw's growling cough continued to pepper the speech.

> . . . the survivors . . . have been herded into a camp con-
> sisting of wrecked huts without doors, windows, light
> or sanitation. By the end of January, 150 cases of
> dysentery had occurred in the camp, but no drugs or
> medical facilities were supplied. The dead had to be
> buried in a corner of the camp.

Max sighed. All things Gwen wanted the world to know – the brutalities, the terrible conditions, the lack of medicine. . . . It was just the list of names that had not got through, but at least he had been in a position to pass on much of what poor Gwen had wanted.

But who had given them such specifics as a figure of 150 dysentery cases? Somebody else must have supplied information to British intelligence. He sucked a sharp intake of breath. Did Robertshaw know something more? No – how could he possibly have known about what happened in Kukong? The BAAG agents there knew only what he had told them: that Miss Gwen Harmison had spoken of making her own way to Chungking rather than wait upon the British authorities in Kukong – that is, the British Army Aid Group – to arrange things. When he arose that fateful morning, she had already gone.

The BAAG chief had swallowed every word.

'We're getting close to the finale,' boomed Robertshaw. Max's eyes tightened. Robertshaw's confidence suggested he had already read the speech – or possibly written it.

> Most of the European residents . . . interned . . . are
> being given only a little rice and water and occasional
> scraps of other food. . . .

Gwen had longed for the truth of conditions in occupied Hong Kong to spur Britain – its government and its armed forces – to redouble his efforts in the Far East, to not just focus on Europe and give up on Asia.

> The names of . . . those captured at Hong Kong . . . of
> interned civilians . . . have recently been received . . .
> lists of names. . . .

Max was listing now, his stomach and chest hollowed out, empty. He bent double over the end of Robertshaw's desk, propped on his forearms.

Dyta came over to him. 'Are you alright?'

The remainder of the speech drifted through his consciousness, the damage already done.

> It is most painful to have to make such a statement to
> the House. Two things will be clear from it, to the
> House, to the country and to the world. The Japanese
> claim that their forces are animated by a lofty code of
> chivalry, Bushido, is a nauseating hypocrisy. That is the
> first thing. The second is that the enemy must be utterly
> defeated. The House will agree with me that we can
> best express our sympathy with the victims of these
> appalling outrages by redoubling our efforts to ensure
> his utter and overwhelming defeat.

He straightened himself up a little as Robertshaw began to speak. 'Ladies and gentlemen, while one of our own Z Force SOE agents was involved, much of the information that the Foreign Secretary just relayed was smuggled to us out of Hong Kong by a civilian – an exceptionally plucky young English woman.' Max sank onto the desk once more. Robertshaw foreshadowed his conclusion with a curt cough. 'Never underestimate what the righteous can achieve.'

His heart pounding, Max stepped slowly back from the desk, as a mandarin would back away from his emperor. Robertshaw's solemn face broke into a half smile. 'Our work is done for another week. Now, you must all go off and relax.'

Max gushed out a sigh. The crowd shuffled towards the door.

'But not you, Mr . . . er, *Spratt*.'

Dyta raised her eyebrows at him as she left, believing he was about receive the expected scolding for fraternising with colleagues.

'Miss Carlisle, would you be so kind as to ask security to put a man outside my office door?' Dyta nodded and closed the door behind her.

Max gripped his sick stomach with both hands.

'Sit down, *Mr Sotherly*. I think we need to talk.'

Chapter 33

Three Weeks Earlier

The metal door to her room crashed shut once more. Foot-steps faded away. The air in the cell thickened, and, once more, Gwen cried into the mattress. The stench had numbed her senses. Week on week, sweating in the torrid summer heat, the mattress collected multifarious bodily fluids.

She had once used bedsheets to cover herself from the man for as long as she could; soon afterwards, all bedding was removed. And they padlocked every piece of her clothing inside the only other piece of furniture in the room, a wooden trunk next to the bed.

The familiar scratching noise ran across the stone floor below her head. The outside latch scraped back for the ninth time that day, and the door again creaked open. They usually gave her five minutes to wash in the bucket next to the bed, but barely a minute had passed since the previous 'guest'. She did not look up from the mattress. They could rape her all they liked, but they could never make her appear to enjoy it.

Eyes shut, body riddled with mosquito bites, she lay there naked on the bed's roll-mat mattress, waiting the next man's touch. Her bruises had begun to fade, for there was now little she could do that warranted a beating. She had resisted her first rapist with violent kicking and biting. He had laughed and returned the favour. He had actively enjoyed the fight and still got what he wanted in the end, so, thereafter, there seemed little point in resisting.

'Gwen?'

She knew the voice. She dare not look. That moment was a dream that must not end.

There had been much time in which to think. The different scenarios, the 'what ifs' of the evening on the restaurant-barge, the argument with Max. For weeks, she had willed him to walk through that door. All the days for which it failed to happen gave her time to bring matters to a conclusion in her mind.

For one thing, were she ever to get out of here, to gain freedom, she promised to spend more time with her parents. Despite her father's encouragement to travel, there was such selfishness in taking off halfway around the planet, never to return.

There was also a great deal to work out about her husband. That illicit kiss in Macao up against a pillar in the Grand Hotel ... her surety that Klaus had seen nothing as he entered the room had begun to dissipate. And had Klaus's sexual interest begun to wane only after that particular evening? Certainly, it was not long after that when his temper snapped. During weeks of enslavement, the mind unearthed long-forgotten details. At the top of the stairs that fateful night, Klaus had rushed his hand back as if ready to strike. Afterwards, she had hectored all through his explanation: he avowed that he held back his hand, motionless in the air, because he rapidly came to the conclusion that he could not, must not and would never, hit her. But she had stepped back anyway. What is more, her memory finally conceded, he then tried to catch her, not push her.

'Gwen? Is that you?' She buried her face in the mattress and wrapped her hands around the back of her head.

After Klaus, Chester and Max had breathed new life into her. Chester was the best of men, and Max ... well. ...

She had considered the whys and wherefores. For example, why had fate killed Chester yet let her live? Chester had saved her – was it so that she could, in a manner of speaking, save Max? If so, she had failed, as she had, in different ways, failed Klaus. She had bored of him as a toddler bores of a new toy.

A hand rested gently on her bare back. 'Darling, it *is* you. I would know your beautiful back anywhere. He laid his jacket down over her body. 'Darling, it's all over. You are safe now. I have come to take you home.'

'I . . . it's all over?' she muttered. 'Has . . . has the war finished?'

'No, it goes on. But you are free. Nobody will hurt you ever again.'

'But they won't let us get out of here. . . .'

'Don't worry, it is all arranged.'

Behind him, the door to her cell was standing wide open.

She cried tears of joy and shame. 'I . . . I cannot look at you. You won't believe what they've done to me.'

'Darling, time is to be the healer. Your inner beauty can never be extinguished, not in my eyes.'

She slowly turned and gazed upon him, scales of mistrust and paranoia fallen from her eyes. She took the handkerchief that he offered her and wiped her eyes dry. She received his embrace as she received life anew.

'I don't understand why you didn't give up on me. I don't understand why you love me.'

'I know.'

They held each other for several tearful minutes before he spoke again. 'You poisoned my character in your own mind, in order to justify yourself. But, perhaps now you can see, I'm not an ogre? Nobody could look after you better, Gwen.'

He withdrew one arm from around her back and held a key up. Then he bent over the trunk on the floor.

'Klaus, how on earth did you get here?'

'Let's get you dressed.' He opened the padlock and picked up the dress she had worn the night she had been kidnapped. 'Here are your shoes and clothes.'

'And then I'm free to go?'

He sat down on the mattress and put his arm around her. 'Yes, my darling. Nobody will even attempt to stop us.'

Reassured, she took the time to wash herself over the bucket.

'To answer your earlier question,' said Klaus, 'I came the same way you did to Kukong. I told the red guerrillas I'm Dutch, just escaped from Stanley, and – for a donation to their funds – they brought me to Kukong. We stopped at the same places you stopped at on the way – the locals told us you had passed through just days earlier.'

She pulled on her knickers and bra. 'But how did you know I was here in this place?'

'That was trickier, even with some help.'

She pulled on her cotton dress and sighed.

Klaus smiled. 'I'd like to tell you it was because I carried your photograph around shops and markets in Kukong – which I did, but to no avail. But really it was because of a meeting I had at the British Army Aid Group headquarters. There's an intelligence officer there I know. He's an associate of poor Chester's – he told me what happened to him. Chester Drake was a good man.'

'Really? I never heard you say anything like that before.'

'Gwen, there was a time when I hated Chester – the night I saw you two kiss. He walked straight out of the ballroom doors and out of my life. They passed me onto another agent who would handle me for a while. In that time, I feared you two were having an affair. And that thought changed me, at least for a time.

'But Chester eventually came back to see me, just after you left home. He apologised for that kiss and assured me that nothing further had happened. I came round to believing him – but, to be honest, even if there had been more to it, I still loved you and couldn't live without you.'

Klaus helped her fasten her shoes.

'Anyway,' he continued, 'ever since then, as I informed Chester of specific matters – various requests for rubber and iron and so on from the increasingly deranged "Third Reich" – he kept me informed as to your plans and movements. Including your intentions to escape to Kukong.'

Her mind jumped back a couple of months. She rushed over to the trunk and peered inside. At the sight of her handbag, she let an audible sigh of relief.

She prayed to God before checking inside.

She beamed a smile at Klaus.

'Something important?' he said.

'Yes, very.' Her cash purse had gone, but there in her handbag was the imperishable toilet roll.

He held a quizzical expression on his face. 'Klaus, you've no idea what this toilet roll means to me.'

He stood up and clasped her hands in his. 'So let's take it safely out of here.'

'But how did you get *in*?'

'The man at the British Army Aid Group headquarters was most helpful. An Australian officer. The best of men. I am told that he founded this B-A-A-G spy agency from nothing. Anyway, he conducted enquiries and then brokered a meeting with a Mr Wong.'

'Mr Wong?' queried Gwen.

'Sorry, but I do prefer to call him by his real name: he is the one they call the "Jade General". He is no more a real general than I am. He is just a gangster, and he adores money. So I paid him three thousand dollars – American: more than the amount he said he had paid for you. A good investment for Mr Wong, you were.'

'But he may kidnap more women!'

'Fear not, darling, the British are on to him. And the Chinese Nationalists have had enough of him, so they tell me. I suspect Mr Wong was already looking for a good opportunity to lose you, his greatest liability.'

Standing by the door, she took a final glance around, and then stepped outside. She peered along the corridor: the guard's desk was unmanned.

'I'll take you to Chungking,' said Klaus.

'But you're a German. They'll intern you.'

'Well, possibly. But not you. And, if I went to the Nazis, they would shoot me. So I like to think the little help I gave to British intelligence will count for something. The war is turning, Gwen. The Americans have hit the Japanese back at Midway. The Russians are pushing back. Rommel has come unstuck in North Africa. It's only a matter of time before Germany loses the war – and we can live in peace, together.'

She hugged him close once again.

'I was once too proud,' he said. 'Perhaps you may concede that you were, too. But now that war has truly humbled us both' – he brushed wisps of her hair away from her eyes – 'there is a chance for us.'

She smiled up from his shoulder.

'I know.'

EXPLORE ASIA WITH BLACKSMITH BOOKS

From retailers around the world or from *www.blacksmithbooks.com*

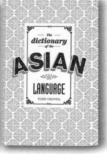